A SUMMER A...

ALSO BY ELIN HILDERBRAND

The Beach Club
Nantucket Nights
Summer People
The Blue Bistro
The Love Season
Barefoot

A SUMMER AFFAIR

Elin Hilderbrand

sphere

SPHERE

First published in Great Britain in 2008 by Sphere
Reprinted 2008 (twice)

Copyright © 2008 by Elin Hilderbrand

The moral right of the author has been asserted.

A CIP catalogue record for this book
is available from the British Library.

ISBN 978-1-84744-224-6

Printed and bound in Great Britain by
Clays Ltd, St Ives plc

Papers used by Sphere are natural, renewable and recyclable
products made from wood grown in sustainable forests and certified
in accordance with the rules of the Forest Stewardship Council.

Mixed Sources
Product group from well-managed
forests and other controlled sources
www.fsc.org Cert no. SGS-COC-004081
© 1996 Forest Stewardship Council
FSC

Sphere
An imprint of
Little, Brown Book Group
100 Victoria Embankment
London EC4Y 0DY

For the brightest star in my sky.

Three things in human life are important. The first is to be kind. The second is to be kind. And the third is to be kind.

—Henry James

A SUMMER AFFAIR

THE INVISIBLE THREAD THAT BINDS HER TO HIM

March 2003

The guilt was like a clump of tar in her hair, warm and sticky, impossible to remove. The more she fingered it, the worse things got. Tar gummed her hands; she tried water but it formed a slick, milky film. She needed scissors, turpentine.

The tar had been real, back when Claire was four or five, back when she and her parents lived in the first house in Wildwood Crest, a shoe box that Claire didn't remember living in, but that her mother was fond of pointing out when they drove through that part of town. Claire had been playing at the edge of the road, which was newly paved; she had been unsupervised (things had been different then with child raising), and when she came inside with the tar weighing down one side of her head, an ooey, gooey, licorice mess, her mother had said with bald matter-of-factness, 'It will never come out.'

Just like the guilt!

On that morning in March, the phone rang early. Claire was exhausted and parched, and the kids were everywhere. Shea had been the baby then, and she was eating the scrambled eggs that had fallen from J.D.'s and Ottilie's plates to the floor. Claire scooped the baby up and grabbed the phone. Siobhan, of course. No one else would call before eight on a Sunday except for Siobhan, who was Claire's best friend and sister-in-law, the wife of Jason's brother, Carter. Siobhan was Claire's soul mate, her darling, her defender, her reality check – and, the night before, her partner in crime. They had been out on the town together, drinking, which happened so rarely that it qualified as a big deal. Siobhan would be calling to talk about it, remember it, relive it, parse it, decon-struct it, moment by moment. A lot had happened.

'Have you heard?' Siobhan said.

'Heard what?'

'Oh, God,' Siobhan said. 'Sit down.'

Claire carried the baby into the front sitting room, which was never used. It was, however, the perfect place to accept bad news. 'What is it?' she said. In their bedroom, Jason was sawing logs; she could hear him through the wall. It was a strictly enforced rule that he be allowed to sleep in on Sunday. Day of rest and all that. Would she have to wake him?

'Fidelma called, from the police station,' Siobhan said. 'There was an accident. Daphne Dixon hit a deer and flipped her car. They flew her to Boston.'

'Is she . . . ?' Claire didn't know how to ask.

'Alive? Yes. But just barely, I think.'

Messy, gooey, insoluble. *It will never come out.*

'She was drunk,' Claire said.

'Smashed,' Siobhan said.

*　　*　　*

4

There had been seven women: Claire, Siobhan, Julie Jackson, Delaney Kitt, Amie Trimble, Phoebe Caldwell, and Daphne Dixon. *One of these things is not like the other.* Daphne was a summer resident – which is to say, very wealthy – who had recently decided to move to Nantucket year-round. Claire knew her slightly. They had met at a pool party, and Daphne and her husband had taken an interest in Claire's glassblowing. They might want to commission a piece someday – who knew? Claire liked Daphne. Or she was flattered that Daphne seemed to like her. She had bumped into Daphne at the dry cleaners (Daphne picking up what looked to be fifty cashmere sweaters). Claire had said, *Come out with us on Saturday night!*

They went to the spacious walnut bar at the Brant Point Grill, where there was live cabaret music. Daphne had been wearing a diaphanous top and a red silk scarf around her neck. It was clear from the beginning of the night that Daphne was letting loose, she was relaxing with the local crowd, she was allowing herself to go a little crazy. This wasn't like the buttoned-up scene in Boston, she said boozily in Claire's ear.

There had been a lot of drinking: countless glasses of chardonnay and a few rosy cosmopolitans for the other women – and margaritas, no salt, for Daphne. At the end of the evening, Claire went to the bar to order herself a Diet Coke before the room began to spin, and Daphne said, 'And a margarita, no salt, for me, please, Claire.'

One Diet Coke, one margarita, no salt, please, Claire told the bartender.

Now, in the sitting room that no one ever used, Claire picked stray yellow flecks of dried egg out of the baby's duck-fuzz hair, her mind racing. Daphne had already had a lot to drink when Claire bought her the margarita. How many drinks had she had, exactly? Claire hadn't been keeping track. Was one more the difference? Claire had wanted Daphne to be happy; she had wanted Daphne to have fun. Claire was the one who invited her along. Daphne had already bought a round of drinks, several rounds; it seemed, in retrospect, that Daphne had been pulling out money all night, leaving lavish tips for the bartender, throwing sixty dollars into the fishbowl on top of the piano for the cabaret singer. Claire had been relieved to reciprocate, to order Daphne a margarita, no salt, and pay for it.

Smashed, Siobhan said.

The margarita wasn't the problem; the margarita itself hadn't done any damage. The problem was that when the night ended, when the bar closed and the seven mothers spilled out onto Easton Street, Daphne had climbed into her car, a Lincoln Navigator. Claire and Siobhan and Julie Jackson got into a cab, and they had encouraged Daphne to join them in the cab. *Come on, Daphne, there's plenty of room! Let us take you home!* In Claire's mind, the details were smudged; what she remembered was that they had encouraged Daphne to get into the cab, but they had not demanded it. They had not said, *You shouldn't be driving,* or *We're not willing to let you get behind the wheel of a car,* though that was what they should have said. The woman had consumed any number of margaritas and then strolled away, across the street and into the darkness, jangling her keys, her red scarf trailing elegantly down her back. Claire had been too intimidated to stop her. Claire had thought, *She is rich enough to know what she is doing.*

Claire sat by the phone, waiting for Siobhan to call back with details from Fidelma, her Irish connection at the police station, who was getting information from her cousin Niamh, who worked as an intensive care nurse at Massachusetts General: *Daphne's going into surgery. It's touch and go. They don't know what they're going to find.* Daphne was going sixty miles an hour down the ridged dirt road that led to her house. Sixty miles an hour – the car must have been rocking like a washing machine. And then the deer, from out of nowhere. She cut the deer in half; the car flipped onto its side. No one saw or heard the accident – the road was lined with summer homes and it was the middle of March. No one was around. Daphne was pinned in the car, unconscious. The person who found her, finally, was her husband, Lock Dixon. After calling her cell phone forty times and getting no answer, he left their ten-year-old daughter, Heather, asleep in the house and set out to find his wife. She was two hundred yards shy of the driveway.

Claire cried; she prayed, working her way around the rosary beads while her children watched *Sesame Street*. She went to church with all three children in need of a nap and lit four candles – one for Daphne, one for Lock, one for the daughter, Heather, and one, inexplicably, for herself.

'It's our fault,' Claire whispered over the phone to Siobhan.

'No, baby, it's not,' Siobhan said. 'Daphne is a grown woman, capable of making her own decisions. We told her to get in the bloody cab, and she refused. Say it with me: *She refused.*'

'She refused.'

'We did what we could,' Siobhan said. 'We did our best.'

Tense hours spun into tense days. Claire's phone rang off the hook. It was Julie Jackson, Amie Trimble, Delaney Kitt, all witnesses.

'I can't believe it,' Julie Jackson said.

'I know,' Claire said, her heart pounding, the guilt rising in her throat like bile.

'She was so drunk,' Julie said.

'I know.'

'And then she drove,' Julie said.

'I should have made her get in the cab,' Claire said.

'Mmmmmm,' Julie said.

'I feel horrible.'

There was a long pause, during which Claire could feel pity rather than a sense of shared culpability.

'Are you going to . . . I don't know, set up meals or anything?' Julie asked.

'Should I?' Claire said. This was what they did when someone

7

was sick or had a baby: one person organized, and everyone signed up to take food. Was Claire the one who should organize? She didn't know Daphne well enough to send over a parade of unfamiliar faces with covered dishes.

'Let's wait and see what happens,' Claire said, thinking, *She has to live and be okay. Oh, Lord, please!*

'Keep me posted,' Julie said. 'And know I'm thinking about you.'

About *me?* This was meant to be comforting, Claire knew, but it gave texture to her shame. People would hear about Daphne's accident and think of Claire.

'Thanks,' Claire said.

Daphne survived the surgery. She was hospitalized in Boston for weeks, though it wasn't clear what was wrong with her. There were no broken bones, no spinal cord injuries, thank God, and no significant blood loss. There was a concussion, certainly, and some other problems that fell under the umbrella of 'head injuries.' There was amnesia of a sort – and here the stories varied. Did she know her name? Did she know Lock and Heather? Yes. But she didn't remember anything about the night out, and when Lock told her who she'd been out with – Julie Jackson, Claire Danner Crispin, Siobhan Crispin – Daphne shook her head. *I don't know those people.* The memory came back, eventually, but certain things were rattled out of place. She wasn't the same; she wasn't right. There was some irreparable damage that had no name.

The guilt stayed with Claire. *She* was the one who had invited Daphne to come out in the first place. She had bought the last, godforsaken drink, when Daphne had already overimbibed. She had tried to cajole Daphne into the cab, but she had not dragged her by the arms the way she should have. She had not called the police or enlisted the help of the bouncer. She turned it over and over in her mind. Sometimes she exonerated herself. How could this possibly be construed as her fault? But the truth was brutal:

Claire had failed to exercise the common sense needed to keep Daphne safe. A sin of omission, perhaps, but a sin just the same. *It will never come out.*

When Daphne came home from the hospital, Claire filled a basket with homemade clam chowder and chicken salad and two novels and a jazz CD and some scented soaps. Something was wrong with Daphne mentally, that was the rumor, but no one knew what exactly. Claire sat in the car outside the Dixons' monstrous summer home for a long time before she summoned the courage to take the basket of goodies to the front door. She was propelled forward by guilt and held back by fear. If Daphne opened the door, what would Claire say?

She knocked timidly, feeling like Little Red Riding Hood with her basket; then she chastised herself. She was being ridiculous! Siobhan liked to point out how ironic it was that Claire was named Claire, or 'clear' – because Claire was blurry. *No boundaries!* Siobhan would shout. All her life, Claire had had a problem figuring out where other people ended and she began. All her life, she'd taken on the world's hurt; she held herself responsible. But why?

Footsteps approached. Claire stopped breathing. The door opened, and Claire found herself face-to-face with Lock Dixon. He was, as everyone knew, a terrifically wealthy man, a billionaire, though it was now rumored he would sell his superconductor business in Boston. It was rumored that he was going to live here on Nantucket full-time and take care of things until Daphne was herself again.

'Hi,' Claire said, and she felt her cheeks bloom. She thrust the basket at Lock, and they both peered in at its jumble of contents. Soup, soap – Claire didn't know what Daphne would want or need, but she had to bring something. Claire knew Lock Dixon casually; they had had the conversation about glassblowing, about Claire's hot shop out behind her house. But would he remember? Claire was sure he would not remember. She was not memorable; she was frequently mistaken for every other redhead on Nantucket. 'This is for Daphne.'

'Oh,' he said. His voice was husky, as if he hadn't used it for days. He looked older to her, balder and heavier. 'Thank you.'

'I'm Claire Danner,' she said. 'Crispin.'

'Yes,' he said. 'I know who you are.' He didn't smile or say anything further, and Claire realized that this was what she had been afraid of. It hadn't been Daphne at all, but Lock. He knew about the margarita and the other ways that Claire had failed his wife, and he blamed her. His eyes accused her.

'I'm sorry,' Claire said. There was a funny smell coming from the basket – the clams gone bad, the chicken salad rancid. Claire was mortified. She should say something else – *I hope Daphne feels better. Please give her my best.* But no, she couldn't. She turned, fled for her car.

PART ONE

CHAPTER ONE

HE ASKS HER

Early Fall 2007

Claire Danner Crispin had never been so nervous about a lunch date in all her life.

'What do you think he wants?' she asked Siobhan.

'He wants to shag you,' Siobhan said. Then she laughed as if the idea was preposterous and hysterical, which, indeed, it was.

Lock Dixon had called Claire at home and invited her to lunch at the yacht club.

'There's something I'd like to talk with you about,' he'd said. 'Are you free Tuesday?'

Claire was taken completely by surprise. When she'd seen his name on the caller ID, she'd nearly let it go to voice mail. 'Yes. Yes, I am. Tuesday.'

It was something to do with the charity, she decided. Since selling his company in Boston and moving to Nantucket year-round, Lock Dixon had graciously agreed to serve as the executive director of Nantucket's Children, the island's biggest

13

nonprofit organization. 'Graciously,' because Lock Dixon was so wealthy he never had to work again. Claire had joined the board of directors of Nantucket's Children right before she became pregnant with Zack, but because of her fall in the hot shop and Zack's premature birth and all the complications thereof, she had been little more than a name on the letterhead. Still, it was the charity, now, that connected them.

But there was an invisible thread, too: the unspoken accusation about Daphne's accident. Did Lock want to revisit the night of the accident now, years later? Claire fretted. She buttoned her cardigan wrong; she nearly locked her keys in the car in the yacht club parking lot.

And yet, once Claire and Lock were seated, overlooking the trim yacht club lawn and the blue harbor beyond, it was he who seemed nervous, worked up, agitated. He wiggled in his wrought iron chair; he fussed over what Claire might order from the menu. ('Get anything you want,' Lock said. 'Get the lobster salad. Anything.') After their orders were placed and small talk was exhausted, there was a dramatic pause in the conversation, a making way, a throat clearing. Claire nearly laughed; she felt like she was being proposed to.

Would she consider chairing the Nantucket's Children Summer Gala the following August?

Claire filled with relief. It felt like laughing gas; it felt like she might levitate. It felt like the invisible thread had been snipped, cut: she was free from the awful weight that attended her connection with Lock Dixon. Was it okay, then, to imagine that the accusation she had seen in his eyes years earlier had been nothing more than a figment of her imagination?

She was so caught up in wondering that she didn't respond. In truth, it would be fair to say she hadn't even heard the question. It was like the time she fainted during track practice, when she was seventeen, and she became convinced that she was pregnant. She was dead certain; she had Matthew ready to sell his guitar so they could pay for an abortion, but she cried herself to sleep, worried that she was going to burn in hell, and she decided to keep the baby. Her mother would raise it while Claire went to college . . .

When Claire went to the doctor, he said, *You're not pregnant. The problem is that you have anemia.*

Anemia! She had shouted the word with glee.

'Chairing?' she said now.

'It's a lot of work, but probably not as much as you think. You'll have a cochair. I know you're busy, but . . .'

Yes, three children and a baby and a glassblowing business put on hold for the foreseeable future so she could focus on her family. She was not the right person to ask. Not this year. Maybe down the road, when she had her head above water. Then it dawned on Claire why he was asking her: The summer gala was a *concert.* Lock was coming to her because they wanted Matthew to perform. Max West, her high school sweetheart, now one of the biggest rock stars in the world.

Claire took in some of the rarefied yacht club air. There were a million thoughts zipping through her mind: Jason would kill her. Siobhan would laugh and call her a pushover (*No boundaries!*). Margarita, no salt. *It will never come out.* Would Matthew do it if she asked? She hadn't spoken to him in years. He might, he just might. Anemia! Nantucket's Children was a good cause. The best cause.

Trumping all those thoughts was this: Lock Dixon was the one person Claire could not say no to. What had happened the night of Daphne's accident hung in the air between them, unfinished business. It hung between them in a way that made Claire feel she owed Lock something.

'Yes,' Claire said. 'I'd love to. Really, I'd be honored.'

Even though she had four children to raise? Even though she hadn't blown out so much as a single goblet since Zack was born?

'Really?' Lock said. He sounded surprised.

'Absolutely,' she said.

'Well, okay, then,' Lock said. He raised his sweating glass of iced tea, as did Claire, and they touched glasses, sealing the deal. 'Thank you.'

Jason was going to kill her.

They had been married for twelve years, together for fourteen. They had met here, on Nantucket, during the hottest summer on record. Jason had been born and raised on the island, he knew it inside out, and he took pride in sharing it with Claire. Each day was like a present: They went clamming naked at sunset on the south shore. They went skinny-dipping in the private swimming pools along Hulbert Avenue (Jason knew which pools had security systems and which didn't). Theirs was, in every aspect, a summer romance. Claire had just graduated from RISD with a degree in glassblowing. She was torn between taking a job offer from Corning and teaming up with a traveling crafts fair and seeing the country. Jason had graduated from Northeastern with a degree in political science, which he declared useless. Four wasted years, he said of college, except for the beer and the proximity to Fenway, and the introduction to de Tocqueville (but she was pretty sure he was only saying that to impress her). He wanted to live on Nantucket and build houses.

They were in love that summer, but what Claire remembered was how temporary it felt, how fragile, fleeting, ethereal. In truth, they barely knew each other. Claire told Jason about her years with Matthew – Max West, *the* Max West of 'This Could Be a Song' – but Jason didn't believe her. Didn't believe her! He didn't believe she could blow glass, either. She showed him her goblets and footed candy dishes; he shook his head in wonder, but not in acknowledgment.

They sailed on Jason's Hobie Cat, they fished for scup and stripers, they dove off the boat into the dark water, they had bonfires at Great Point and slept under the stars, they had sex with the wild abandon of two twenty-year-olds who had nothing to lose.

16

They hung out with Jason's brother, Carter, who was a chef at the Galley, and Carter's girlfriend, Siobhan, who hailed from County Cork. Siobhan wore square glasses and had dark freckles across her pale nose, like pepper over mashed potatoes. Claire fell in love with Carter and Siobhan as well as Jason, and one night she was drunk and bold enough to say, 'What if I don't go to Corning after Labor Day? What if I stay on Nantucket and marry Jason? And Siobhan, you marry Carter, and we raise kids together and live happily ever after?'

They had laughed at her, and Siobhan told her to piss off – but she, Claire Danner, had been right, and they were now, all of them, Crispins. Ten strong, including the kids. It was storybook – except that it was tough, frustrating, boring reality. Claire and Jason had gone from being two kids with no tan lines and sand in the cracks of their bums to being Mom and Dad, the heads of a minicorporation, the Csrispin family of 22 Featherbed Lane. Jason had worked for Eli Drummond for years, and on the weekends he slaved on their own house as well as the hot shop for Claire out back. Then Jason hired four Lithuanian guys and went out on his own. Claire cultivated five clients with erudite and expensive taste in art objects made of glass. She gave birth, in quick succession, to J.D., Ottilie, and Shea. Claire worked erratic hours – after the kids went to bed, before they woke up. Then, when Shea hit preschool, Claire worked more. Everything was okay, fine, good at times, but there were bumps. Jason started smoking at work – smoking! – and trying to hide it with beer or breath mints. Jason became resentful when Claire turned him down for sex. She tried to explain to him what it felt like to be pawed by three kids all day. She was their slave, their employee; she worked for them. Was it any wonder that when the end of the day came, she wanted to be left alone? Jason had never been intellectually curious (after that first summer, he never mentioned de Tocqueville's name again), and over time he became incorrigibly sucked into the television. Claire found the TV maddening – the channel surfing, the sports.

Jason drove a pickup that was as huge and black as a hearse, a gas-guzzler he affectionately called Darth Vader. *Darth Vader?* Claire said, incredulous that she had married a man who treated his truck like a fraternity brother or a pet. *The kids like it,* Jason said. The truck, the love affair with the tube, the sneaked cigarettes, and the early morning breakfasts at the Downyflake so that Jason could touch base with his subs and hear about new business – all of it served to push Claire to the brink.

But there were also many wonderful things about Jason. He worked hard and provided for his family. He prided himself on being simple and straightforward, honest and true; he was the right angle of a T square, the bubble in the level, always locating the center. *What you see is what you get.* He adored the kids. He had a foot soldier in their son J.D. J.D. helped Jason with projects around the house: rolling paint onto walls, turning the screwdriver while sucking intently on his bottom lip. *I'm Dad's wingman.* They built a go-cart using an old lawn mower engine; they went scalloping together and pulled cherrystone clams out of the wet, marshy sand with a tool Jason had fashioned from a piece of PVC pipe. *You'll never go hungry with the Crispin men around!* Jason was exemplary with the girls, too – father of the year. He delivered Ottilie and Shea to dance lessons, he bought them bouquets on the day of their dance recital, and he whistled louder than anyone else in the audience. He tirelessly explained that *Ottilie* was an old-fashioned French name. *We wanted something unique,* he said, beaming with pride.

When Claire got pregnant with Zack, things were going smoothly. She was working on a huge commission for her best client, Chick Klaussen: a sculpture for the entry of his offices on West Fifty-fourth Street in Manhattan. She planned to be finished with the commission right before the baby was due. Jason was happy because he was, deep in his soul, a procreator. He would have had ten kids if Claire was willing, a stable of kids, a posse, a football team, a tribe: the Crispin clan.

When Claire was thirty-two weeks along, she was in the hot shop working on the Klaussen commission. She had a week or two of work left at the most. *At the most!* she promised Jason, even though her doctor wanted her to stop. Too hot in there, he said. Not safe for you or the baby. Claire was working very hot, it was finish work, shine and polish, she was not drinking enough water, and she fainted. She hit the floor, cut her arm, broke two ribs, and went immediately into preterm labor. On the MedFlight jet, they told her she would most likely lose the baby. But Zack had lived; they took him by emergency C-section, and he spent five weeks on a respirator in the NICU. He lived, Claire healed.

Jason was shaken to his core. He had been standing there as they sliced Claire open – Claire, whose body had sucked in two bags of IV fluid in less than thirty minutes, so advanced was her dehydration – and he had fully expected them to pull out a stillborn. But then, the cry. It was a revelation for Jason; it was his born-again moment, the moment when an adult man who thought he knew everything learned something about the human condition. He sat next to Claire's bed as Zack spent the first of thirty-five days in the NICU, and he made Claire promise she would stop working.

For a little while, he said. *Have a studio finish the Klaussen commission.*

This was as close as he came to blaming her. But no matter – Claire blamed herself, as she had blamed herself for Daphne's accident. Her blood type was the rare AB positive: the universal acceptor. And that was all too fitting. Give her the blame, the shame, all of it: she had no boundaries, she would take it on. She agreed to stop working; she gave the Klaussen commission to a glass studio in Brooklyn to finish.

Zack captured Jason's heart – and Claire's heart, too – because they came so close to losing him. Even now, seven months later, Claire woke up in the middle of the night, worrying about the lasting effects of her fall. She watched Zack, willing him to respond to her in an age-appropriate way, wishing that his eyes would show

19

that glimmer, that promise that her other kids had shown: intelligence, motivation, determination. Since Zack's birth, she had lived with the whisper, *There's something wrong with him.* She constantly badgered Jason: *Do you think something happened when he was born? Do you think there's something Dr. Patel isn't telling me, or something she didn't see?* To which Jason always responded, 'For Chrissakes, Claire, he's fine!' But that sounded to Claire like denial. It sounded like Jason was blinded by love.

How was she going to tell Jason about the gala? Claire waited through dinner – fried chicken, Jason's favorite. She waited through bath and stories for the girls and a shower and homework for J.D. She waited until Zack had his bottle, until Jason was relaxed on the sofa, remote control in hand. The TV was on, but Jason had not committed to anything yet. Now was the time to tell him! This was their life now, but Claire could remember Jason naked and grinning with a clam rake in his hand, his sun-bleached hair shining like gold.

'I had lunch with Lock Dixon today,' she said. 'At the yacht club.'

He heard her, but he wasn't listening. 'Did you?'

'Doesn't that surprise you?'

Jason changed the channel. Claire resented the TV, all fifty-two bright, chirping inches of it. 'A little, I guess.'

'He asked me to cochair the summer gala.'

'What's that?'

'You know, the Nantucket's Children thing. The event. The concert. The thing we went to last month.'

At this past year's gala, while Jason lingered at the back bar with his fishing buddies, Claire had applauded as the two cochairs floated up onto the stage to accept bouquets of flowers. As if they had been named prom queen. As if they had won an Academy Award. Claire had been caught up in the glamour of it all. The mere fact that she had *sat down* for a *civilized lunch* at the yacht club made Claire believe that if she agreed to cochair the summer gala for Nantucket's Children, her life would be more like that and less like it was now. Claire never ate lunches like the one she had had today. Lunch for her was a sleeve of saltines that she kept in the console of her Honda Pilot and stuffed blindly into her mouth as she picked the kids up from school. If she was at home, lunch was a bowl of cereal that she poured at eleven thirty (it was break-fast *and* lunch), which grew soggy before Claire finished it because the baby cried, or the phone rang, or the crumbs under her feet pushed her past her already-high threshold for filth and yuck and she capitulated and pulled out the vacuum. If Claire agreed to cochair the gala, her life might take on a distinguished quality, the golden glow that accompanied a life devoted to good works. How could she explain this to Jason?

'He asked you to chair it?'

'Cochair it. I'd have help.'

'I hope you said no.'

She stroked Zack's soft head. 'I said yes.'

'Jesus, Claire.'

Was it so wrong? She and Jason had spent the past seven months living in reverence of their own good fortune. Wasn't it time now to think of others? To raise money for kids whose parents were working themselves sick with three jobs?

'It's a good cause,' she said.

Jason huffed, turned the volume up. And that, she supposed, was the best she could hope for.

'You're a complete idiot, Clairsy. A bloody fool.'

This was Siobhan, the next morning on the phone, after Claire had told her, *Lock Dixon asked me to chair the summer gala for Nantucket's Children, and I capitulated like a soldier without a gun.*

'I'm not a fool.'

'You're too much yourself.'

21

'Right,' Claire said, losing enthusiasm. 'Jason is not amused. Have I made a whopping mistake?'

'Yes,' Siobhan said.

Claire had spent the past twenty hours convincing herself that it was an honor to be asked. 'It will be fun.'

'It will be work and stress and heartache like you've never known.'

'It's for a good cause,' Claire said, trying again.

'That sounds rather canned,' Siobhan said. 'Tell me something true.'

I did it because Lock asked me, Claire thought. But that would send Siobhan through the roof. 'I couldn't say no.'

'Bingo. You have no boundaries. Your cells don't have membranes.'

Correct. This had been a problem since childhood: Claire's parents had battled constantly; their problems came in thirty flavors. Claire was the only child, she held herself accountable for their misery, and her parents did nothing to dissuade her from this. (Things *had* been different then with child raising.)

She was an easy mark, too easy. She could not say no to Lock Dixon, or anyone else, for that matter.

'I want you to serve on my committee,' Claire said. Siobhan and Carter owned a catering company called Island Fare. They did big events like the Pops concert on Jetties Beach, as well as hundreds of smaller cocktail and dinner parties, lunches, brunches, picnics, and weddings, though they had never catered the summer gala. Claire was asking Siobhan to be on the committee because Siobhan was her best friend, her darling, but right away Claire sensed tension.

'Are you asking me to *cater* the gala?' Siobhan asked. 'Or do you expect me to slave with you on it while some other mick gets the job?'

'Oh,' Claire said. Of course, if it were up to her, Siobhan and Carter would cater the event, but Claire didn't know if being cochair gave

22

her the power to hire anybody, and even if she did have the power, she wasn't prepared to wield it yet. What if she hired Carter and Siobhan and someone called it nepotism (which, of course, someone would)? Worse still, what if Claire hired Carter and Siobhan and her fellow board members expected a deep discount that Carter and Siobhan either didn't want or couldn't afford to provide? God, how awkward! She'd been in charge for five minutes and already she was facing an impossible situation.

'Listen,' Claire said. 'You don't have to – '

'No, no, no, I will.'

'But I can't promise anything about the catering.'

'That's okay.'

Claire wasn't sure, exactly, where that left things. Was Siobhan on the committee? Would she come to the meeting at eight o'clock on Wednesday, September 19? She would not, Claire decided. She would forget about the meeting, and Claire didn't call to remind her.

So when Claire Danner Crispin reached the top of the narrow staircase of the Elijah Baker House (a grand house, built in 1846 for Elijah Baker, who had made a fortune fashioning ladies' corsets out of whalebone) and stepped into the office of Nantucket's Children, she found only . . . Lock Dixon. Lock was sitting behind his desk in a blue pinstripe shirt and a yellow tie, his head bent forward, so that Claire could see the bald spot on top. He was writing on a legal pad, and he didn't seem to have heard Claire on the stairs (impossible: she was wearing clogs). Rather, he had heard her and simply had yet to acknowledge her. Claire felt self-conscious. She should have called Siobhan and dragged her along, no matter how uncomfortable or unethical it was.

'Lock?' Claire said. 'Hi.'

Lock raised his head. He was wearing half spectacles, which he whipped off immediately, as if they were some kind of secret. He smiled at Claire. It was a real smile, it broke his face open, and

Claire felt the air in the room crackle, practically, with the power of that smile. It sent an electric current through her heart; it could have brought her back from the dead, that smile.

Claire took the smile as her reward for saying, *Yes, I'd love to. Really, I'd be honored.* When you were a cochair of the summer gala, people were glad to see you walk in the door. Or grateful. Or relieved.

Lock stood up. 'Hi, Claire, hi, hi. Here, let me get you a – '

'I'm fine, I'm fine,' she said. 'Are we meeting here, or in the . . .'

The Nantucket's Children office consisted of two rooms divided by a hallway, and at the end of the hallway was a powder room and a small kitchen. One room was the actual office, where Lock worked and where Gavin Andrews, the office manager-bookkeeper, had his desk, and across the hall was the board-room, which held a large, round table and eight Windsor chairs. Every detail of the Nantucket's Children office transported one back to the whaling heyday that put Nantucket on the map: the floor was fashioned from 150-year-old pine boards, and the door-ways were topped with leaded transom windows. With the old-fashioned charm, however, came old-fashioned conveniences or the lack thereof. The board meetings were stifling in the summer and freezing in the winter, and every time Claire used the powder room, the toilet backed up.

Tonight, however, the office was unusually inviting. Because it was September now, it was dark outside. Through the window at Lock Dixon's back, Claire could see all the way up Main Street: Nantucket Town was twinkling like a child's toy village. Lock worked with the light of one desk lamp and the blue glow of his computer. Half a sandwich – turkey, stuffing, and cranberry sauce – sat on white butcher paper on his desk blotter, which meant it was eight o'clock and he had yet to make it home. Claire's mind flickered to Daphne. If Lock spent every night at the office, did Daphne make dinner for herself? Did she read magazines, take baths, watch TV? Daphne was never quite right in public after her accident, but what about in private? Was she better or worse? Their daughter, Heather, was at boarding school. Andover. It had been a much-debated topic among Claire's circle of friends: How did Heather Dixon get into the best prep school in the country with solid B grades and an attitude problem? It was field hockey, everyone concluded, and they were probably correct. Heather Dixon was quite an athlete, but Claire believed that Heather Dixon got herself into prep school out of the sheer will to escape her mother. It had killed Lock to see Heather go, and it was odd, too, that he should head a charity called Nantucket's Children when his own child didn't really qualify as such. Heather Dixon rarely came back to the island; this past summer, Claire heard, she had attended a camp in Maine.

'Let's just meet in here,' Lock said. His voice startled Claire. She had been so busy thinking about him, she forgot he was in the room. 'It's cozier.'

Cozier? Claire thought. She was blushing as Lock pulled a chair up to his desk for her. 'Cozier' made it sound like the two of them were about to snuggle under a blanket together. But Lock was right: the office was cozy, with the low light and the faint smell of woodsmoke floating in through the cracked window, and the classical music coming from the Bose radio.

Now that she was a cochair, maybe she would have more calm and quiet hours like this. This office – its architectural detail and distinguished period furnishings combining to convey a scholarly air, a well-heeled doing-of-noble-works – stood in direct opposition to the scene Claire had left at home. At home, there had been dinner to make: tacos, her only home run, and late corn from the farm and a green salad with ranch dressing, which she had painstakingly made from scratch (fresh herbs picked from the garden, onion finely minced). Jason, as ever, wandered in the door with five minutes to spare, smelling of Newport Menthols, and the kids jumped into his arms and tackled him. How could Claire deny

them his attentions? This was his time of day. She could not interrupt routine just because she had a *meeting*. Hence Claire was left
to shuttle everything from the kitchen to the dining room table,
trying not to look like she was hurrying. Jason ended his rough-
housing session by picking Zack up and putting him in his high
chair, which was helpful because when Claire tried to do this, Zack
pitched a fit. Dinner went well, which meant there were only sixty
or seventy reminders to eat up, and Claire stood immediately after
grace and buttered corn for the girls, got up twice to refill milk,
and then, when she sat down again, spooned pureed carrots into
Zack's mouth, which was an exercise in one step forward, two
steps back. Zack had not yet gotten the hang of eating solids. He
pushed most of the food back out of his mouth with his tongue;
it dribbled down his bib or landed on the tray of his high chair,
where he liked to put his hands in it. Claire, in an attempt to create
an environment of art appreciation for her children, made refer-
ences to Jackson Pollock. Jack the Dripper, Zack the Dripper. But
the kids were, for the most part, grossed out. J.D. (at nine, Claire's
eldest) called Zack 'the mental patient.' Claire hated when J.D.
used that term, not because Zack was old enough to understand
it, but because it echoed Claire's private fears. *There's something
wrong with him.*

Sitting in the office, Claire realized she was starving. With all
that had happened during dinnertime, she hadn't had a second to
eat her own food.

Lock noticed Claire staring at the uneaten half of his sandwich.
'Are you hungry?' he said. 'Do you want . . . I don't know if it's
rude to offer someone your leftovers, but I haven't touched this
half, I swear. Would you like it?'

'No, no,' Claire said quickly. 'I ate at home.'

'Oh,' Lock said. 'Right. Of course. Well, how about some wine,
then?'

'Wine?' Claire said. At home, Jason would be dealing with bed-
time. This normally went like clockwork: Bath for the younger

three while J.D. finished his homework, then a shower for J.D. Then stories for the girls and Zack, which worked if Jason remembered to give Zack a bottle. The bottle had to go into the microwave for thirty seconds. Would Jason know this? She should have reminded him; she should have written it down. Claire eyed the phone on Lock's desk. She should call home and check on things. Of course Pan, the Thai au pair who had come to live with them after Zack was born, was in the house, too, but Pan rarely came out of her room at night. Still, if Jason got into a jam, he would go to Pan and she would prep Zack's bottle and rock him to sleep.

'I'd love a glass of wine,' Claire said.

One of the good things about being cochair of the summer gala and attending evening meetings, Claire thought, was that Jason would get more hands-on time with the kids.

'Wonderful,' Lock said. He disappeared into the hallway and came back with two glasses dangling from his fingers and a chilled bottle of white.

Very strange, Claire thought. *Wine in the office.*

Lock held up the bottle to her like a sommelier. 'This is a viognier. It's a white from the Rhône valley. It's my favorite varietal.'

'Is it?' Claire said.

'My wife finds it too tart. Too lemony. But I love its brightness.' He poured Claire a glass and she took a sip. Wine, like classical music, was one of those things Claire wanted to learn more about. She had tried to interest Jason in a wine-tasting class offered through the Community School, but he'd refused on the grounds that he never drank wine, only beer. This wine was bright, it was grassy – should she say that word 'grassy,' or would she sound like a complete ass? She wanted to make Lock happy (she could hear Siobhan shouting, *No boundaries!*), and hence she declared, 'I love it.'

'You do?'

'I love it. It tastes like a meadow.'

Another smile from Lock. She had spent the past five years certain

27

that he hated her, blamed her – but here he was, smiling! It warmed her to the pit of her stomach.

'I'm glad you like it,' Lock said. He poured himself a glass equal to Claire's. Was this okay – drinking wine in the office, alone, with Lock Dixon? Had the meetings with his former cochairs gone this way?

'Is Adams coming?' Claire asked. Adams Fiske, a mop-haired local attorney and one of Claire's dearest friends, was president of the board of directors.

'He's in Duxbury this week,' Lock said.

'I invited my sister-in-law, Siobhan,' Claire said. 'But I doubt she'll remember.'

'Okay,' Lock said. He sounded like he couldn't have cared less. He raised his glass. 'Cheers!' he said. 'Here's to the summer gala!'

'To the summer gala,' Claire said.

'I'm so glad you agreed to cochair,' Lock said. 'We really wanted you.'

Claire blushed again and sipped her wine. 'It's my pleasure.'

Lock was sitting on the edge of his desk. He was wearing khaki pants, loafers without socks, a leather belt with a silver mono-grammed belt buckle. His tie was loose and the top two buttons of his shirt were undone. Claire found him newly fascinating – but why? She knew nothing about him, other than that he was a rich man. That was interesting. Or rather, it was interesting that he had taken this job (which Claire, as a member of the board of direct-ors, knew meant that he made $82,000 a year) even though he was so rich he never had to work again.

'I think we've found someone to be your cochair,' Lock said.

'Oh,' Claire said. 'Good.' This was good; Claire certainly couldn't shoulder all of the responsibility of the summer gala her-self. And yet she was nervous about having a cochair. Claire was an artist; she worked alone. There was some sense in which she could call Jason her cochair – the cochair of the family – but if Claire got home tonight and found J.D. on the computer (unshowered, his homework incomplete), the girls lying in bed with tangled hair (you had to comb it out carefully), and Zack zoned out on Jason's lap in front of *Junkyard Wars,* she would throw her arms up in frustration. 'Who is it?'

'Isabelle French,' Lock said. 'Do you know her? She joined the board in the spring.'

Isabelle French. Did Claire know her? She pictured a woman with her hair up, wearing dangly earrings and some kind of funky Indian-print tunic that reminded Claire of the Beatles in their psychedelic years. That was what Isabelle French had been wearing at the gala. She had been drinking a cosmopolitan, she had been dancing; Claire had seen her come off the dance floor pink-faced and breathless. Claire wondered if she was remembering the right woman.

'I . . . think so,' Claire said.

'She's very nice. She's eager to get more involved.'

'She lives . . . ?'

'In New York.'

'Okay. Does she . . . ?'

'Work? No, I don't think so. Other than doing things like this, I mean.'

'Does she have . . . ?'

'Kids? No, no kids.'

There was a beat of silence between them. The charity was called Nantucket's Children; it was for people who cared deeply about children, which generally meant having one or more of your own.

'No kids?' Claire said, wondering if Adams Fiske had been brazen enough to put someone on the board solely because of her pocketbook.

'No kids,' Lock confirmed.

'Is she . . . ?'

'Divorced,' Lock said. 'From a guy I went to college with at

29

Williams, actually. Though that has no bearing. I haven't seen Marshall French in years, and honestly, I know Isabelle only slightly. Adams was the one who brought her aboard. But I know that she's very nice. And eager.'

'Great,' Claire said. And then, lest she not seem eager herself, she pulled a notebook out of her bag – a notebook she had bought for this very reason – and said, 'Should we get to work?'

The Nantucket's Children Summer Gala: The goal was to sell a thousand tickets. The evening started with cocktails and passed hors d'oeuvres. Cocktails were followed by a seated dinner, during which Lock showed a PowerPoint presentation of the programs that Nantucket's Children funded. By the time dinner ended, the guests had (presumably) imbibed a few drinks and the wheels were greased for the auction. The trademark of the Nantucket's Children Summer Gala was that they only auctioned off *one* item (one fabulous item, expected to go for at least fifty thousand dollars). The brief auction gave way, finally, to a concert by a performer or band that had highly danceable hits, like the Beach Boys (2004), like the Village People (2005), like Frankie Valli and the Four Seasons (2007). With underwriting, the event made well over a million dollars. That money was distributed to the twenty-two initiatives and programs set up exclusively for island kids.

'The most important element, no matter what anybody says, is the talent,' Lock told Claire. 'It's what sets our event apart. Anyone can put up a tent. Anyone can hire a caterer and throw together an auction. But we get music. That is what makes us sexy. That is why people come.'

'Right,' Claire said.

'And rumor on the street is that you know – '

'Max West,' Claire said.

'Max West,' Lock said. Again the smile, this time hyped up with admiration. Well, yeah, of course. Max West was a superstar; he was right up there with Elton John, Jon Bon Jovi, Mick Jagger.

He'd had more than thirty hits. He'd been singing for nearly twenty years, since the summer after his and Claire's high school graduation, when he played the Stone Pony in Asbury Park and an agent heard him, and . . . yeah. Rock star. Claire's heart had been broken. God, had she cried, every night after the show, back behind the club, where it smelled like empty beer bottles and trash – she had cried and held on to Matthew's neck because she knew it was ending. She was going to RISD, and he was going to . . . California. To record an album. They had been different people then. He had really been a different person – Matthew Westfield – before he became Max West and played the inaugural parties in Washington, before he played for Princess Diana, before he sold out Shea Stadium six nights in a row, before he recorded a live album in Kathmandu, which went double platinum. Before he got married, twice, and went into rehab, three times.

'Yes, I know him. We went to high school together. He was my . . . boyfriend.'

'That's what someone told me,' Lock said. 'But I didn't – '

'You didn't believe it?' Claire said. Right. No one ever believed it at first. Claire and Matthew had been best friends since seventh grade, and then, one night years later, when they were old enough to be horny and curious, Matthew had kissed her – on a school bus, at night. They were in the chorus together, returning from a trip to the old-folks' home. Not only was Matthew in the chorus, but he was also the lead tenor in the barbershop quartet, and that was the music the old people had liked best. 'Sweet Rosie O'Grady.' They clapped like mad, and Matthew hammed it up, bowing, and kissing an old woman's hand. Standing on the top riser in the soprano section, Claire had felt unaccountably proud of him. So on the dark bus heading back to school, they sat together as they had a hundred times before, and Claire rested her hand on Matthew's thigh, then her head on his shoulder, and the next thing she knew, they were kissing.

'It's not that I didn't *believe* it,' Lock said. 'It's just that, I don't know . . . he's so famous.'

'But he wasn't then,' Claire said. 'Back then he was just a kid, like the rest of us.'

'The question is,' Lock said, 'can we get him?'

'I can try.'

'For free?'

Claire sipped her wine. 'I can try.'

Lock leaned toward her. His eyes were bright. He had very kind eyes, Claire thought. Very kind or very sad. 'You would do that?'

'All I have to do is track him down,' she said. She wrote on the first line of the first page of her notebook: *Find Matthew*. That would be the hard part, finding him. 'I haven't talked to him in years.'

'Really?' Lock said. Now he sounded worried and possibly even suspicious. 'Do you think he'll remember you?'

'I was his high school sweetheart,' Claire said. 'You don't forget your high school sweetheart, do you?'

Lock was staring at her. Claire felt the trill of the piccolo travel right up her spine, and the bass notes of the tuba reverberate in her stomach. Being with Lock, alone, in this 'meeting,' was messing her up. Or maybe it was thinking about Matthew that was making her feel this way – like a teenager, like she was forming a crush, like the world was filled with outlandish romantic possibilities.

'What else?' she said.

Before he could answer, Claire's eye caught on something on the bookshelves to the left of the twenty-paned window. It was a glass vase with green and white tiger stripes and a star-shaped opening. It was one of Claire's pieces, right there in her direct line of vision, but she hadn't noticed it until that second. It was like not recognizing one of her own children. She stood up and took the vase off the shelf, turned it in the light. Two summers earlier, when she was between commissions, she had made twelve of these vases for Transom, a shop in town. The colors varied, but they all had tiger stripes or leopard rosettes. The *Jungle Series,* she called it. Claire's glassblowing career had been all about custom-made, one-of-a-kind commissioned pieces for very wealthy patrons, so it had been fun, and liberating, for Claire to do these vases, which were light, easy, whimsical. Transom had sold out of the vases in only two weeks.

'Where did you get this?' Claire asked.

'In town. At that shop . . .'

'Transom?'

'On the corner there, yes.'

'You bought it?'

'I bought it.'

'You bought it . . . for yourself?'

'For myself, yes. For the office. We kept flowers in it for a few weeks, but I prefer it empty. It's a work of art by itself.'

'Oh,' Claire said.

'I'm a big fan of your glass.'

Now Claire was suspicious. 'How much of my work have you seen?'

'We're friends with the Klaussens,' he said. 'We've seen the *Bubbles.*'

'Ah,' Claire said.

'And I read *GlassArt,* so I've seen your pieces in there. And I'm familiar with the museum pieces.'

'The one piece,' Claire said. 'At the Whitney.'

'And the vases at the museum in Shelburne,' Lock said. 'They're beautiful.'

'Wow,' Claire said. Her face bloomed hot and red; two posies would be appearing on her cheeks. She was embarrassed and flattered – Lock Dixon knew her work. *Knew* it, knew it. He read *GlassArt,* which had a circulation of about seven hundred.

Lock cleared his throat. 'This is going out of order a bit, but I wonder if you would be willing to put a piece up for bid, as the auction item.'

'At the gala, you mean?'

Lock nodded.

Claire shook her head, confused. The auction item at the gala was something outrageous, something money couldn't buy: a week in a castle in Scotland with golf at St. Andrews, or an Italian feast for twelve cooked by Mario Batali.

'I don't get it. We have to make money.'

'Right, so the piece would have to be on par with the *Bubbles* series.'

Claire returned to her chair and polished off her wine. Because she hadn't eaten anything, her head was vibrating like a tuning fork. 'I don't work anymore. I shut down the hot shop when my son was born.'

'But as I understood it, that was temporary? A sabbatical rather than retirement?'

Claire put her hands to her face to cool her cheeks. Lock Dixon knew more about her – much more – than she would have guessed. Claire was curious. He understood this how? From whom? Claire herself didn't know when she would resume working. The hot shop behind the house was now shuttered and locked, cold and dormant. Claire looked at the shop with longing – of course she did, glassblowing was in her blood – but also with a sense that she was a woman with her priorities straight. She had four children who needed her. She could go back to glassblowing once she had them all safely in school.

'I'm not working anymore,' Claire repeated.

'So you won't do a piece for the auction?'

Claire stared at him. Was he taunting her? Was he daring her to say no? He poured her more wine, which she gratefully accepted.

'I'm not working,' she said.

'Just think how that will bolster the price,' Lock said. 'You haven't produced anything in over a year – it will be nearly two years by next August, right? This would be your triumphant return.'

'But art is subjective. What if I make something and nobody likes it?'

'You're a genius.'

'Now you're teasing me.'

'Tell you what,' he said.

'What?' Claire said.

He was quiet, looking at her, the hint of a smile on his face. Claire was confounded. He was teasing her and she was enjoying it. Her sensibilities were aroused, her intelligence piqued. Lock Dixon was, perhaps, the only person in the world – short of her handful of patrons – who cared if she started blowing glass again. But he couldn't egg her into it just because he was a man, a wealthy man, a man who had poured her a glass of wine, a man whose wife Claire had unintentionally wronged. He couldn't make her do it. She *did* have boundaries!

'What?' she said again.

'I'll bid fifty thousand dollars on it myself.'

'What?' Claire said, incredulous now.

He bent over to look her in the eye. His face was so close she could have kissed him. Just the fleeting thought of kissing him put the color back into her cheeks. She pushed him away mentally and backed up a few inches in her chair.

'You will not.'

'I will. Fifty thousand dollars. If you create a piece for the auction, a real Claire Danner Crispin original, museum quality, one-of-a-kind, whatever your mind's eye comes up with, I will bid fifty thousand dollars on it myself.'

Claire shook her head. He was kidding. He had to be kidding: fifty thousand dollars was the sum of his take-home pay as executive director.

'You're nuts,' she said.

'Maybe I am,' he said, in a way that seemed to have meaning, and although Claire was high from the wine, she didn't let him undermine her resolve.

35

She stood up. 'I don't work anymore,' she said, astonishing herself. She wanted to give back to the universe, she wanted to act in kindness – but even she had her limits.

The kids were all asleep when Claire got home, and she checked on them one by one, rooting around like a raccoon in the dark. They seemed reasonably clean, the girls' hair was combed, and J.D.'s homework was complete, though stuffed into his backpack like garbage. Claire smoothed out the pages of long division and tucked it in neatly. In the nursery, she pulled the blanket over Zack's shoulders and stroked his cheek. God, how she worried about him! He *was* healthy, despite having been a preemie; her pediatrician, Dr. Patel, reassured her of this again and again.

In their bedroom, Jason was waiting for her. He wanted sex all the time, even after so many years of marriage. Tonight would have been a good night to indulge him with a serious, creative effort, but sex seemed too tame for Claire's mood. Her meeting with Lock Dixon had gotten her gears turning. She wanted to pore over her back issues of *GlassArt*. She wanted to go into the hot shop – museum-quality piece! – and sketch until dawn.

'Come to bed,' Jason said.

Thinking about the hot shop suddenly felt illicit. 'How were the kids?'

'Fine. Come to bed.'

'Don't you want to know how my meeting was?'

'How was your meeting?'

'It was amazing,' she said. He didn't ask her to elaborate, and Claire thought, *Why bother?* Her definition of amazing was completely different from Jason's definition of amazing. Jason was a contractor; amazing for him was the plumber showing up on time. It was a thirty-nine-inch striper caught with a fly.

'Come to bed, please, Claire. Please, baby?'

'Okay,' she said. She brushed her teeth, then took her time

washing her face and moisturizing, then wiping down the granite vanity and the bowl of the sink, hoping that Jason would fall asleep. But when she crawled into bed, Jason had his light on. He was facing her side of the bed with his hands out, like she was a basketball he was about to catch.

'The kids didn't wear you out?' she asked.

'Naw, they were great.'

'You read to them?'

'I read to Zack. Ottilie read to Shea. J.D. did his homework, then read his chapter book.'

'Good,' Claire said, relaxing. 'So, the meeting . . .' She paused – not because she was hesitant to admit that it had only been her and Lock at the meeting, but because Jason's hands were already traveling up inside her camisole. He wasn't interested in what had transpired at her meeting. Claire grabbed Jason's wrists, but he was persistent, and she let him go. Their sex life was robust, but there was a part of their marriage that had withered, if it had ever existed at all. What was it? They didn't talk. If Claire said these words now to Jason, *We don't talk,* he would tell her she was being silly. He would say, *We talk all the time.* Yes, about the kids, about what was for dinner, about the car being serviced, about Joe's fortieth birthday next week, about what bills needed to be paid, about when he'd be home from work. But if Claire tried to explain her meeting with Lock and its many tangents – Matthew, how it felt to think about Matthew, how it felt to think about Daphne and the accident, Lock's interest in Claire's glass and his request that she come out of retirement on behalf of the auction item – Jason would glaze over. Bored. She would be keeping him from what was really important – the sex! Furthermore, he might grow angry at what Claire told him: Who was *Lock Dixon* to tell his wife to start blowing glass again? It was easier for Claire to keep her mouth shut, to indulge Jason physically and try to quiet the agitation in her mind.

Find Matthew. Museum-quality piece. Silver belt buckle. The

37

Jungle Series. *Whalebone corsets. Viognier that tasted like a meadow. Fifty thousand dollars. Classical music: she really should learn more about it.*

She closed her eyes and kissed her husband.

CHAPTER TWO

HE HAUNTS HER

The Crispin children started waking up at six thirty. They awoke in reverse order to their age – Zack first, then Shea. At four and a half, Shea was very challenging. J.D. and Ottilie had always been labeled 'the big kids,' which left Shea and Zack as 'the babies,' but Shea did not appreciate being called a baby, nor did she like being lumped in with Zack. As a result, she was constantly trying to distinguish herself; everything had to be done 'the Shea way.' Her pancakes had to be cut with a chef's knife because she liked 'square pieces'; otherwise the pieces would be called 'ugly' and were therefore inedible. She would not sit next to Ottilie at any meal, and she would not have her hair styled like Ottilie's, nor would she wear any of Ottilie's hand-me-downs. Ottilie, for her part, was preternaturally beautiful, with long hair streaked the colors of fine wood – mahogany, heart pine, Brazilian cherry. She was, at the age of eight, already a teenager, already using her

ballet training to swing her hips provocatively. Ottilie was preco-
cious, brilliant, adept at sweet-talking her parents, her teachers,
her legions of friends. And J.D., Claire's oldest, was a golden child,
reading three grades above level, a leader on the ball field and the
basketball court, an altar boy at Saint Mary's. He was pleasant and
easygoing and respectful. If Claire received compliments about
her parenting, it was because she had great kids. But they were
great on their own; they had been born great. Claire didn't want
to take any credit.

She did, however, try hard as a mother. She would say she'd
always tried hard, had always put her children's needs before her
own – but now that there was no glass in her life, she channeled
all her frenetic, creative energy into parenting. Her kids were only
going to be young once; she wanted to enjoy them. She now had
time to pack healthy lunches, to volunteer in all three classrooms,
to chaperone field trips, to read *Harry Potter* aloud at night, to
make every practice, every ball game, and every ballet lesson early
or on time. She was more focused; her house was cleaner; her kids,
she thought, were happier now that they had her full attention. Her
parenting wasn't perfect, but it was earnest and well intentioned.

Just look at Claire this morning: She made breakfast for four kids
(bacon, buttermilk pancakes, chocolate milk, vitamin pills). She
chose clothes for four kids (the only one she could truly dress
anymore was Zack; with the other three, the struggle was what
matched, what was appropriate for school, what was clean). She
packed lunch for three kids (J.D. liked strawberries, Ottilie demanded an obscene amount of mayonnaise on her sandwich, and
Shea was 'allergic' to strawberries – the only 'fruit' she would
eat without a fight was canned mandarin oranges). Claire kept
track of homework, library books, permission slips, and whatever
equipment – cleats, gloves, skates, goggles – they needed for their
after-school activities (there was a color-coded schedule taped to
the fridge). It wasn't always the well-oiled machine that Claire

dreamed of. Often, there were extenuating circumstances: someone had a 'stomach ache' or a luridly loose tooth; it was pouring rain, or blizzarding sideways, or Zack had one of his inexplicable screaming fits and the noise pushed them all to the edge of insanity. *Mom, make him stop!* Many times, Claire stood in her own kitchen and thought, *I can't believe I make it through the morning, much less the rest of the day.* Many times, Claire felt like a triage nurse: What needed her attention first?

This was the life she had chosen. She repeated certain thoughts like a mantra – *Good mother! Only young once! Enjoy them!* – as she shepherded them out the door.

Claire drove the kids to school. She took two to the elementary school and one to Montessori. Zack was strapped into his car seat, crying for his bottle, which none of the other three deigned to give him. Shea plugged her ears. The car was always loud, but Claire made a point to call Siobhan anyway. Siobhan had stopped at two kids, but Liam and Aidan were total hellions and fought incessantly, and Siobhan's car was just as noisy.

'I woke up this morning and checked my calendar,' Siobhan said. 'I see I missed your meeting last night. How was it?'

'Oh,' Claire said. The meeting had been a scant twelve hours earlier, and yet it had slipped down the drain with the dishwater. Her excitement had vaporized. But something lingered, some feelings about Lock Dixon. Could she share these feelings with Siobhan? She and Siobhan were married to brothers; they were frank with each other about their marriages. They loved to complain – *sneaking cigarettes, too much TV, always bugging me for sex* – and they loved to one-up each other when they complained. (Because Siobhan and Carter worked together, she claimed they were twice as sick of each other at the end of the day.) Siobhan had a crush on the Korean UPS man; Claire thought the twenty-year-old who picked up her trash was cute. They talked about other men in a funny, harmless way all the time. But Claire decided not to say anything about Lock, if only

41

because she couldn't tell what her feelings were, exactly. 'It was fine. We talked about preliminary stuff.'

'Do you have a cochair?' Siobhan asked.

'I do. A woman named Isabelle French.'

'Isabelle French?'

'Yeah. Do you know her?'

Siobhan was quiet. This was very strange. Claire checked her phone, thinking it had cut out.

'Are you there?' Claire said.

'Yep.'

'Is everything okay?'

'We did a luncheon for Isabelle French this summer,' Siobhan said.

'You did? Where does she live?'

'Out in Monomoy. But not on the harbor. In the woods. On Brewster Road. Between Monomoy and Shimmo, really.'

'Okay, so what's the deal? Did she not pay her bill? Was she a total bitch?'

'No, she was fine. With me.'

'Was she rude to Alec?' Alec was Siobhan and Carter's Jamaican head server. 'Did she use a racial slur?'

'No,' Siobhan said. 'She was fine, agreeable, very nice. There was just this awful moment when she was out on the porch chatting away, and a coven of witches were in the kitchen slicing her to ribbons. I guess there was an incident in New York. She was at some big party and she drank too much and she kissed some woman's husband on the dance floor, and it turned into this big thing where no one would speak to her and she stopped getting invited to things. She used to sit on the board of one of the big hospitals, but I guess they asked her to step down. It didn't sound too good.'

'They were talking about her behind her back in *her* kitchen?' Claire said.

'Yeah. It made me nauseated, honestly.'

'Did they know you were there, listening?'

'I'm the caterer. Did they care?'

'So, do you think it's bad that she's my cochair?'

'No, I don't think it's bad,' Siobhan said. 'Just so you know, her own people don't like her.'

Claire and Zack walked back into the house at ten past eight, and the silence was like a big sigh of relief. Pan sat at the counter eating a bowl of Cocoa Puffs, a cereal forbidden to the children.

Why does Pan get to eat it?

Well, Pan is an adult.

Pan was twenty-seven years old, from an island off the southwest coast of Thailand, in the Andaman Sea. Pan had arrived after Zack was born to work as an au pair, although Claire liked to think of it as a 'cultural exchange.' With Zack's difficult birth, and with the demands of a fourth child, having an extra set of hands in the house seemed wise. Having Pan around allowed Claire to be a better mother. Pan played creative games with the older children, she cleaned and straightened, she prepared mouthwatering Thai food, but she was the best, perhaps, with Zack. In Thailand, apparently, babies were never put down. They were constantly carried and therefore they did not cry. When Zack was with Pan, he was held and carried. When Zack was with Claire, and Claire, out of necessity, set him down – *I have to get dinner ready, sweetie* – he howled. Sometimes it was so bad that Pan came out of her room and picked him up, and although Claire was then relieved, she was also suspicious. Maybe Zack's problem was that he was coddled, spoiled, soft. Maybe all of Pan's nurturing had quelled Zack's natural desire to explore, to learn, to interact. Or maybe Pan held him all the time because she, too, sensed there was something wrong.

'Here,' Pan said. 'I take.' She stood up from her stool and reached for Zack.

'You finish. I've got him.'

'I take,' Pan said. Zack was no fool. He lunged for her.

43

'Okay,' Claire said. And then, like an automaton: 'I have a hundred things to do.' Such as the breakfast dishes – plates sticky with syrup, cups with chocolate sludge coating the bottom – and then the counters and the stools. Then Claire went upstairs. The kids nominally made their beds, but Claire had to remake them. She was put out by the thought of her children climbing into a sloppy bed. She liked crisp, clean sheets and a neatly folded comforter. She flushed the toilet in the kids' bathroom, put all of the toothbrushes into the plastic cup, and rinsed the dried toothpaste out of the sink. But what she realized was that she was watching herself do these things rather than just doing them. She was doing them and at the same time wondering what Lock Dixon would think if he were watching her. Or Matthew. God, she had to find Matthew.

She got started on the laundry. If she missed a day of laundry, it spiraled out of control. Did any of these details matter to anybody but Claire? The details that ruled her life, the five thousand tasks that cropped up in her day like obstacles in a video game – if Claire died or got sick, or took on a consuming project such as the summer gala, and these tasks didn't get done, what would happen? Would the house get run into the ground? Would her children become derelicts? In her heart she believed the answer was yes. Her efforts mattered. She threw a load of darks into the machine.

At ten o'clock she tried to do some yoga on the floor of her bedroom. She unrolled a mat and positioned herself in downward dog. The room was filled with sunlight, and being in downward dog felt good. She wondered again about Lock Dixon. If he could see her this second, would he be impressed by her flexibility? (No. Even Claire's ninety-two-year-old grandmother could do downward dog.) She was too lazy to get herself into another position, and honestly, it had been so long since she'd made it to yoga that she'd forgotten all the positions, anyway. If she tried one now, it would be incorrect and offer no real benefit.

She sat up. Her head was buzzing. She hadn't eaten anything;

she had forgotten herself. And that was the reason Claire was so thin; it had nothing to do with yoga.

The phone rang. Would it be Lock? One thing about cochairing the summer gala was that the phone would ring and it would be Lock, or Isabelle French – or Matthew! – instead of Jeremy Tate-Friedman, her client from London, telling her he'd had a dream about an orchestra that played instruments made of glass. Would Claire, for the right price, consider making a glass flute, one that actually worked? (Her career had been subject to – indeed, dependent on – the eccentricities of a handful of very wealthy people.) Claire checked the caller ID: it was Siobhan. But Claire didn't pick up the phone; she had too much on her mind. It was still Lock. Okay, this was pitiful. The man was following her around her own house like a ghost who had unfinished business with the living. Why? What did he want? He wanted her to create a museum-quality piece of glass for the auction. He wanted her to burst out of retirement, like a woman jumping out of a cake, in front of a thousand paying guests. Break the shackles of motherhood, emerge from the cave where she had been shutting herself away like a hermit. She had been out of the hot shop for months and – *Just admit it, Claire!* – she missed it. A part of her yearned for it. People like Jeremy Tate-Friedman called, and Elsa, the woman who owned the shop Transom, called. (Would Claire produce another *Jungle Series*? The vases had sold so quickly!) But these people did not provide the right impetus for Claire to return to the hot shop. Lock, somehow, had pushed a different button. He had used the element of surprise. He read *GlassArt;* he knew not only her piece at the Whitney but her piece at the Yankee Ingenuity Museum in Shelburne, Vermont, as well. He appreciated her work, and hence he appreciated her, Claire, in a way that few other people did. Who would have guessed? Lock Dixon was a fan. He had always made her nervous; Claire thought this was because of Daphne and the accident.

But maybe not.

* * *

Claire wondered if Lock Dixon had ever seen the inside of a hot shop. If he was willing to pay fifty thousand dollars for a piece of glass, then he must know something about the craft. Maybe he had been to Simon Pearce; there were two studios now where you could watch the guys blow out a few goblets, then go upstairs to a fancy restaurant and eat a warm goat cheese salad with candied pecans. Or maybe Lock had seen glass blown in Colonial Williamsburg or Sturbridge Village, or on a school trip to Corning. She would ask him the next time they were alone. Would they ever be alone again? Why did she care? Did she find Lock Dixon attractive? Well, he was twenty pounds overweight and balding on top, so no, he wasn't Derek Jeter or Brad Pitt, and he wasn't a twenty-year-old hunk, like the kid who worked for Santos Rubbish. He wasn't as handsome as Jason (who had a washboard stomach and a thick head of blond hair). But Lock had nice eyes – and that smile. There had been something between them last night in the office – a connection, an energy – that had not been present during lunch at the yacht club or at the handful of board meetings that Claire had attended. A spark, something that caught fire and smoldered. Claire's interest, her desire. But why? This was the kind of question Siobhan *loved:* Why this person and not that person? Why now and not before? Why did love, lust, romance, even the real, deep, and true stuff you felt for your husband, always mellow (and then, in some cases, sour)? And if the mellowing was inevitable, did that mean you simply gave up that tingling, stomach-swooping, giddy, God-I'm-in-love-or-lust feeling forever? Were you left with your hopeless crush on George Clooney or the UPS man? Siobhan could talk about this stuff for hours as she filled phyllo with lobster meat and fresh corn, but until today, these questions had never interested Claire. Until today, she couldn't have cared less.

Claire's hot shop was locked up like Fort Knox. When she worked, the furnace ran night and day, and so the term 'hot shop' was something of an understatement. Jason called it the Belly of

Hell. Jason had built the hot shop for Claire because there was no glass studio on the island. He'd started out reluctantly. *One expensive hobby,* he called it. They spent tens of thousands of dollars on the pot furnace, the glory hole, the punties, the benches, the molds, the shaping tools, the colored frit, the annealer. A small fortune. Eventually, however, Jason became fascinated with the construction of the hot shop. He was building the only glassblowing studio on the island. For his wife, who was trained in the craft; she had a degree from RISD! She could make things – vases and goblets and sculpture – and sell them. Now the hot shop had paid for itself, and Claire had made enough money from the whims of her kooky patrons to pay off the car and plump the kids' college funds.

She could not believe she was doing this. She glanced back at the house, stealthily, feeling like a criminal as she unlocked the heavy metal door. But why? There was nothing wrong with blowing glass again. Pan would take care of Zack, and the other kids were at school all day, so . . . why not? But there was guilt. It had to do with her fall. Claire should never have subjected herself to the heat when she was so far along in her pregnancy. She should have been drinking more water. The doctor had warned her! And it was Zack who had paid the price. *There's something wrong with him.*

Still, she stepped inside. She was an alcoholic opening the liquor cabinet; she was a junkie visiting her dealer. But that was ridiculous! She had, after all, come into the hot shop plenty of times in the past year – to get tools, to go over her books with the accountants, to show Pan the pieces she'd made as a beginner – but Claire had never come in with the intention of starting up again. When she turned off the heat, she did so in the name of her family. She had four kids, a husband, and a home that needed her.

Claire stood in the center of the shop and looked around. *Just admit it!* She was dying to get back in there.

Claire's attraction to molten glass was atavistic; it was coded somewhere on her DNA. She was drawn to the flame, to the unsafe temperatures, to the blinding light. A blob of molten glass on the end of a blowpipe contained her life's meaning, even though it was hot and dangerous. She had burned herself and cut herself too many times to remember; she had scars with stories she'd forgotten. But she loved working with glass the way she loved her children – unconditionally, and despite the real possibility of failure. Molten glass fell to the floor, she marvered incorrectly and came out with something lopsided, she blew a piece too thin, she necked incorrectly and could not transfer the piece to the punty, she cooled a piece too quickly and it shattered in the annealer. There was nothing about glass that was forgiving; it was a craft, but also a science. It took precision, concentration, practice.

She found a half-empty sketchbook on her worktable. *Museum-quality piece?* The piece at the Whitney was a sculpture of thinly blown-out spheres – so thinly blown that they had to be placed in a soundproof room – all of which held hints of prismatic color and interlocked like soap bubbles. The sculpture was called *Bubbles III*. (*Bubbles I* and *II* were housed in the private galleries of Chick and Caroline Klaussen and Chick Klaussen sat on the board of the Whitney.) The Yankee Ingenuity Museum displayed a set of nesting vases with differently shaped openings. When you looked down into the vases, it was like looking into a kaleidoscope. Claire had done the vases in sea colors – turquoise, cobalt, jade, celadon. Claire and Jason and the kids had traveled to Vermont to see the vases on display. The vases were lovely and well displayed in the small, rustic museum, though they didn't compare to the *Bubbles* at the Whitney. Claire couldn't do another in the *Bubbles* series for the auction; that would be like Leonardo repainting the *Mona Lisa*. But Claire could possibly create another set of nesting vases. Would they be worth fifty thousand dollars?

The door opened and the room filled with breeze. Claire turned. Pan stood in the doorway. Claire felt like she'd been caught.

'Where's Zack?' Claire said.

'He sleep,' Pan said.

'I'm thinking about working again,' Claire said.

Pan nodded. She was still very brown from the summer. She wore a black tank top and khaki capri pants and a thin silver chain with a tiny bell on it around her neck. Claire had paid twice already to have this chain repaired after Zack had yanked it off. Claire suggested Pan not wear the chain while she was working, but Pan ignored this advice and that was fine. The chain and the bell were part of Pan's persona, part of her magic. Pan was short and lithe, and her glossy black hair was cut into a rounded pageboy. She was both adorable and androgynous. With the silver chain and the tiny, tinkling bell, she reminded Claire of a wood sprite.

'What do you think?' Claire asked.

Pan tilted her head.

'About me working?'

Pan shrugged. Possibly she didn't understand the question, and certainly she didn't understand what Claire's working again would entail.

Claire shook her head. 'Never mind,' she said.

Pan left, but Claire lingered for another few moments on the bench, paging through her sketchbook. Once upon a time, she had made an elaborate pair of candlesticks for Mr. Fred Bulrush of San Francisco. The pulled-taffy candlesticks. She had come upon the design by accident, holding on to the gather with tweezers while rolling the blowpipe; she had twisted and pulled the molten glass, then rolled it into blue and purple frit that she'd scattered on the marvering table. She was like a kid with clay, and she thought she'd end up with a kid's mess, but the colors blended beautifully and the form cooled a bit and Claire recognized it as a candlestick stem. She added a foot and blew out a small bowl, and when it came out of the annealer, she thought, *This is really cool.* It looked, to Claire, like a psychedelic Popsicle. It was Jason who thought it looked like pulled taffy. He liked it as much as Claire did, but then he said, *What are you going to do with one candlestick?*

And Claire thought, *Right. I'll never in a million years be able to make another one.*

She tried again and got close – the color wasn't quite identical and the twistiness was off – but that was what made it art. She took a picture of the candlesticks and sent it to Mr. Fred Bulrush, a mysteriously wealthy man – a former associate of Timothy Leary's – who loved Claire's work because he believed it contained what he called 'the elation and pain' of her soul. Bulrush paid twenty-five hundred dollars for the pair.

What about turning the idea upside down? Upside-down candlesticks: a chandelier. Claire had always wanted to do a chandelier. What about a pulled-taffy chandelier that would cascade from the ceiling like party streamers, each strand ending in a lightbulb the size of a grape? God, it could be utterly fantastic. Would Lock like that?

Two o'clock came and Claire picked up J.D. and Ottilie at the elementary school, then Shea at Montessori. J.D. and Ottilie had Little League at three, and Shea had soccer at three thirty. Claire had snacks and drinks for everybody, J.D. and Ottilie's mitts, hats, and uniform shirts, Shea's cleats and shin guards. The kids piled into the car with their lunch boxes, their backpacks, and assorted art projects. J.D. had a flyer for an open house, which wafted like an autumn leaf into the front seat.

'How was school?' Claire asked.

J.D. ripped open a bag of Fritos. Nobody answered. Claire checked the rearview mirror; Shea was struggling with her seat belt.

'What did you do today?' Claire said. 'J.D.?'

'Nothing,' J.D. said.

'Nothing,' Ottilie said.

'Shea?'

'I can't get my seat belt buckled.'

'J.D., will you help her, please?'

J.D. huffed. 'Of *course*,' he said.

Claire smiled. She was not Julie Andrews, these were not the von Trapp children, these were children who had apparently done nothing during a whole day of school – but everything was okay. She had gone into the hot shop, but the fact of the matter was, she liked her life the way it was now. She was consumed with making sure the kids had what they needed. Because she had spent so much time mooning over her sketchbook, she had forgotten to put the laundry in the dryer, and she hadn't done anything about dinner, so things would be insane when she got home, and there would be Zack to deal with because Pan was off at five. Claire didn't have time to create a museum-quality piece. And yet the feeling remained, the tug. The pulled-taffy chandelier was the most exciting idea she'd had in a long time. Claire turned into the parking lot of the town recreational fields. The rec fields were the site of the summer gala; they were the only place big enough to accommodate the tent and a concert for a thousand people. Claire wondered if there was any reason she would see Lock Dixon at the rec fields, and decided the answer was no.

The soccer fields were a great place to get a glimpse of 'Nantucket's children.' On Shea's team alone, the kids spoke five languages – there were two Haitian girls, a Bulgarian boy, a pair of Lithuanian twins whose parents were deaf (they spoke English, Lithuanian, and Lithuanian sign language). The diversity was amazing, it was exciting; the soccer program was well organized and impeccably administered. It was funded by Nantucket's Children.

When Claire saw her own group of friends – Delaney Kitt, Amie Trimble, Julie Jackson – she felt the way men must feel about their fellow soldiers: *We're all in the foxhole together, fighting the same war.* Raising young children, enjoying them, because they would only be young once.

Claire walked up to Julie Jackson. Julie was a natural beauty; she had curly blond hair and was even thinner than Claire (kickboxing).

Julie Jackson had three kids, she sold stationery and occasionally hosted an at-home show, and she served on the board of the ice rink. When Claire saw her, she thought, *Committee!*

'Hey,' Claire said.

'Hey!' Julie said. 'How are you? Did you bring the baby? God, I haven't seen him in forever. He must be getting so big.'

'Yeah,' Claire said. Her good mood was like a balloon that she accidentally let go – floating away, up over the trees, out of sight. Claire didn't bring Zack to the soccer field on purpose. She didn't want the other mothers to see him and sense something wrong and then confer with one another about whether it was because he'd been *so premature*. 'He's home with Pan.'

'So, what's new?' Julie asked.

'Oh, not much,' Claire said. How to broach the subject? She should send an e-mail, she decided. But that was cowardly – and this was the perfect place to ask. They were overlooking a veritable United Nations on the six-and-under soccer team. 'I agreed to cochair the summer gala. The benefit for Nantucket's Children? Hey, you know, I would love to have you serve on the committee. Would you consider it?'

Julie Jackson had her eyes glued on her son, Eddie, who had the ball. Julie didn't answer Claire, and Claire debated whether to repeat herself. Claire suddenly felt like she'd asked Julie Jackson to join her on the chain gang.

'Do you know what I'm talking about?' Claire said. 'The summer gala? It's held right here, in August . . .'

'I know,' Julie said. 'Lock Dixon's thing. Was he the one who asked you?'

'Yes,' Claire said. She found herself flustered at the mention of Lock's name. Julie had been in the cab the night of Daphne's accident. Was she making a connection? 'They want me to get Max West.'

'Oh, right,' Julie said. 'I forgot you knew him.' Did she say this ironically, or was Claire just too sensitive?

'Yeah,' Claire said.

'I can't take on one more thing,' Julie said. 'I just can't.'

'Right,' Claire said. 'I understand.'

'Me, either,' Delaney Kitt said.

'Me, either,' Amie Trimble said. 'Ted would kill me. It always seems harmless to join this committee or that committee, but it ends up being hundreds of hours and thousands of dollars.'

'Yeah,' Julie said. She grinned at Claire. 'But it's great that you're doing it, Claire. You're a good egg, making time in your life for this.'

'*Such* a good egg,' Delaney echoed.

'It's going to be so much work,' Amie said. 'Better you than me!'

Claire was late getting home from the rec fields because there was an injured bird on the side of the road. She saw it there, the sparrow or wren, hit by a car, maybe, or nipped by someone's dog, injured, struggling, but not dead. The kids were limp and exhausted in the backseat; they didn't see the bird, and Claire thought, *Keep going!* She only had five minutes to get home in time to relieve Pan. But no, she couldn't ignore it. When she pulled over and said, 'Look at that poor little bird,' the kids perked up a little, but they did not get out of the car.

Claire knelt by the bird. Something was wrong with its leg and its wing. It hopped lopsidedly. Claire heard a car horn. Amie Trimble slowed down.

'What are you doing?'

'Injured birdie patrol,' Claire said.

Amie shook her head, smiled, drove off.

Claire reached out to pick up the bird, but the bird was having none of it. It hopped out of her reach, and Claire hurried down the sandy border of the road chasing it. Julie Jackson drove by. Claire stood up and looked at the back of Julie's car. Claire was the only person she knew who would stop for a bird, she was the only person she knew who would agree to cochair something as colossal and consuming as the gala – but instead of making her feel virtuous, she felt like a bloody fool. *You're a good egg, making time in your life for this.* She *didn't* have time – *Get back in the car!* – but she could not in good conscience leave the lame little bird here. She sneaked up on the bird and got a hand under it. The kids were cheering her on now from the car. This was all the little bird needed: it got aloft, flew away. Claire was relieved. She headed back to the car. The kids were clapping.

A few days later, Claire and Siobhan went on one of their rare girls' nights out, just the two of them, eating cheeseburgers and *frites* and drinking wine at Le Languedoc. There was a viognier on the wine list, and Claire's mind flickered to Lock and how she had wanted, more than anything during that meeting, to please him. She ordered the wine, but she did not bring up the topic of Lock Dixon with Siobhan, because if she had, Siobhan would have teased her. Siobhan had something of the schoolyard bully in her. She taunted, she poked, she prodded; she was always making out-landish suggestions and daring Claire to join her. It was commonly understood that Siobhan was naughty and Claire was nice; Claire was sweet and Siobhan was spicy; Siobhan carried the pitchfork, Claire wore the halo. Siobhan cursed like a sailor and danced on tabletops. Claire carried spiders outside instead of smushing them in a paper towel like a normal person. Siobhan was the one people wanted to be stuck with on a deserted island; Claire was the choice if the plane was going down and there was only one parachute. She would hand it right over.

'Let's go to the Chicken Box,' Siobhan said now. 'Find a couple of hot guys and go dancing.'

'No way,' Claire said.

Siobhan frowned. Her darling square glasses slipped down her nose. 'You're no fun,' she said, inhaling her wine. 'Why couldn't I have gotten a sister-in-law who was fun? You're a boring bore.'

Yes, Claire felt like a boring bore, but she also felt virtuous, and doubly so because she knew Siobhan wouldn't go looking for trouble on her own, and she was correct. They paid their bill; they went home to their husbands.

The next day, at hockey practice, Siobhan's son Liam got slammed against the boards and suffered a gruesome break in his arm. Carter flew with Liam to Boston, where he was going to be operated on, while Siobhan stayed home with Aidan and cried and worked her way around the rosary beads.

Surgery, she said. *Jesus, Mary, and Joseph. Cutting up my baby. Putting him under.*

Claire went to the grocery store while the kids were at school, with the idea of getting a chicken to roast to take to Siobhan and Aidan, as well as some Oreos and ice cream to cheer them up. The store was quiet and nearly empty.

Claire was relieved that she and Siobhan had not misbehaved the other night. Unlike the Crispin brothers, Claire and Siobhan were Irish Catholics and hence were united in the belief that when you did something bad, something bad happened to you.

But what if that *weren't* true? Claire thought as she wandered down frozen foods in search of Häagen-Dazs. What if things weren't connected? After all, Siobhan had behaved like a saint, and Liam still got hurt.

Claire heard a harsh laugh. She looked up and, at the other end of the aisle, saw Daphne Dixon. Oooooooooohhhh. Very bad. Claire could spend hours having conversations in the Stop & Shop with nearly anyone, but Daphne Dixon was someone Claire did her best, now, to avoid. She wanted to duck behind the tall display of dog food and disappear, but Daphne spotted her. The laugh, which sounded like the cackle of a satanic rock star, seemed to be aimed at Claire.

'Hi,' Claire called out. She waved but made no motion forward. She could get away with just this, perhaps – a wave and pivot – and at the expense of Siobhan's ice cream, she was out of there. She did get a gander at Daphne, however, and was surprised to find that she looked fabulous. She'd had her hair colored so that it was very dark, and she wore a white tank top and a quilted jacket and a gold medallion necklace that glinted against her tan breastbone.

The first time Claire had ever laid eyes on Daphne Dixon had been ten years earlier. Claire was pregnant with J.D., and she and Jason were at a pool party. Claire was miserable, first of all because she was wearing a maternity bathing suit the size of a circus tent, and second, because everyone was drinking Coronas and margaritas except for her. Jason, who had never gotten the hang of being a sympathetic partner in pregnancy, was especially drunk. He pointed across the pool at Daphne Dixon, who was wearing a tan bikini that made her look nude, and said, 'That woman has beautiful tits.'

She may indeed have had beautiful tits, and Jason may only have been making an innocent observation as he claimed, but once you heard your husband say that a woman had 'beautiful tits,' you could never give that woman a 100 percent endorsement.

Somehow, though, Daphne had won Claire over. Later, at that same party, Daphne cooed over Claire because she was pregnant. Daphne and Lock had a five-year-old daughter named Heather, and Daphne confided that she had very much wanted a second child, but she'd suffered complications after Heather was born. When she found out Claire was a glassblower, she went wild. She loved glass; she was a devotee of Dale Chihuly. She would love, someday, to see Claire's work. Okay, Claire thought. (Claire worshipped Chihuly, too.) Daphne knew what she was talking about.

A year or so later, Daphne and Heather started spending more time on the island. Daphne enrolled Heather in the elementary school, and Lock commuted to Nantucket from Boston on the weekends. Claire saw Daphne every so often and they chatted about preschools and swim lessons and the commissions Claire was working on. Then Claire got pregnant with Ottilie, and Daphne, again, was interested and attentive. She even dropped off a tiny pink sweater at the hospital with a note that said, 'As soon as you're ready for a girls' night out, call me!'

The Daphne Dixon that Claire remembered from those days was extremely normal and good-hearted. She was lovely, really.

Claire stopped in the chicken section and threw the biggest roaster she could find into her cart. She was afraid to look behind her.

'Claire?'

Claire turned, very slowly. Daphne was right there, inches from Claire's face. Claire could smell Daphne's perfume and something else: vinegar. The salad dressing, maybe, from Daphne's lunch. Claire thought it again: *Ohhhhhhhhhh, very bad.*

'Hi,' Claire said. She hadn't seen Daphne Dixon in ages; her voice should convey more excitement. Instead it contained false enthusiasm, dread, the old, useless guilt, and fear that what was coming was not going to be pleasant. 'Daphne, how are you?'

'Fine fine fine fine fine fine fine,' Daphne said, in a way that made Claire, like J.D., think, *Mental patient.* 'I'm fine. Lock told me you're chairing the gala this year.'

'Yes,' Claire said. 'I am.'

'You know why they asked you, right?' Daphne said. 'Right right right?'

'Right,' Claire said. 'Because – '

'They want Max West,' Daphne said. 'But Lock doesn't think you'll be able to deliver.' They'd been talking for ten seconds, and already Daphne had landed a jab. The most pronounced result of the car accident was that Daphne had lost the filter between the appropriate and the inappropriate. She had lost her ability to finesse social situations, to turn a blind eye, candy-coat, lie. 'So Lock has a call in to Steven Tyler, from Aerosmith. We knew him a little in Boston.'

'Okay, but I'm pretty sure that – '

'And the other gal, Isabelle French? She's making some calls to

57

people on Broadway. Though frankly, I think she's pretending to be more connected than she actually is.'

'I've never met her,' Claire said. 'We have a meeting, though, next week.'

'I want you to tell me if Isabelle French makes any overtures toward my husband. Will you tell me?'

'Overtures?'

'If she touches him, or if they spend time alone together. I want you to call me. Between you and me, that woman is a viper. Here, I'm going to give you my card.' Daphne rifled through her purse, which was also quilted. She was wearing jeans and a pair of suede Jack Rogers sandals. She looked great, but this was just plain old deception. Daphne pulled out a business card and handed it to Claire. It was white, with Daphne's name and various phone numbers printed in navy. Claire had never known anyone to have a business card just for herself, as a person. It was unusual, right, an affectation of the wealthy? The card should read *Daphne Dixon, Crazy Person* or *Daphne Dixon, Mental Patient* so that you would know never to dial the numbers. Even if you did see Isabelle French grabbing Lock Dixon by the necktie and planting a kiss on his lips.

'Okay,' Claire said. 'Will do.'

'I mean it, Claire,' Daphne Dixon said. She tucked her very dark hair behind one red ear. Why was her ear so red? Agitation? She was standing so close to Claire that Claire could see the delicate purple veins of Daphne's ear. 'I want you to call me if you see anything, if you *suspect* anything. When I say "viper," I mean *viper*. She kissed another woman's husband in front of everyone on the dance floor of the Waldorf-Astoria ballroom last spring. And it is a well-known fact that Isabelle French wants to fuck my husband.'

Claire laughed. She did not find that statement funny at all, but there was no point in further engaging the woman. Agree – *Yes, Daphne, you bet! I'll let you know!* – and extricate yourself from the conversation. Get the hell out of there!

'You bet,' Claire said. She pushed her cart all the way to the ham, bacon, smoked sausages, pickles, and sauerkraut. She could feel Daphne Dixon behind her, but she was afraid to check. She stopped, feigning interest in sauerkraut, thinking that rather than have Daphne Dixon shadow her through the store, she would let Daphne pass her. She fingered a package of sauerkraut – Claire liked it, but no one else in the house did – and then she studied a jar of kosher dills.

'Pickles?' Daphne Dixon said. Claire was so spooked, she nearly dropped the jar. Daphne was right up against her back. 'You're not pregnant again, are you, Claire?'

Again, Claire laughed. 'No,' she said.

'You're sure? That was one of the things I said to Lock. The problem with asking you to cochair is that you're always getting pregnant.'

'I'm not pregnant.'

'At least you're having sex,' Daphne said. 'Which is more than we can say about yours truly. And if you're having orgasms, then you're really one up on me.'

Claire was annoyed to find her interest piqued by these statements. Lock and Daphne didn't sleep together? So *did* Lock have a thing for Isabelle French? Was Claire stepping right into the middle of a messy situation? Friend from college, divorced . . . what if it had been Isabelle at the cozy meeting the week before, and not Claire? Would something have happened between them? But Claire had to cut bait here. Daphne was like an unsightly piece of toilet paper that Claire had dragged out of the ladies' room on her high heel.

'Do you ever shower?' Daphne said. She sniffed in Claire's general direction, and Claire looked down at her clothes: yoga pants, ratty sneakers, a white T-shirt that had turned pale gray and had a juice stain on the sleeve that looked like a gunshot wound. She had done some yoga positions that morning, she had attempted the sketch of the chandelier, she had had twenty phone conversations about Liam's arm – what the doctor had said, the impending surgery – but she had not showered. Should she explain to Daphne about Liam, Siobhan, Children's Hospital, the roast chicken? She didn't smell like flowers, certainly, but did she stink? It was true that you couldn't smell yourself. Maybe she did stink. But Daphne stank, too – like vinegar.

'I do shower,' Claire said, 'though I haven't yet today. I haven't had a chance.'

'That's the other thing about Lock asking you to chair the gala. Everyone knows you're stretched out like old gum. Four kids, one of them a baby, and you let your career go down the tubes . . .'

'My career didn't go down the tubes,' Claire said.

'Lock and I love your glass. But now it's gone.' Daphne snapped her fingers. 'Dust. Vapor.' She took a deep, dramatic breath. 'We need the gala to succeed, Claire. We need someone who can give it a *dedicated effort.*'

Claire felt tears prick her eyelids. And that was the problem, now, with Daphne: she told you the unadulterated truth about yourself until you cried. She didn't do it to be mean; she simply couldn't help herself. Minutes earlier, Claire had been thinking about how things weren't connected, how there was no tit for tat, no retribution for one's actions visited on one from above – but maybe she was mistaken. This verbal assault right now was one small piece of payback for everything that had happened the night of Daphne's accident. The irreparable damage that had no name was this: Daphne was now rude, and not only rude but mean; she forgot things easily; she repeated herself a hundred times – whole thoughts and ideas as well as individual words. It became a verbal tic, this repetition; it became a stutter. She had remarked to Julie Jackson, while her head was still swathed in bandages, 'I can see everything now. Everything is crystal clear.' But that seemed to mean she had complete disregard for the rules of polite society, for small talk, for being thought of as kind and amenable. Instead, she was sharp-tongued and venomous; she was notoriously brutal. Nobody liked Daphne Dixon anymore; she set out to sting people, like a wasp. She was her own doppelgänger now, after the accident. She was a bowl of cream gone rancid.

It was always Claire who stuck up for her.

She's not that bad, really. When she's on her medication, she's perfectly fine.

The guilt, old and useless, was tar in her hair; it was an invisible thread snarled around her heart. Claire had bought the last drink, she had not *absolutely insisted* that Daphne get into the taxi, and a woman's personality had been forever altered. Daphne was somebody else now, and Claire blamed herself.

Here, in the chilly outer ring of the Stop & Shop, Claire was receiving her just deserts: Daphne was holding up a mirror and forcing Claire to look. How can you chair the gala when you can't even get a shower? When you were careless in the hot shop and put yourself into preterm labor? When you won't face the fact that your baby isn't now, and may never be, right? How can you give it a dedicated effort?

'My nephew broke his arm playing hockey and was medevaced to Boston,' Claire said. 'I have to go. I want to make Siobhan some dinner.'

Daphne's face softened. 'Oh, God,' she said. 'How awful. By all means, go, go. Let me know if there's anything I can do to help.'

Claire looked at Daphne. Her ears were pink again, like a regular person's ears. She was, at that second, her old self – but that was part of the problem, too, the inconsistency. Daphne bounced like a tennis ball between two frames of mind. Which personality were you going to get? Claire was no dummy. She was being given a pass, and she was going to take it.

'Okay, I will,' Claire said. 'See you later, Daphne.'

CHAPTER THREE

HE ASKS HER (AGAIN)

When Claire walked up the stairs of the Elijah Baker House for the second gala meeting, she found Lock Dixon sitting at his desk much as he had been two weeks earlier, minus the sandwich. He was wearing a pink shirt this time and a red paisley tie; the classical station was on, featuring harpsichord music. The office was dark but for the desk lamp and the blue glow of Lock's computer. Claire checked her watch, confused. It was five after eight.

'Where is everybody?' she said.

And at the same time, Lock said, 'Didn't you get my message?'

'What message? No.'

'The meeting was canceled. Postponed, to next week.'

'Oh,' Claire said. 'No, I didn't get it . . .'

'We should have tried your cell phone. I told Gavin that, and he looked around the office for the number, but to no avail. I'm sorry. Adams has the flu and Isabelle couldn't call in tonight, so we bumped the meeting back to next week. I feel bad that you had to come all the way into town for nothing.'

For nothing – well, in a way it was for nothing, but Claire didn't regret it. She turned to survey the rest of the office. 'Is Gavin here?' she said.

'No,' Lock said. 'He left at five.'

'Oh,' Claire said. 'Well, you and I could talk over some things . . .'

And at the same time, Lock said, 'Would you like a glass of wine?'

'Viognier?' Claire said. She worried she was pronouncing it wrong, though she had practiced at home in the shower: vee-og-nyay. 'Yes, I'd love some.'

When Lock returned from the kitchen with the wine, he said, 'Have you given my proposition any thought?'

'Your proposition?' she said, immediately blushing.

'About the auction item,' he said. 'About your triumphant return as an artist.'

'Oh,' she said. She took a deep breath, then sank into the chair opposite his desk. He sat on the edge of his desk, close to her. 'I wasn't sure if you were serious or not.'

'Of course I was serious.'

'Fifty thousand dollars?'

'Your *Bubbles* sculptures are worth several times that.'

'Right, but . . .'

He sipped his wine and shook his head. 'Never mind, then. It was just a thought.'

'It was a really nice thought,' Claire said. 'I'm flattered that you believe my work might be worthy.'

'Worthy?' Lock said. 'It's more than worthy.'

'Hardly anyone on this island knows me as a glassblower,' Claire said.

'Oh, come on. Of course they do.'

'I mean, they know that's what I do – or did. But practically nobody's seen my work. The vases, yes, but not my real work.'

'That's a shame,' Lock said.

'I have a select clientele,' Claire said. 'Five people. I'm what you call "extreme boutique."'

'You should be as famous as Simon Pearce,' Lock said. 'One good thing about doing the auction would be the exposure.'

'But that's not what I want,' Claire said. 'I never wanted to be Simon Pearce. Mass-produced and all that.'

'Of course not. You're an artist.'

Claire looked at her hands. They had been callused for so many years, callused and sore, cut and burned. They were just starting to look like a normal woman's hands, red from the dishwater, streaked with Magic Marker – but was this a good thing? She didn't know. Talking about working again tore her in half. It had felt wonderful to open the sketchbook, and the image of the pulled-taffy chandelier would not leave her alone. But then Claire thought of the kids, especially of Zack: Should she explain to Lock how Zack had weighed two pounds seven ounces when he was born and spent the first five weeks of his life on a respirator? How now, at eight months, he wasn't crawling yet, whereas her other children had been cruising around, holding on to the furniture? Dr. Patel had told her not to worry. *Kids develop at different paces, Claire.* Claire wanted to see a specialist, but she was terrified of what he would say. She was certain there was something wrong and it was her fault. Her doctor had warned her.

'I can't do it,' she said.

Lock looked at her for a long while with an inscrutable expression on his face. 'Okay,' he said.

Claire felt tears coming on. What was *wrong* with her? She suddenly felt very sad and sorry for herself. She tried to stop; crying in front of Lock was embarrassing. At home, it seemed, one of the children was always crying. Claire was the one who plucked the tissues, wiped the noses, kissed the bumps and bruises, scolded the perpetrator. She did not cry, she realized, because there was no one to comfort her. Jason was as emotionally feeble as the children. If he were watching her now, silently weeping, he would be baffled.

Lock offered her a handkerchief. Claire blotted her face, thinking how charming it was that there was still a man in the world who carried a handkerchief.

'Are you okay?' he asked. 'Did I hit a nerve? I didn't mean to – '

'No,' Claire said. 'It's okay.' Lock handed her her wine. She took a sip and tried to collect herself. 'Can I ask you a question?'

'Shoot.'

'Why do you work here? I mean, you're . . . you don't have to work, right?'

Lock gave her another one of his incredible smiles. 'Everyone needs something meaningful to do. I sold my business so I could move to the island permanently, but I never meant to stop working. I never meant to have a life where all I did was golf and talk to my stockbroker. That's not me.'

'No,' Claire said. 'It's really none of my business . . .'

'I looked around the island to see where I would be happiest. I looked at buying a real estate development company, but that felt a little empty at this point in my life. There was a woman who cleaned rooms at the hospital when Daphne was there for physical therapy. Her name was Marcella Vallenda. Do you know her?'

'No,' Claire said.

'Dominican woman. Four kids, three teenage boys, always in trouble, and a daughter. Husband was a deadbeat, alcoholic; he worked some days, and some days he spent at the Muse, playing keno. I got to know Marcella a little bit. She worked three jobs, she developed a cocaine habit to stay awake, basically, but the house was a hellhole, and the daughter, Agropina, found a rat in her cereal bowl . . .'

'Oh, God,' Claire said.

'It happens,' Lock said. 'I had no idea until I met Marcella, but it happens here, just like everywhere else. I wanted to give Marcella money, but money doesn't help – it goes right to drugs. What she needed was programs, and that was how I found Nantucket's Children.'

'I never heard that story before,' Claire said.

'Well, everybody wonders why I'm here, but few are brave enough to ask. You asked.'

'Oh,' Claire said.

'Raising money for Nantucket's Children is the most important job I've ever had.'

When Claire stood up, her legs wobbled. She was feeling weepy again. Okay, she was hormonal; she hadn't been right since she stopped nursing Zack. But no, it wasn't that; it was something bigger. In her universe, an apocalyptic decision was being made. It wasn't because of Lock's spiel about making a difference, or the rat in a little girl's cereal bowl, at least not completely. Claire was making this decision because she wanted to. She felt like a person she had nearly lost in a crowd: her old self.

'I'll do the auction piece,' she said.

'You will?' he said. 'Are you sure? Now I feel like I goaded you into it.'

'I'm sure,' she said. She waited, not breathing. Was this moment loaded for him, or was the emotion all in her mind? She had, after all, just made a monumental decision. Lock was standing before her, larger than life, a god of sorts, a person who could make things happen.

'I should go,' she said.

'But wait,' he said. There was something in his voice that held her there.

'What?' she whispered.

'Thank you,' he said.

He thought she was doing it for him, or for the cause. But she was doing it, ultimately, for herself.

'No,' she said. 'Thank *you*.'

When Claire got home, Jason was awake, watching TV with Zack asleep on his chest. Because the whole world was now transformed, Claire looked on them tenderly. Her husband and her baby. They knew nothing about her.

'How was the meeting?' Jason asked.

'Oh,' Claire said. 'Fine. I have to try to find Matthew tomorrow.'

'He's on tour in Southeast Asia,' Jason said. 'I saw it on *Entertainment Tonight*.'

'You did?'

'Yeah. The sultan of Brunei attended one of his concerts. It was a pretty big deal. The richest man in the world dancing to "This Could Be a Song."'

'Funny,' Claire said. She sat carefully in the chair next to Jason. 'Listen, there's something I want to talk to you about.'

Jason's attention was back on the TV. *Deal or No Deal.*

'Jase?'

'Mmmmmm.'

'I'm serious. I have to talk to you.'

Jason emitted air that was part sigh, part huff. She was horning in on his date with asinine TV.

She had rehearsed a line in the car. Give it to him straight. Skip the cushioning remarks; he didn't want to hear them. But Claire found the raw words hard to say. Jason was glaring at her. He had only muted the TV; he had not turned it off.

'What?' he said.

'I'm going back to work.'

Instinctively, it seemed, he squeezed Zack. Right. The guilt was so automatic, Claire's fingers started to tingle. (She had regained consciousness on the Medflight jet with Jason stroking her hair. *They don't know about the baby,* he had said. *They don't know about the baby.*) Now, the accusation was loud and clear in Jason's silence: her work had nearly killed their son. If he had his way, she would never set foot in the hot shop again. She had overheard him telling Carter that he wanted to dismantle it, bomb it, burn it down.

'*What?*' he said.

'I'm going back to work. For one project.'

'Did Chick call?'

That was the right question. Chick Klaussen had flown to Boston to see Claire in the hospital. He was racked with guilt that Claire had gone down while working on his piece, and Claire was racked with guilt that she had to ask a studio to finish it. She'd told Jason that she would only return to work for Chick, but both of them knew Chick would never ask.

'No,' she said. 'Not Chick. I'm going to create a piece for the gala auction.'

'Jesus, Claire,' Jason said.

'Lock asked me,' she said. 'He thinks it will bring in a lot of money.'

'It's too much to ask,' Jason said. 'You're already chairing the damn thing.'

'I know,' Claire said. 'But I'm ready to go back. I want to get back in there. I miss it. It's who I am.'

'It's a part of who you are,' Jason said.

'An important part.'

'And what about the kids?'

'They'll be fine. I have Pan to help me. It's not going to take a lot of time.'

'Sure, it is,' Jason said. 'They're not asking you to make cupcakes for a bake sale, Claire. They want an auction piece. Something intricate.'

'What I make is my choice.'

68

He shuddered, jarring the baby. Zack started to cry. Bitterly, Jason said, 'Great. You woke him up.'

Claire said, 'I was hoping you would understand. I was hoping you would get it. I'm ready to go back.'

'Here.' Jason held Zack out to her. Zack clawed the air like an upside-down bug. Jason said, 'It hasn't even been a year. Zack is still a baby, and a baby needs his mother. You should have said no. Not just to the glass, but to all of it. The whole thing. The gala.'

Claire took the baby and kissed his forehead. She didn't know how to respond, and it didn't matter. Jason went back to watching TV.

There was no predicting how happy the idea of going back to work would make her. Claire was both her old self and a new person. She was more energetic with the kids, solicitous, playful. She kissed J.D. on the cheek and he freaked out, and Claire laughed merrily and kissed him again and tickled him under the arms until he said, 'Mom, quit it!' with a big grin on his face. She bought a new sketchbook and a set of number two pencils; she sharpened the pencils and stroked the heavy, creamy paper. She then spent two hours sketching the pulled-taffy chandelier in meticulous detail. It was going to be nearly impossible to execute by hand, on her own, but this galvanized her.

Siobhan called just as Claire was ready to take a break.

Siobhan said, 'How's the *work* going?' She had been skeptical when Claire told her the news. She didn't understand why Claire would work if she didn't have to; she didn't understand why Claire was going back to slave over a project that she wouldn't even get paid for. *You're a bloody fool, Clairsy! No boundaries!*

Claire said, 'It feels better than a hot stone massage.'

Siobhan said, 'Oh, come on!' and laughed.

'Really,' Claire said.

'You're soft in the head,' Siobhan said.

It felt good to have a mission. Setting the two hours aside for 'work' made the rest of her day go more efficiently: She did not languish in useless yoga positions, and she did not spend precious minutes trying to entice Zack to pick up a Cheerio. She accomplished more. She found herself with a spare hour before pickup, and when was the last time that had happened? She could cut Pan a break and take Zack for a walk to the beach. But she wanted to return to Lock on Monday with a gift, a surprise, a thank-you for the change he had brought about in her life, and so she took the phone into her room and locked the door. She rifled through her address book, which was filled with the torn corners of envelopes and assorted 'We've Moved' announcements – Claire did herself the favor of dating these things, but she never found time to write them down.

Matthew Westfield (aka Max West): there was a cell phone number, which Claire knew to be useless. The last time Claire had tried to contact him was two years earlier, on behalf of Siobhan's brother, Declan, in Dublin, who wanted concert tickets. She had been unable to reach Matthew on the cell phone that time, and so she left a message for him with his agent, Bruce, in L.A., and sure enough, tickets arrived by DHL on Declan's doorstep. But the last time Claire had actually spoken to Matthew was nearly a dozen years earlier. He had called her from the Minneapolis airport. He was on his way to Hazelden for rehab.

'I can't beat it, Claire,' Matthew had said then. 'The bottle. I can't fucking beat it.'

The bottle, Claire thought, should have been easier than the cocaine – but in the past twelve years, Matthew had been in three times for alcohol abuse. Claire thought back to high school. In those days, she was the only one who could get away with buying beer. She put her hair in hot rollers and wore her mother's long black skirt and sensible flat shoes – she looked, Matthew used to say, like one of the Amish, but she never once got carded. They drank in fields, in the woods, and, in summertime, at the quarry, where Matthew, plastered, used to dive into the jade green water from the highest outcrop of rocks. He had been so cavalier; he had thought himself indestructible. They drank at the beach or at one of the empty rental houses on the street across from the beach. They wandered the boardwalk, ogling its carnival atmosphere – the blue and green neon spokes of the Ferris wheel, the strings of round lights outlining the Kettle Korn, taffy, and Slushee stands, the hundreds of kitschy shops (*Greetings from Wildwood!*) – with a sense of hilarious wonder. The drinking had been innocent, a mood enhancer, and it was rebellion, too, of course. It was usually only part of the night and not the night itself (though there were exceptions to that, nights when either she or Matthew, or both of them, drank so much that they puked until dawn). For the most part, the nights of their youth had been about music. Matthew took his guitar everywhere; he slung it over his back and placed it next to them on the beach or in the grass when they made love. He sang to their group of friends, to strangers, he sang to Claire, he sang to himself. There had been plenty of times when Claire grew jealous of the music, when she accused Matthew of being obsessed with it. Music was his drug back then.

It surprised Claire that alcohol had reached out and grabbed Matthew, as an adult, by the neck. Why him and not her? Of course, his life – in the interim between their last month together, August 1987, and the present – had contained excesses such as Claire could only imagine. Matthew had told her about some of it – the drugs, the alcohol, the girls, the parties, the complete lack of scruples characteristic of a rock-and-roll tour bus. There was not one wholesome thing about his Stormy Eyes Tour: not one night where he drank water and went to bed early, not one sentence uttered without a swear word, not one steamed vegetable, not one breath of air that didn't contain the sweet suggestion of marijuana smoke. It was all vodka and tits, he said. And pressure. That was the real monkey on his back: the pressure.

Claire had spoken to Matthew in the Minneapolis airport, as he awaited his escort to Hazelden, for nearly an hour. Mostly it was him talking, reminiscing, apologizing.

I should never have let you go. We were happy.

Happy, she said.

Your father hated me.

He did not.

Your mother thought I sang off-key.

Don't be silly. She thought you had the voice of an angel.

Remember when I sang at the Pony? Things were simple then.

Simple, Claire said. She laughed. *Remember when you let me play the tambourine?*

You were a regular Tracy Partridge.

She could hear him smiling.

I miss you, he said. *If you ever need anything, anything at all . . .*

Or if you ever need anything, she said.

Ask, he said.

Ask, she said.

So. She had an ancient cell phone number and Bruce's number in L.A. Call Bruce! It was only October. If Max called her back in three weeks or a month or even two months, that would still leave plenty of time to book him as the talent. Or she could write to Matthew's mother, Sweet Jane Westfield, who still lived on East Aster Road in Wildwood Crest. Claire got a Christmas card from her every year. Sweet Jane was the one constant in Matthew's life; if Jane received a note from Claire, she would pin it to her corkboard over the sink (Claire could see the corkboard plain as day, as well as the crocheted cover that went over the teakettle) and she would mention it to Matthew when he called, which he did every Sunday.

Claire would do both. She found Sweet Jane's address in her book and handwrote a note in large print, explaining that she needed to get ahold of Matthew. She wanted Matthew to play a short concert here on Nantucket to benefit a children's charity. *It's*

72

not for me, Claire wrote. *It's for the island kids. Would you please have him call me? My number is . . .* In a PS she mentioned that her kids were doing well – no doubt Sweet Jane still had Zack's birth announcement pinned to the corkboard – and she asked after Monty, Sweet Jane's cat.

Next she dialed Bruce Mandalay, Matthew's agent. Bruce Mandalay was the person who'd discovered Matthew at the Stone Pony. It came as a surprise because although there were always agents and managers and record producers at the Stone Pony (thanks to Springsteen and Bon Jovi), they were normally easy to pick out. They had slick hair and diamond earrings; they wore suits. Bruce Mandalay looked like a manager at a box factory; he was *or-di-nary.* Paunchy, balding, with rimless glasses and a mustache and sturdy wing-tip shoes. He was soft-spoken, nonthreatening to the point of invisibility. Matthew had signed with him because he was serious, smart, sensible. Bruce thought the song 'Parents Know' could be a single; he offered to put the money up himself to have Matthew record it professionally in New York. Matthew did so, and then, almost immediately, Bruce hooked him up with Columbia. Just like that, Matthew shot toward the stars.

When Matthew went to New York to record the single, he'd insisted Claire come along. She rode in the back of Bruce's Pinto from Wildwood to Manhattan. Bruce had treated her nicely, better than she had thought a tagalong girlfriend would be treated. At a rest stop, Bruce bought her a cheeseburger and a Coke; he asked her about college. She told him, 'RISD,' and he said, 'Impressive.' He had five daughters himself, he said.

But as Matthew became more important to Bruce, Claire became less important. When she showed up backstage at the Beacon Theatre eighteen months later (Max West was opening for the Allman Brothers), Bruce didn't recognize her. Was she that forgettable, or were there just so many girls by then that Bruce couldn't keep track? Claire had been out of touch for so long now that she might have to remind Bruce who she was, but that was okay. There had been hundreds of girls for Matthew, possibly even thousands, including two wives and one unfortunate mistress (the most famous actress of modern times), but Claire had the distinction of being the first girl, the one Matthew had loved before he was famous.

'Hello? Bruce Mandalay.'

'Bruce?' Claire said. 'This is Claire Danner calling.'

There was a pause. Well, the request for tickets had been two years ago. And it was possible that Claire had an inflated view of her importance in Matthew's history.

'I'm Matthew's – '

'Yes,' Bruce said. 'Claire, yes, hello.' His voice sounded the same, very calm and metered. He was a nonagent agent; nothing got him excited or riled up. Being Max West's agent must have made him a rich and powerful man, but you would never know it. Claire wondered about his five daughters. They had been younger than Claire, but by now they were all grown. Bruce might even be a grandfather. Claire didn't have time to ask. She had to pick up the kids from school in fifteen minutes.

'I have a favor to ask, Bruce.'

'Tickets?' Bruce said. 'Max is in Southeast Asia. He's not playing in the States again until spring.'

'It's not tickets,' Claire said. It was so much more than tickets that she wasn't sure how to ask. A free ninety-minute concert on a baseball diamond for a thousand wealthy summer people who might not even dance. She'd eaten a salami sandwich for lunch, and now she had heartburn.

'No?' Bruce said, and his voice sounded both interested and wary.

'I'm the cochair of a benefit here on Nantucket,' Claire said. 'It's called the summer gala. It's cocktails and dinner for a thousand people. And traditionally, there's a concert.'

Silence.

'It's a charity event,' Claire said. 'A thousand dollars a ticket,

74

and all the money goes to this organization I'm involved with called Nantucket's Children.'

Silence.

'I want Matthew – Max, I mean – to play it.'

Silence.

'For free.'

Had Bruce hung up? She wouldn't have blamed him if he had.

'It's August sixteenth, a Saturday,' Claire said. 'Here, on Nantucket. Nantucket is off the coast of – '

'I know where Nantucket is.'

'Okay,' Claire said. She took a deep breath. 'What do you think?'

She heard the shuffling of papers. Bruce Mandalay cleared his throat. 'Hollywood Hospice, Doctors without Borders, Save the Children, the United Way of Orange County, the Metropolitan Museum of Art, Dade County SPCA, the Druckenheimer Center for the Elderly of Saint Louis, the Kapistan School for the Blind, the Red Cross, the Seattle Symphony, the Redbone fishing tournament for cystic fibrosis, the Home for Retarded Citizens of Rock City, Iowa, the Conservancy Project at Estes Park, the First Baptist Church of Tupelo, the Jackson, Mississippi, Botanical Gardens, the Cleveland Clinic, Arthur Ashe Youth Tennis and Education, DATA – that's Bono's thing in Africa – the Mount Rushmore Restoration Concern – '

'Okay,' Claire said. 'Stop. I get it.'

Bruce sighed. He was a nonagent agent and he had bought the cheeseburger and the Coke for Claire so long ago, when she had no money for lunch herself – but he wasn't exactly kind, either. Maybe he had been kind at one time, but representing Max West through twenty years of meteoric success had made him . . . a realist. It was hard to be a realist *and* kind.

'Claire . . . ,' he said.

She should never have called. She should have mailed the letter to Sweet Jane and waited to hear back. Jane Westfield *was* sweet, she *was* kind, she had known Claire since Claire was twelve years old, she wouldn't give Claire a song and dance . . . but what, really, did Claire know? Maybe she would. Claire felt like she was going to cry. It was rejection, plain and simple, and the thing was, she deserved it – for being so smug, for assuming that she had been an unforgettable influence in Matthew's life. *You don't forget your high school sweetheart, do you?* But maybe you did. She hadn't seen Matthew in forever and a day.

Lock doesn't think you'll be able to deliver. She couldn't deliver. She experienced vestiges of an old hurt – Claire, out behind the Stone Pony, hugging Matthew, holding on to him for dear life, knowing she was going to lose him – and it was combined with the hurt she was going to feel when she told Lock Dixon, who admired her and believed in her, that she couldn't get Max West.

'It's okay,' she whispered. 'I get it. All those people want him.'

'Those are just the requests from this month,' Bruce said. 'This is what's come in since he's been gone. He turned down *Bono,* Claire. And nearly all of the organizations are willing to pay . . .'

'I know,' Claire said. 'I just thought I'd ask.'

'You were right to ask,' Bruce said.

He was quiet again, and Claire thought, *Please let's just end this call.* Did he expect her to make nice and ask about his daughters now?

'Do you know who I work for?' he said.

'Who?' Claire said.

'Max West.'

'Right.'

'He's like my own son,' Bruce said. 'I know everything about him. For example, I know he's in Brunei right now, jonesing like crazy because the sultan is Muslim and his kingdom is dry.'

'Right,' Claire said. There were only ten minutes until pickup; she had to hang up. 'Listen, would you do me a favor? If you talk to Max, will you tell him I called and just *ask* him? Tell him it's really, really important to me . . .'

'I don't have to ask him,' Bruce said. 'I know everything about him. If I tell him you called and asked for this crazy, inconceivable thing, I know what he'll say.'

'What?'

'He'll say yes.'

'What?'

'He'll say, *For Claire Danner, yes.* Free concert, no problem, sure. Saturday, August sixteenth. You're lucky because he happens to be free. He flies to Spain a few days later. So, yes, he'll be there.'

Claire stood up from the bed. She started to bounce – she couldn't help herself – but she didn't want Bruce to know she was bouncing.

'Really?' she said. 'You think?'

'I don't think,' Bruce said. 'I know. He'll be there.'

CHAPTER FOUR

HE SURPRISES HER

On Sunday, Jason and J.D. spent all day scalloping, and on Monday night, Claire sautéed the scallops for dinner and served them with risotto and asparagus. Claire wanted Jason to be happy about dinner because he was not happy to hear she had another gala meeting.

'Is this what it's going to be like?' he asked. 'Two, three nights a week, you at meetings? Leaving me with the kids?'

'They're your kids, too,' Claire said. 'It will be good for you to spend time with them. It will be good for them to spend time with you.'

'Just answer my question,' Jason said. 'Is this what it's going to be like?'

'Only at first,' Claire promised blindly.

'I told you, it was a mistake. You should have said no.'

'Well, I can't back out now, can I?'

'No,' Jason said grudgingly.

'No,' Claire said. There had been a crackled message on the machine, left late Friday night while Jason and Claire were at Joe's fortieth birthday party. It was Matthew, calling from Brunei, saying he was coming to Nantucket in August.

'I can't wait to see you again,' he said. 'God, this is going to be great!'

Even Jason was impressed with Claire for locking up Max West so quickly, so easily, and for free. Claire had let the news slip after a couple of glasses of champagne at Joe's birthday party – *Looks like Max West is playing the gala* – and voilà! Five people agreed to be on her committee, including Julie Jackson's husband, Brent. Hurray! Claire might have been a rock star herself. Joe's wife put a Max West CD on the stereo and everyone danced, and Claire heard Jason say, 'Yeah, he'll probably stay with us. He's crazy about Claire. They dated, you know, in high school. They nearly got married.'

So there was no backing out now.

The kids regarded their dinner plates dolefully. Even J.D., who had been so proud of bringing home two bushels of scallops, didn't want to eat them.

'Do we have to?' Shea asked.

'Yes,' Jason said. He was snarfing down his food, but Claire just picked at her plate, not unlike the kids. She had called Lock that morning and said, *I have something to tell you!*

He'd said, *Great, what is it?*

I'd like to tell you in person. She waited a beat, two, three. He sounded like he was shuffling papers. Did he get it?

He said, *Can you meet tonight?*

As Claire climbed the stairs of the Elijah Baker House, she felt weightless and sick. The symptoms were the same as heatstroke: shallow breathing, hot, dry skin, rocketing heart rate. She was going to pass out. How was she getting one foot in front of the other? She was climbing the stairs to meet with Lock – that was all. The thought that it might be something more was completely inane. Affairs only happened in novels and on TV – but that wasn't exactly true, was it? Every winter, someone on Nantucket had an affair – the circuit judge, or the high school chemistry teacher, or the woman who gave private piano lessons – and everyone else heard about the gory details: caught in bed with a manager from the Atlantic Café . . . threw her belongings into the front yard. Siobhan was a big fan of the Annual Affair Story. She was the first to castigate the couple – for having an affair, and for getting caught.

Immoral, sneaky, deceptive people, Siobhan said gleefully. *Stupid! Careless!*

What always crossed Claire's mind was how brave the person must have been, and how unhappy. Claire was not brave (she hadn't had the courage to suggest a night meeting herself; she had merely willed Lock to do it). And Claire wasn't unhappy. She loved her kids, she loved Jason, she had Siobhan and a host of other friends, she had full-time help and a newfound zest for her work. She was not unhappy.

And since she was not brave and not unhappy, nothing would happen. She would tell Lock the incredible news about Matthew – it was such big news, it *should* be announced in person – and then she would leave.

The office was so dark that Claire thought it must be uninhabited, and immediately she panicked. Had Lock forgotten? If he had forgotten, she would be wounded, but also relieved. She would slip out of the office and try to forget that anything interesting had ever transpired there. But then she rounded the corner into the office, and there was Lock at his computer, working. The desk lamp was off, as was the radio. There was very little light and no music – and no sandwich, no wine – but Lock was there, at the computer, wearing his glasses. Claire studied him: He was just a person. A balding, slightly overweight middle-aged man with deep eyes and a magnetic smile and (maybe this was the most attractive thing about him) an unquestionable authority.

'Hi,' Claire said.

He took off his glasses and rubbed his eyes, as though he were having a dream that was too good to believe.

'I saw you coming down the street,' he said.

'Did you?'

'I did. I've been watching for you for . . . oh, about five days.'

'Oh,' Claire said. She was tongue-tied and jumbled up. Had he really just said that? Had he meant it? She wanted to say something equally sweet back to him, but it was as if she was holding an instrument she didn't know how to play. No matter what she said, she would strike the wrong note.

He stood up and she approached the desk. She thought they were taking their places: she would sit in the chair and he would sit on the edge of the desk. But he bypassed the desk and came toward her. She stopped. He stopped. Lock looked at her, and her stomach dropped away – whoosh! – gone. He touched Claire's cheek, then ran his thumb across her lips. He kissed her.

Ohhhhhhhhhh.

It was so deeply entrenched as a fantasy in Claire's interior life that she couldn't believe it was actually happening.

Lock Dixon kissed her only once. Then he pulled away. Claire thought she might fall over backward. She was afraid to move, afraid to speak. She was in a bubble where all that mattered was that Lock had kissed her and might kiss her again.

'Claire,' he said. He spoke her name with wonder and respect, as if it was a beautiful name, as if she was a beautiful woman. Was she a beautiful woman? She hardly ever felt beautiful. She was too harried, too often in her yoga pants, with her wild red hair in a bun. Jason came after her in bed all the time, but did he think she was beautiful? If she asked him, he would laugh and say something patronizing. The part of their marriage that had dissolved was the part where he told her she was beautiful; it was the part where they held hands at dinner or had a drink together in front of the fire. It was the part where, when she said she had something to talk to him about, he turned off the TV instead of merely muting it. The part of their marriage that had dissolved was the breathlessness of moments like this one.

'I don't know what to say.' This, the truth, from her.

He nodded. 'I'm going to kiss you again. Okay?'

She nodded. He kissed her more deeply, for longer, a full second, then two. Her mouth opened. She tasted him. It was heaven. She was twelve years old. This was her first kiss.

It stayed innocent like that: just the kissing. No part of their bodies touched except for their lips, their tongues. It was sweet, and intoxicating. Claire ached for him. Did he ache for her? She had no idea. She knew enough about relationships, though, to pull back first.

'Is this wise?' she said. Now she sounded like the person she knew herself to be. 'What if someone finds us up here in the dark?'

'Someone like who?' Lock said. He touched her face again. He held it with both his hands so that her face felt small and delicate, like a child's face, a doll's face.

Like Gavin Andrews, Claire thought. *Or Daphne. Or Jason. Or Adams Fiske.* But she didn't speak; she was too rapt by Lock's hands on her face and, in the next second, by his kissing her. They were kissing again. Claire's mind was a tornado. Why was this happening? Why her, of all people? Had he had feelings for her for a while, or were his feelings newly hatched, like her own feelings? Would this go any further? Lock Dixon had an unquestionable authority, he was a leader, a commander, he knew what he was doing at all times. Claire didn't have to be brave; he would be brave for both of them. She would be swept up behind him on horseback, and he would gallop them across the fields. And if he knew she was thinking all these preposterous things, he wouldn't want to be kissing her anymore. At the same time that Claire's

mind was mowing down all her previous convictions and expectat-
ions, she was present in the physicality of the moment. She was
kissing him, tasting him, feeling the heat of his palms on her face,
then in her hair, then against her back. He pressed himself against
her, and she took a stutter step backward and he caught her. She
pulled away.

'What are we doing?' she said.

'Right,' he said. 'I don't know.'

'Okay,' Claire said, relieved. 'Good.'

'Do you want to stop?' he said. He sounded concerned, almost
scared. 'Am I pressuring you into something you'd rather not be
doing?'

'No, no, no . . .'

'I don't have an explanation,' he said. 'I am as stunned as you
are. It's like someone cast a spell on me. From the moment you set
foot in here, for the first meeting.'

'The first meeting,' Claire said. 'But not . . . before? Not at
the lunch? Not two years ago or five years ago? I've known you
awhile.'

'But not really,' Lock said. 'Right?'

'Right,' Claire said. 'I thought you hated me.' She remembered
his eyes when she showed up at the front door with that basket for
Daphne. That horrible look.

'Hated you?'

'Because of Daphne. The night of her accident, I bought her
last drink. And then the cab. We asked her to join us, we begged
her, but she refused.'

'And you thought I *hated* you?'

'Blamed me, yes. I blame myself.'

'Because you're that kind of person. A caring person. You
would worry. You would blame yourself for something that was,
very clearly, not your fault.' Lock loosened his tie. His white shirt
was turned back neatly at the cuffs; his watch glinted in the lamp-
light. 'I've known for a long time that you're a good person, good

83

like the rest of us aspire to be. And I've admired your work. But then you walked in here and we spent time together and suddenly it dawned on me that I am a lonely man.'

Claire's mind flickered to the half-eaten turkey and cranberry sandwich on white butcher paper. To the daughter, Heather, at Andover – studying, eating, playing field hockey, and sleeping, all under the supervision of people who were not her parents.

'I have been lonely for so long,' he said, 'but I didn't feel lonely until I spent that hour with you.'

'So I made you feel lonely?'

'You made me feel unlonely. And then you left and I couldn't stop thinking about you.'

'I had the same problem,' Claire said.

'I am not like this,' he said. 'I have not kissed a woman other than my wife in twenty years.'

Really? Was this true? Claire thought of Isabelle French.

'What about Isabelle French?'

'What about her?'

'I saw your wife at the grocery store. She seemed to think there might be something going on between you and Isabelle French.'

'She said that?'

Claire looked at the floor. Now she had the weirdly unpleasant feeling that she'd betrayed Daphne's confidence. Which felt like a worse offense, somehow, than kissing Lock.

'Yes,' Claire said.

'Daphne doesn't always realize what she's saying.'

This was a generous spin on the way things were, but Claire wasn't going to argue with Lock about Daphne's state of mind.

'I have no feelings for Isabelle French,' he said. 'Other than compassion.'

'Compassion?'

'Bad divorce,' Lock said. 'And some subsequent bad decisions.'

'I haven't met her yet,' Claire said.

'You will.'

'Yes.' This sounded sort of like a discussion about the gala, which was odd because they were standing very close to each other, closer than normal people would stand. Claire was inside Lock's orbit; she was a captive of his magnetic field.

It's like someone cast a spell on me.

Was this total bullshit? God knows, it sounded like it. If Jason had heard Lock speak those words, he would have guffawed and choked on his spit. He would have questioned Lock's sincerity, and possibly his sexual orientation. But that was how Claire felt, too. She had attended the lunch at the yacht club terrified of Lock Dixon, but after the first meeting, she was thinking about him in a whole new way, thinking about him all the time. He'd wooed her, somehow.

And now they were kissing and she didn't understand it, and he didn't, either, apparently, and that came as a relief. He was not a brave horseman after all. If it did turn into something more, it would be the two of them, bumbling their way through the dark, which felt like something Claire might be able to handle.

Since they were on the topic of the gala, sort of, Claire decided to bring up the ostensible reason she was here.

'I got Max West,' she said. 'He'll do it for free.'

'I know,' Lock said. 'I heard.'

'How?' Claire said. 'How do you know?'

'Someone told me.'

'Who?'

'I promised not to reveal my source. It was someone you were at a party with over the weekend.'

So, one of twenty-five people. It was a very small island.

'I thought you'd be shocked. You didn't think I could do it.'

'Of course I did.'

'So you're proud of me?'

'I'm proud of you.' He leaned forward and kissed her on the forehead.

'I started sketching the chandelier,' she said.

'That's great,' he said.

'It is great,' Claire said. 'I've been wanting to get back into the hot shop. I just needed a push.'

'I'm nothing if not pushy,' he said. He checked his watch. 'I should get home.'

Stupidly, this pierced her. Claire had thought he would try to persuade her to stay. Didn't he want her to stay? Didn't he want to kiss her some more? She had only been having an affair for twenty minutes, and already she was jealous.

'Okay,' she said. Thank God for words like 'okay,' employable in any situation, even when what you meant was the opposite of 'okay.' Claire had to get out of there; she was in danger of sinking into an emotional quagmire. She hadn't taken her jacket off and hence she couldn't busy herself with putting it back on. There was nothing left to do but turn and go. Was that what she should do?

'So I'll see you . . .' She wanted to know if this was it. Would there be more, and if there was to be more, then when, and where?

'We have a meeting Wednesday night,' Lock said.

'Right,' Claire said. She had mentioned Wednesday's meeting to the people who had volunteered for the committee; she would have to call and remind them. 'I'll see you Wednesday, then.' She turned to go, yes, go – and he took her arm. He pulled her to him. She filled with elation. He wasn't ready to let her go. He kissed her so gently that she emitted a sigh, and then he kissed her more hungrily. He wanted her, she could feel him wanting her, she could feel his arms around her, trembling – with fear or lust or in an attempt to hold himself back, she had no idea, but she loved it. The person she was – a good person, a person committed to kindness, who showed up with a basket of soup and soap, a peace offering – did not do things like this. But Lock's trembling, his kiss, was a drug, a rush, an attraction too powerful to resist. Claire thought of Jason, and of her kids, and they seemed distant, but sweet, too, and simple and safe.

What was she doing? She was too easy. She was the Universal Acceptor.

Lock pressed her up against the wall. He ran his hands up inside her sweater. He touched her nipples, lightly, with his palms. She gasped. His touch was electric. She should go now. She'd asked for this in her mind and here it was: amazing, foreign, scary. Because what came next, what happened now? This was all still relatively innocent; it had yet to take on heavy, cumbersome labels like 'adultery' or 'cheating.' This was leading to serious trouble, to something Claire would regret, something she would not be able to wish away or undo. And yet she didn't want to stop. She didn't want to pull away. She didn't want to. His hands were on her waist; he tugged at her belt loops.

You made me feel unlonely. . .

'We should go,' she whispered.

'Yes,' he said.

They did not stop. They kissed. He touched her. She was afraid to touch him, so she kept her hands on his arms and noted how strong and solid his muscles were and how soft his shirt was. She ran her fingers up his arms to his shoulders. She touched the collar of his shirt and the back of his neck, and he pulled back and said, 'It has been so long since someone touched me like that.'

Claire felt wistful, thinking of Lock, who was rich, yes, who had unquestionable authority, who was good-hearted and right and smart, but who was so lonely. He was not Derek Jeter or Brad Pitt, but despite this, Claire was sure he could have had any woman he wanted, and he had picked her. She touched his ears and the very short hair on the back of his head. She was manhandled four times a week by Jason, but she understood Lock's longing.

'Really,' she said. 'We should go.' Claire did not know anything about affairs, but she was an expert when it came to finesse and timing. These were the gifts of a glassblower – knowing not to blow a piece out too thin, knowing when to back off, when to cool a piece down. She felt that way now. They couldn't go any further.

He released her reluctantly. The reluctance was what she savored. 'I'll see you Wednesday,' she said, and she slipped down the stairs.

As Claire descended the stairs of the office into the crisp, smoky autumn air, she felt like she was filling up with bubbles, or feathers. Lock Dixon had kissed her; they had kissed. He did not hate her, after all; he *liked* her. God, she couldn't believe it. She had been thinking of this, of him, but carefully, circumspectly, because never once had she allowed herself to believe that he might reciprocate her feelings, her intense curiosity, her nascent desire. What she'd had, basically, was a crush, and crushes were never mutual – but yes, tonight, yes. Claire floated to her car, feeling as if she would explode in a burst of light, or flower petals, or paper confetti. She wanted to tell someone, and that of course meant Siobhan, but even as Claire palmed her cell phone, she knew she could never tell Siobhan. Siobhan – although she was Claire's best friend and the closest thing to a sister Claire had ever had – would not be able to handle this news. This was not some half-baked fantasy about the trash boy or the UPS man knocking on the door and Claire or Siobhan inviting him in. This was not Siobhan putting a dare out there, and then jumping out of harm's way at the last minute. This was real; this had *happened*. Claire could not tell Siobhan. She could not tell anyone.

On Tuesday, Claire broke her own rules (she didn't even know she had rules, but as she climbed the stairs of the Elijah Baker House, her heart hammering, she knew this was *not wise,* showing up the very next day, out of the blue). And yet she couldn't help herself. Bruce Mandalay had sent Claire a fax at home – the contract and rider for Max West's performance – and Claire wanted to drop it off for Lock or Adams to peruse. Matthew was playing for free, but there were some things in the paperwork that concerned Claire. He was bringing Terry and Alfonso from his band (bass and drums – he never played without them), and they needed to be paid ten thousand dollars apiece. In addition, Nantucket's Children was in charge of hiring four contract musicians, who also had to be paid. There were pages of production notes, which Claire could not make heads or tails of – spotlights, instruments, amps, sound systems, microphones. The rider specified that the band had to be put up in five-star accommodations, with all kinds of food and drink, down to the cherry Italian ice, Nilla wafers, and Quik chocolate milk, which made Claire laugh because it reminded her of late-night trips to the 7-Eleven twenty-five years earlier. The most alarming thing was a clause at the end of the contract, which Lock was supposed to sign, regarding the fact that, because of Matthew's drug and alcohol problems, Bruce couldn't ensure the performance. A Post-it note was stuck to this page, written in Bruce's hand: *He's doing this as a personal favor to Claire, and wild horses won't keep him away, but . . .*

But it was Matthew. He was always at the mercy of his addictions.

Claire wanted to give the contract and rider to Lock as soon as possible. This was business. It was all in the name of attacking her line items before the meeting. She had every reason to be stopping by the office, and yet she felt obvious, as if she was throwing herself at Lock's feet.

The classical music was playing. Claire knocked on the door frame and poked her head in. Her eyes went right to Lock's desk – empty.

'Claire?'

Gavin Andrews looked at her expectantly from behind his desk.

'Hi, Gavin. How are you?'

'Me?' Gavin said. He looked down at his red-and-navy-striped tie – like something a prep school kid would wear – as if checking on himself. 'I'm fine.'

Claire didn't actually hear him say 'fine'; she was too busy scanning the office – no Lock – and at the same time trying to discern if Lock was in the boardroom or the kitchen or the bathroom. No, he wasn't here. She felt relief first, then deflation.

'Is Lock here?' Claire asked pointlessly.

'He's at lunch with some donors,' Gavin said. 'What can I help you with?'

Claire regarded Gavin. She didn't like him, and it had nothing to do with his being a pale replacement for Lock. Gavin was best described as smug, snooty, and condescending. Also, he was hard to pin down. Who was he? How old was he? Claire put him at thirty-five, though he might have been thirty-two, or thirty-nine. He was exceptionally good-looking, with blond hair and clear green eyes and smooth-shaven cheeks, and like Lock, he always wore a shirt and tie. But he was persnickety and critical; the one time Claire had engaged him in a personal conversation, he told her that as a rule he never dated a woman more than three times. More than three times, he said, and they started sniffing around for a wedding ring. Gavin lived in his parents' house out by Cisco Beach. His parents were older; they lived in Chicago and only made it to Nantucket for the month of August. The parents had money, though it was unclear how much of this trickled down to Gavin. He was forever complaining of the high cost of living on Nantucket (though Claire assumed he lived rent free), and he was always approaching the board with a pay raise, which Lock supported, saying, *He is very organized. And fastidious.* Overall, Claire regarded Gavin with suspicion – he was living here on Nantucket in his parents' house, working as a glorified secretary, wasting all his obvious potential: his looks, his articulateness and poise, his college education. Why? He was perfectly nice with Claire and the other board members, though Claire sensed him looking down his nose at her. He thought, as did Daphne Dixon (maybe they even

90

talked about it), that Claire was sloppy and unkempt, that she was a flaky artist who reproduced like a rabbit – all those children! And she was married to that carpenter caveman, who smoked and spat and fished and drank Bud Light out of cans and drove a black pickup named Darth Vader. (Pompous laughter, barely stifled.)

Gavin was Claire's opposite: he looked like he went home and showered at lunchtime, his shirt and pants were crisp like the pages of a new book, and he was single-minded in his devotion to Lock Dixon and the seamless administration of Nantucket's Children.

Claire dropped the contract on his desk in a way that was probably rude. 'You heard we got Max West to play the gala?'

He nodded once, solemnly. 'Lock told me. Congratulations.'

'Don't congratulate me. Congratulate us. We should make a lot of money.'

'Indeed, we should.'

'Do you like Max West?' Claire asked. 'Have you ever seen him in concert?'

'I listen to classical, Claire, you know that.'

'But not *only* classical?'

'Only classical. And jazz, every once in a while, on the weekends.'

'But no rock music?' Claire said. 'No blues, no rap, no country? No music with words?'

Gavin smiled at her. The classical music came across as an affectation, as did the red and white Mini Cooper that Gavin drove. The sight of him in that car bugged her, though she couldn't say why.

'This is the contract and the rider. I'd like Lock to look at them, go over them with Adams, whatever the usual procedure is.'

Gavin straightened the papers. 'They will go most directly into Lock's in-box.'

'Thank you, Gavin.' Claire beamed as warmly as she could.

'Is there anything else?'

Claire eyed the clock. It was ten minutes to one. Lunch with donors? Had he left at twelve, or twelve thirty? What if she left right now and missed him by a matter of seconds?

'I have some questions about the catering. The catering of the gala.'

'Mmmmmm,' Gavin said. 'What would those be?'

Claire paused. She didn't know how to handle the whole catering question. Claire had asked Siobhan to sit on the gala committee automatically, right away, because Siobhan was her best friend and Claire wanted to include her. But it would be truly awkward if Siobhan sat on the committee and for some reason she and Carter didn't get the catering job. Right? Anyone could see the tough position Claire was in. She wanted to proceed fairly, but the more she thought about it, the clearer it became that Claire would somehow have to secure the catering job for Siobhan. Claire eyed Gavin. Was it safe to spill her guts to him about this? It was not, she decided.

'My sister-in-law is interested in bidding the catering job,' Claire said. 'You know Siobhan and Carter, right? Island Fare?'

Gavin nodded once, briskly.

'So what is the procedure?'

'They are free to submit a bid,' Gavin said. 'We have two bids in already.'

'You do?'

'It's a big deal, the gala,' Gavin said. As if she didn't get it.

'Can I see the bids?' Claire asked.

'Well, technically, yes. I mean, you are the cochair. But I'm going to have to ask you not to share the content of the bids with Carter and Siobhan. If you were, for example, to tell Siobhan what the price per head was, and then she came in a couple of bucks under, that would fall outside the parameters of fair business practices. To keep your nose clean, I would suggest you not look at the bids. In fact, I would suggest you delegate catering to someone else. That's why you have a committee!'

'Right,' Claire said reluctantly. How to explain to Gavin that

92

Siobhan was Claire's best friend and Claire could not deny her the catering?

'Can you tell me who gave you the bids, at least?' Claire asked.

'I could,' Gavin said. 'I certainly could. You are the cochair. But what you have to ask yourself is, do you really want to know? Wouldn't it be better, from an ethical standpoint, to wash your hands of this? Because, you know, here in this office, we insist things be done in an aboveboard way.'

Claire gazed at the wall next to Gavin's desk. Only eighteen hours earlier, Lock Dixon had pressed her up against that wall. What would Gavin think if he knew? He would never believe it – and if he'd seen it with his own eyes, he would have fainted dead away.

We insist things be done in an aboveboard way. Gavin was weaselly, Claire decided. And self-important. He was the kind of guy who assumed that any woman he went out with more than three times would want to marry him, and now he was treating the catering bids as if they were the Pentagon Papers. But unlike three weeks ago, when Claire had known nothing about the gala, had done nothing and contributed nothing, she now felt she had some clout, some bargaining power. She had delivered Max West promptly, and free of charge. Surely she could lobby on Siobhan's behalf?

'Is it really that big of a deal?' Claire asked.

'I'm just trying to keep everything on the up-and-up. You don't want your integrity called into question, do you?'

Her integrity was becoming a tender spot already. 'God, no,' she said. 'You're right. Forget I asked.'

Gavin nodded again and got back to work, effectively dismissing her.

'You'll show Lock the contract?'

'When he gets back.'

'Okay.' She couldn't really delay another second. Did she want to delay? Did she want to see Lock? Yes, desperately, but now she would be too nervous, she would be tongue-tied, and Gavin, with his sharp, discriminating eye, would detect something fishy afoot, something fishier than the catering bids. *Get out of there!* 'Good-bye!'

The following night, Wednesday, there was a real meeting. Jason grumbled and Claire snapped at him for grumbling. He was angry that Claire had gone back to work, and she was angry that he was angry. She was more than angry; she was disillusioned. Jason didn't value her career – and not only did he not value it, but he hated it. He had told his own brother that he wanted to *bomb* Claire's hot shop. Bomb it – like a terrorist! When Claire had heard him say those words, they had not seemed as egregious as they did now. Jason had asked Claire to give up her career; he made her feel like her career was evil. He did not appreciate or respect her work. Lock was responsible for getting Claire back into the hot shop. That was a bond that went beyond the kiss in the office.

As she grabbed her purse, Jason said, 'Have fun at your meeting.'

'Thanks,' Claire said with open hostility. 'I will.'

Claire could see the lights of the Nantucket's Children office blazing from half a block away. Then she saw Brent Jackson, Julie's husband, and Brent's friend Edward Melior (who had the distinction of having once been engaged to Siobhan) heading toward the office from Water Street. Claire waved and they all climbed the stairs together, and Claire was glad she was entering the office with these handsome, successful men (Brent and Edward were both real estate agents) rather than alone. The office was a hive of activity. Adams Fiske was there, shaking hands, pounding backs, directing people toward the boardroom. Francine Davis was there, one of Claire's recruits, as well as Lauren van Aln, and the biggest coup, Tessa Kline, who was an editor at *NanMag,* the island's biggest, glossiest magazine. She would give them great press. Right away, it was a party of sorts, all these people, a veritable who's who of year-round islanders, and Claire was so overwhelmed and so pleased with herself for gathering these fine souls that she nearly forgot to look for Lock. There he was, in the corner, talking to a woman Claire didn't recognize. The woman was attractive, wearing a red silk Chinese jacket and jeans. She had the sort of long, straight hair that distracted men, and the hair was loose, which seemed like a come-on, a call for attention, on a woman in her forties. Why not pull it back or pin it up? The hair – a pretty light brown – was making some kind of statement, and Claire didn't like what it was saying. She felt as if her own hair – true, deep red and naturally wavy – was a Brillo pad in comparison. It was Ronald McDonald hair. She felt immediately defensive, not only about her hair, but about Lock's talking to an attractive woman. Claire realized – just as Lock turned and looked at her (blankly, as though he didn't recognize her) – that the woman was Isabelle French. Here, in person. Claire was taken aback; she had expected that Isabelle would call from New York. She had been ready for a disembodied voice, not an intriguing flesh-and-blood presence.

Lock said, 'Claire!' and waved her over in a way that made her feel like his servant.

She tried to smooth the wrinkles in her mind. When she was working and she blew out a piece too thin, or she marvered lopsidedly, the best thing to do was start over – go back to the crucible and get a new gather. She could do that now, with Isabelle: start fresh, with a glob of molten possibility that could be coaxed into something divine.

The room seemed to part as Claire made her way toward Lock and Isabelle.

Lock said, 'Claire, *this* is Isabelle French, your cochair. Isabelle, Claire Crispin.'

Claire smiled. She and Isabelle clasped hands like two heads of state. Claire could imagine the caption beneath their official photograph: *Gala cochairs meet for the first time.*

'It's a pleasure to meet you,' Isabelle said. Her voice was smooth and rich and a touch smoky, like some kind of complicated sauce. 'I know your work, of course.'

That was a nice touch, Claire thought. *I know your work.* It made Claire feel like Gertrude Stein.

'Thank you,' she said. 'It's nice to finally put a face to the name.' This was the woman in the Indian-print tunic whom Claire had seen at the benefit. Claire remembered seeing her one other time before that, from across the room at a board meeting – but Claire could never have guessed from either of those previous sightings that they would someday be shackled together.

'Let's get started,' Lock said. 'Will everyone take a seat?' He pulled out a chair for Isabelle and took the seat beside her. Claire felt a twinge of jealousy. Absurd. She remembered Daphne Dixon: *If she touches him, or if they spend time alone together, I want you to call me. . . .* But who was the real threat? Why, it was Claire! Claire was the only woman Lock had kissed other than Daphne in twenty years. But Lock Dixon hadn't pulled out *her* chair. *Okay, stop,* she thought. *Back to the crucible.* She needed to remember why they were there – to help people like Marcella Vallenda, to raise money, to fund programming, to improve people's lives.

Claire wanted to get away from Lock, but the chairs were filling up quickly . . . She felt a momentary panic, as if this was a child's game, the music was going to stop at any second, and she would have to grab a seat . . . and the only seat remaining was to Lock's right. Claire sat down; now she and Isabelle were flanking him. To Claire's right, thankfully, was Adams Fiske, with his mop of brown curls and glasses sliding down his nose. Claire adored him unconditionally. His youngest son, Ryan, was J.D.'s best friend. Adams was in Claire's foxhole; he would watch her back.

Isabelle cleared her throat. 'I've written up an agenda for the meeting,' she said. She opened up a luscious calfskin portfolio and took out a sheaf of papers, passed them around. Claire felt the first drop of poison sully the new waters of her relationship with Isabelle. She had written up an *agenda*? *All right,* Claire thought.

That made sense. She wouldn't travel all the way from New York City on a Wednesday in October to show up at a meeting unprepared. So, the agenda. Claire glanced at Lock, who had put on his bifocals. Forty-eight hours earlier, they had been making out like a couple of teenagers in the other room, but now that seemed like a figment of Claire's imagination.

The first line item on Isabelle's agenda was 'Talent.' *Discuss talent possibilities. Assign talent point person. Create talent and production budget (including travel and accommodations).*

Isabelle tucked her long hair behind one ear, then tossed the ends over her shoulder. It was a move from her personal theater, Claire could tell, and she knew she'd see a lot of Isabelle's hair tossing between now and August. Another drop of poison in the well.

'Since the gala is, in essence, a concert,' Isabelle said, 'I thought we'd start by discussing talent.'

Claire opened her mouth to speak, but Brent Jackson beat her to it. 'We got Max West,' he said. 'Max West has agreed to play for free.'

Isabelle turned to Lock, slowly, deliberately. Claire and everyone else in the room watched, fascinated. Had Lock not *told* Isabelle about Max West?

'Max West?' Isabelle said. 'Max *West?*' She might have said his name with awe and admiration – or disbelief – but what Claire heard was disdain. 'Do we *want* Max West?'

Claire leaned against the back of her Windsor chair so that she could feel every one of her vertebrae, and she pressed her feet flat to the ground and simultaneously tried to lower her pelvis. She was creating her own yoga position. This distraction lasted for a few seconds before the shouting in her head began. *Do we* want *Max West?* That was like asking if they wanted Billy Joel, John Cougar Mellencamp, Tom Petty. Max West was probably the biggest cross-generational rock star in the *whole world.* He was right up there with Jimmy Buffett and Elton John. *Do we want Max West?*

Was she kidding?

'Hell, yes,' Brent Jackson said. 'That's why I'm here. I love Max West. Everybody loves Max West.'

Isabelle tilted her head back so that her nose pointed up. 'I'm not sure he's right for our demographic,' she said. 'Our leading donor demographic is fifty-five to seventy. That's the biggest money. They don't want to hear Max West. They want to hear Broadway.'

Adams said, 'With all due respect to our demographic, since Max West is willing to play for us for free, we are going with Max West.'

'I think that's a mistake,' Isabelle said. 'I really do.'

So there you had it: the well was poisoned. Claire *hated* Isabelle French. Siobhan had tried to warn Claire, but Claire had not heeded this warning – she had felt *sorry* for Isabelle French! (*Bad divorce*, Lock had said. *And some subsequent bad decisions.*) But now Isabelle was making Claire look like an ass in front of Adams, the committee, and Lock. Overriding Claire's embarrassment, her humiliation, her indignation (should she recite the litany of charitable organizations that wanted to get Max West and had no prayer? Should she inform Isabelle that Max had turned down *Bono?*), was mounting anger at Lock. He should have told Isabelle about Max West before the meeting started, and he should be defending Claire now. It had never crossed Claire's mind that there was a person alive who would not want Max West to play the benefit. Claire was completely blindsided. She was mute with rage.

Lock said, 'I guess we could look into other options . . .'

'No,' Claire said. All this time she had been staring into her lap, and there was a reason for that – she knew her face would be discolored. Her skin was milky white, but now she would have a red spot – round as an apple – on each cheek. She looked up at Brent Jackson and Tessa Kline, the magazine editor – *God, what must she be thinking?* – then turned to Isabelle and Lock. 'No way. If you make me cancel Max West after calling in this favor, I will quit.' She rose from her chair to show she was serious, but was this a threat? Did anyone *care* if she resigned as cochair? Did Lock care?

Lock said to Isabelle, 'Claire brought us Max West. He's a friend of hers from high school.' He made it sound like Claire was a cat who had dropped a dead mouse at their feet.

'Forget it,' Claire said. She felt like a nine-year-old, a seven-year-old, a four-year-old. 'I'll call him back and tell him we don't want him. I'll tell him he doesn't hit our demographic.'

'I've been talking to people, too,' Isabelle said. 'Kristin Chenoweth, who is the hottest voice on Broadway right now. And Christine Ebersole is considering us, too. I've known her manager for years.'

'Christine Ebersole?' said Lauren van Aln. 'Never heard of her.'

'How old are you?' Isabelle said.

'Thirty-one.'

'Well, that's why.'

'I've never heard of Kristin Chenoweth,' Brent Jackson said.

'She's starring in the revival of *South Pacific,*' Isabelle said. 'Her face is on every bus and billboard in the city. She is *h-o-t.*'

'What is your objection to Max West?' Claire said. 'If I may ask. He has eight platinum albums. He has thirty-one Top Forty hits. He has mass appeal. He is a bona fide celebrity, everyone knows him, and he will put ticket sales through the roof.'

'Nobody's going to pay a thousand dollars for someone they've never heard of,' Francine Davis said.

There was silence. Everyone was waiting for Isabelle to speak. When she did speak, she looked at Lock, though Claire was the one standing, demanding an answer. But Isabelle appealed only to him. 'Max West is a *rock* star,' she said. 'His songs are loud and some of them have an edge. Do we really want our elegant evening to end with screaming guitar?'

'It's mostly acoustic guitar,' Brent Jackson pointed out. 'And incredible vocals.'

'I think he's tawdry,' Isabelle said. 'He's common, lowbrow. He will make the event seem cheap. We're not selling tickets to Fenway; this is an upscale event. We should get an upscale performer.'

'You have a point,' Lock said.

'I was asked to deliver Max West,' Claire said. 'I have delivered Max West, but now I'm hearing we don't want him. I'm hearing he's not suitable. Is that how everybody feels?'

'No!' Brent Jackson said. 'Why are we even having this conversation?'

Why indeed? Claire thought. She was glaring down at the bald spot on Lock's head with such heated vitriol that she expected it to catch fire. 'Do we want Max West or not? I'm happy to cancel him and walk.'

Adams took Claire's arm. 'Don't cancel him. We're in the business of making money for this organization, and I think the best way to do that is to take the biggest star power we can get. Max is a coup for us, and he's willing to do it for free. In my mind, there's no question. Maybe we lose a few old folks who think his music is too loud, but we'll pick up younger people.'

'We're making a mistake,' Isabelle said. 'What about the man's personal life? The drugs, the drinking, the rehab, the affair with Savannah Bright splattered all over the tabloids. Is this a person we want representing a charity for *children?*'

Claire put her hands to her burning cheeks. She couldn't decide which of many nasty things to think first. *What do you know about children? Do you even know who Big Bird is? And what about kissing another woman's husband on the dance floor of the Waldorf-Astoria in front of eight hundred partygoers? What about the letter that came a week later asking you to rotate off the board*

100

of Manhattan East Hospital? Are you *the right person to represent a charity for children?*

'We are sticking with Max West,' Adams said. Adams was always conciliatory, always open to other points of view and extending any debate, but tonight his voice was firm. 'I don't want to talk about it any further.'

Isabelle laughed derisively. She waved her hand. 'Fine,' she said. 'I'll pull my other lines out of the water. But let it be noted that I think we're making a mistake.'

'So noted,' Adams said.

'He's, like, the biggest name in the business,' Brent Jackson said.

Isabelle's smile was so fake it looked painful. 'Okay,' she said. 'Fine.'

Claire sat back down. Technically, she had won her point, and yet she felt defeated. Her own cochair wasn't happy about Max West, and Lock had come dangerously close to rolling over on it – and this after he had *asked* her to pursue Matthew in the first place! Isabelle had gotten her shots in, calling Matthew tawdry, common, lowbrow, and cheap, and because Matthew was Claire's friend, because they had grown up together and shared a history, Claire now felt like she was the skanky ex-girlfriend of a motorcycle drug lord. She wasn't cut out for this kind of jockeying, or the politics.

Claire didn't want to fight with Isabelle; she didn't want to compete to see who would be the alpha dog, though wasn't that what Isabelle was doing? Wasn't that the point of her creating an agenda in the first place? Isabelle was asserting her control, taking charge. It hadn't crossed Claire's mind to write up an agenda for the meeting. Claire had thought that Lock would run the meeting, or Adams would, but not her and certainly not Isabelle.

Isabelle said, 'We'll make Claire the point person for the talent, then. Okay with you, Claire?'

'Fine,' Claire said. 'I already delivered the contract and the rider.'

Adams held them up. 'I have them right here. I will look them over.'

Next on the agenda were the invitations. Isabelle knew a graphic designer in New York who would do them gratis. She said this word, 'gratis,' instead of 'for free,' and Claire shuddered. The graphic designer, Isabelle said, was young and hip; he lived in Nolita. (Claire understood that this was a neighborhood in Manhattan, but she didn't know where it was because the last time Claire had been to New York, Nolita hadn't existed.)

'We need to revamp the invite design,' Isabelle said. 'It's fusty. The past few years the invites have been straight out of the retirement home.'

Perfect for our demographic, Claire thought.

Isabelle reached into her portfolio. 'I've copied the invitation list for each of you to look over. Please add people, delete people, make notes by anyone you know who has died, or worse still, divorced.' She looked up for a laugh but got none. Claire felt marginally better. 'This list is stagnant. It needs freshening up. We don't want it to be the same old people.'

The same old thousand people, Claire thought.

'Like I said, having Max will bring in some new faces,' Adams said.

'Yeah,' Brent Jackson said. 'Like me. Finally, someone I'd pay a thousand bucks to see.'

Isabelle sniffed. 'Is it all right with everyone if I spearhead invitations?'

People nodded. Fine, fine. Though what was the point of having a committee if they weren't going to be given jobs?

'Item three,' Isabelle said. 'Catering.'

Claire had been prepared, coming into this meeting, to do battle regarding the catering. She was so stunned after fighting about

Max West, however, that she couldn't remember how she had planned to broach the catering question.

'There were problems with the catering last year,' Isabelle said. 'Some people said their steaks were raw, and some said theirs tasted like shoe leather.'

Claire tried to keep the eagerness out of her voice. 'Maybe we should switch caterers,' she said.

'Absolutely,' Isabelle said, and for a split second, there was harmony. Palpable relief around the table. The cochairs agreed! 'Do you have anyone in mind?'

Claire paused. Did she dare say it? 'I know someone who's interested in putting in a bid.'

'Who's that?'

'Island Fare.'

'Never heard of them,' Isabelle said.

'Really?' Claire said. She pressed her back against the chair again and did the thing with her feet and her pelvis in an attempt to keep her mouth shut, but that was impossible. 'The owner, Siobhan – she's my sister-in-law – said she catered a lunch at your house last summer.'

'Oh,' Isabelle said. 'Well, I threw a lot of catered luncheons last summer. I don't remember who I used for each one.' There was silence around the table. If the rest of the committee hadn't hated Isabelle French before, they did now. Claire tried to keep her expression neutral. She had never had an enemy before, or even a rival; she wasn't used to feeling pleased when someone said something completely asinine.

Adams cleared his throat. 'They're very good,' he said. 'They cater the Boston Pops every year.'

'We don't want to use the same people as the Pops,' Isabelle said. 'We want to distinguish ourselves.'

'It would be different food,' Claire said. 'It seems to me we want the most creative, delicious food at the best price. Yes or no?'

The table murmured yes. Edward Melior piped up. 'I think Siobhan would be great.'

'Let's have them give us a bid,' Adams said. 'I happen to have two other bids here, though one of them is from the catering company we used last year.'

'Well, forget that,' Isabelle said. 'They were awful. Half our table had their entrées, but the other half had to wait, and by the time their food came, the rest of us were finished.'

Things were looking good for Siobhan, Claire thought, and she'd barely had to say a word. 'Edward, will you take charge of catering?' she asked. She knew he would pick Carter and Siobhan because he and Siobhan had once been in love and engaged to be married, and everyone in the universe knew he still carried a flame for her. The only person who would not be thrilled about this situation was Carter – he didn't like Edward – but Siobhan wanted this job, and here was one way for her to get it without Claire's having to perform subterfuge with the paperwork.

'My pleasure,' Edward said.

'Item four,' Isabelle said. Was it Claire's imagination, or did it sound like she was wearing down? 'Auction item.'

Lock had been sitting, this whole time, still as a statue, his hands folded on top of his legal pad. He had not written a single note, and he had not (as Claire had hoped) looked meaningfully in her direction. Possibly he was afraid to speak. He had a cochair to his left who was making the meeting difficult and unpleasant, and a cochair to his right whom he had kissed two days earlier. Claire was hurt that he wasn't placing himself solidly in her corner, but perhaps he was afraid to show his hand. He had feelings for Claire but couldn't let anyone know it, so he would let Claire flounder and take Isabelle's arrows. Or he was exercising his usual good judgment and listening to everyone's opinions before weighing in. Claire should admire his impartiality instead of letting it bother her.

'I have a few spectacular ideas for an auction item,' Isabelle said. She did the tucking-and-tossing thing with her hair again. Claire was certain that none of Isabelle's 'spectacular ideas' included a museum-quality piece of glass conceived and fashioned by Claire Danner Crispin. If Lock hadn't told Isabelle about Max West, then he certainly hadn't told her about Claire's coming out of retirement for the auction item. Claire had considered bringing the sketch of the chandelier, but in the end she had been too afraid. Art was subjective and always included the possibility of failure. Already there had been a few nights, before she drifted off to sleep, when she imagined Pietro da Silva, the island's best auctioneer, starting the bidding on her piece and looking over a sea of people, all of whom were sitting on their hands.

'Since we're not going to ask Kristin Chenoweth to perform,' Isabelle said, 'we might ask her to donate private singing lessons.'

'Singing lessons?' Tessa Kline said skeptically.

'Her face is plastered across every subway station in the city,' Isabelle said.

Edward Melior shrugged. 'What about orchestra seats to the show, with a meet and greet afterward?'

'Or dinner,' Tessa said.

'I'm willing to ask,' Isabelle said gamely.

Claire's breathing was shallow. No one was going to want her glass. It wasn't sexy; it wasn't interesting.

'I also have a friend willing to donate his G5,' Isabelle said. 'That's a private jet. I could ask for a round-trip anywhere in the United States with twenty people onboard for a cocktail party.'

'That sounds incredible,' Edward Melior said.

'Incredible,' Claire echoed. She felt like a complete ass. Lock had led her to believe that people would want her glass – but compared with singing lessons from a Tony Award-winning actress, or a cocktail party on a private jet flying to Palm Beach or over the Rockies, what Claire was offering up felt like a crayon drawing.

Lock Dixon tapped his pen against his notebook, like a judge with a gavel. 'Claire and I have already discussed the auction item,' he said. 'And she has agreed to create a museum-quality piece of glass that we will put up as the auction item.'

Claire felt her cheeks burning, as obvious as two circles of red felt. This was quite possibly the most mortifying moment of her entire life. Why had she let Lock talk her into this? She had no boundaries. Her cells, as Siobhan so adroitly pointed out, had no membranes. When she looked up, there would be a table full of uncomfortable looks and throat clearings and scratching of heads, literal and figurative. Museum-quality glass? Huh?

Tessa Kline shrieked. 'Oh, my God!' she said. 'Claire? You'll do it?'

'Um,' Claire said, 'I told Lock I would. I don't have an idea yet, though.' Here, she thought, in addition to her cheeks burning, her nose would grow. 'Plus, let's face it: art is subjective. People could hate what I do.'

'But you're a genius!' Tessa said. 'Claire has a piece in the Whitney Museum, you know.'

'I told her this would be her triumphant return,' Lock said. He sounded, at that moment, proprietary and proud, and although Claire was elated, she was also worried. Would everyone now guess that there was something between them? 'Back after a two-year hiatus.'

'But Claire has a point,' Adams said. 'Art is subjective. I would hate to see her spend a lot of time and energy creating something and then not have it go for what it's worth.'

'It would be embarrassing for me,' Claire said. 'And bad for Nantucket's Children. If we didn't get the money, I mean.' In the two weeks since the gala auction item had first been mentioned, it had jump-started Claire's career and caused a rift in her marriage – and now Claire found herself backpedaling about it.

'We already have a guaranteed bid of fifty thousand dollars,' Lock said.

'We do?' Adams said.

'Yes,' Lock said. 'From Daphne and me. Whatever Claire

creates, we'll pay fifty thousand dollars for. And we can culti-
vate other bidders.'

'Precisely,' Tessa said. 'I'll do a feature article in the magazine,
with a photograph. Museum-quality piece. People will go *crazy*.
The homes on this island have gotten so out of control with their
movie theaters and their sculpture gardens and six-thousand-
dollar shower curtains – I'll bet there are a bunch of people who
would jump at a chance to own a major work by Claire. It would
be one-of-a-kind, right?'

'Yes,' Claire squeaked.

'One-of-a-kind. And she's been out of commission for a couple
of years. That makes it even more special. I say we go for it,' Tessa
said. She grinned at Claire. 'I say, go home and get blowing!'

Brent Jackson laughed at this, and Edward Melior started to
applaud. Lock said, 'Great. Tessa, will you head the auction committee? You're the right person to get news about the piece out
there.'

Claire turned to Adams. 'Do you think it's a good idea?'

'You seem to have the full confidence of our executive director,'
Adams said. 'And Tessa is right about the summer people having
a bad case of one-upmanship. The question is how you'll find the
time.'

Of course, along with the waking nightmares, that was the
question.

Claire glanced over at Isabelle, who was quietly tucking her papers into her calfskin portfolio. What did Isabelle think of Claire's
creating a museum-quality piece of glass for the auction? Did she
think it was a good idea or a bad idea? *I know your work.* But did
she *like* Claire's work? Did she consider blown glass to be *art,* or
did she consider it a hobby, like pottery, or knitting? Strangely,
Claire found herself seeking Isabelle's approval, her endorsement.
But Isabelle didn't respond; she looked exhausted. She had flown
in for this meeting with her neatly printed agenda, but things
hadn't gone her way. Claire should have been pleased, but she

was plagued with self-doubt. What if Max West *was* perceived as tawdry and common? What if hiring Siobhan to cater *was* unethical? What if Lock *was* the only one bidding on Claire's piece? Did Claire really know how to run a benefit better than Isabelle French, who had done it for larger organizations, in the most sophisticated city in the world? It was silly to think so.

If Claire was a reluctant victor, Isabelle was a stoic loser. She crumpled the agenda in her fist in a way that seemed more resigned than angry.

'I'm tired,' she said. 'And starving. There is still PR and marketing to discuss, but should we save it for next time?'

'Next time,' Lock agreed, and the rest of the committee seemed relieved. People packed up.

'Dinner?' Claire heard Lock say.

'God, yes,' Isabelle said. 'Where?'

'I made a reservation at Twenty-one Federal,' he said.

'Is Daphne coming?' Isabelle asked.

'No. She wanted to see you, but she didn't feel well enough to come out.'

Claire tried to remain calm. Lock was taking Isabelle to 21 Federal for dinner. This really, really bugged her, but why? After all, Isabelle had arrived from out of town. Tessa and Lauren and Francine were lingering by the door. They were waiting for Claire; they wanted to talk to her about the meeting, and she needed to thank them for coming. She should thank Brent and Edward, too. They had been supportive. But Claire could not tear her attention away from Lock and Isabelle. Lock was taking Isabelle and her beautiful hair out for dinner.

Adams took Claire by the elbow. 'Let's go grab a drink.'

'Oh,' Claire said. 'I don't know . . .'

'Claire?'

This was Lock's voice. Claire turned too eagerly.

'Do you want to join Isabelle and me at Twenty-one Federal?' he said. 'We're going right now, for dinner.'

Did Claire want to go to Twenty-one Federal with Lock and Isabelle? God, no! It would turn into an uncomfortable extension of the meeting – or it would be Lock encouraging Claire and Isabelle to get to know each other. Claire would rather go out and belt back a couple of stiff drinks with Adams and the rest of the committee. But she didn't want to turn Lock down. What if he took it as a rejection? Maybe she and Lock would outlast Isabelle; maybe they would return to the office alone or drive somewhere in Lock's car. If she said no to him now, when would she see him again? Would he call her at home? Or would she have to create an excuse to swing by the office? If she swung by during the day, Gavin would be around. But what reason could she possibly fabricate to stop by at night?

'Come out for a drink!' This was Tessa calling across the room. 'We'll go to Water Street, okay, Adams? We'll meet you there.'

'Okay,' Adams said. 'Claire?'

'Have you eaten?' Lock asked.

Claire felt like she was being pecked at by chickens. But why? She could either go for drinks with Adams, Tessa, and the gang, or she could go to dinner with Lock and Isabelle. The fact was, she could have stood there all night deliberating and still not have come up with the answer, which proved to Claire only one thing: she was losing her mind.

'I ate earlier,' she said to Lock, though this was, of course, a lie. Or a partial lie: at dinner with the kids, she had eaten the two puckered ends of Shea's hot dog. 'I should really get home. The baby doesn't do well without me.'

'Come out, just for one drink,' Adams said.

Claire put on her coat. She was finding it hard to breathe here in the Elijah Baker House. She felt like she was wearing a whalebone corset.

'Next time,' she said. She faced Isabelle and Lock and gave them a (believable?) smile, shook Isabelle's hand, and said, 'Thanks for running the meeting. You have my e-mail, right? Well, if not, Lock

109

has it. He'll give it to you. Or you can call me. I have to go. I'll see everybody later, okay?' Claire wedged her way past Lock and Isabelle – who were looking at her as if she was nuts, which she was – and then around the table, jingling her keys. She meant it: she was leaving.

When she finally made it out onto the cool street, she could almost hear the skin of her face hisssssssssss, the way a hot mold hissed when she dropped it into the water basin.

She took her cell phone out and called Jason's cell phone. He answered on the first ring, in a whisper. 'Hey, baby.'

She was so happy to hear his voice, she nearly wept. 'Hey,' she said. 'I'm on my way home.'

CHAPTER FIVE

SHE SURPRISES HERSELF

Claire slept with Lock for the first time a week later.

After the meeting with Isabelle French and the committee, Claire walked away thinking, *I am done with Lock Dixon.* It was all adolescent nonsense, anyway, and what were they *doing,* two reasonable, married adults? Claire climbed in bed with Jason and thought, *I am happy here. I am happy!* That Lock Dixon had showed an interest in her was flattering and would be left at that.

How to explain what happened? Claire had always thought of adultery as a country she either wasn't brave enough or didn't want to visit – until someone handed her a passport and a ticket, and suddenly she was on her way. Lock called Claire on her cell phone, which he had never done before. She was driving home from dropping the kids off at school; she had only Zack in the car and he was drifting off to sleep. Claire was so certain it was Siobhan on the phone that she picked it up without checking the display and said,

111

somewhat glumly (because she wasn't exactly giddy about giving up Lock; in fact, it left her feeling deflated), 'Hey.'

'Claire?'

It was him. She was flustered. She couldn't later remember what he had said – something to the effect that he knew she'd found the meeting difficult, it would get easier, Isabelle would loosen up, she had been nervous and was going through the wringer with the divorce.

Okay, Claire said. *Right, I could tell. Whatever, it was fine.*

And then, after what seemed like a significant pause, Lock said, *Would you mind stopping by the office tonight?*

Tonight?

Are you busy?

No, she said. *Well, yes, always busy, but I can come in. Swing by.*

Great, he said.

Then there was silence. This was the time for Claire to renege, but she didn't. She could 'swing by' the office – it sounded both casual and proper. He had something to give her, there was something for her to sign, proofread, consider. But she did not ask what it was.

Okay, she said finally. *I'll see you tonight.*

See you tonight, he said.

Claire waited until Jason got home from work to tell him.

'I have a meeting tonight.'

'Jesus, Claire!'

'I know, I'm sorry. It should be short.'

'I can't believe this,' Jason said. 'Why can't you meet during the day when the kids are at school and Pan is working? Why does it always have to be at night?'

'Sorry,' Claire said. 'It will be quick. I'll be back by nine.'

'Promise?'

'Promise.'

After dinner, Claire gave the younger three kids a bath, got the girls into their bedroom with books, and dressed Zack in his pajamas. She handed him to Jason, who was zoned out in front of *Entertainment Tonight*.

'Can you make his bottle?' Claire asked.

'Why can't you do it?'

'I can do it, but I have to get ready.'

'Get ready for what?'

'My meeting.'

'Why do you have to get ready for a meeting? You look fine.'

'I'd like to change.'

'Why?'

Claire was shaking from anger, frustration, guilt, nerves. 'Forget it,' she said. 'I won't go. Give me the baby.'

Jason scowled. 'You're acting like one of the kids.'

'*I* am?'

'Go get ready for your meeting,' Jason said. 'I'll take care of things here. Again.'

Claire went into the kitchen and fixed Zack's bottle. She couldn't do this. She could not leave her home, her kids, she could not even leave her infuriating husband to go to Lock. She wasn't cut out for it; it required guts that she didn't have. She felt something pop inside her – the bubble of expectation that had been expanding every second since Lock said, *See you tonight*. He would be there, in the dark office, waiting for her. When she came up the stairs, he would smile.

Claire brushed her teeth and changed into jeans and a cashmere sweater. She did nothing with her hair and she did not put on perfume. Earrings? No. Earrings would be a red flag.

'Okay,' she said to Jason. 'I'm going to my meeting. I'll be back by nine.'

He said nothing. She hesitated. He hadn't even heard her. Or he had heard her and was ignoring her. *Stop me!* she thought. But she only wanted him to stop her so she would have a reason to go

113

in anger. As it was, she was going to have to take this step of her own free will. The decision was hers.

'Jason?' she said.

He was wrapped up in *Jeopardy!* He waved.

When Claire reached the office, she was shaking. She couldn't keep herself from shaking, even though she'd told herself that nothing had to happen, that it would all just be very innocent. Gala business. *We insist things be done in an aboveboard way.*

Lock was at his desk with two glasses of wine already poured, but they didn't even get to the wine until afterward, after he had taken her, with insane hunger, incredible electric urgency, up against the wall. It was fast, animal-like, there was clawing and biting. They were like a pile of gasoline-soaked rags that someone took a match to, they went up in flames, whoosh, just like that; they were two crossed wires that caused an explosion. Boom. Hot. Claire had no thoughts other than thoughts about her body and what it wanted. He touched her here, he kissed her there, she could not get enough, she did not want it to end. His body was so different from Jason's. Jason was lean and muscular; he had six-pack abs that he was very proud of. Lock was softer, pudgier in the midsection, his chest was hairy – it was so foreign to Claire – but his arms were strong and he touched her with skill and desperation. He caressed her body, then grabbed it; he sucked, then bit. He was a man who had not made love in a long time, and his unchecked desire was touching, heartbreaking almost. Claire wanted to hand herself over: *Yes, take me, gobble me up, it's okay.*

She had landed. Welcome to Adultery.

When it was over, Claire slid to the ground, stunned, and Lock, too, despite the lack of decorum, sat on the floor next to her and pulled her head into his lap and gently stroked her hair.

'How are you?' he whispered.

'I don't know,' she said.

'Me, either,' he said.

'I'm all messed up,' she said.

'I know,' he said.

She was grateful that it had happened quickly, so quickly that there had been no time for deciding – yes, no, right, wrong. When she thought back on it later, it seemed like an act of nature visited upon them – a tornado, a bolt of lightning. Lock.

She cried on the way home. Her whole body shook, despite the glass of wine, whose purpose all along, she realized, had been to calm her nerves. She was sad because she had done something very wrong: She had betrayed not only her husband but her own set of values. She was an adulteress. Then, too, she was sad because the sex had been amazing, it had been transporting, she was a hostage to it, to him, Lock. She was sad because she had to leave him. He would stay at the office, get cleaned up, and go home to Daphne, while Claire would go home to her kids. And Jason. She said, *When will I see you again?* He said, *I'll be in touch.*

It continued. They met once a week, twice a week; they arranged it by text message or by e-mail. Claire couldn't explain it, she didn't understand it, she was a captive of the country: *Adultery.* Lock had infected her, he was something she'd caught, he was a sickness – maybe, like the common cold, it would wear off in a week or two, but maybe it would linger and grow like cancer. It would kill her. Claire couldn't decide if the worst thing about adultery was the guilt or the fear. The guilt was debilitating. It was worse than the guilt she harbored about Daphne and worse than the guilt that attended Zack's birth. Those had been accidents, mistakes. They had been unintentional. This affair was deliberate, the most deliberate sin she had ever committed. As a child, she had memorized the act of contrition: *O my God, I am heartily sorry for having offended you . . .* A priest once told her that sinners only thought about God after they had sinned, not before. This was Claire. She slept with Lock, she begged for

115

forgiveness, as contrite as all the world, and then she slept with him again.

Claire was plagued by memories of her own parents. Her father, Bud Danner, had owned an electronics store in Wildwood. He was a heavy drinker and a wild philanderer. He had not, in the words of Claire's mother, 'been faithful for five minutes.' After work, he would go to the bar, where he caroused with a string of trashy women. Claire remembered her mother crying, her mother blaming herself, her mother so angry at her father that Claire thought she would kill him. She screamed, she threw things, he walked out – he seemed to have no shortage of places to go – and then Claire's mother would smack herself in the face again and again. It was awful. It was the worst thing Claire had ever witnessed, her mother's self-loathing. Claire had promised herself she would never be this way. She would not blame herself for things beyond her control. But of course she did, all the time. She had inherited her parents' worst traits, their most despicable behavior. She certainly never believed she would follow in her father's flawed footsteps and *cheat.* And yet here she was. As Claire spoon-fed Zack pureed squash, as she bathed the girls and folded their pretty clothes, as she chose peaches and rib-eye steaks at the grocery store, she recognized herself as a liar. She wasn't the person her children thought she was; she was someone with a secret life. Even worse than feeling guilty was forgetting to feel guilty. The guilt should have been part and parcel with the adultery; it should have been constant. To not feel guilt was monstrous. Guilt and no guilt: these were the worst things.

We're going to hell, Claire whispered in Lock's ear one night.

There is no hell, he whispered back.

The only thing worse than the guilt was the fear of getting caught.

One night, after Claire came home from being with Lock, Jason said, 'You smell funny.'

Panic seized Claire by the knees. 'I do not.'

116

'You do. You smell funny. Why do you smell funny?'

She didn't look at him, though he was sitting up in bed, staring at her. 'You smell funny all the time,' she said. 'You smell like cigarettes.' She got right into the shower.

One day, she couldn't find her cell phone. Where was it? Claire looked everywhere – throughout the house, under the kids' beds, in the drawers, in each of her purses, in the car, outside in the frosty grass, in the hot shop. Where was it? Had Zack taken it? She looked in the toy box. Had she left it at the supermarket? She called the supermarket; no one had turned in a phone. She called Siobhan. Siobhan said, 'Call the phone, silly. See if anyone answers.'

Claire called the phone. Jason answered. Claire said, 'What are you doing with my phone?'

Jason said, 'I have no idea. I didn't even know I had it until just now, when you called me.'

Claire's stomach contracted until it was a tight ball of fear. This sounded like a lie. Had he taken her phone to check on her? Had he seen all the phone calls to the Nantucket's Children office, or to the strange number that was Lock's cell phone? Had he seen the texts? Meet me here, meet me there? Claire should have deleted them, one and all. She was such a *bloody fool,* such an innocent – she had not followed the most basic rule in covering her tracks. She got in the car and drove to Jason's work site, thinking of how to reasonably explain herself. The worst thing would be if Lock called while the phone was in Jason's possession. But there was an easy explanation: gala business. There were always questions about the gala that needed to be asked or answered.

Still, when Claire got the phone back, she erased every call with a sick and pounding heart. The fear was the worst thing.

Claire wanted to go to confession, but confession was only held on Saturdays at four o'clock, and every Saturday at four o'clock J.D. had a Pop Warner football game at the Boys & Girls Club, and

Claire could not miss a game. It would be worse to miss her child's football game than not to confess to her adultery, she decided, though her desire to confess was pressing. She wasn't sure she could actually hand the truth over to Father Dominic, the priest who had baptized all four of her children and had administered J.D.'s and Ottilie's First Communions. Claire adored Father Dominic, she'd had him to the house for dinner numerous times, and twice the two of them had gone to the movies together – once to see *Chicago* and once to see *Dreamgirls* (Father Dominic was a big fan of musicals; Jason could not abide them). The longer Claire went without confessing, the more convinced she became that she would not be able to say the words *I'm committing adultery* to Father Dominic. She would have to wait for a visiting priest, whom she didn't know and who didn't know her, or she would confess to Father Dominic to a gamut of general sins and hope that adultery was covered among them. But somehow Claire understood that confessing would not be confessing unless she confessed to Father Dominic about Lock Dixon. Anything short of this would be a cop-out and would not count. And so she went. She left the Pop Warner game at halftime, telling Jason she had a migraine and had to go home.

He said, 'Will you take Zack with you, please?'

She said, 'I can't.'

He said, 'I can't watch Zack and Shea – *and* Ottilie and J.D.' Ottilie was cheerleading, adorable in her *N* sweater and her blue and white pleated skirt. Shea was kicking a football on the sidelines, chasing it, kicking it again. Zack was whining, clawing at Claire's neck. Claire could not in good conscience leave Jason with all of the kids, but she had to get to church.

'Okay,' she said. 'I'll take Zack.'

Father Dominic was stunned to see Claire and Zack sitting in the front pew when he exited the confessional; the surprise registered on his face. A slender, pretty young woman hurried out of the church, and Claire wondered what *she* had confessed and whether it was anywhere close to as appalling as what Claire was about to admit to. Father Dominic said nothing; he simply gestured to the empty booth, and Claire carried Zack in and knelt. She wished fervently that she had been born a Protestant because at that moment, owning up to this enormous sin, saying it out loud to another human being, seemed a beastly punishment.

She started in with the act of contrition. *O my God, I am heartily sorry for having offended you, and I detest all my sins . . .* Zack clawed at her neck. He needed his fingernails cut: it felt like he was drawing blood. Claire took a deep breath. She eyed Father Dominic, whose head was bowed in prayer. She was trembling, as terrified as she'd ever been in her life. What was she afraid of? She was afraid he would hate her. He saw her, not every week, but many weeks, in church with the kids. He thought her to be a devout person; he had called her daily when Zack was in the hospital in Boston and had prayed with her over the phone. Now he would see her for who she truly was.

'I'm committing adultery,' Claire said. She expected Father's head to pop up, she awaited his aghast expression, but he was still. She was grateful for this stillness, this posture of acceptance. 'I'm having an affair with Lockhart Dixon.' Claire said his name because not to say his name felt like holding back a part of the truth. Claire had no idea if Father Dominic knew Lock – Lock was a member of Saint Paul's Episcopal. They might have known each other through one of Nantucket's Children's programs.

Father Dominic remained still. Claire closed her eyes. 'That's all,' she whispered. Zack started to cry.

When Father Dominic raised his head, his expression was blank. In regard to confession, Father Dominic had once claimed that there was a hole in the back of his head. People's sins drained out nearly as soon as they entered, he said. But Claire was pretty sure that wouldn't happen today.

Father Dominic said, 'You will stop? You came to confess, so you understand what you're doing is wrong. Will you stop?'

Tears fell – Zack's, and Claire's own. Of course he would ask her to stop, or demand it.

'I don't know if I can,' she said.

'You can, Claire,' Father Dominic said. 'You must pray for strength.'

'I can pray for strength, but I don't know if I can stop seeing Lock. I could tell you I'm going to stop, but I would be lying.'

Father Dominic shook his head, and Claire felt an argument rising in her. It was the argument that ran like ticker tape through her mind. Did the adultery automatically make her a bad person? Did the good things that she did – caring for her kids, washing Jason's T-shirts, chairing a benefit that would bring important programs and enrichment into the lives of hardworking families, being a kind and thoughtful friend, helping injured birds on the side of the road rather than letting them suffer – did these things count, too? Or did only the sins count? Was there some kind of moral accounting that would put her ahead? Because she didn't feel like a *bad person* or an *evil person*. What, anyway, did Father Dominic know about heart-stopping passion?

Zack was still crying; his cries reverberated against the walls of the confessional booth. Claire said, 'Can you give me my penance?'

'You have to stop,' Father Dominic said. 'Then I can give you your penance.'

She had to stop. She repeated this in the car on the way home. Zack screamed in the backseat, screamed and kicked his legs; his cries were echoing inside her. She was not a barroom urchin addled by drink, like her father; she was a reasonable woman. She had to stop.

By the time she got home, she did have a headache, so she took some Advil and lit a fire and poured a glass of wine, all with Zack snuggled against her chest, on his way to sleep. She had a pot of chili on the stove, and corn bread, and homemade applesauce. At five thirty, it was pitch black outside and the kids and Jason came home, their cheeks rosy from the cold and the exercise.

Jason did not ask how she was feeling, but he did taste some chili from the wooden spoon and declared it delicious. J.D. stripped off his pads and his sweaty long underwear while Ottilie set the table in her cheerleading outfit.

Jason touched Claire's back and said, 'This is how I always sort of imagined it. Our life.'

The fire, the pot of chili, her children at home on a chilly fall evening. What was not to love? *She had to stop.*

Claire nodded. Her heart was a bad apple, soft and rotted. 'Me, too,' she said.

PART TWO

CHAPTER SIX

HE LOVES HER

It was boom or bust, their business, and it was starting to wear on Siobhan. She slaved through the summer and fall, fielding phone calls from impetuous brides-to-be and their mothers; she woke up in the morning knowing she wouldn't see the boys for five min-utes because she had a sit-down lunch for fifteen people at noon, cocktails for a hundred in Brant Point at six, and a dinner buffet in Pocomo at six thirty. (Could she really be two places at once? She would have to be.) This all-hell-has-broken-loose, wild-ass chaos was slightly preferable to suffering through the winter and spring, making good on all the dinners for eight that Island Fare put up for bid at charity auctions, and constantly worrying about money and illegal staff and getting jobs and money again. The business made a profit, but life was expensive. Liam had hockey, which had cost a fortune even before he broke his arm and took an eight-thousand-dollar jet ride to Boston, where he underwent two surgeries and incurred bills from a three-day hospital stay and five subsequent weeks of physical therapy. That was behind them now, but there was the mortgage, heating oil, and Christmas approaching, and Siobhan was beginning to suspect that Carter had a gambling problem. The man loved sports, but that was hardly unusual; God knows Siobhan had seen a pub full of men, including her father and her five brothers, scream bloody murder at the telly when rugby was on, or even worse, cricket. Carter spent so much time in the confines of the hot kitchen, it was healthy for him to have some release, and Siobhan was glad it was sports and not porn on the Internet. He was in a football pool, she knew that, but then the other night at dinner he announced that he had lost twelve hundred dollars on the Patriots game. Twelve hundred dollars! Siobhan nearly sprung a leak. She knew nothing about sports in this country and even less about the gambling that attended the sports, but she had assumed it entailed a bunch of guys throwing twenty bucks onto the bar. Twelve hundred dollars was six lovely dinners out; it was an entire weekend in Stowe or New York City.

Don't overreact, Carter had said. *It's not exactly a fortune.*

It damn well is so, Siobhan had countered. She was the one who counted the beans. When Carter decided to quit his job as head chef at the Galley Restaurant and start a catering business, it was because of the kids, because of the flexible scheduling, being his own boss. That was all well and good, but there would be no barter up in lifestyle if money kept flying out the door. For Siobhan, owning a business meant anguish and indigestion day in and day out.

They did one big job in November: the private Montessori school dinner auction. Siobhan liked doing this dinner. Because it was her only big job between wedding season and the holidays, she was able to give it time and careful attention, and each year, it was a masterpiece. This year the theme was the Far East. Siobhan dropped the boys at school and went straight to the catering kitchen, which was located in the back half of a commercial building out by the airport. It started to snow on her way there, which brightened her mood. Siobhan was a fan of layered sensory stimulation. She unlocked the door to the kitchen, made herself a cup of Irish breakfast, and put on a Chieftains CD, which Carter did not tolerate at home. The first snow of the year was falling in feathery bits out the window. Siobhan pulled her notebook out of her purse. She was in charge of the appetizers and dessert; Carter would do the entrée. Her appetizers were duck, mango, and scallion spring rolls for one hundred, sesame-crusted rare tuna on cucumber rounds with pickled ginger and wasabi for one hundred, and jumbo shrimp satay with peanut dipping sauce for one hundred. For dessert, she was making a complicated passion fruit and coconut cream parfait with macadamia nut brittle, which Carter called her crazy as Larry for even attempting. But hey, this was her masterpiece. Would he rather she was at home, picking up the boys' disgusting excuse for a bedroom, or lamenting the many ways she might have spent the money that he had flushed down the loo with the disappointing Patriots? Siobhan loved Carter, and she had sworn on the altar that she would always love him, yes, but he was bringing her down.

The tea was steaming, the Irishmen keening, the snow piling up. *Don't think about a weekend in Stowe!* Siobhan started with the peanut sauce. Technically, Siobhan's mother had taught her to cook, though the porridge and cabbage and finnan haddie of Siobhan's youth in no way resembled the delights that now came out of her kitchen. She was all about flavor and color and decadence; she was Liberace playing poolside, candelabra ablaze, while her mother's cooking was like the parish organist, dutifully banging out another funeral dirge.

As Siobhan sautéed onions and garlic and ginger in peanut oil, the phone rang. She looked around the empty kitchen, confused. It was the kitchen phone and not her cell phone, which was unusual. On her way to answer the phone, she saw the machine held six messages. Six!

'Hello?' she said.

'Siobhan? Is that you?'

The voice. She laughed, not because she was amused, but because she was caught off guard.

'Edward?'

'Hi,' he said.

Well, he would be more nervous than she was. Edward Melior, her former fiancé. They lived on the same island, which was four miles wide, thirteen miles long, and yet she rarely saw him. Maybe once or twice a month they passed each other in their cars. Edward always waved, but Siobhan never realized it was him until he was in her rearview mirror. What was becoming more common was that Edward would attend an event Siobhan was catering – she had a way of sensing when he was going to be there – and she would stay in the tent, or give the whole thing to Carter. It wasn't that she was avoiding Edward Melior; she just didn't want to have to offer him a canapé.

'Hi,' she said. 'What's up?'

'How are you?' He said this the way he always said it: How *are* you? As if he really wanted to know. He really did want to know; he had a zealous interest in other people. He remembered their names, their children's names, their situations – if they were thinking of buying a new car, or if they were caring for an elderly parent, or if their dog had just died. This was stuff he cataloged in his brain. It was unusual how much he remembered, how much he genuinely cared. It was feminine. But that was why he was a great (and wealthy) real estate agent. People lapped it up.

'Oh, I'm fine,' Siobhan said breezily. She recalled the flowers Edward had sent to the house when Liam broke his arm. They were pink calla lilies, Siobhan's favorite, about fifty of them, fantastically expensive. She got rid of them before Liam and Carter came home from Boston. She hadn't sent a note for the flowers, which was monstrous, but dealing with Edward was tricky. He loved her still. He took every communication from her as a sign that they would reunite.

They had been together during Siobhan's first four years on the island. When she was scooping ice cream and making sandwiches at Congdon's Pharmacy, he was handling rentals at the real estate office upstairs. Edward was charmed by Siobhan's accent (which she found ludicrous); he fell in love immediately. Because Edward had far more money and knew far more people than Siobhan did, he assumed the role of Henry Higgins to her Eliza Doolittle. He believed he'd 'discovered' her. Looking back, Siobhan was annoyed at how she'd played along with this notion. She became the pantry girl at the Galley and then the garde-manger, and then a line cook at lunch. Edward always referred to her as a chef, which wasn't accurate, but she never corrected him. He, meanwhile, had acquired a broker's license and was thinking of going out on his own, which sounded to Siobhan like a reckless idea. The Nantucket real estate market was a gold mine, a diamond mine; brokers were printing their own money, yes, but Edward was such a good, sweet, accommodating guy that Siobhan feared he would get swallowed up. (She came by this doomsday attitude honestly – she was Irish!) Before Edward set up shop, they got engaged – on a perfect autumn afternoon at Altar Rock. Edward had champagne and berries and melon and pink calla lilies, and he got down on one knee and presented a whopper of a ring. *Will you be my wife?* Siobhan laughed, covering her mouth, and nodded, because who would say no to such a beautiful, well-orchestrated proposal? It was only after the engagement was a publicly known fact, after it had been in the newspaper, after Edward's parents had thrown a party at their house on Cliff Road, that Siobhan began to falter. She didn't believe in Edward, and she realized that Edward didn't believe in her. Why else would he tell people she was a chef, when in fact she stood at a sauté pan for twelve hours a day making goat cheese omelets and lobster eggs Benedict? She grew less fond of the idea that she was a piece of Irish white trash that Edward had picked

129

from the rubbish bin, and she became increasingly annoyed by Edward's interest in her every thought and mood. She had grown up in a family of eight children; no one had paid attention that closely to Siobhan, ever. She yearned to be left alone with her interior life rather than to explain it.

And, too, there was a new sous-chef at work, a cute guy who had come from Balthazar in New York, whose knife skills put even the head chef's to shame. And – funny thing! – his last name was Crispin. Siobhan called him Crispy; he called her Trouble. *How're you doing there, Trouble?* His first name was Carter, which made him sound rich, though clearly he wasn't, and Siobhan liked that. She was growing sick of Edward and his discretionary income and the way he bought things just because he could. This kind of waste offended her Irish sensibilities.

'How are the kids?' Edward asked. Siobhan smelled the garlic and ginger turning bitter and she hurried back to the stove and killed the heat. 'How's Liam's arm?'

'Fine. All better. Just fine.' Siobhan reached for the curry powder, the peanut butter, the soy sauce. She could chat and cook all day, but not with him. 'What can I do for you, Edward?'

'I've called and left a bunch of messages for you,' he said. 'On your office phone?'

'I just saw them this second,' Siobhan said. 'Honestly, Edward, this is the first time I've set foot in the kitchen since Columbus Day.'

'I'm calling about the summer gala for Nantucket's Children,' Edward said. 'I'm the head of the catering committee and we'd like you to submit a bid. It's a bar bid, plus passed hors d'oeuvres, sit-down dinner, dessert sampler at the table. A thousand people. Can you give us a bid?'

'I can,' Siobhan said uncertainly. She had several thoughts at once, and she tried to arrange the thoughts neatly in her mind, the way she'd seen Carter arrange cards in his hand when he played poker. She had been waiting for this request for quite a while.

Claire had asked Siobhan to be on the gala committee back in September, and Siobhan had said yes, thinking this meant she and Carter would nab the catering job, but when Siobhan mentioned the catering, Claire backpedaled. And Siobhan had thought, *There's no flipping way I'm going to sit on the committee if we don't get the job* – and so she hadn't attended any of the meetings, and Claire hadn't asked why, and the whole topic was left suspended. This might have made their friendship awkward, but Claire and Siobhan's friendship encompassed such vast territory that the summer gala catering question registered as no more than a tiny pinch.

'We'd like all the bids submitted by the first of the year,' Edward said. 'Though I won't lie to you: it's going to be a while before we decide. Most of my committee lives in New York, and so I have to get everyone the bids, ask them to review the bids, then find time to set up meetings . . . A decision will be made sometime in the spring.'

'I'll fax you a bid,' Siobhan said. 'I'm doing the dinner auction for the Montessori this weekend, but I can probably get it to you before Thanksgiving.'

'Great,' Edward said. 'You know, I was thinking of going to that dinner auction.'

'Why would you?' Siobhan said. 'You have no children.'

'Well, you know me. I like to support island causes.'

Yes, she knew him. She knew he would go to the dinner auction now because she would be there. And he had probably volunteered for the catering committee because he thought it would mean they would work together. Again, Siobhan's anger flared: Why hadn't Claire *told* her? Maybe Claire had wanted Siobhan to be surprised; maybe Claire thought Siobhan would be *happily* surprised. Maybe Claire thought Siobhan wanted to have a fling with Edward. It was true that Siobhan occasionally mouthed off about having a fling with the produce guy at the grocery store or the UPS man – but that was just mouthing off. It was a way for her to throw darts at Carter's picture without actually hurting him.

'I'll fax you the bid,' Siobhan said.

'Or drop it by my office,' Edward said. He paused. 'We already have two other bids, by the way.'

'Will do. Thanks, Edward.'

'Take care, Siobhan.'

She hung up. That last tidbit from Edward was meant to be what, a taunt? Knowing Edward, it was purely informative. He would never do anything unethical, like ask her to sleep with him in exchange for the job. Ha! This was so outrageous, Siobhan laughed. Then the awkward feeling set in that followed each time Siobhan saw Edward or accidentally thought about him. She still had the engagement ring Edward had given her. It was in a secret compartment in her jewelry box, tucked into a blue velvet bag. The ring was magnificent, two and a third karats in a platinum Tiffany setting; it had cost Edward ten thousand dollars. It was too big for Siobhan to wear while she was working – had he not considered her career when he bought it? – and so she had worn it on a chain around her neck for a while. But within the gritty, foulmouthed funk of the restaurant kitchen, the ring had seemed ostentatious. Siobhan was afraid it would fall into the bisque; she was afraid one of the (sketchy) dishwashers would yank it off her neck as she walked to her car in the dark, after service. So she started leaving the ring at home, right around the time that Carter Crispin arrived, and this started the fight that broke Siobhan and Edward up.

When Siobhan and Edward split, the ring bounced around a bit. In one impetuous moment, Siobhan threw the ring at Edward; he picked it out of the crease in the sofa where it had landed and took it home. He returned a few days later to talk, but Siobhan turned him away. He left the ring in its soft velvet bag on her doorstep with a note: *I bought this for you. It's yours.*

Siobhan had wanted nothing more than to return the ring, but she could not endure another confrontation with Edward. She mailed the ring to Edward at his office. Again the ring appeared on her doorstep. Siobhan got it: the ring caused Edward pain, he didn't want it, and he didn't need the money he would get if he returned it.

Fine, she thought. It went into her sock drawer first, then into the secret compartment of her jewelry box, a hiding place straight out of the mystery stories her boys liked to read. The ring, when she thought about it, irked her. It was like a pesky tag in her knickers, a pebble in her shoe, a popcorn kernel between her back molars. She should sell it, pawn it; it would still fetch thousands and thousands of dollars, which she, unlike Edward, could really use. But she couldn't bring herself to sell it, stupid as that sounded, and if anyone asked her why (which no one would, as no one knew she had the damn thing except, possibly, for Edward), she would say it was because she wasn't ready to let it go. Whatever that meant.

Damn Edward for calling and ruining her pleasant morning! Damn Claire for meddling!

As she was filling and wrapping the spring rolls, Siobhan called Claire. It was nearly noon. Now that Claire was 'back at work,' she told Siobhan she was 'only available' at lunchtime.

'Hey,' Claire said, her mouth full.

'Edward Melior?' Siobhan said.

'Excuse me?'

'Edward is heading your catering committee?'

'Oh, yeah,' Claire said. 'Jeez, I forgot about that. Are you pissed at me?'

'A little.'

'Well, don't be. He volunteered for it.'

'Yeah, and you didn't tell me.'

'I didn't want to freak you out.'

'What freaked me out was being caught off guard.'

'Well, I'm glad he finally contacted you,' Claire said. 'You're going to give him a bid, right?'

'Yes.'

'He'll take you as long as you're lower. Even a little bit lower. You know that.'

'I know. But I don't know what lower is, do I?'

'No, you don't,' Claire said. 'I don't know, either. I didn't look at the other bids.'

'No, of course not. You're as pious as the pope's mother,' Siobhan said. She considered mentioning Carter's gambling loss but decided against it. Twelve hundred dollars was not the end of the world; he claimed it had been tip money, anyway, his own discretionary income. *Don't overreact, baby.* If Siobhan told Claire about it, Claire would worry and the whole thing would get blown out of proportion. 'How's it going in the shop?'

'Ohhhhhkay,' Claire said. 'Still trying to finish the vases for Transom. They're not as easy as I thought they would be, and Elsa wants them in time for Christmas. And I have to start the chandelier for the gala auction. That's what I really want to be working on.' Big sigh. 'Lock keeps telling me I'm an artist, not an artisan.'

'Lock has a warped perspective,' Siobhan said. 'He has nothing else to spend his money on other than museum-quality glass. Well, and private school tuition. And wax for his Jaguar. And cuff links. And Daphne's meds.'

'And viognier,' Claire piped in.

'What?' Siobhan said.

'Nothing,' Claire said. 'It's his favorite wine.'

'Ooohhh,' Siobhan said. 'Nice that you know his favorite wine. I wasn't sure Lock Dixon even drank wine. He has such a pole up his ass.'

'He does not,' Claire said.

'Yes, he does,' Siobhan said.

'No, Siobhan, he does not,' Claire said. 'He's nothing like that. You don't know him.'

'Sure, I do. He's as self-righteous as the born-agains.'

Claire said, 'I have to go.'

Siobhan rolled up another spring roll, eight rows of eight, sixty-four. They were all plump and perfect, like swaddled babies. 'Call me later,' Siobhan said. She hung up.

Siobhan prepped the marinade for the satay, thinking, *Edward Melior, pink calla lilies. It's too late to write a note for them now. It would look shoddy.* Thinking, *Viognier. It's his favorite wine.* Not Edward's, but Lock Dixon's. Lock Dixon kept telling Claire she was an artist, not an artisan. Siobhan was a caterer, not a chef, not a genius; she had scored Bs and Cs during her years with the nuns. She sometimes got so caught up in the mood of things that her common sense suffered. Her husband had managed to gamble away four figures right under her nose. Right under her nose. *It's his favorite wine.*

Was something going on between Claire and Lock Dixon? Never! And yet, it sounded like it. But Claire was a straight arrow; she was all caught up with being good and kind and sending positive energy out into the universe. She was all about her kids and the lofty precepts of art, and besides all that, she had a sex life with Jason that was directly out of *Cosmo.* Claire would *never* have an affair. And if she were, impossibly, having an affair, she would never keep it from Siobhan. Claire told Siobhan everything; she told Siobhan about her menstrual cramps, her hangnails; she told Siobhan when the mail arrived or the toilet backed up. *It's his favorite wine.* Such a curious statement, and Claire had said it so proudly, so proprietarily. Claire and Lock Dixon? Never! And yet . . . it sounded like it.

Siobhan catered the Montessori dinner to enormous kudos, she got Edward the bid for the gala, she kept an eye on Carter's gambling, she delivered the boys to and from their endless hockey practices. At Christmastime she went crazy around the house, cooking and decorating: she baked figgy puddings, she made smoked salmon dip with homemade parmesan pepper crisps, she did a ginger-bread house with the boys, even though they had outgrown it and did little more than eat all the candy. Her gift to her friends this year was wreaths made out of dried hydrangea and the giant pine-cones that fell from the firs out by Tupancy Links.

Siobhan went on several pinecone-collecting missions, all of them bewitching and romantic. She wrapped herself in a candy-striped merino scarf and carried a woven basket as she wandered through the firs on cold afternoons, with the promise of Christmas carols at home, and a hot buttered rum to warm her up. She was a girl from a fairy tale in those moments as she gathered only the largest, most perfect pinecones, the only person for miles, alone on this pristine part of the island.

Imagine her surprise when, on her way home with an overflow-ing basket of plump piney beauties next to her, she passed Claire's car. Siobhan was heading out of the evergreen forest and Claire was headed into it. Claire was driving way too fast, so that when Siobhan came around the bend on the dirt road, Claire's car was right there on top of her; they nearly collided. Siobhan gasped at the near miss, then gasped again at the fact that it was Claire's car, Claire at the wheel with somebody in the passenger seat – a man. Lock Dixon. Or at least Siobhan thought it was Lock Dixon. All she could say for sure was that the man was wearing earmuffs and Lock was famous around town for wearing earmuffs (pole up his ass). Siobhan knew Claire recognized her car – how could she not? – but Claire didn't stop. She and Lock Dixon barreled into the deserted forest that Siobhan had just left.

Siobhan drove on, stymied. In the months since Claire had agreed to chair the gala, there had been two or three meetings a week, always at night. Jason complained to Carter, and Carter passed the complaints on to Siobhan. *Seems a bit excessive, doesn't it? All those meetings. Don't you ever chair anything like that.*

Never, Siobhan said. *It's too much bloody work.*

What were Claire and Lock Dixon doing driving into the forest together at one o'clock on a December afternoon? They weren't going to collect pinecones, that was for sure. Siobhan considered following them. What would they be doing?

Later that afternoon, Siobhan called Claire at home, and Claire said, 'Hey, how are you?' As though nothing had happened.

'Did you not see me?' Siobhan demanded.

'See you what?'

'Up at Tupancy. Coming out of the woods. In my car. Jesus, Claire, you nearly ran me over.'

Claire laughed, but Siobhan was her best friend, had been for fucking centuries, and she could tell it was a fake laugh. 'I don't know what you're talking about.'

'I saw you, Claire,' Siobhan said. 'And you had Lock in the car.'

Again, the laugh, one key off-tune. 'You're crazy, baby.'

Siobhan huffed. This was insane! She would know Claire in a dark cave with a paper bag over her head. 'So you're denying that you were at Tupancy today?'

'Tupancy?' Like Siobhan was crazy. 'I haven't been to Tupancy since the dog died.'

She was denying it! But why? Claire could have come up with any number of plausible stories. Claire could have told Siobhan *anything* and Siobhan would have decided to believe it – but to deny ever having been there when she had nearly crashed into Siobhan was an insult to the friendship, and stupid besides. It could only mean one thing: Claire and Lock were having a torrid affair. This was betrayal at its most exquisite.

But no, Siobhan thought. It just wasn't possible. Claire was too much the choir girl. She had been born with a nagging conscience. She felt guilty when she missed a week of church, when she killed a housefly; she felt guilty when it *rained*. Having an affair was not something Claire was capable of.

So what, then, was going on? Siobhan meant to find out.

137

When he was younger, he used to pinch himself all the time. The money came rolling in, but it wasn't the money that was exciting; it was the girls, so many girls, and guys, too, for that matter, and limousines and rooms at the Four Seasons with their fluffy towels, their waffled robes, the Veuve Clicquot chilling in a silver bucket, the bouquets of roses, a garden's worth of roses thrown onto the stage. It was the deference, the respect shown to him by everyone from record execs to heads of state to Julia Roberts – she and her husband were fans and owned every album. Of Max West's, Matthew Westfield's, a kid from Wildwood Crest, a scruffy beach town in New Jersey. *Down the shore,* that was where Matthew had grown up, with a father who took off when Matthew was five, and a sainted mother who worked as the church secretary and who got most of her information about life outside of Wildwood from the magazines she picked up at the grocery store checkout. What was he, Matthew Westfield, doing onstage with seventy thousand people waving their arms in front of him? They were worshipping him; he was no longer a punk kid from New Jersey, but a god. He could have whatever he wanted – women, drugs, guns, an audience with the pope (he went once and tried to persuade his mother to join him, but she wouldn't travel to Italy, not even for the Holy Father).

He was in Thailand now, in Bangkok, hunkering down at the Oriental Hotel. Outside his room were two butlers (they had these for every guest) and two armed guards (these were only for him, since he had cavalierly suggested that a Muslim girl in the crowd in Jakarta rip off her *hijab* for him, inciting Muslim rage and necessitating a quick exodus from the country). It was winter in America but hotter than Hades here in Thailand. It was too hot to do anything but sit in the air-conditioning, drink the chilled champagne, smoke the delightful Indo weed they took as a parting gift from Java, and just generally seek oblivion. Because wasn't it the sad truth that Max West, a person who could have whatever he wanted, wanted only oblivion. Some time in the great black box. A poor man's peace.

They had sent some girls up, a group skinny and giggling, wearing short skirts and noisy earrings and makeup meant for white women. They were all beautiful, but very young, a couple of them maybe only fourteen, maybe not even menstruating yet. They clung to one another like schoolgirls, and this made Matthew melancholy. He gave the girls a wad of *baht* and sent them away. The butler looked at him questioningly, and Matthew said, 'Too young.' Less than an hour later, there was a knock at the door and a lone girl stood there glowering at him. She *was* older – twenty or twenty-one – and she had a knowing, Western look: jeans, a black T-shirt, silver hoop earrings. Flip-flops, toenails painted and embedded with rhinestones. She looked smart, and bored with him already; she was a college girl, maybe, looking for some extra cash. Matthew liked her right away.

'Sawadee kop,' he said, and he grinned. It was his rule to know how to say 'hello' and 'thank you' in every country he visited.

'Can I come in?' the girl said. Her English was perfect, with very little accent.

Her name was Ace (probably not spelled that way, but the Americanized version of the name suited her; she was cool like a tightrope walker, a pool shark). She walked in, allowed Matthew to pour her a glass of champagne, and made herself comfy on the sofa. He poured himself a glass; then, seeing that this would not be enough to slake his greedy thirst for the stuff, he poked his head outside and asked the butler for two more bottles. He understood that what he was doing was wrong, everything about it was wrong, but he was on his way now, growing warm on the inside, jonesing for the weed and the dose of amnesia it would bring, wondering about the girl. Who was she? What was she doing here? Where had she learned English?

Matthew was, technically, married. His wife, Bess, was back in

California, living in their glass castle in Malibu with their two border collies, Pollux and Castor. Bess had been a substance-abuse
counselor at the place in Pennsylvania that Matthew had tried in
between stints at Hazelden. She had not wanted to marry a rock
star, and especially not one with the seemingly incurable addictions that Matthew had, but she had been undone by her desire
to save him. After six years of marriage, she was now operating
on a zero-tolerance rule, and she had announced – upon hearing
his slurred voice on a call from Irian Jaya – that if he was indeed
drinking on this tour (*which is what it sounds like, Max*), then she
was finished with him. Professional credentials aside, she could
not take another go-round with the booze. Detox didn't help,
twenty-eight days didn't help (there had been eighty-four days
sum total), because the problem was hardwired, it was connected
to what Bess called his 'deep-seated unhappiness,' which she suspected had been caused in childhood by his father's desertion.

Bess had developed a strong friendship with Matthew's accountant, a man named Bob Jones, and Matthew assumed the avenue
Bess would now pursue was one that would lead her to Bob Jones's
house. She would be an accountant's wife; she would live a life opposite from the one she currently led. Instead of spending 90 percent of her time alone, walking on the beach, preparing elaborate
meals for the dogs, and eating only hummus herself, she would
live a life with constant companionship. She would cook nour-
ishing things for Bob Jones, they would do everything together:
watch TV, have sex, sleep until they were wakened by the gentle
California sun. The nice thing about Bess was that she wouldn't
take Matthew's money. She didn't want money. It was useless, she
liked to say, in getting the things that really mattered.

Matthew had to admit, he didn't feel any deep-seated unhappiness about the impending breakup of his marriage. Except, of
course, that he and Bess had been trying to have a baby, an en-
deavor that would now go out the window; Bess would, instead,
have a baby with Bob Jones. A baby that could count and add,

rather than a baby genetically predisposed to drinking gin. Matthew wouldn't even mind it if Bess was pregnant now. He liked the idea of having a son or a daughter in the world, and Bess would be a wonderful mother. Her priorities were straight, and drinking, drugs, and rock and roll were all at the bottom of the list.

These, of course, were the thoughts of a man on his way to getting drunk. The butler appeared with two more bottles of very cold Veuve Clicquot, and as Matthew submerged them in ice, he studied himself in the mirror. There were pictures of Max West all over the room, on CD covers, on posters, in newspapers and magazines, but none of these photographs showed what Matthew really looked like. He looked puffy in the face, he thought, and sort of gray-skinned, despite all this tropical sun. His hair was still deep brown, though greasy, and it stuck up in spikes. He had brown eyes that had been described as 'soulful' and 'deep,' but the whites around them were red, tired, sore-looking. In the skin on the end of his nose he had a pockmark, very small, which he had acquired at age seven with the measles; his stylist usually covered it up with makeup, but it always comforted Matthew to see this little divot, this small imperfection that announced his authentic self. Matthew heard a rustling sound and, in the mirror, saw Ace uncross her legs and then cross them again on the sofa, in impatience. She was not amused by him, nor impressed. He was not a world-famous rock star. He was a mess.

He had had a sponsor on this trip, a sponsor who was supposed to stay by his side every second of the day, except when Matthew was onstage, and even then, Jerry Camel lurked in the dim wings. Jerry was a good guy, he was good company; Matthew had no complaints about Jerry or the ardent way that Jerry loved Jesus. Jerry Camel was a childhood friend of Bruce Mandalay's; he was being paid by Bruce to *keep Max West sober!*

Jerry Camel, however, contracted a near-fatal stomach virus while they were hiking up to see the mystical jewel-colored volcanic pools on the Indonesian island of Flores. There was no hospital on Flores,

141

and so Jerry was helicoptered to Denpasar in Bali and then to Singapore. Matthew, who had been sneaking long pulls off the native guide's flask of hooch, did not catch the near-fatal stomach bug. Alcohol had saved his life!

But it was killing him, too, he acknowledged as he popped open both bottles of champagne, handed one to his Thai co-ed, and drank from the other one himself. Why insist on formalities like glasses? Ace didn't seem to mind. She chugged from her bottle. Matthew would be found dead in a hotel room not unlike this one, he was sure of it, especially with Bess now gone. He would die alone, the unintentional victim of his own hand, just like Hendrix, Morrison, Joplin, Keith Moon. Addictions were an occupational hazard, Max West liked to say, though Bess called this the ultimate cop-out.

Matthew rolled a joint and was freshly pleased that he had company. The rest of his band – Terry, Alfonso, the good family men that Bruce had insisted he surround himself with long ago – were on an all-day tour of Bangkok: the floating markets, the palace that held the Emerald Buddha, the temple called Wat Po with a hundred-foot-long reclining Buddha, and a famous silk merchant's house that was filled with the finest antiques in Southeast Asia. The rest of his band tolerated a toke or two of delightful bud, but they would lynch him if they knew he was drinking.

So, Ace. Matthew smiled at her as he lit up the joint, but he suddenly didn't have the energy for small talk – where she was from, what she was about. He wanted to know these things but couldn't bring himself to ask. *A deep-seated unhappiness.* Matthew tried to imagine the unhappiness residing in him. Was it thriving somewhere in his dark recesses, growing, mushrooming? Was it really due to his father's leaving? Matthew didn't remember his father and never wondered about him. In his mind, his childhood had been fine; he'd been loved by his mother and doted on by his four older siblings. His adulthood had been a fantasy, every wish – material and nonmaterial – fulfilled. He wrote songs, he

142

sang, he played the guitar. He regarded Ace, the smooth, brown suede of her skin, the silky line of her black hair, the tender, pale inside of her wrist. She was beautiful and indifferent (he appreciated the indifference more than the beauty), but Matthew knew he wouldn't sleep with her. It was what he'd expected to do when he let her in, it was what she expected, but Matthew was all done with empty relationships and with touching beautiful girls who meant nothing to him.

A deep-seated unhappiness. Matthew let the champagne flow down his throat, stinging him, nearly choking him. While Max was in Brunei, the strangest thing had happened. Bruce had called to tell Max he would be going to Nantucket Island in August to sing for Claire Danner.

Claire Danner? Max had said.

I thought you would want to do it, Bruce said. *I wasn't wrong, was I?*

No, Max said. *Not wrong. Of course I want to do it.*

It was weird the way things happened, the way the world worked, so bizarre and unpredictable that Max could barely handle it sober. No sooner had Bruce said the name Claire Danner than Max was suffused with tender, painful memories of himself as a teenager. And Claire. God, the two of them had been so unformed, but somehow perfect. In Matthew's mind, Claire Danner wasn't even a person anymore, she was an idea: hand-holding, falling asleep on the beach wrapped together in a blanket; she was his innocence, his sight, his voice. He had learned how to sing by singing to her. They hadn't known the first thing about love, and that had been better, that had been best – they were innocent. They didn't know when or how to hide their feelings, and so they shared everything. They were kids; they had been happy even when they were miserable. *Claire Danner,* Bruce said. Max hadn't seen her in many, many moons, and yet in his mind, she was right there: her milky white skin, her red ringlets, her tiny ears like delicate shells. She had pale eyelashes, skinny wrists; her second toe was longer than her big toe. She had a silent sneeze that made Max laugh every time. She couldn't drink beer because it made her vomit (he could attest to this), so she had to drink wine coolers. Did they even make wine coolers anymore? He'd started to believe, in the weeks since Bruce had said the words 'Claire Danner,' that Claire Danner was the woman he'd known and understood best in his life. Better than either of his wives, and certainly better than Savannah. And he had left her. He had thought he had no choice: he was going to California to become a rock star, she was off to college, she was going to be an artist, a wife, a mother. She belonged to someone else now, and he had belonged to many someone elses. But there was a way – wasn't there? – in which he would always belong to Claire Danner. Max West, like most rock stars, had built a career on the premise that we were all, in our hearts, seventeen years old.

He passed the joint to Ace. She inhaled with her eyes closed.

'And guess what?' Matthew said. 'I'm going there this summer to sing for her.'

Ace tilted her head. 'Where?' she said. 'Who?'

'Nantucket,' he said. 'Claire.'

Did he feel guilty? Yes and no. It was tricky emotional terrain, and the best thing about his love affair with Claire Danner Crispin was that before she came into his life, he had feared himself emotionally dead. The part of his life where his feelings mattered was over. It had ended, not during the months following Daphne's accident (because those were the most emotionally turbulent months of his life), but in the months following those months, after Daphne had 'recovered.' 'Recovered' was not the right word, implying as it did that something lost had been found. Daphne had survived the accident, yes, but the best parts of her were gone. Her charm, her sense of humor, her devotion to him, Lock, and their daughter,

Heather. Gone. These things were replaced with anger, suspicion, and a cruel frankness that left Lock, Heather, and everyone else who came into contact with Daphne breathless. Lock would lie in bed – after Daphne had told him that she married him for his money, that she stayed married to him for his money, that he was a piss-poor lover and she had faked every orgasm with him since 1988 – and wonder: If the car had crashed differently, if Daphne had hit her head harder, or less hard, or at another angle, might things have turned out the opposite way? Might he have been left with a sweet and loving pacifist for a wife? Why did it happen one way and not another? The loss of the Daphne he had fallen in love with was the first blow, and this was followed by Heather's exodus to boarding school and then to a camp in Maine. She had even spent the past Thanksgiving with the family of a friend, in Turks and Caicos.

These things happened, and Lock's well of happiness and love dried up, and then eventually his sadness and disappointment and anger dried up, too. He felt nothing; he was a desert.

It was easier to live this way than he had thought. He immersed himself in work. He loved his job, liked it better than the career he'd built for twenty years at Dixon Superconductors in Boston. He enjoyed being on Nantucket, part of a community where he could make a difference. He garnered genuine satisfaction from fund-raising and from administering those funds for Nantucket's Children.

Contrary to popular belief, there were kids on this island who were truly needy, as needy as kids in the inner city, kids who lived in basement apartments that housed fourteen people, who only made it into the shower once a week, who got the majority of their clothing and shoes and toys and furniture from the 'take it or leave it' pile at the town dump, whose parents worked so hard, for such long hours, that the kids were left to play foosball at the Boys & Girls Club until eight o'clock at night with only a bag of pretzels for dinner. Lock's circles were wide enough now to include people like this; everyone who knew Lock respected him and thought he was a good man. He was doing a job that needed to be done, even though he never had to work again. He was steadfast with his wife through the maelstrom of her attacks; he was solid. A rock. A desert. He had no feelings. Things were not good, but they were easy.

How to explain about Claire? He had known her for years; she was a face in the background. He had never thought her particularly beautiful; he had never been partial to redheads or women with a Victorian pallor. He had always admired Claire's glass, but that was solely an appreciation for her work. Something about the curves of the pieces struck him as sensual, and her use of color resonated with his own personal aesthetic. He thought her work was good, technically, and he thought it was beautiful. The *Bubbles* sculpture displayed in the foyer of the Klaussens' summer home had captured his imagination the way marbles and kaleidoscopes had as a child. He made a point to see the Bubbles sculpture in the Klaussens' Park Avenue apartment, as well as the piece at the Whitney. And then one year, on their way to ski at Stratton, they had detoured to the museum in Shelburne. But Lock's admiration for Claire's work was disembodied from the artist; it didn't explain his sudden fall to her feet. It happened to him like an accident, like a crash, a blow to the head, on the night of the first gala meeting. There was something about Claire that night – she was nervous, earnest, and yet confident (about Max West, about her glass). She had been wearing a jade green T-shirt that plunged to her breasts, and tight jeans; her hair curled in tendrils around her face, and she wore a perfume that made something inside him stir when she walked into the room.

Woman, he thought. Perfume, hair, breasts, smile. And a smile in her voice. When she was talking about Max West, she said, *Back then he was just a kid, like the rest of us.* She was drinking wine and her cheeks flushed; she was a woman and a girl at the same time. When she stood to look at her own work on his shelf – a vase – she brushed past him; he noticed her scent again, and her jeans. She picked up the vase and turned it gently – and at that moment, Lock's fascination with her was born. She had *made* that vase; she had blown it out with her own lips. This aroused him. He was shocked – because along with his emotional life, his sexual life had also died. Daphne wanted sex in spurts and bouts: twice a day for a week, and then not again for twelve months.

But watching Claire, whole parts of him were suddenly alive with possibility. He might have been seeing her for the first time. Boom, a blow to the head, a blow to the heart. She took the job as gala chair, not because she was power-hungry or needed her name in lights, but because she wanted to help; in this, they were the same. She was darling. He wanted her.

It started out slowly. One kiss, another kiss, more kissing – if she had had any hesitations, she would have asked him to stop, right? He had been through university before the age of date rape and 'No means no,' but he was the father of a girl (now a teenager), and hence he understood. He moved things along with Claire very slowly, though there was a tide of ache and longing in him to push it faster. They kissed and he touched her breasts, her delicate nipples, and she gasped as if she'd been burned. He pulled away immediately: Had he hurt her? Had he pushed things too far? She said, *If you stop, I'll kill you.* And they laughed.

He felt guilty – not for himself, but for her. She had a husband, Jason Crispin, and she said she loved him. Lock wanted to know what she meant by this. How did she love him, how much did she love him, and if she loved him, why was she willing to be with Lock? Because she *was* willing. All through the fall, through the holidays, and into the winter, she met him. Some nights they stayed in the office; some nights they met in the garden at Greater Light, now a preserved (but little visited) historic site, and they made out like teenagers, with Claire sitting on the chilly cement steps as Lock reached into her blouse, then into her jeans. Sometimes they drove in Claire's Honda Pilot beyond the water tower or to the end of Capaum Pond Road, where they grappled for each other over the children's car seat, their feet muddling the pages from coloring books and empty juice boxes on the floor of the car. Lock was reluctant to make love in the car, not because it was uncomfortable (though it was), but because the children's presence was almost palpable. The Honda was a piece of Claire's actual life, it was an extension of her home, and Lock felt like an intruder. But Claire loved to have him in her car; she got a delicious satisfaction, she said, from remembering their coupling as she drove the children to school. And so they went out in the car frequently because, more than anything, Lock wanted to make Claire happy. Unlike Daphne, Claire could be made happy, and this was what satisfied Lock the most, what filled him up. Claire smiled, she laughed, she giggled. *I feel like a kid again,* she said. *You've changed my life.*

He had gotten her back into the hot shop, back to work. He hadn't thought of it as a come-on; if he thought of it at all, it was as a public service. The world, in his opinion, should not be without the art of Claire Danner Crispin. When he asked her to create a piece for the auction, he was pretty sure she'd be thrilled, flattered. He had not, at that time, understood why she had stopped working. He thought the break was temporary, a maternity leave. Now he knew the whole story, and while there was much that Lock wanted to say in response, he kept his mouth shut. He was glad he had gotten her back into the hot shop, working again.

You would have gone crazy, he said. *Spending the rest of your life sponging countertops.*

Oh, I don't know . . . , she said.

But it was clear she loved being back at work. She was fired up again, she said.

Lock had a harder time convincing her that neither the fall nor Zack's early delivery was her fault.

I was the one who fell, she said. *I was dehydrated. I wasn't drinking enough water. The temperature was unsafe, I knew that. My doctor warned me . . .*

She talked all the time about Zack. Lock had only seen Zack once, in passing, though Claire described him as very needy and 'way behind' where her other kids were at his age. Lock thought it sounded bad, or potentially bad, and in an attempt to help, he gave Claire some information about Early Intervention (Nantucket's Children funded them every year) as well as the name of a doctor in Boston. Lock thought Claire would be grateful for this information, but it immediately became clear that she resented it.

'You think there's something wrong with him!'

'I don't even know him, Claire. I haven't spent five minutes with him. I only gave you the information because you seemed concerned and I wanted to help.'

This turned into an argument. For the first time, they parted on bad terms. Claire was sobbing about Zack – there was something wrong with him, it was her fault, she knew it – and there was Lock, rubbing her nose in it, giving her the number of a doctor in Boston, and of Early Intervention. *If I thought he needed Early Intervention,* she screamed, *I would have called them myself!* Lock had only been trying to help. He facilitated things like this all the time; it wasn't his job to make a diagnosis, only to put people with problems in touch with people who could solve the problems. He'd tried to explain this to Claire, but she was having none of it. She drove off.

Lock didn't hear from Claire for five days. Five empty, nearly unbearable days. He was distracted at work; every time the phone rang, he stopped what he was doing and watched Gavin, listening. Was it Claire? No. Every time he heard the door open at the bottom of the stairs, his heart leapt. No. He sent Claire one (vague) e-mail of apology, then another. She did not respond, but this wasn't entirely surprising. Claire rarely checked her e-mail. Finally he decided he would stop by her house. This decision was both rash and carefully thought out. On the one hand, he didn't want to see her cheerful, bustling household and feel bereft and lonely because his own home was as chilly and white as an empty icebox. After Siobhan had run across the two of them, together, in Claire's car, they had made a rule about seeing each other during the day: they wouldn't do it except in the name of legitimate gala business. There was, of course, a lot of legitimate gala business: Claire was working on production for the concert; she and Isabelle were back-and-forthing on the invite design, possible underwriting, and assignments for the committee members. Before the argument, Claire and Lock had had lunch on two occasions, once with Tessa Kline of *NanMag*. Tessa was doing a feature spread on Nantucket's Children and Lockhart Dixon, executive director, and the annual summer gala, and Claire Danner Crispin, gala cochair and local artisan.

'I've always wanted to do a really in-depth piece like this,' Tessa said, 'and bring in all these different, intersecting elements.'

They were at lunch at the Sea Grille, and Lock and Claire were sitting next to each other on the banquette while Tessa faced them, firing questions. At one point, Claire nudged Lock with her leg and he shifted away from her. They talked all the time about how important it was to 'be careful.' Siobhan already harbored suspicions; they couldn't have any more close calls. If they got caught, it would ruin everything: Claire's marriage, her family life, Lock's marriage, his reputation, and the reputation of Nantucket's Children.

The affair was a grenade. Pull the pin, and everything got destroyed.

But Lock couldn't stand thinking of Claire upset by something he'd done. He couldn't let another day go by without seeing her.

He decided to go to Claire's house under the pretense of dropping off a stack of underwriting letters that Claire had to sign and mail out, ASAP. Before the argument (and it couldn't accurately be called an argument because they hadn't fought or even disagreed – he had inadvertently offended her), Claire had asked

150

him, all the time, to stop by and see her. It would be sweet, she said, and romantic, if he surprised her sometime.

Come in the early afternoon, Claire said. *Jason is never home.*

Lock wasn't worried about Jason. He had actually bumped into Jason at Christmastime at Marine Home Center, where they were both buying tree stands. They stood in line together and made small talk.

Jason said, 'Claire is really into that thing the two of you are working on.'

'Mmmm,' Lock said. 'Yes. The gala.'

'Should be a hoot,' Jason said.

The man was affable enough, Lock thought. He had a toughness, a masculinity, that Lock lacked, but part and parcel with those traits was what Lock could only think of as ignorance. Lock wasn't saying that Jason was stupid, but he wasn't polished or worldly, and there were things he didn't know or understand about Claire.

Once, after a few glasses of viognier at the office, Claire said, in regard to Jason, 'Half the time, I'm his mother, and the other half I'm his sex slave.'

Lock said, sweeping her hair aside so he could kiss the back of her neck, 'You deserve better, you know.' It was Lock's opinion that Jason treated Claire like a feudal servant, and while he was angered by this, he was also grateful for it. The holes that Jason left were ones that Lock could fill. He could tell Claire she was beautiful, he could talk to her about her work, he could appreciate her, treat her gently, tenderly. He could clip poems out of the *New Yorker* or copy passages out of novels and know that the words and the sentiments were fresh. Claire kept the clippings in an unmarked folder.

'I love Jason,' she said. 'But he's not you.'

What did that mean? Lock took it to mean that he was giving Claire something she lacked, something she needed.

Claire had sex with her husband often. She used this word

'often,' though she didn't qualify it. For Lock and Daphne, once a month would have been often; before the accident, they had had sex once or twice a week. Lock feared that 'often' for Claire meant even more frequently than that, but he couldn't bear to dwell on it. When he and Claire were together, he couldn't allow himself to become distracted by whether Claire had been employed as Jason's sex slave the day before or even that very day. She never said a word. Her passion for Lock was pulsing and vocal every single time, and he was happy with that.

Well, he had no choice. Jason was the husband, the father of her children.

Lock went to Claire's house after a lunch with the head of Marine Home Center to discuss a yearly giving plan. On his way back to the office, he decided he would drop off those underwriting letters, which did indeed have to go out. They were behind the eight ball as it was.

Lock knew Claire's neighborhood, though he wasn't exactly sure which house was hers. (Odd, he thought, that he didn't even know which house his lover lived in.) Daphne had been to Claire's house once for a women's cocktail party or a baby shower and Lock had dropped her off, but that was ages ago, back in another lifetime. He turned onto Claire's road – Featherbed Lane, an unfortunate name – his heart skipping, his lunch trying to find a way to comfortably settle. He was crossing a threshold, stepping over the line, into Claire's actual life. Her house, on cozy, comfy Featherbed Lane. It was different from Claire's stopping by the office; the office was public space and she belonged there now as much as he did. She would never dream of going to Lock's house, that cold white palace on the edge of the water. She wouldn't want to see Daphne, and Lock didn't blame her.

He identified the house right away. There was something distinctive about it, which he had forgotten: an alcove around the front door. When Lock had dropped Daphne off long ago, it had been summer, the roof of the alcove had dripped with ivy and clematis (though now, in January, they were bare, brown vines), and on the step had sat a wide-bottomed green bottle with the word 'Crispin' imprinted on the front. Claire's car was in the driveway and there were hockey sticks leaning against the garage door, and a basketball trapped in an icy puddle. The day was very bright and cold. Lock squinted despite his sunglasses. He wore earmuffs – this had become something of a joke around town, people pointing out that since he was losing his hair, he really needed a hat – and an overcoat and wing-tip shoes. He felt like a salesman as he approached the door. He felt like a Jehovah's Witness.

The house was a work of art. It was trimmed with mahogany and copper flashing; the light fixture next to the door was an antique. The front door was salvaged from somewhere – probably a farmhouse in Vermont. Lock knocked. He should have called first, though that belied the principle of 'stopping by,' which was what Claire had said she wanted him to do. She wanted him to surprise her. Well, here he was. Surprise!

Lock heard a shuffle, a whispery noise, nearly imperceptible beneath his earmuffs. And then the door opened a crack. Lock saw a sliver of dark hair, one dark eye, a glint of silver. He heard a noise like a tiny bell.

'Yes?'

Now he really felt like a Jehovah's Witness, a vacuum salesman. 'Hi, I'm Lock Dixon. I work with Claire. Is she here?'

The door opened a little wider, revealing a girl, the Thai au pair. The lifesaver. The real reason Lock and Claire were able to conduct an affair. 'She out back,' the girl said. 'Hot shop.'

'Are you Pan?'

She nodded; the bell around her neck tinkled brightly. The door opened a little wider. 'Okay you come in?' she said.

'Okay, I'll come in,' he said. And then, just like that, he was in Claire's house. To the left was a bench covered with bright

153

cushions, and a pendant light with a stained-glass shade. A door led to a silvery powder room. The floors were maple, and to Lock's right was an unusual twisting staircase, with balusters made from what looked like the staves of an oak wine barrel. The house was warm and it smelled like onions and ginger. He loved the house instantly and hated himself for loving it. His eyes darted around, as if he was a robber casing the joint, as he followed Pan into the great room: stone fireplace with a smoldering log, honed limestone countertops, Oriental rugs, a deep, red couch, exposed beams, cherry cabinets, copper pots, dried flowers, a large oval chalkboard that said: *Shea, 4 P.M. pickup rink! Milk!* Pan stirred something on the stove; it smelled wonderful. Behind the sofa were a few toys: a plush tiger, a plastic phone on a pull cord, some wooden blocks. Lock placed his stack of underwriting letters on the countertop next to a pile of mail. To hear Claire talk, he would have thought the house was a shambles. He expected drawers open, piles of laundry mounded on the club chairs, an inch of dust on the bookshelves, soggy breakfast cereal clogging the drain of the sink. But the house was orderly and clean and comfortable and splendid in every detail. The door to the mudroom was open and Lock could spy parkas and boots, a pair of ballet slippers hanging from pink satin ribbons; he heard the churning of the washing machine. The room smelled like woodsmoke, ginger, laundry detergent. His eyes filled with tears unexpectedly. He had dreamed of saving Claire from this place, but she was already safe. This was a home, and he was the wrecker. What was he doing?

'These are for Claire,' Lock said, indicating the pile of letters. 'I'm just dropping them off.'

Pan nodded as she moved vegetables around with a wooden spoon. She saw him watching. 'You hungry?' she said. 'You want?'

Lock raised a hand. 'I just ate,' he said. 'Thank you.' He should go. When Claire was ready to speak to him again, she would call him. He turned toward the door. Now, however, Claire would know he'd been here and hadn't made a point to see her, and what kind of message would *that* send? He cleared his throat. 'Can I see Claire? Is she out back?'

'Hot shop,' Pan said. 'Working.' This seemed to be an admonishment for him to leave; certainly Claire would not tolerate anyone disturbing her when she was working.

'I see,' Lock said. So he really should go. But it had taken such an effort, emotionally, to come, to cross the line, and he would almost certainly never do it again, so . . . he would see her. He would insist. 'I'll go out back,' he said. 'Okay?'

'Claire working,' Pan said. 'It not safe.'

True enough. It wasn't safe. But Lock said, 'Please? It's okay. She wants to see me.'

Pan stared at him. Had he just tipped his hand to the Thai au pair?

She shrugged. 'Okay. Be careful. Hot shop hot. Hot shop bright. Wear gogglc.'

He smiled. 'You bet.'

He left the house by the back door and traversed the slushy, muddy backyard to the hot shop, which was smaller than a guest cottage but bigger than a shed. It billowed white smoke like a nuclear reactor. He had often envisioned Claire at work in the shop, and now he would see her. He knocked on the metal door. There was no answer. She was busy, or she couldn't hear him. He waited, shivering and tapping his foot against the cold, wondering if Pan was watching him out here. He looked back at the house; the windows were steamed. He knocked again, more forcefully.

'Claire!' he called. The property abutted the public golf course, and his voice echoed out over the frozen fairway. Was this a good idea?

He tried the knob, and it turned. Should he just enter, then? Surprising her was one thing, but what if he scared her so badly she burned herself or cut herself? Well, he didn't have all day, he needed to get back to the office, and since he was determined to show his face, he pushed into the hot shop.

'Claire?' he called out. Jesus, was it hot! Lock whipped off his earmuffs and unbuttoned his coat. It had to have been well over a hundred degrees in there. The furnace was roaring like a dragon. Lock's eyes were drawn to the dazzling brightness; it was like looking at the inside of a star. He closed his eyes, and amorphous green blobs danced around. Be careful! He had been here ten seconds and already he'd burned his retinas. When he opened his eyes again, he saw Claire across the room – in a white tank top and jeans and clogs. If he hadn't known it was her, she would have been unrecognizable. Her hair was gathered in a very tight bun and she wore large plastic welder's goggles. She was just stepping away from the furnace with a molten blob of glass on the end of a pipe; she turned the pipe deftly so that the blob became a uniform sphere, a perfect globe of yellow jelly. Lock yanked at his tie – it was sweltering, nearly unbearable in here. How did Claire stand it? He noticed she was sweating; her tank top was damp and clung to her. She hadn't seen him yet, and he wasn't sure how to announce his presence without scaring the bejeezus out of her. He was fascinated, too, by her movements, by the way she held the pipe, by the way she manipulated the hot glass. The glass was like a living thing on the end of the pipe, with a mind of its own; it wanted to go one way, Claire coaxed it another. She held the pipe to her mouth and blew, and the blob expanded like a balloon. She made it look effortless. She twisted the pipe some more; she lay the balloon against a metal table and rolled it and shaped it and opened the end with a pair of tweezers. Then she turned back toward the furnace. Lock tried to duck out of sight, but he wasn't fast enough. He didn't want to scare her, true, but he also didn't want to stop watching her. She saw him then – her mouth opened, and she jerked the pipe. The vessel on the end of the pipe jerked also and immediately became lopsided. Claire dumped the pipe, vessel-end down, into a bucket of water, causing a lot of steam and hiss. At the same time, Lock's spirits were dampened. He had made a mistake in disturbing her; he had ruined her work.

He wanted to leave, hastily, but he was here now and she knew it, so he took a few hesitant steps forward.

She closed the furnace door and immediately the room dimmed and grew cooler. She pushed her goggles to the top of her head and blinked rapidly, as if she thought she might be hallucinating.

It's me, he thought. *Surprise!* Stopping by had backfired. The five days of silence had been a message. She was finished with him.

But then she smiled. 'I can't believe it,' she said. 'Can-*not* believe it.'

'I'm here,' he said. 'I dropped off those letters.'

'Letters?' she said.

'For the underwriting.'

'Fuck the underwriting,' she said. She looked around the shop. 'This place is safe. The only person who ever comes in here is me.'

'Well, then,' Lock said, moving toward her and putting his arms around her waist, 'I can tell you the truth. I came for you.'

They kissed. She tasted like metal and sweat; her lips and the skin of her face were very hot, as if she had a fever. It was different, but not unpleasant. When they both went to hell and they kissed, this was what it would be like.

'I'm revolting,' she said.

'You? Never.'

'My hair?' she said. 'And God, I stink.'

Her hair was matted against her forehead and there were marks on her face where her goggles had clamped against her skin. She smelled sour and musky. And yet she had never been more beautiful. In fact, Lock would have been hard-pressed to remember a time he had ever found any woman more beautiful than Claire

157

was right now, working, sweating, smiling in her hot shop. She was a queen.

'I'm sorry about the other day,' he said. 'About giving you those numbers. I just thought – '

She put her hand over his mouth. 'Forget it. I was too sensitive. I shouldn't have stormed off.'

'And then you didn't call . . .'

'You didn't call *me*.'

'I didn't feel like I could call you,' he said. 'I did send an e-mail. Two, in fact.'

She didn't respond. He wasn't sure if this meant she had read them or not, but it didn't matter. What the five days of silence had shown him was that he was in love with her. He might have been in love with her for a while, but he had never felt compelled to say it. To say it would be the ultimate in *not safe*.

'I'm in love with you,' he said.

Her eyes were wet – or it was the perspiration, or a trick of his vision in this heat. But no, he was right: she was crying.

'You must be,' she said. 'You came.'

He squeezed her as hard as he could, fearing she would melt in his arms like butter, she would slip away, disappear. The molten glass on the end of her pipe, that hot, pulsing, living thing, that organ she controlled and expanded with only her breath – that was his heart.

They did not kiss much more and they certainly didn't go any further. The hot shop was too hot, and there was Pan waiting in the house, and the whole fact of Lock's trespassing on her (and Jason's) territory. And, too, there was a sense that the purpose of this afternoon's visit was deeper and more meaningful than their previous couplings. He had shared something, he had given himself over, and now everything was changed. It had been elevated. He was in love. She owned him. He was hers.

'I have to get back to the office,' he said.

'I know,' she said. 'But one thing, please? Will you come up and see Zack?'

'Where is he?'

'Upstairs, asleep. I just want you to look at him.'

'Why?'

'Just because he's my baby. I want you to see him. Please?'

They entered the house together, though not touching. Pan was sitting on a barstool at the counter, eating her lunch. She watched them silently as they climbed the stairs.

They entered the nursery, painted butter yellow. It had an alphabet rug and gauzy drapes, a walnut crib and matching changing table, shelves of board books, an upholstered rocking chair, a basket of plush animals. Heather had had such a nursery – her nursery was redecorated now and served as Daphne's 'study,' though Daphne did no actual work in there that Lock knew of, other than writing angry letters to the editor of the *New York Times* about the liberal slant of the paper's journalism. This nursery was cozy, like the rest of the house; it soothed the soul. It gave Lock peace to walk in behind Claire, to gaze down on the sleeping baby, a beefy redhead with Claire's pale skin. He was snuggled under a blue blanket, working a pacifier.

'This is Zack,' Claire whispered.

What did Lock think about this sleeping baby? Claire was knitting her fingers together nervously. She thought there was something wrong with her child, and it terrified her; she was scared, despite the fact that Gita Patel, a very good pediatrician, had said that Zack was fine, normal, healthy. For some reason, Claire wanted a diagnosis from Lock; her fears about Zack were the one thing she wanted him to assuage. It was the only thing she had ever asked him for.

Zack's hair was red and curly like Claire's, and his long, curved eyelashes were red. His skin was white like plaster or powder or snow or pure marble. His eyelids flickered back and forth; he sucked rhythmically on the pacifier. He was Claire's child, her baby, and Lock felt a surge of love for him. If there was something wrong with this child, Lock would help Claire find it, fix it, cure it.

'He's beautiful,' Lock said. 'He's perfect.'

CHAPTER SEVEN

HE LEAVES HER

To: isafrench@nyc.rr.com
From: cdc@nantucket.net
Sent: February 10, 2008, 10:02 A.M.
Subject: The invite

Isabelle –

Thank you for sending me the mock-up of the invite. It's lovely, really, with the peach and the mint green, very elegant without being tired or fusty. I just wanted to address a few points. First of all, it seems you have renamed the event. 'Une Petite Soirée' does have a certain Continental charm, but Nantucket isn't Paris, nor is it Saint-Tropez, and the event has been called the 'Summer Gala' for so long that I think, to avoid confusion, we should stick with it. So please change 'Une Petite Soirée,' to 'Summer Gala.'

I noticed Aster forgot to include *where* the event was being held, so we need him to add a line after '6–10 P.M.' that reads,

'Town Recreational Fields, Old South Road.' Lastly, would you mind changing my name so that it reads 'Claire Danner Crispin' instead of 'Mrs. Jason Crispin.' Without getting into the particulars of my marriage, suffice it to say that nobody on this island or anywhere else in the world knows me as 'Mrs. Jason Crispin.'

Thx! Claire

To: cdc@nantucket.net
From: isafrench@nyc.rr.com
Sent: February 10, 2008, 10:05 A.M.
Subject: The invite

Dear Claire,

Regarding the three points made in your e-mail of a few moments ago: I chose the title 'Une Petite Soirée' very carefully. Granted, Nantucket is not Lyons, nor is it Aix-en-Provence, but 'Une Petite Soirée' will lend the event an understated elegance it desperately needs.

Secondly, describing the location as 'Town Recreational Fields' adds a Sunday-softball-game feel to our event that we would do best to avoid *at all costs,* and so I simply deleted the location when I gave Aster the information in the first place, figuring we would decide on a name for the location that would be more savory to our demographic than 'Town Recreational Fields.' We might simply say, 'Under the Tent, Old South Road.' This sort of makes it sound like a traveling circus, but it is an improvement on 'Town Recreational Fields,' just as 'Une Petite Soirée' – you understand the translation, yes, 'A Simple Affair'? – is a vast improvement on 'Summer Gala.'

As for our monikers, the way I have them written – 'Mrs. Marshall French' and 'Mrs. Jason Crispin' – is how it is standardly done in

New York. I agree, it is a bit old-school Emily Post (and believe me, with the divorce I am going through, I am personally loath to use the name 'Mrs. Marshall French'), but I am even more hesitant to buck tradition, especially in light of our demographic, who will, no doubt, appreciate the invitation worded formally.

Thx! Isabelle

To: isafrench@nyc.rr.com
From: cdc@nantucket.net
Sent: February 18, 2008, 11:21 A.M.
Subject: The invite

Isabelle –

Sorry it has taken me sooooooooooooo long to respond. My kids are all sick and my husband is on deadline with a job, and wouldn't you know it, my au pair is on vacation in the Grand Canyon, leaving me to mastermind our daily survival. Time being of the essence, I will cut to the chase:

- I do understand the translation, thank you for asking. 'Une Petite Soirée,' a simple affair, is a whimsical name for a certain kind of party, but not this party. I'd rather not be ironic – there is nothing small nor simple (nor French) about the event. And as I've said before, there is great danger in changing the name of an event that is as established as ours is.

- We *have* to use 'Town Recreational Fields' because that is the *name* of the *venue*. Granted, it is not glamorous, granted my children do play baseball and soccer there, but it is the only venue *big enough* to host this kind of event and it is *generously donated* to us by the town, and hence the town must be named on the invite. To say, 'Under the Tent, Old South Road,' is cruelly uninformative. Old South Road is three miles long; I can just picture our demographic puttering along, trying to locate the peaks of a tent above the trees.

- Thirdly, it is the twenty-first century and it is okay, now, for women to use their own names. There is no reason why you should have to use your ex-husband's name, just as there is no reason why I should have to use my husband's name. I will use my maiden name as well as my given Christian name because that is how I am known, professionally and personally: Claire Danner Crispin. I am not willing to bend on this, and I thank you in advance for your kind indulgence.

Thx! Claire

To: cdc@nantucket.net
From: isafrench@nyc.rr.com
Sent: February 18, 2008, 11:24 A.M.
Subject: The invite

Dear Claire,

I will inform Aster of the nature of our discussion.

Thx! Isabelle

To: isafrench@nyc.rr.com
From: cdc@nantucket.net
Sent: February 28, 2008, 3:38 P.M.
Subject: Urgent question!!!

Isabelle –

Today in the mail I received the sample invite, and I noticed that – although it is utterly beautiful – only one of the changes we talked about had been made. I am still listed as 'Mrs. Jason Crispin.' And the location is described as 'Under the Tent, Old

South Road.' You said you would give the changes to Aster. What happened????

Claire

To: cdc@nantucket.net
From: isafrench@nyc.rr.com
Sent: February 20, 2008, 3:41 P.M.
Subject: Urgent question!!!

Dear Claire,

I said I would inform Aster as to the nature of our discussion. He was willing to bend on the name of the event in order to be consistent with years past (I, however, was dismayed, believing, as I do, that 'Une Petite Soirée' is a far superior title for the evening). Aster did not see the need to incorporate the other two changes.

Thx! Isabelle

To: isafrench@nyc.rr.com
From: cdc@nantucket.net
Sent: February 28, 2008, 8:24 P.M.
Subject: Sense of entitlement?

Isabelle –

I hope I will not offend you when I say that Aster Wyatt, gracious as he was to design the invite gratis, is not in a position to make decisions on behalf of Nantucket's Children, and I am infuriated that he has done so. Please, I must insist, change my name to read, 'Claire Danner Crispin.' If you want to leave the location as vague as it is, be my guest, but get ready for the ensuing chaos.

Thx! Claire

To: cdc@nantucket.net
From: isafrench@nyc.rr.com
Sent: February 28, 2008, 8:27 P.M.
Subject: Sense of entitlement!

Dear Claire,

Actually, Aster Wyatt is on the gala committee, he was appointed by me, and I made him the chair of invitations, hence all final decisions on the invitation were made by him. He did design the invite for free, though the printing costs for 2,500 invites (including invite, oversize envelope, response card, and response envelope) came to just under six thousand dollars. (A vellum insert printed with the committee members' names will be extra, but I do think we should include it once our committee is firmed up.) The invites just came back from the printer; I sent you one straightaway. But you'll agree with me that we can't incur any *additional* expense by going back and changing your name (which, I will point out, is not misspelled or inaccurate) just because you don't like it.

Thx! Isabelle

Fwd: LDixon@nantucketschildren.org
CC: AFiske@harperkanefiske.com
Sent: February 28, 2008, 9:00 P.M.
Subject: Sense of entitlement!

Have you seen this??? Can you believe it??? I am going to be listed (underneath Isabelle, by the way, even though I am first alphabetically, and whose decision do you think *that* was?) as 'Mrs. Jason Crispin.' It is so disgustingly *Mayflower,* I think I might puke.

To: cdc@nantucket.net
From: AFiske@harperkanefiske.com

Sent: March 1, 2008, 8:14 A.M.
Subject: Sense of entitlement!

Six grand is too much money as it is, Claire. We can't go back and fix them. On the bright side, Jason will love it.

Adams

To: AFiske@harperkanefiske.com
From: cdc@nantucket.net
Sent: March 1, 2008, 9:45 A.M.
Subject: Sense of entitlement!

Jason won't understand it! He'll see the name 'Mrs. Jason Crispin' and think someone is calling him a woman.

To: isafrench@nyc.rr.com
From: cdc@nantucket.net
Subject: Disgusting sense of entitlement
(Unsent)

Isabelle –

I find working with you difficult and unpleasant. I understand that you are going through a very painful divorce and hence I am willing to give you some extra rope. What I'd like you to understand, however, is that Nantucket is different from Manhattan. Nantucket, at its core, is a small town, casual and humble, even in the busy summer months. We do not need (or want) all the trappings and pretensions that might attend a benefit such as the gala in Manhattan (or Cannes, or Nice, either, for that matter!). I do not need (or want) a title like 'Mrs. Jason Crispin.' Even my children's friends call me Claire. It does not matter if the location of the gala is referred to as the 'Town Recreational Fields,' because that is, in fact, the venue's name. I am sorry if that is too down-home-church-social for you. I am sorry if Nantucket in general is too unpolished and loosey-goosey for you. However, remember this: The quiet, modest, relaxed nature of the island is the very reason why so many esteemed people have sought it out as their summer refuge. As an *antidote* to the big city, not a summertime version of it.

Thx! Claire

Bid for Nantucket's Children Summer Gala: Island Fare Catering, Carter and Siobhan Crispin, Proprietors

Including full bar, champagne fountain, passed hors d'oeuvres, stationary hors d'oeuvres, sit-down dinner, dessert sampler: $225 per person

Caterer's Note: The following menu has been written for success. It is a challenge for even the largest, most sophisticated catering operation to serve a sit-down dinner to one thousand people successfully. (We heard complaints that last year's entrées were, in turn, cold, undercooked, and overcooked.) Our focus is fresh, seasonal food (locally grown, raised, and fished, when possible) that can be eaten at room temperature, as at a picnic. We will offer modest portions of three entrées to ensure that we please everyone, and we guarantee elegant and creative presentation.

Passed Hors D'Oeuvres

Coconut shrimp, curried mango chutney

Chilled gazpacho 'shots'

Smoked chicken and avocado quesadillas with corn salsa

Wild mushroom and Roquefort in phyllo

Gougères

Crispy fried pork wontons with sweet-and-sour apricot dipping sauce

Stationary Hors D'Oeuvres

Raw bar with freshly shucked oysters and clams, mignonette sauce

Jumbo shrimp with horseradish, mustard, and cocktail sauces

Brie *en croûte* with pecans and plum chutney

Chilled vegetable crudités with chive and pine nut dip and roasted red pepper hummus

Seated Dinner

Grilled beef tenderloin with Gorgonzola cream

Mini lobster roll

Wild rice salad with portobello mushrooms and dried cranberry vinaigrette

Traditional Caprese salad: Sliced Bartlett Farm tomatoes, buffalo mozzarella, fresh basil

Corn bread with honey butter

Dessert sampler

Brownies and blondies, chocolate-dipped strawberries, éclairs, Key lime bars, homemade marshmallows, brown sugar fudge, peanut brittle, chocolate mint truffles

Business Briefs, *The Inquirer and Mirror*, February 25

Lockhart Dixon, executive director of Nantucket's Children, confirmed yesterday that rock-and-roll icon Max West will perform at the charity's annual Summer Gala, to be held on August 16 at the Town Recreational Fields.

'We're thrilled with this opportunity,' Dixon said. 'Max West has agreed to donate the performance; otherwise we would never have been able to afford such an esteemed name. Our gala cochair, Claire Danner Crispin, is a childhood friend of

Max West's. She was able to get him to commit, and we are very grateful.'

Tickets to the event start at $1,000 per person and include cocktails, dinner, and a 90-minute concert by West.

'It's sure to be the social event of the summer,' Dixon said.

Gavin Andrews was stealing from Nantucket's Children, though he didn't think of it as *stealing* per se, nor did he think of it as *embezzling*. Rather, the image that came to his mind was that of skimming off the top, as harmless as a child putting his finger through the icing on a cake.

He had started 'skimming' back in October, when donations rolled in for the annual appeal. He would get ten or twelve checks, totaling eighty-five hundred dollars, and he would deposit eight thousand, taking five hundred in cash in his pocket. The check amounts were recorded in a file on the computer, but the deposits were made at the bank, and the only record of them was the deposit slip (which Gavin threw away) and the bank statements, which it was Gavin's responsibility to reconcile. His skimming would be caught eventually, by an auditor, but the auditor only came once every two years and he had come in September and had found everything on the up-and-up, in perfect order, balanced to the penny. Lock was pleased with Gavin, said he expected nothing less, patted him, literally, on the back. Two weeks later, Gavin started the skimming. By the time the auditor returned, Gavin would be long gone.

No one else would catch him. The board of directors did have a treasurer, an elderly man named – you had to love this – Ben Franklin, who lived in Lincoln Park in Chicago, not far from Gavin's parents. In fact, Ben Franklin and Gavin's father, Gavin senior, belonged to the same social club, and it was for this reason that Gavin knew Ben Franklin was, in his waning years, losing it. Mr. Franklin was the only board member who had volunteered to be treasurer. He was the father of nine children and the grand-father of twenty-six, and Gavin believed he desired to be treasurer less to manage the finances than to escape the chaos of his summer household. Old Ben expected Gavin to hand him the budget and investment balance in the minutes before each board meeting. Ben Franklin came to only three meetings a year – June, July, and August – and the rest of the time, Gavin sat in as treasurer and presented the budget himself.

Lock was the only person Gavin had to worry about, but Gavin had worked at Nantucket's Children for nearly as long as Lock had, and Gavin knew his boss as intimately as a spouse. (This might have been presumptuous on Gavin's part. What, after all, did he know about having a spouse? So let's say this: Gavin spent more time with Lock than Daphne did.) Gavin knew the following things: Although Lock was a businessman, his predilections ran toward interacting with people and building relationships. He could schmooze, he could negotiate with such a deft touch that the other party did not realize he was doing Lock's exact bidding. Lock was persuasive and confident and smart, and that was how he had built his fortune. Lock was not, however, a numbers man. Looking at rows and columns of figures made his head swim and his eyes cross until he begged Gavin to bring him an Advil. Gavin learned this early on and kindly suggested that Lock leave the annoying minutiae of the banking to him. Lock was grateful, and Gavin had spent years earning his confidence. The books were perfect, the auditor pleased. Gold star.

Gavin's decision to steal, embezzle, skim, did not come lightly. Even though his path was clear and his plan foolproof, he was still terrified of getting caught. Getting caught would pretty much end the life he now led – meaning his job and the use of his parents' enormous house, not to mention his relationship with his parents, with Lock, and with everyone else he knew. So why do it? To be blunt: Gavin felt somebody somewhere owed him something. His life had not worked out the way it was supposed to. He had been born the only child of wealthy parents; his life should have been easy. One of his problems was that he had peaked too early. He had been voted Best Looking by his graduating class at Evanston Day School, but his parents had not been impressed by that distinction; they had seen it as one more thing they had given him. (*You were born with very good genes,* his mother said.) Gavin then attended the University of Michigan, where he nearly got lost; it was impossible to stand out in the sea of blue and maize that populated Ann Arbor. Gavin would never forget his first football game in the Big House, gazing at all those other bodies and feeling his insignificance, as some people did when contemplating the infinite number of stars in the heavens. The defining moment of college came when Gavin was having sex with a beautiful freshman named Diana Prell in the broom closet of an Irish pub. He couldn't remember how they had ended up in the broom closet, but he remembered that it had been Diana's idea, that she had led him in there. When the sex was over, however, she accused him of having forced himself on her. She did not go so far as to press charges, but the term 'date rape' was silently attached to his name. He pretty much lost the few friends he had, but he kept going to parties, anyway, and took up smoking so that he would have something to do, a group of people to bond with, if only for bumming a cigarette or a light. His resentment and alienation grew; he felt something underneath his surface starting to rot.

After college, Gavin senior set up a job for Gavin at Kapp and Lehigh, an accounting firm in Chicago, and it was there that his life of white-collar crime began. He succumbed to what he now saw was classic peer pressure when he was approached by a group of second-year hires who had an embezzlement ring going. He could have blown the whistle, or he could have turned a blind eye, but he so desperately wanted acceptance by this group that he performed the most dangerous of the jobs – moving funds from one account to another and changing the amounts in the switch, then placing the difference in a slush fund that everyone in on the scam split. They got caught after only a few months, not because of Gavin, but because of another fellow, who fingered everyone in the ring. Because they were all recent hires, very young, and incredibly stupid, and because the amount embezzled was less than ten thousand dollars, Kapp and Lehigh fired them but did not, mercifully, press charges.

Still, Gavin was left in a state of disgrace, and he was unhirable. His parents were at their wits' end. Gavin lived at home that winter, jobless, listening to mournful jazz and spending his parents' money on finely tailored clothes that, as far as he could tell, he would never again have a reason to wear. In the summer, he trailed his parents to Nantucket, and in the fall they suggested he stay and try to make his own way. Either Gavin's parents thought the sea air and cold, gray winter would be fortifying for his character, or they simply wanted him banished, tucked away on an island where they didn't have to deal with him in the day-to-day. Gavin was allowed to live in the house overlooking Cisco Beach for free, but he had to find a job and pay for the utilities.

Nantucket was a small place, and this suited Gavin, but he had a hard time finding a way to distinguish himself. He babysat paintings in an art gallery for a few months but found it too boring; he waited tables at the Brotherhood but found it too messy and hot. Then he found Nantucket's Children, and something clicked. (This was odd, his parents thought, because he disliked children.) His skill set, as it turned out, was exactly that of a fastidious administrator. He was prompt, he was neat, he was impeccably polite, and he never forgot a thing. He built himself a persona – the tiny red ladybug of a car, his penchant for classical music and foreign films and Italian shirts from the Haberdashery – but lately he had begun to feel hemmed in by his own identity. He wanted friends instead of acquaintances, he wanted to be invited out to see a band and drink beer at the Chicken Box, he wanted to be talked to instead of wondered about. His closest friends now were Rosemary Pinkle, a recently widowed woman he knew from the Episcopal church, and Lock's wife, Daphne Dixon, who liked to gossip as much as he did.

He was stealing, not because he needed the money (though the utility bills for a six-thousand-square-foot house weren't cheap, and his raises at work never garnered him as much butter as he hoped), but because he wanted a change. He would stockpile the cash and save it for his escape. When the time was right, he would flee the country – for Thailand or Vietnam or Laos, where he would find a beautiful girl and live freely, without judgment.

Here was one thing that surprised Gavin about the stealing: it enhanced the quality of his day-to-day life. He went from floating mindlessly through the thousand and one tasks of his day, to sitting on the edge of his seat, noticing everything, taking nothing for granted. He was aware of the five hundred-dollar bills in his pocket; he was aware of the crumpled deposit slip buried in the trash can; he could feel the pressure of his fingertips against the computer keyboard as he typed in the deposit amount. He could feel the sharp zing of the air against his clean-shaven cheek; he could hear Lock, across the room, drawing and expelling breath; he could pick apart each individual note of the Chopin polonaise that was playing on the Bose radio. Which note would be playing at the moment he was discovered? It gave him a chill to wonder.

The phone rang and Gavin nearly jumped out of his rolling office chair. Lock looked up.

'Too much caffeine at lunch?'

'Double latte,' Gavin confirmed.

'If it's Daphne, tell her I'm out,' Lock said.

Gavin nodded. This was a standard request. Although Gavin regarded Daphne as a comrade in the quest to keep life interesting, he did not tell her that her husband routinely refused her calls.

'Nantucket's Children.'

'Gavin?'

Gavin licked his teeth and stared straight ahead at the free-standing coatrack – like a prop straight out of *Dragnet* – draped with Lock's Burberry overcoat and Gavin's (nicer) cashmere jacket from Hickey Freeman. It was Claire Crispin . . . again.

'Hello, Claire.'

'Hi. Is Lock handy?'

Handy. She always said this – maybe because her husband was a carpenter – and the phrase drove Gavin apeshit. Was Lock handy? No, he wasn't handy; he couldn't even change the toilet paper roll in the bathroom. (Gavin had used that joke once, then wearied of it.) He had wearied of Claire in general and yet she was always around, calling Lock, popping in. She would stop by at eight fifteen on her way back from dropping the kids off at school, looking like death on a stick – in her stretched-out, shapeless yoga clothes, wearing no makeup, her hair in a haphazard bun. Gavin would never be seen looking that way in public; he didn't like to look that way in private. Claire always had something to pick up or drop off or something she wanted Gavin to pull from the files, or she wanted Lock's ear on a conflict she had had via e-mail with Isabelle French. It was so tiresome, Gavin didn't pay close attention. More often than not, Claire would call later that day, and when Gavin answered the phone, she would say, 'Hi, it's Claire. Did you miss me?'

And Gavin would think: *How can I miss you when you won't go away?*

He usually tried to muster a little chuckle, and then Claire would say (wearing his patience down to a frayed thread): *Is Lock handy?*

Now, Gavin said, 'Please hold.' He pushed the button on the phone and said to Lock, 'It's Claire.'

'Okay,' Lock said. 'Great. Put her through.'

Lock did not take Daphne's calls, but he always took Claire's. What did that say? Gavin watched Lock closely. His eyes did seem to brighten when he said hello, and his voice seemed to take on a tender tone, and then Lock swiveled in his chair and faced the twenty-paned window, which put his back to Gavin. It was a gesture Gavin knew well, in many incarnations: Gavin kept his hands in his jacket pockets when he went to the bank with a deposit, and he did all of the banking computer work with the screen tilted away from Lock's desk, most often when Lock was at lunch. These were the ways of a person with a secret. Turn your back. Speak in short, innocuous phrases that give nothing away, as Lock was now doing: *Yes, I see what you mean. Okay. Not right now. You bet. Yep, me too.*

Gavin narrowed his eyes at Lock's turned back. Affair? It just wasn't possible. Claire came in all the time looking like she had just spent six weeks in Outward Bound but hadn't had time for her back-to-civilization shower. This was not the way a woman presented herself to a lover (Gavin had bedded fourteen women in his lifetime, none of them special, but all of them clean). Besides, Claire wasn't Lock's type – and it wasn't only the fact that she looked like she got dressed in a dark closet. She was too casual a person for Lock, she was too comfortable and chummy; she wasn't refined. If Gavin had suggested to Daphne that Lock was having an affair with Claire Crispin, Daphne would have laughed wickedly and unleashed an invective about Claire that would have made even Gavin uncomfortable, and 'unwashed' would have been the nicest of it. Daphne worried about Lock and Isabelle French, and she was correct to worry because Isabelle French was classically beautiful and polished . . . and newly single. (Gavin was interested in Isabelle himself, though she was way, way, way, way, way out of his league.) But Isabelle hadn't been to the island in months, and she rarely called. When she did call, Lock sometimes asked Gavin to take a message; otherwise the conversations were terse, with Lock conveying unmistakable impatience.

No, Gavin told Daphne with full confidence. *Nothing is going on between Lock and Isabelle French.*

But now there was this vibe, this near *certainty* that Lock, like

Gavin, had a secret. Look at him, tapping his foot against the ancient radiator. That was a nervous tic. Gavin recognized it because he monitored himself for nervous tics all the time: the humming, the knuckle cracking, the licking of the teeth, the compulsive checking of his pants pocket: Was the cash still there, all of it? It took a criminal to recognize a criminal, and Gavin recognized a criminal.

'Okay,' Lock said to Claire. 'I'll follow up. Yep, see you.' He hung up.

'How is Claire?' Gavin said. He asked as nonchalantly as possible. Maybe he was just projecting: doing a bad thing came so easily for him that he assumed it would come easily for others.

Lock smiled. Fondly? Guiltily? Gavin couldn't tell.

'Oh,' he said. 'She's fine.'

Carter won nineteen hundred dollars on March Madness – which was, he informed Siobhan, a basketball tournament, and a very big deal in America. Siobhan was beside herself about the gambling, even at the win, even after Carter pulled five bills off his wad of hundreds and said, 'Go shopping.'

Siobhan did exactly that, despite the fact that she should have put the money right into the bank to hedge against future losses, despite the fact that she should have thrown the money in Carter's face and told him, point-blank, that he had a problem. The month of March had been dismal for Siobhan – there was no work, only an endless string of hours spent with the kids at the ice rink eating cardboard pizza and stale popcorn and drinking flat diet soda. Claire had been strange and distant – working all the time in the hot shop on the project for the summer gala, attending her 'meetings' at night. Twice now, when Siobhan had called to see if Claire wanted to go to 56 Union for a glass of cabernet and a pile of crispy, hot *frites,* Claire had turned her down, saying she had a 'meeting.'

Siobhan said, 'Who goes to these meetings? Everyone? Or just you and Lock?'

There was a pause. Then Claire said, 'There's a committee.'

Her tone of voice contained the accusation that while technically Siobhan was on the 'committee,' she had yet to attend a single meeting. And wouldn't attend, either, Siobhan thought haughtily. Until they were offered the catering job.

The fact of the matter was, things between Claire and Siobhan had not been right since the day Siobhan caught Claire and Lock heading into the forest at Tupancy Links and Claire flat-out denied it. It was an egregious lie – but it wasn't the lie, per se, that bothered Siobhan. It was that the lie covered up a slew of other lies. What were all the meetings for? What happened at these meetings? Jason was perhaps too close to see the writing on the wall, but Siobhan could read it. Something was going on. Why wasn't Claire owning up to it? Claire was hiding something, and Siobhan was offended and hurt by this; she was angry at Claire and angry at herself. Siobhan was too sarcastic, maybe, or too tough – the result of learning to survive as one of eight children – and Claire was as soft as the center of a fancy chocolate. She was afraid to confide in Siobhan. Siobhan was dying to ask Claire, How do you feel about Lock? Do you like working with him? You spend a lot of time together. Do you have feelings for him? Claire's relationship with Lock seemed to be reaching beyond the normal, beyond the everyday; it seemed to have taken on an intimacy that overstepped the appropriate. But Siobhan was not brave enough to bring it up with Claire. And so they were at an impasse. Claire would not confide in Siobhan about Lock; Siobhan would not confide in Claire about Carter's gambling or anything else. Their friendship was suffering. It had been a brutal winter.

Siobhan took the five hundred dollars from Carter, stuffed it in her jeans pocket, and went into town. As she was leaving the house, Carter said, *Buy yourself something pretty!* Like he was a gangster and she his moll. What a joke.

Saturday afternoon in the middle of March: Federal Street was deserted – the place was a ghost town – and yet there, parked on the street, was Claire's car. Siobhan saw it as she walked into Eye of the Needle. This was Claire's favorite store; maybe they would bump into each other and go to the Brotherhood for a Baileys. But Claire was not in the store. Siobhan stepped outside and called Claire's cell phone, and it went straight to voice mail. Instinctively, Siobhan knew that Claire was at the Nantucket's Children office on Union Street – she just knew it. Why not go and see for herself, and end the questions once and for all? Siobhan felt like Nancy Drew, girl sleuth; she felt like Angela fucking Lansbury.

Siobhan scooted down Federal Street, charged with an energy it was hard to describe. She was going to catch her best friend at . . . what?

Siobhan saw Claire tripping down the front steps of the church. Siobhan checked her watch. Four thirty. Mass was at five, but Claire was leaving the church, not going into it, and every good Catholic knew there were only three reasons to go to church in the middle of the afternoon: wedding, funeral, confession. Siobhan didn't see a bride and groom, nor did she see a hearse.

'Claire?'

Claire whipped around. Guilty. Caught.

'Hey,' she said weakly.

Siobhan glanced, pointedly, at the church. 'What are you doing?'

Claire said, 'What are *you* doing? God, town is dead.'

'Were you at confession?' Siobhan asked.

Claire looked behind her at the church, as though surprised to find it there.

'Yeah,' she said. 'I was. You know, I try to get J.D. and Ottilie to go, but they won't, so I figure, lead by example or whatever. A little repenting never hurt anyone.'

179

Claire was the easiest person in the world to read. Now she had two hot spots on her cheeks. Siobhan, girl sleuth, had another clue. Although she had been raised in County Cork, and Claire had been raised in godforsaken coastal New Jersey, their Catholicism was the same. Siobhan hadn't been to confession since she was twelve years old, and she knew Claire hadn't, either. It would have to be a *pretty big sin* to send her there.

'I'm out shopping,' Siobhan said. 'Do you want to go somewhere and get a drink? Do you want to talk?'

'No,' Claire said. 'I can't.'

'Just one drink. Come on. I feel like I never see you anymore.'

'I have to get home,' Claire said. 'Jason, the kids, dinner. You know what my life is like.'

Siobhan nodded, they kissed, and Claire boogied for her car. Siobhan headed around the corner, ostensibly to check for 'something pretty' at Erica Wilson. But she really just moved out of sight so she could catch her breath from the shock. Claire at confession.

You know what my life is like.

But did she?

There was a song the kids liked about having a 'bad day,' and when it came on the radio, Claire was required to turn up the volume, and the three older children sang along while Zack cried. Claire hated the song; it taunted her. The spring – a season of rebirth and new hope – was turning out to be a disaster for her. She had one bad day after another, after another.

Take, for example, what was going on in the hot shop. For months she had been trying to get started on the pulled-taffy chandelier for the gala auction. But it was all false starts and wasted time. She blew out a beautiful globe, which was to be the center of the chandelier, the body; it was colored a transcendental pink, the most luscious pink Claire had ever achieved because of the pains-taking way she had crushed the frit with a mortar and pestle. The globe was perfect, it was Platonic, it was as thin and wondrous as the *Bubbles;* she was back on track, hitting her stride. But then the perfect, Platonic globe shattered in the annealer, and when Claire saw this, she cried for three days. She cried with Jason; she cried with Lock. Both of them pretended to get it, but they didn't get it, not really, and she was vexed because they both, ultimately, expressed the same sentiment. *It's okay. You'll do another one, and the second one will be even better.* They used the same tone of voice; they were, in those moments, the same man. Disturb-ing. Claire tried to explain that it wasn't just the globe that was broken; it was her confidence and her will. She did, however, try again, and the result was probably just as good, lacking only the luster of perfection that the first globe had acquired in Claire's mind. Toward this second globe she acted like an overprotective mother. When it was cool, she set it gingerly in a crate filled with straw, and from time to time she revered it, like it was Baby Jesus lying in his manger.

With the body of the chandelier finished, she moved on to the arms. The arms of the chandelier had to arch and curve. They would have the same pulled-taffy nature as the candlesticks she had made so long ago for Mr. Fred Bulrush – all that twisty, col-ored glass – but they had to fall like tendrils from the globe, they had to drip. That meant Claire had to pull each arm by hand and get it to curve and bend just the right way, twisting it at the same time. It was impossible, it was beyond her, like certain positions in yoga; she couldn't make the glass do what she wanted it to do. She tried sixty times to get one graceful, arabesquing arm, and when she finally had it, the one arm, she wept some more because she could see how incredible the chandelier would be if she ever finished it, but she wasn't sure she had the patience to make seven more arms. In fact, Claire pulled another arm beautifully within her next ten tries, but because she was working by hand and not with a mold, this second arm did not correspond with the first. The angle of the curve was too sharp; if she attached these two arms to the globe now, one arm would look broken. More tears.

Lock said, 'There was no guaranteeing that it was going to come easily. In fact, one of the reasons this piece is so valuable is that it is so difficult. We're paying for your blood, sweat, and tears.'

Claire nearly swore at him. This was a piece for an auction, it was a *donation,* and it was consuming all of her time. It had been a mistake to return to the hot shop; she had lost her touch, the chandelier was beyond her, and yet it was the only thing she wanted to do. So there you had it: she had set herself an unattainable goal, and all it brought her was frustration and heartbreak.

Jason was right. She should have let him bomb the hot shop or shoot it full of arrows. Burn it down. Put Darth Vader into gear and run it over.

Claire placed the globe for the chandelier and the one peerless arm in the crate and set them on top of her filing cabinet, out of the way. She would think about the chandelier later; the best thing to do when the glass wasn't cooperating, her instructors used to tell her, was to walk away. Take a break. Claire took Ottilie and Shea to get haircuts – and then, as a super-duper special treat, manicures. Claire got a manicure herself, but the mere sight of her hands reminded her of the chandelier, and she left the salon with two giggling girls and a heavy heart. The chandelier called out to her. It haunted her. It was a baby she'd abandoned in a Dumpster, screaming for her. Talk about waking nightmares! Claire managed to make it through dinner, but after the kids were asleep, she went back into the hot shop and fashioned a tiny, bell-shaped cup onto the end of the one and only arm. This was where the bulb would go. It was sweet and precious, this tiny cup, like the blossom of a lily of the valley. Claire felt good about the project for about five minutes; then she started in on another arm. Forty-seven tries later, she was in tears again. She climbed into bed next to Jason, who woke up momentarily and said, 'Jesus, Claire, just forget about it. You're making yourself crazy.'

To: isafrench@nyc.rr.com
From: cdc@nantucket.net
Sent: March 27, 2008, 1:32 A.M.
Subject: Auction item

Isabelle –

I am having a very hard time producing an item for the auction. I planned to make a chandelier, which I thought would be a real winner, but it isn't turning out as I had hoped. I know it's late in the game as far as these things go, but I wondered if you might be able to scare up another auction item. Perhaps we should revisit the singing lessons, or loge seats to *South Pacific,* followed by a meet and greet with Kristin Chenoweth. With everything I have on my plate right now, the idea of having to produce this piece of art is bone-crushing – it's keeping me up at night. (As you can see, I am writing this e-mail at one in the morning. I am losing sleep!) Will you please help me explore other options?

Thx!
Claire

To: cdc@nantucket.net
From: isafrench@nyc.rr.com
Sent: March 28, 2008 7:32 A.M.
Subject: Auction item

Dear Claire,

I have the fullest confidence that you will create a breathtaking piece for our auction. The sentiments of the committee during our initial meeting are ones that I share: you are an island artistic treasure, and having your masterpiece to auction is a coup for Nantucket's Children indeed. Dinner with Kristin, although a fabulous idea, might have been an option for us back in October, but by now she has donated away all her time for the next calendar year. I really do think we will have to stay our course with your magnificent piece.

Thx! Isabelle

To: isafrench@nyc.rr.com
From: cdc@nantucket.net
Sent: March 28, 2008, 9:12 A.M.
Subject: Auction item

What about the G5?

To: cdc@nantucket.net
From: isafrench@nyc.rr.com
Sent: March 28, 2008, 9:13 A.M.
Subject: Auction item

What about it?

To: isafrench@nyc.rr.com
From: cdc@nantucket.net
Sent: March 28, 2008, 9:35 A.M.
Subject: Auction item

The round-trip flight anywhere? The cocktail party onboard? I thought that was the best idea of all! Is it still available?

To: cdc@nantucket.net
From: isafrench@nyc.rr.com
Sent: March 28, 2008, 9:37 A.M.
Subject: Auction item

No.

Claire should abandon it, declare it beyond her reach. They still had four months until the gala. They should certainly be able to come up with another option. Claire was positive that Isabelle was insisting on the chandelier as a means of revenge. The damn thing would sap Claire's energy and steal her time, and then, *then,* to cap it all off, no one would bid on it except for Lock, and Claire would look like – indeed, *be* – a failure. Abandon it! It was giving her one bad day after another. Her frustration with the chandelier was creeping into the rest of her life. She was late for pickup two days in a row, and she missed most of J.D.'s first Little League game.

Some part of Claire felt she deserved the torment the chandelier was causing her. She deserved it because she was a liar and a cheater. She was having an affair with Lock Dixon.

She wondered if, after a certain amount of time passed, the intensity of her feelings for Lock would fade. Would the sparkle wear off? Would he seem familiar? Would she begin to notice the twenty pounds he had to lose, or the shiny bald spot on top of his head, or the words he routinely used to show off ('pernicious,' 'occult')?

No. Every day, every meeting, Lock Dixon seemed more amazing to Claire, more mysterious and unattainable – and therefore desirable – than ever. She was in love with him and it was making her miserable. When she couldn't be with him, which was nearly all the time, she was a hostage to her longing. She couldn't enjoy anyone else – not her kids, not Siobhan, not Jason. She counted hours, minutes, she rearranged her schedule, she skipped things, blew them off, so she could spend one more bittersweet hour with Lock.

One night, Claire and Lock sat at the table in the conference room, holding hands. They were naming the things they would do if they were free in the world together.

185

LOCK:

Play cards.

CLAIRE:

Fly to Spain.

LOCK:

Where in Spain?

CLAIRE:

Ibiza.

LOCK:

Take you shopping. Watch you try on clothes.

CLAIRE:

Eat Big Macs.

LOCK:

Go to the movies.

CLAIRE:

Ride a Ferris wheel.

LOCK:

Climb the Eiffel Tower.

CLAIRE:

Climb Mount Everest. No, scratch that. Too hard.

LOCK:

Go fishing. In Ibiza.

CLAIRE:

Build a campfire, roast marshmallows.

LOCK:

See a concert.

CLAIRE:

Who?

LOCK:

Tough decision. Anyone past or present? Frank Sinatra.

CLAIRE:

Love it. My turn. Share the Sunday paper. You can have the Business section.

LOCK:

Stand in line together at the post office.

CLAIRE:

We could do that now, if you wanted to.

LOCK:

But I would have to be holding you from behind, with my chin resting on top of your head.

CLAIRE
(fighting back tears):
Oh.

LOCK:

Your turn. What else?

CLAIRE:

Sleep in the same bed. Just once. One night.

They were both quiet after she said that. It was a fun game, and funny, but demoralizing, too. All the things they wanted to do together but couldn't. The simplest things: stand in line at the post office, share a pew at church, shop for a new watch, pick out a video. As they sat in silence, their hands squeezing, stroking, squeezing again (*Don't let me go!*), Claire wondered how bad her life would be if she left Jason and married Lock. She wondered this all the time, and the answer was: Bad. Very bad. The kids would hate her, they would side with Jason, their lives would become a mess that even therapy couldn't straighten out. Claire would lose all her friends, including Siobhan, she would lose her position in the community, and she was certain that Lock, once he was married to her, would become disenchanted.

Still, she wondered. Because it was on nights like these – nights when, instead of frantically making love, they talked and floated around in their fantasies – that Claire didn't think she could stand it another day. She was in love with the man. She wanted to be with him.

Claire was at Hatch's, the liquor store, on a Saturday afternoon of cold and driving rain. Jason had the kids at home, and Claire wanted out, just for a few minutes. The weekends were murder, a wasteland of No Lock, of Claire's trying at home, trying to cook something nice, trying to be engaged in family life. *Want to play Parcheesi, Mom?* Okay, sure, she could do that. It would be fun. They played five games with Zack whimpering and stuffing the colored pegs in his mouth. Jason sat right there alongside them, watching a bowling tournament on TV.

Is there any beer? he asked.

Claire checked the fridge. They were out of beer. Instead of telling Jason, *Sorry, honey, no,* instead of yelling or taking the moral high ground because she had just spent two hours entertaining the kids while he moldered in their midst, she saw this as her opportunity.

Before he could protest, she snapped up her car keys.

Liquor store, she said. *Be right back.*

She stood in front of the towers of white wine with a bottle of viognier in her hands. Hatch's was busy, a rabbit warren of activity, wet people buying cigarettes, scratch tickets, snack food, the newspaper, beer, wine, champagne, vodka, gin, scotch, Cuervo Gold, whatever helped them through. The door had a lovely little bell that rang every time someone went in or out. Claire didn't want to leave the store; she didn't want to go back to her house. She was a woman in a movie, a character from a Bruce Springsteen song. She went out for a bottle of expensive French wine and never went back.

'Claire?' a voice said. 'Is that you?'

Claire swiveled.

A person in a green raincoat, holding a dripping Burberry

umbrella. A woman, familiar, but there was a split second when Claire was stymied. Who? Then the medicine ball to the stomach. Daphne.

'Hi!' Claire said like a maniac.

Daphne took the very same bottle of viognier that Claire held in her hands off the shelf. Claire was suffused with heartache, and then fear, and then heartache again. Daphne was picking up Lock's wine, or their wine together, wine for an afternoon by the fire, wine for whatever dinner plans they had tonight. Out? In? Which would be better? Which would be worse? Claire shifted her own bottle of viognier behind her back, but this movement must have seemed furtive because it drew Daphne's attention.

'You drink viognier?' she asked.

All the time, Claire wanted to say. *It's my favorite varietal.*

But this was out of the question.

Claire gazed at the wine bottle in her hands. 'I just picked this up,' she said. 'I don't really know what it is.'

Daphne stared at Claire for a second. Was she suspicious? Would she know that Claire and Lock drank viognier in the office all the time? Or was she simply stunned by Claire's ignorance?

'How *are* you?' Daphne said. 'How's everything going with the gala planning?'

Trick question? You never knew with Daphne.

'Fine,' Claire said. She sounded very nonchalant to her own ears. Disinterested, even. 'Things are falling into place bit by bit.'

'I'm glad for that,' Daphne said. 'I finally convinced Lock to get away.'

Claire nodded. What was Daphne talking about? Get away? From her? Or . . . what? Claire was confused, but she kept right on nodding. *Whatever you say, Daphne, you bet!*

'We're going to Tortola a week from Friday,' Daphne said.

'Tortola?'

'It's one of the British Virgin Islands.'

189

'Oh, right,' Claire said. 'I know what it is. I just didn't realize . . .' She couldn't continue.

'We're going for a week.'

'With Heather?' Claire said. What must her face look like? She was, as far as she could tell, still upright, though her legs were threatening to buckle. The wine was dangling from her hand like a club. 'Is it her . . . spring break?'

'We're going alone,' Daphne said. 'Just the two of us. It's time. We need it. We'll go see Heather first, for the weekend. Then we'll fly out of Logan to the Caribbean. We're staying at this ultrachic new place called – '

'It sounds fabulous,' Claire said, then realized Daphne wasn't finished. But no matter – Claire was finished. *Finished!* When she got into her car, she would decide if she should cry or vomit, but she couldn't do either right now.

'I'm surprised Lock didn't mention it to you,' Daphne said. 'He is so anxious to get away, the vacation is all he talks about.'

'Well, with this weather,' Claire said, 'who can blame him?'

'Exactly,' Daphne said. 'And what about you?' Her nose wrinkled, and Claire wondered if she was about to make another nasty comment about Claire and the shower. Well, if she did, Claire would smack the nose right off her face. Okay, this was bad, a bad thought, a bad series of thoughts, a bad, *bad* situation – facing her lover's wife in the liquor store, both of them buying the same bottle of wine, Lock's favorite fucking wine, and then the news of the vacation. Unspeakably bad.

'What *about* me?' Claire asked.

'Are you going away?' Daphne asked. She took a stab. 'Disney?'

'No,' Claire said. 'Not this year.'

'That's too bad,' Daphne said. 'I suppose it's hard, with the kids.'

'Hard,' Claire agreed. She widened her eyes, as if remembering

190

something. 'I have to get Jason some beer,' she said. 'That's what I came for.'

'Oh,' Daphne said. She seemed disappointed at Claire's retreat. 'Okay. Well, enjoy the viognier!'

'Thanks,' Claire said, backing away. 'Enjoy Tortola!'

Claire's emotions were so complicated, she didn't even know where to start. Lock was going to Tortola with Daphne, alone, for a week. *It's time. We need it.* And he hadn't even bothered to tell her himself. She had to hear it from Daphne. This was awful. This was the low point. Every minute of every hour since Claire had returned home from the liquor store, she had chastised herself. One of the rules of having an affair was that you weren't allowed to feel this kind of jealousy. Claire could not be jealous of Daphne. Daphne was Lock's wife. She had legal ownership, the history, the name, the home, the child. Of course he would go on vacation with Daphne. How could Claire protest? She could not. Agreeing to an affair meant agreeing to a relationship without claims; she had no rights to him. That she should feel utterly betrayed was backward. It was Daphne who should feel betrayed, but Daphne would spend a week with Lock alone, at some ultrachic new resort. They would be making love on a wide, soft bed, not on top of a conference table. It was horrible to contemplate – Lock and Daphne together romantically, sexually. But what a hypocrite she was! She slept every night next to Jason, she made love to him, she even had orgasms – but it was not attended with the same heartbreaking desire that she felt for Lock. What she experienced with Jason was exercise, it was fondly going through the motions, it was empty. She and Lock had talked about this carefully. They had agreed: they would both be happier together, sharing the paper, eating Big Macs, fishing in Ibiza. The happiness brought about simply by talking about these things was impossible to conjure now. Tortola. *Just the two of us. We need it.*

* * *

191

Claire's phone rang on Monday morning at eight fifteen. She was in the car, on her way home from dropping the kids off at school. She checked the display. Lock. She threw the phone as hard as she could at the passenger door. The phone broke into its component parts. Zack started to cry.

Finished!

In the driveway, Claire put her phone back together with trembling hands. It rang again. Lock. Again, she ignored it. She handed Zack off to Pan and went about the tasks of her day.

Finished!

The calls came every hour. Claire lasted until four o'clock. Pan watched the kids; Claire took her phone out to the hot shop. She didn't bother with 'hello.'

'Why didn't you tell me earlier?'

'I was afraid.'

'Afraid of what?'

'That you'd be angry.'

'Any idea how grossly humiliating it was to hear it from Daphne?'

'I was horrified. I would have called you Saturday if I could have.'

'You should have told me yourself. Back whenever it was that you made the plans. A month ago? Two months?'

'I am so sorry, Claire. I am prostrate at your feet.'

'Are you?'

'Yes! God, yes. I love you.'

'You didn't tell me, why? Because you didn't think I could handle it?'

'No. I knew you could handle it. But I didn't think you'd like it.'

'You're right,' Claire said. 'I don't like it. It's not fair, but I don't like it.'

'I know,' he said softly. 'I don't want you to like it.'

'So you're trying to make me jealous, then? Is that why you're going?'

'No,' he said. 'I'm going because Daphne wants to get away someplace warm, and I can't blame her, and I have guilt, Claire, and one of the ways to assuage my guilt is to throw Daphne a bone, and Tortola is that bone.'

'Couldn't you have bought her something? A diamond ring?'

'She wanted to get away.'

Well, that was something Claire understood. The island was frigid, gray, rainy, and miserable, without a single sign of spring except for a few hardy crocuses. Maybe Claire and Jason *should* go away. They could one-up Lock and Daphne and go to Venezuela or Belize. But Jason would never agree to it; he didn't even like to go to Hyannis.

'Okay,' Claire said. 'I understand.'

'Do you?'

Did she? No!

'Yes,' she said.

She understood, but that didn't mean she wasn't filled with jealousy, fury, and longing. Lock had promised he would stay in touch by e-mail, but after checking her e-mail fifteen times in the first four hours of his absence, Claire gave up. She didn't have time to pine after someone like this; she didn't have time to go into her home office, log on to the computer, punch in her secret password, and wait while the computer told her there were no new messages in her in-box. She had to put her heart in a crate of straw along with the newborn chandelier; she had to tuck it away in the storage closet until Lock came back. She should take advantage of this time apart and use it to spend time with her children.

Zack was turning one. Her baby! Zack had made some progress. Instead of sitting like a potted plant before crying to be picked up, he scooted forward on his butt if he really wanted something. Claire threw a small party for his birthday. Siobhan and Carter and the boys came over, and Claire made spaghetti and homemade meatballs and a beautiful salad and golden crispy garlic bread. She went to great pains to make a cake that looked like a giraffe, because although Zack couldn't say the word 'giraffe,' it was the one animal he was able to identify. When Claire asked, 'Where's the giraffe, Zack?' he pointed right to it. It was his favorite animal! Claire made a template out of paper, she cut the cake just so, she dyed the icing yellow and brown, she placed gumdrops for the eyes.

'It's a gorgeous cake,' Siobhan said. 'Must have taken you forever.'

Claire said, 'Yeah, it did, but I found myself with some extra time this week.'

Siobhan stared at her, and Claire busied herself with the salad dressing.

The birthday dinner was a success, Claire decided, despite the fact that Zack cried when they sang, despite the fact that he was more interested in chewing the wrapping paper than in the presents inside. Claire drank four glasses of the blasted viognier and it made her teary. She had no idea if Lock remembered that it was Zack's birthday, though back in the fall he had asked Claire to write all the kids' birthdays down so he could memorize them. Claire had not predicted how emotionally fraught Zack's birthday would be – because contained within the celebration was the unspoken fact that they had almost lost him, that he'd been born so early, so unprepared for life outside the womb. Only two pounds seven ounces, he'd fit in Jason's palm; he wore a diaper the size of a cocktail napkin. No one mentioned her fall in the hot shop or the jet ride to Boston, or the five weeks in the hospital. Was Claire the only one who remembered? She looked at Zack and thought, *I am so sorry, buddy.*

The party was lovely, the food delicious, the cake charming. Zack was fine, Claire told herself. He was whole and healthy and loved.

As Claire was clearing the dishes, Siobhan, who had consumed no small amount of wine herself, wiped the lenses of her glasses on her dinner napkin and said, 'Guess who I caught going to confession last week?'

Claire's heart went into a free fall; she said nothing. Jason and Carter said, 'Who?'

And Siobhan said, 'Claire.'

Claire set the dishes in the sink and turned on the water, full blast, and hot.

Carter said, 'Got something on your conscience, Claire?'

Siobhan said, 'Something big, I'd say.'

Steam rose from the sink. Jason said, 'Hey, now, leave her alone. You know Claire, always stopping her car so the guinea hens can cross, instead of running them off the road like the rest of us do. She's as pure as the driven snow.'

They all laughed at that, and the matter was forgotten. When, at the end of the night, Claire kissed Siobhan good-bye, Siobhan tasted bitter, like antiseptic.

And even later, when Jason came to bed, he stroked Claire's hip and said, 'I understand about the confession. We're lucky to have him, you know? We're lucky the little guy is alive.'

The next morning, Claire took Zack to Dr. Patel's office for his twelve-month shots. Claire had checked her e-mail – nothing – and she checked her cell phone every twenty minutes for a text message. Surely Lock could send a text message?

Zack was gaining weight, he was getting taller, and his eyes looked good, as did his ears, nose, and throat; his lungs were clear, his reflexes automatic. He screamed during the shots, yowled so that Claire tensed every muscle in her body, but then she held him and gave him his pacifier and he calmed down.

Gita Patel smiled at Claire and said, 'He looks great. Do you have any concerns?'

'I look at him,' Claire said, 'and I feel something isn't right.'

'Something like what?' Dr. Patel said.

'Like he's not developing fast enough. He can't walk. He doesn't crawl on his hands and knees. He cries all the time. He doesn't have any words. He isn't active or engaged like my other kids were.'

Dr. Patel put a finger out. Zack grabbed it. She held his hands and he took a few steps down the examining table. She tickled his feet, and he smiled, then started crying.

'See?' Claire said.

'He's fine, Claire,' Dr. Patel said.

'He was so little when he was born,' Claire said. 'He was intubated for so long. I shouldn't have been in the hot shop. It was irresponsible.' She picked Zack up and hugged him. 'I feel so guilty.'

'He's fine, Claire. He's going to be fine. Kids develop at different rates, even siblings. Okay? If I had any doubts, I would tell you, but I don't.'

'You're sure?'

'I'm sure.'

Dr. Patel put her hand on Claire's arm, and this gesture and the words were so comforting that Claire nearly said, *I have a lover, Lock Dixon, and he's in Tortola with his wife. I miss him. I need him. Father Dominic says I have to stop, but it's beyond me. Sometimes I can't believe this is really me because I am not like this. I'm a good person, or I always had been until this thing. Can you help me?*

'Thank you,' Claire said.

Bad day followed bad day. Lock was away, still away. How was he filling all those hours with Daphne? Claire thought of Daphne, breasts spilling out of her bathing suit, swimming in a pool with an infinity edge while some cute British butler brought her a planter's punch. Claire considered e-mailing Lock and telling him about the visit with Dr. Patel; he would be interested in this, he would be happy to hear Claire repeat Dr. Patel's words, but no, she would not contact him first. He had yet to send her a single e-mail. So . . . if he was wondering how things here were going, let him wonder!

Siobhan called to say that Carter had had an unexpected windfall, and to celebrate, they were throwing a drinks party. Martinis and munchies, Saturday night. This raised Claire's spirits. Lock was with Daphne in Tortola, but Claire had a wild, rollicking party to attend. She would get perniciously drunk.

Claire was all keyed up for Saturday night. Carter and Siobhan threw the best parties on the island, and all of Claire's friends would be there, the people in her foxhole. She looked in her closet for something to wear; she yearned for something new, although she never had time to shop. She put on jeans and a jade green cashmere sweater and pearls. She tried not to think about Lock. As she got ready she drank a glass of wine and Jason drank a beer and they listened to Max West on the stereo in their room. Jason was wearing jeans and a black shirt and a black blazer and his cowboy boots. His hair was damp and mussed, and Claire ran her hands through it, smoothing it. He smelled good, his face had a day or two of growth, which was how she liked it – scruffy – and he had a tan from working outside. It had been weeks since he'd come home reeking of cigarette smoke, she realized. She should be grateful for that. Jason was handsome, he was sexy, and she could see this and know it intellectually, but it was hard to make herself feel anything.

'Do you want to fool around?' she asked, thinking it must be a balmy night in Tortola, and Lock and Daphne would be on their way out to dinner, ordering grilled lobster and conch fritters.

Jason glanced at his watch. 'We don't really have time, do we?'

Claire blinked at him, stunned. In fifteen years, he had not turned away from even the slightest chance of getting lucky. They had been late for all sorts of things because of Jason's libido; they were famous for being late.

She shrugged. 'I guess not.' She touched his collar. 'You look good tonight, Jase.'

'You, too,' he said.

Claire poured a second glass of wine into one of Zack's plastic cups and drank it on the way to Siobhan's house. They took Jason's truck. It was warm enough to crack the windows, and Jason hummed along to the Allman Brothers on the radio. Claire looked at his profile, as familiar to her as her own face. He was her husband, they had built a family together, a house together, a life together – and yet they had nothing in common anymore, did they, except their mutual efforts to sustain what they had created. They were alone, out of the house together for the first time all week, and they had nothing to say. Claire could ask him about the job, but he didn't want to talk about work; she could revisit, for the hundredth time, the encouraging things that Dr. Patel had said about Zack, but the words lost their effect every time she repeated them. She wanted to ask Jason why he had turned her down, back in the bedroom. Was he angry with her? Had he noticed her foul mood of the past ten days and connected it to Lock's absence? Did he know what was going on? Had he lost interest in her, finally, this week – had his desire for her dried up? Was he consumed with stress, about the house in Wauwinet or about something else? She was flabbergasted to find that she had no idea what he was thinking about.

'Does your back still hurt?' she asked.

'A little,' he said.

'Did you take a painkiller?'

'Three Advil, right when I got home.'

He was driving very fast, as though anxious to get to the party. (To see his brother and smoke dope in the basement?) Claire wanted to get there, too, but she couldn't stand to fritter away this time alone. If they didn't find each other right now, their marriage would end. This was an exaggeration – it was a manifestation of

198

Claire's own guilt and stress, and the two glasses of wine taking hold of her senses, and the lingering sting of being turned down – but she felt it, deeply. Did they have *any* common ground? What had they talked about when they first met, when they were dating, when they were married but had not yet had children? They had been so focused on getting set up, getting situated and organized for the rest of their lives, that they had overlooked the fact that their relationship was based on . . . nothing. Well, there was physical attraction, a mutual love for the island, a desire to raise a family. But was that it? Shouldn't there be a shared passion for something else – even if it was just for watching *Junkyard Wars*? (Claire hated it.) She wanted to travel with the kids – take them to Machu Picchu and to Egypt to see the Pyramids – but would that ever happen? She wanted to read novels and see films and talk about important ideas. Claire was reading a book of short stories by an Aboriginal writer that Lock had recommended, but whenever she started explaining the book to Jason, he glazed over.

She looked around the dark truck. It was a mess – coffee-stained napkins, sections of old newspaper, CD cases from his prized Grateful Dead bootlegs, fishing lures, breath mints, keys to God knows what, a rubber duck with the beak chewed off, which had been around since Shea was a baby, the anglers' club hat that had belonged to Jason's father, Malcom. She picked up the hat. 'Do you miss your dad?' she asked.

Jason closed his eyes for a split second. 'You know, I was just thinking about him today.'

'Were you?'

'Yeah, it's so strange you asked me. I was thinking about my tenth birthday and how he took me to play my first round of golf at Sankaty. He had a winter membership that year and it was too cold to walk it, so he spent thirty bucks on a cart and he brought along a thermos of coffee with Baileys or something in it that he let me sip from.' Jason swallowed. 'It was special, you know, because he was showing me that I was growing up.' He shook his head. 'It's

199

like sex. How many rounds of golf have I played, but I'll always remember that first time.'

'I miss your dad, too,' Claire said.

'He was a great guy,' Jason said. 'The greatest. You know, I want to do something like that for J.D.'s birthday. Maybe I will. See if I can take him for nine holes at Sankaty.'

'Minus the Baileys,' Claire said.

'Right,' Jason said.

Claire relaxed in her seat. She thought of Malcolm Crispin, Jason and Carter's father, a great old, salty guy, who worked for the water company for forty years, who loved golfing and fishing and grilling big, fat steaks and drinking red wine and smoking cigars on the deck of the anglers' club. Malcolm died of mouth cancer when J.D. was a baby, but he'd given Claire a strand of pearls – the ones she was now wearing – for delivering the first Crispin grand-child. Siobhan had been pregnant with Liam when Malcolm died, and she'd never gotten over the fact that Malcolm hadn't lived to see Carter's children, or that Claire had gotten the pearls. But even Siobhan's resentment was born of the fact that they were all one clan, the Crispins. Those ties counted for something.

Jason pulled up in front of Carter and Siobhan's house; there were cars lined up all the way down the street. Claire drank down the rest of her wine.

Jason opened his door and climbed out.

Claire said, 'Jason?'

He peered in at her.

'Thank you for telling me that story,' she said. 'About the golf with your dad. It was nice.'

He shook his head. 'It's weird,' he said. 'It's like you read my mind.'

At that moment, Tortola seemed very far away. Claire felt better. They went inside.

*   *   *

The party was lovely. The living room was clean and cozy and lit only by votive candles. People carried drinks in frosted glasses, and jewel-like canapés. There was conversation, laughter, the sexy strains of Barry White floating down from the in-ceiling speakers. Siobhan was across the room wearing something new, something slinky and pink that left one of her shoulders bare. She was surrounded by people. Claire tried to catch her eye, but when she did, Siobhan gave her a half wave that felt like a brush-off. Claire's good mood was like a basket of fruit balancing on her head; it teetered precariously.

Claire poured herself a glass of wine, and then another glass; she talked to people she had seen only in passing since Christmas – Julie Jackson, Amie Trimble, Delaney Kitt, Phoebe Caldwell, Heidi Fiske.

Where have you been hiding yourself?

No, not hiding, Claire said emphatically. *Just so busy. Beyond busy. Now that I'm back at work.*

How is the baby? He must be getting so big!

So big, she echoed. *He's doing great, just had his first birthday. He's nearly started crawling. He's fine.*

She drank, she chatted, she did not eat nearly enough, though the food was to die for – guacamole with fresh corn, mini Asian crab cakes that were sweet with coconut milk, scallops wrapped in bacon with horseradish sauce.

'Yum!' Claire said to Siobhan as Siobhan passed by with succulent Chinese ribs. Siobhan gave Claire a pointed look over the top of her square glasses. Claire's good mood tumbled. Was Siobhan mad? Claire thought back: They hadn't talked in two days. Claire had left a message, or maybe two, which Siobhan hadn't answered. This was unusual, but Siobhan was busy. She was throwing a party! Claire threaded her way through the crowd until she spotted Siobhan offering a rib to Adams Fiske. Claire tapped Siobhan on the shoulder.

'Hey.'

'Hey,' Siobhan said flatly.

'What's wrong? Are you mad at me?'

Siobhan nodded toward the hallway, where it was dim and quiet. Claire followed, her heart scuttling.

'What is it?' Claire said.

'I spoke to Edward.'

'And?'

'You don't know?'

'Know what?'

'He gave the catering job to someone else. For the gala.'

'He did *what?*'

'He gave it to À La Table.'

'Genevieve?'

'Genevieve.'

'I can't believe it.'

'It gets better.'

'What?'

'Because Edward wasn't even the one who told me. I found out from Genevieve herself. I saw her at the farm market, and you know her, she couldn't keep herself from spilling it, she was *so happy!* She just had to tell me: she got the catering job for the Nantucket's Children Summer Gala!'

'Oh, shit.'

'So I went home and I called Edward and he confirmed it, he took their bid. They came under by nearly forty dollars a head.'

'Oh, shit.'

'You didn't know this?'

'I had no idea.'

'Because I asked him if you knew, and he said he sent you an e-mail.'

'Oh,' Claire said. 'Well, he might have. I haven't checked my e-mail . . . in a couple of days.'

Siobhan took a step closer to Claire, so that the edge of the platter of ribs nudged Claire in the stomach. Siobhan's glasses slipped down her nose, and her face flushed pink. 'Edward knows nothing about food and even less about wine. You could serve him peanut butter on a cedar shingle and he'd say it was delicious. Or a glass of vintage lighter fluid. *Why* did you put him in charge of catering?'

'He volunteered. And I thought he'd pick you. I was sure of it.'

'But he didn't pick me, did he?'

'Oh, Siobhan, I'm sorry.'

'Sorry? You're sorry? That's all you're going to say?'

'What else do you want me to say? Tell me and I'll say it.'

'You were wrong to put Edward in charge of catering. It was a gross error in judgment on your part. You were sure he'd pick me, but if you had any common fucking sense, or better still, if you had just *asked* me, I would have pointed out that Edward has just been *waiting* all these years for a chance to screw me over, for an opportunity to *humiliate* me the way he feels I humiliated him by breaking the engagement and marrying Carter. Otherwise, why would he have picked Genevieve? She sucks! Her food tastes like shit, she actually makes an appetizer using Froot Loops, and she hasn't timed an event correctly since she got into the business. He picked her because he *knows* she's my rival; he *knows* I detest her. It would have been better if he had chosen some fancy-pants New York caterer. But Genevieve! The reason she came forty-dollars-a-head under is that she hires her sixteen-year-old daughter and her daughter's friends to serve.'

'I am so sorry,' Claire said. 'I was wrong to put Edward in charge.'

'Don't just feed my words back to me, Claire. I find that very patronizing.'

'At the time, at that meeting, he was singing your praises, telling everyone how great you were, and I thought it was a sure thing.' Claire reached out and touched Siobhan's arm, but Siobhan pulled away suddenly and nearly dropped the platter of ribs. Claire was pretty drunk – she didn't seem to be handling this situation the right way – but Siobhan might have been drunker.

'You know what the worst part is?' Siobhan said. Her voice wavered and her eyes filled with tears. 'You're different. Since you took this stupid job as cochair, Claire Crispin, you are a different person.'

'I'm not different,' Claire said.

'You lied to me about being at Tupancy back at Christmastime,' Siobhan said. Her voice was now a furious whisper. 'I saw you, you nearly fucking ran me over, and then you denied ever being there.'

Claire scoffed, though inside her, discomfort bloomed. She had been at Tupancy with Lock, they had been seeking a private spot, and it had been startling to come across Siobhan, so startling that Claire drove on, convinced that she was mistaken. *What should I do?* she asked Lock. And he said, *Deny it.*

'I can't believe you're taking me to task for something that happened back before Christmas,' Claire said.

'Admit that you were at Tupancy,' Siobhan said. 'Admit that Lock was in your car.'

'Lock?' Claire said.

'Then a few weeks ago, I see you at confession.' Siobhan leaned forward. 'Fucking *confession,* Claire. What was that about?'

'I told you, I – '

'Do you take me for an idiot, Claire?'

There it was, Claire thought. Siobhan suspected something was going on, but she had been left in the dark. Claire hesitated, thinking, *I should have told her before. I should have picked a quiet time and place and told her.* How much less excruciating would the past few months have been if she'd had a repository for her thoughts, her feelings, the delicious and the evil, the confident and the insecure? Claire should have told Siobhan about Lock before, but Claire couldn't tell her now because Siobhan would be furious – perhaps fatally so – that Claire hadn't confided in her from the beginning.

What? she would say, her Irish ire up. (*Woot?*) *You didn't trust me?*

And the truth would be out there between them, stinking and obvious.

Claire didn't trust her.

She couldn't tell Siobhan now, in the middle of the party. Maybe someday soon . . . but no, never. Claire would never tell, not even with Siobhan pushing her up against the wall. As long as it was just Claire and Lock, contained in a cell, it was not real; after they left each other, it vanished, it never was, it could not be pointed to or proved. There was no paper trail, not one physical, tangible object that implicated the two of them. If a tree falls in the forest and no one is there to hear it, does it make a noise? No, Claire decided. As long as nobody knew, it was safe. If it stayed secret, nobody would get hurt. But somehow, Siobhan had gotten hurt. She knew that Claire had a new heart. *You are a different person.* Ironic that Siobhan had noticed, but not Jason. And yet Siobhan was closer to Claire in nearly every way, and Claire felt just as bad, if not worse, about betraying Siobhan.

How to keep herself from spilling this, like the ribs, all over the place?

'I've been upset about Zack,' Claire said, which was true. 'His birthday brought it all back. And then, on the way here, Jason and I were talking about Malcolm . . .'

Siobhan snorted. 'Malcolm?' she said. 'Ah, yes!' She turned away with her tray of ribs. 'By the way, nice pearls!'

Claire was about to follow her (and say *what* to make things right, she couldn't guess) when she saw something that rendered her temporarily speechless: her husband and Julie Jackson coming down the stairs. The stairs were lit with small votive candles on each end, but as far as Claire knew, that was just decoration and not an invitation to ascend the stairs. As far as Claire knew, the upstairs was dark and deserted except for Liam and Aidan, who were sleeping.

Claire felt like she was going to vomit. Julie Jackson was the most beautiful woman Claire knew. She was touching Jason's arm, leaning into him, holding on to him. She was wearing a short skirt and a pair of very high heels and she was having a hard time getting down the stairs. Claire thought back to Jason's turning her down in the bedroom. *We don't really have time, do we?* She thought of him racing over here in an unprecedented hurry. What on earth would Jason and Julie Jackson have been doing together, alone, in the dark upstairs? Claire might have looked to Siobhan for a reality check, but Siobhan had stormed off. Claire drank what was left of her wine and approached Jason. She knew her cheeks were pinking; she felt like her face was going to explode. Her eyeballs felt like hot glass, and her lips were stretched into a fake smile that made her teeth chatter. Julie squeezed Jason's arm and ducked out, toward the kitchen.

Jason said, 'Hey, babe.'

'What were you doing upstairs?' Claire asked.

Jason laughed and took a swig of his beer. 'You should see your face.'

'I asked you a question.' She could not believe the rage inside her. While Siobhan had been raking her over scorching emotional coals, her husband had been upstairs, hiking Julie Jackson's skirt and bending her over in the guest bedroom. There wasn't a doubt in Claire's mind. She lowered her voice to a whisper. 'You were fucking her.'

'Whoa!' Jason said. His eyebrows shot up.

'Don't deny it,' Claire said. 'The two of you were upstairs alone together. I'm not stupid, Jason.'

Jason set his beer bottle down on the table behind him with a thud. 'I was showing her the half-round trim detail in the master

206

bedroom,' he said. 'She and Brent are starting their addition and she asked to see it.'

'Oh, yeah, I bet,' Claire said.

'Are you accusing me of cheating on you?' Jason said. 'Is that honestly what you're doing?'

His voice was very loud, and although they were separated from the rest of the party by a wall, the people going to and from the bathroom could see them and maybe hear them – and Adams and Heidi Fiske were peering at them from the doorway of the living room. Making a scene at a party like this was a very bad idea; everyone would be talking about it in the morning.

Jason grabbed Claire's arm. 'Let's go ask Julie what we were doing upstairs. Come on, right now, so you can hear it for yourself. Let's go find her.'

'No,' Claire said. 'God, no.' The last thing she wanted was some kind of messy confrontation in the kitchen with everyone watching. Claire would never be able to look Julie in the eye again.

'You just accused me of fucking her,' Jason said. 'After fifteen years of being together, thirteen years of marriage, and four kids at home. You think I would desecrate all that by fooling around with one of your friends at a party? Is that how little you think of me?'

'She's very pretty,' Claire said.

'*You're* very pretty!' Jason was screaming now. 'This has nothing to do with pretty! This has to do with you accusing me. This has to do with you not trusting me – me, Jason Crispin, your husband! Do you honestly think I would *cheat* on you?'

He was hot now, hopping mad. First her best friend, now her husband. Why tonight? What had she done wrong?

'You didn't want to fool around at home,' Claire said.

'We were going to be late,' Jason said. 'And my back is killing me.'

'Then you drove like a bat out of hell . . .'

'So you thought what? That I couldn't wait to get here so I could take Julie Jackson upstairs?'

207

'Well . . . ,' Claire said.

'Do you really think I'm having an affair?' Jason said. 'Do you really think I'm that kind of lowlife? That kind of skunk?'

'It's dark upstairs,' she said. 'Pitch-black. What was I supposed to think?'

'You think I'm a cheating scum. Like your father! Come on, we're leaving.'

'No.'

'We're leaving. I'll get our coats.'

Claire sat down on the bottom step and held her burning face. In the other room, the music was getting louder, couples were probably dancing, and Siobhan had probably popped the cork on a bottle of vintage Moët, but Claire and Jason Crispin were leaving.

Jason threw her pashmina at her. 'Here.'

'But Siobhan . . .' Siobhan would really be mad at her now, for picking a fight at her party, for leaving early.

'Let's go,' Jason said.

They marched out of the house, slamming the door. When they were on the sidewalk, Carter stuck his head out.

'Jase, man, where are you going?'

'My wife's dragging me home.'

'Already? Dude, we still have food coming. I'm grilling sirloin . . .'

'Sorry, man,' Jason said. He climbed into the truck and Claire climbed into the truck and they sat there, cold and silent and seething.

Claire said, 'You stay.'

'No,' Jason said.

'Fine, then I'll stay.'

'No,' Jason said.

'You can't tell me what to do,' she said. 'You don't own me.' She kicked her high heel at the glove box. 'I hate this truck.' Jason said nothing, and this infuriated her. 'I think it is so stupid the

208

way you've named this truck Darth Vader. Ever considered what an imbecile it makes you seem like to drive a truck named Darth Vader?'

Jason deftly extracted the truck from their parallel parking place and gunned it for home. Claire braced herself with one hand against the dash. When they passed under a streetlight, Claire saw Jason's face. His mouth was a pinched line.

When they screeched into the driveway, Jason yanked the keys from the ignition. His eyes were filled with tears. He said, 'I call the truck Darth Vader because the kids like it. They think it's funny.'

Claire stared at him, defiant. She would not be a shrinking violet; she would not wilt. But Jason, in tears? This was new, this was awful, this was something she had done. She bowed her head. Jason was not an imbecile. He was not stupid, small-minded, backward, or limited. He was a man who liked to see his kids smile, who liked to hear squeals of terrified delight (Shea) when he revved the truck's engine in a menacing way. And Jason was not a cheater. When Claire had seen Jason coming down the stairs with Julie Jackson, she had thought: *I know what that means.* She had seen herself. Claire was cheating, Claire was lying, Claire had had sex with Lock Dixon on the conference table in the Nantucket's Children boardroom – she'd had sex with Lock, countless times, in her own car, the Pilot, which she now did not allow Jason to ride in. Claire had projected her behavior onto Jason; she had splattered it all over him like paint.

Claire was the skunk.

The following morning, Claire woke up with the worst hangover of her life. It wasn't just the alcohol, although her head hammered with pain and her stomach squelched and she released foul gas that Jason certainly would have complained about, had he been in bed. But Jason's side of the bed was empty, smooth; it had never been slept in. He had spent the night in the guest room, which they had agreed never to do except in case of marital emergency, because J.D. and Ottilie were both old enough to construe what this meant, and neither Claire nor Jason wanted stories, true or false, about their sleeping arrangements leaving the house. So the fact that Jason had spent the night in the guest room indicated that matters were dire indeed. Claire had insulted him; she had called his love, and his character, into question, and what offense was worse than that? Once they were inside the house and once Pan had slipped away to her room, Claire tried to explain that she had been upset by her conversation with Siobhan and she'd been drinking her fourth or fifth glass of wine, and when she'd seen Jason and Julie coming down the stairs, she'd jumped to conclusions. She'd accused him, yes, but she was sorry and she begged him to take into consideration the circumstances.

The circumstances are, Jason had said, stumbling over his own soapbox, located six feet from the TV, remote control in hand, *that you suck.* He'd turned the set on and begun hunting for *Junkyard Wars*.

Claire, meanwhile, got a glass of water for herself and said, *Come to bed. I'll make it up to you.* She was not used to fighting with Jason. They had divided up their life into his territory and her territory; they ruled peacefully, side by side, and their common ground – the marriage – rarely came up as a topic of conversation the way it had tonight. Tonight, their marriage was the Gaza Strip. But even so, Claire was pretty sure she could win Jason over in the usual way.

No, Jason said.

You're turning down sex, again? she said.

I'm sleeping in the guest room, he said.

She had alienated her husband and she had alienated her best friend. The first had happened suddenly; the second had been taking place slowly, over the course of six months. Claire felt despicable; her heart was pumping out black blood, sludge, sewage.

She could barely lift her head off her pillow or move her feet to the floor.

Could she go back to six o'clock last night and start over? Could she go back to that lunch at the yacht club and politely decline, say to Lockhart Dixon, *Thank you so much for thinking of me, but I have to decline*? Could she simply stay in bed all day, as she used to in college, on any one of the mornings when she woke up full of hungover regret: she had done six tequila slammers, hooked up with a frat boy from URI whose last name she didn't know, and then stopped by Cumberland Farms at two in the morning and chowed two hot dogs with chili and onions – but at least back in those days, despite her regrettable behavior, she could sleep.

Now she heard Zack upstairs, crying. God only knew where the other kids were. It was Sunday, Pan's day off. Insult to injury.

Claire pulled on her yoga clothes, brushed her teeth, and climbed the stairs. Her head felt like a glass ball blown out too thin, one that was sure to shatter in the annealer. Zack was howling. J.D. was on the computer in the hallway playing the god-awful race car game – he was obsessed with it. Jason allowed it because the game wasn't violent. Wasn't violent but *was* so hypnotizing that J.D. didn't seem to hear his brother screaming in the other room.

'Do you not hear your poor brother?' Claire said.

'What do you want *me* to do about it?' J.D. said. 'He doesn't want me. He wants you.'

Claire felt like smacking him, but J.D. was unconsciously mimicking his father. It was *Jason* who spoke to Claire like she was his feebleminded servant, Jason who conveyed the preposterous idea that Claire was the only person in the family responsible for Zack – perhaps because she was the one who had almost killed him. Claire peered into the guest room. The bed was empty and made up.

'Have you seen Daddy this morning?' Claire asked.

'He went to work,' J.D. said.

211

'Work?'

'Deadline, he said.'

'Right, but it's Sunday. Day of rest.'

J.D. did not see fit to respond to this; he got sucked right back into his game.

'Where are your sisters?'

He did not answer this, either. Claire went into the baby's room and lifted Zack out of his crib. He was red-faced and nearly inconsolable, hiccupy, hysterical. He was the saddest baby Claire had ever seen, and even after she picked him up he bellowed and struggled for breath, perhaps because he sensed she was not really there.

Ottilie came out of her bedroom wearing her nightgown over her jeans. There had been one inexplicable morning when she'd asked to wear this exact ensemble to school.

'Come on down in a few minutes,' Claire said. 'I'm going to make breakfast.'

'I'm not hungry,' Ottilie announced.

'Doesn't matter,' Claire said. 'You have to eat.'

'I'm not hungry because Shea threw up in her bed and the smell made me lose my appetite.'

'Shea threw up in bed? No, she didn't.'

Ottilie nodded her head at the closed bathroom door. 'She's in there.'

Claire put her ear to the door. She heard Shea, gagging and spitting.

She knocked. 'Shea, honey, are you okay?'

Moaning.

'And it's all over her bed,' Ottilie said. 'And there's some on the rug. It smells disgusting.'

'Okay,' Claire said, thinking: Jason working (to spite her, to punish her), Pan's day off, one kid screaming, one kid puking, two kids aggressively unhelpful. Hurting head, heavy heart. No best

212

friend anymore, and lover in Tortola. It felt just, though; it felt right. Claire thought of Father Dominic. This was her penance.

Claire jimmied open the door to the bathroom. She rubbed Shea's back while Shea expelled the contents of her stomach into the toilet. (And Ottilie was correct, it did smell disgusting. It made Claire want to vomit herself; all those mini crab cakes churned in her stomach.)

'Any idea what it was, honey? Did you eat too much candy last night? Or too much greasy popcorn?'

'No,' Shea moaned.

No, which made Claire fear it was a virus that would mow down the family.

She stripped Shea of her pajamas and put her, naked, teeth brushed, into the bed in the guest room. The guest room linens were among Claire's most valuable possessions – crisp, white, about six thousand thread count, embroidered with sage green thread around the edges. There were ten pillows on the bed, including two foam slabs encased in European shams that were emblazoned with the letter C. The guest bed was an extravagance; it was fit for a Turkish pasha, and Shea was so delighted to be allowed to snuggle, naked, beneath the fine, smooth cotton and the green chenille blanket and the fluffy down comforter that she seemed to perk up immediately. Either that, or she was experiencing the imminent sense of wellness one felt after vomiting. Claire hoped, prayed, that Shea would not vomit on the sheets. On the guest room nightstand was a glass pitcher and cup for water, which Claire filled in the bathroom. She set it down for Shea.

'Don't drink too much right away, okay, honey?'

'Okay.'

'And if you feel sick, you have to promise me you'll run to the bathroom.'

'I promise.'

Claire looked at her daughter. Her red hair was damp and matted

213

and her round cheeks were flushed pink. Only her slender torso and two toothpicky (but deceptively strong) arms were visible above the bed's fluff. Shea was a miracle, Claire thought, and her eyes filled with tears. All of her children were miracles, especially the one whimpering in her arms.

'I love you,' she told Shea.

'I know that,' Shea said, unaware of or unimpressed by Claire's gush of emotion. 'Can I watch TV?'

Yes, there was a TV in the guest room, hidden in a cabinet opposite the pencil-post bed. With so many amenities for guests, it was amazing they didn't have more visitors (the idea of four kids frightened many off). But Matthew would stay in this room in August. Claire really did not want Shea to throw up on the million-dollar sheets. She went to the linen closet and pulled out a bucket, placed it by Shea's bed.

'Just in case,' she said.

A note from Jason on the kitchen counter said, *Working*. Claire poured herself coffee, then a glass of water, and she took three Advil. It was a beautiful day outside, sunny, springtime; they only got two or three days like this, and they should be taking advantage of it. Picnic at Great Point, a walk around Squam Swamp, something outside, wholesome, as a family.

She hugged Zack, kissed his eyelids, his nose. 'I love you,' she said. 'Can I put you in your high chair, please? So I can get breakfast?'

He clung to her. He would not be set down. It was impossible to deal with frying bacon, mixing up pancake batter, or stirring chocolate powder into milk when she didn't have hands. She poured J.D. and Ottilie bowls of cereal and then called upstairs for them to come down. She tried to interest Zack in a banana, but he just stared at it.

'Banana,' she said. 'You eat it.' She took a bite, then regretted it. 'See?'

Claire eyed the phone. Should she call Jason on his cell and try apologizing again? Should she call Siobhan? It wasn't even seven-thirty yet, and unlike Claire's kids, Liam and Aidan had been known to sleep until noon on the weekends, so no, she couldn't call Siobhan. (And what would she say when she did call? Should she promise to call Edward and deal with the catering issue? She couldn't! She had delegated the catering to Edward, he and his committee had made a decision, and now Claire's hands were tied.) The other, more substantive issue rested like a boulder between them. Claire hadn't told her about Lock; Claire wasn't going to tell her about Lock.

Claire called up to J.D. and Ottilie again – she could hear the goddamned Doppler effect of the race car game – but she knew they wouldn't come down, and when they did come down and found cold cereal, they would complain. So forget it. Breakfast was a lost cause.

She slipped into the home office, Zack heavy against her chest, and switched on the computer.

'Computer,' she said, pointing to the screen.

Lock was due home in the morning. Finally, finally. There was no way he had expended the psychic energy on her that she had on him. She was angry at herself, but helpless, too. She couldn't control her thoughts, and as had been demonstrated last night, she could only marginally control her words and actions, and they all led back to him.

She opened her e-mail. There was the ill-fated message from Edward, copied to Isabelle and Lauren van Aln and the two women from New York who were also on the catering committee. There was no e-mail from Lock.

Claire squeezed Zack, kissed his hair. Upstairs, she heard Shea retching.

She had never felt so lonely in all her life.

*   *   *

She fell asleep across her bed with Zack next to her, which was, she realized when she woke up, a precious gift, despite the fact that she had left the other three children – one of them sick – unparented. She checked the clock: it was nearly ten. There were no sounds from upstairs, which alarmed her. Better she should hear the zooming of the godforsaken race car game or Shea retching, if only to know the kids were still alive. She poked her head into the kitchen. Everything was just as it had been – Jason's infuriating note, two uneaten bowls of Cheerios. She tried to feed a few Cheerios to Zack, who had resumed his position on her shoulder – she was a pirate, he was her squawking parrot – but he clamped his mouth shut.

Upstairs, the computer was abandoned, J.D.'s room empty (bed unmade, pajamas in a pile on the floor instead of in the hamper), and the girls' room empty and reeking. Claire had forgotten to strip the bed of the vomited-upon sheets. She, the Laundry Queen, had forgotten the second most important thing, after getting Shea situated. Now the room smelled sour and vile, the odor made worse by the fact that the day was warm and the girls' windows closed.

But first, the children. The door to the guest room was shut tight and there was no noise leaking from within, not even the muted babble of the Cartoon Network (Claire hated it and would only allow it in her weakest moments). Claire eased the door open, resolved that what she would find inside would not be to her liking – and there she found Shea, asleep upright against the unforgiving bolster of the C pillows, and at the foot of the bed, Ottilie and J.D., quietly drawing. It was adorable, really – when was the last time Claire had seen the two of them doing quiet, productive work together? It had been years. J.D. was sketching with a set of sharp pencils. He was drawing houses; he wanted to be an architect. Ottilie was coloring with a set of special markers that Claire had ordered from a catalog. When Claire entered, the kids looked up and smiled shyly, knowing that although they hadn't eaten a bite of breakfast, there was no way she could be anything

216

but happy with them. They were doing creative work *and* keeping watch over their sick sister. Model children, two more miracles, or so Claire would have thought had her eyes not landed swiftly on Ottilie's special, ordered-from-a-catalog fuchsia marker, which had the cap off and was bleeding ink, in a perfect circle, onto the precious white duvet cover.

The duvet cover was ruined. It was such a stupid thing, in comparison with everything else, but it was the thing that made Claire's throat tighten; it was the thing that nearly made her cry.

'Come down to breakfast,' she sniffled.

At ten thirty, the phone rang. Claire was upstairs trying to strip the vomity sheets off the bed with Zack clinging to her neck, and the sound of the phone took her by surprise. She zipped downstairs to get it. *Siobhan,* she thought, and her heart lightened. Or Jason. Or . . . Lock. But no, it was Sunday, he would never in a million years call her house on a Sunday.

The called ID said, *Unknown Number.* Telemarketer, she thought, her heart sinking. Zack started to bang his head against her breastbone and cry. It was not a good time to take a call. But Claire was grateful that anyone wanted to talk to her, even a salesperson. She picked up the phone.

'Hello?'

'Claire?'

It was a man. It was Lock? It was not Lock, but the voice was as familiar as Lock's voice. It was ringing the same bells in her head.

'Yes?' she said.

'It's me.'

She paused, then said tentatively, 'Me who?'

'Matthew.'

'Oh,' she said, astonished. *Matthew?* Really, it was Matthew? 'Oh, God, I can't believe it.'

'You got my message?' he said. 'Back in . . . ?'

'October. Yes, I got it.'

'I'm home now,' he said. 'Well, not home home, but in California.'

Zack was crying. Claire couldn't hear Matthew. She said, 'Can you hang on a second?'

'Is this a bad time?'

'No!' she said. 'No, God, no.' The voice all of a sudden made sense; it clicked, that famous voice. It had been so long. 'I have to talk to you. I mean, I need a friend, and all of my other friends, and my husband, for that matter – well, I've pissed them off. I'm pretty much persona non grata around here.'

'That makes two of us,' he said.

'Hold on one second,' she said.

She set the phone down and tried to shush Zack, but he was in a full-blown tizzy; there was nothing she could do with him. But she wanted to talk to Matthew; they had known and loved each other long before Jason or Siobhan or Lock had come into her life, and there was a reason he was calling now, this morning. It was a sign; it was what she needed.

She buckled. She had no choice. She knocked on Pan's bedroom door.

Pan opened the door a crack. She was wearing a gray athletic shirt and black panties and her hair was in her face. She had been asleep.

'I am so, so sorry,' Claire said. 'But can you please, please hold him for ten minutes? I have to take a very important phone call.'

Pan did not respond, and Claire thought maybe she was sleepwalking. Zack lunged for her, and Pan reached out instinctively, took Zack, and shut the door.

'Thank you!' Claire said to the closed door. 'Thanks, Pan! Ten minutes!'

She hurried back to the phone. 'Are you still there?'

'I'm here.'

'Thank God,' Claire said. She moved outside and settled on the top step of the deck, where she sat in the sun. She was warm, outside, for the first time in months. 'Thank God you called me.'

'Tell me what's happening,' Matthew said. 'Tell me everything.'

Only then did Claire cry. Max West was a rock star, yes. He had played for the sultan of Brunei, the Dalai Lama, an amphitheater full of Buddhist monks. He had won Grammys and met presidents. But he was her childhood, her adolescence; he was a part of her, he was who she used to be, and he was who she still was, somewhere deep inside. Back when they were friends, before they were lovers, he would come to her house on Saturday mornings and help her with her chores: dusting and vacuuming the front of the house. Before he had his growth spurt, he would stand on top of the vacuum, and Claire would push him around the living room. He showed up, one time, in the middle of the night and found Claire asleep with her hair wrapped in treated paper to straighten it, and they both laughed until they nearly wet their pants. His junior year, he drove a 1972 yellow Volkswagen Bug that had no turn signals and no ignition, and even in February when it was fifteen below zero, he had to crank down his windows and stick his arm out so that oncoming traffic would know he was turning. He had to run alongside that car to get it started, and Claire was right there with him, running, pushing, hopping into the passenger side. He worked as a busboy one summer at a seafood restaurant on the boardwalk, and Claire would meet him after his shift, and once in a while he would pull lobster tails from behind his back. *They were extras. A gift from the cook.* They used to eat the lobsters with their bare hands in the dunes, looking at the black ocean. On those nights of the pilfered lobsters, the breeze in her face and Matthew's bare leg knocking against hers and the hour growing so late that the lights of the boardwalk were shutting down behind them, she felt something rare. She thought to herself: *I never want my life to change.*

But change it did.

'I'm okay,' Claire sobbed. How had she gotten here? So far

away from that dune in Wildwood. She lived somewhere else now, and she had four children and a husband and a career and a house and a best friend and a lover and this unwieldy commitment that was causing her so much angst – but the gala was also bringing Matthew back to her, and along with Matthew, these memories. They gave her strength, if only because they were reminding her of who she was at her core. But this second, she was like Zack; she couldn't stop crying, despite the sunshine. 'You talk first. You tell me.'

'I'm drinking again,' Matthew said. 'I'm drunk now.'

'Ohhhhhhh,' Claire said, through a blockage of teary snot in her nose. 'Oh no.'

'Yes,' he said. 'I was away for months, on tour. I was in Asia – remote Indonesia, far-flung islands with dragons – and I was in wildest Borneo, where there are still cannibals. It was a freak show. I thought I could handle it. But then my sponsor got sick and left me on top of a volcano in Flores, where the lakes were pink, purple, and turquoise because of mineral deposits. The lakes were mind-blowing, they were like something Disney came up with, but they were *real* – and then my sponsor, Jerry, Christian fellow, got really fucking sick, and I could tell you that that was when I lost my way, but the fact of the matter is, I lost my way well before that. I started drinking in the airplane bathroom before we even left LAX, and basically never stopped.'

'No.'

'Yes. When I came home to California, Bess divorced me. I let her down, she said. She wasn't willing to do it anymore. And I said, "You knew I was vulnerable. You should have come with me."'

'Yes. Why didn't she?'

'She hates touring. Hates it. She's a homebody. She didn't want to leave the dogs.'

'Ahhhh,' Claire said, sniffling. 'The dogs.'

'So we're done. It's over. She's going to marry my accountant and have children. I'm giving her three million dollars, even though she claims she doesn't want it. And she doesn't want the house, even though she helped design it and decorate it in that Zennish Bess way, but I can't live in it – it's *her* house – so we're selling it. But she's there, for the time being, with the dogs – she's taking custody of the dogs, of course – and I'm renting a place in the hills, trying to keep myself to two gin and tonics per hour.'

'Oh, Matthew.'

'I know. This is the bottom. Everyone thought the bottom was when Savannah and I got caught coming out of the Beverly Hills Hotel . . .'

'That was pretty bad.'

'That was just a media blitz, except for the fact that the husband took a contract out on me with the Belarussian mob. They tried to kill me.'

'Well, no one's threatening to kill you now,' Claire said. 'So this is better.'

'It's worse,' he said. 'Because I am, very slowly, killing myself.'

'You have to stop,' Claire said.

'I can't stop.'

Right. She had seen it in the tabloids: in and out of rehab, where he was treated and deprogrammed, medicated and talked to, but as soon as he got out, as soon as he was left to his own devices, he sought the very thing he was trying to stay away from. Claire understood it now, better than she ever had before, because she was addicted to Lock. She was unable to give him up, despite the fact that staying with him was ruining her life.

'You can't stop,' she whispered.

'It's a disease,' he said.

Claire thought back to Labor Day weekend, 1986, a few nights before their senior year was to begin. There was a late-night party in an empty rental house, thrown by their friend E.K., whose mother was a real estate agent. There was beer; there was strip poker. Claire, for some reason, was the only girl at the party after midnight, or the only girl playing strip poker, and Matthew did not want her to take her clothes off, but that was the game, so she took them off, unconcerned, because E.K. and Jeffrey and Jonathan Cross and everyone else were her good buddies, buddies since nursery school – they were like brothers. Claire sat in the circle practically naked, feeling skinny and sexless – they were her brothers! – but Matthew got quietly upset, he drank and drank and drank, and when the sun came up and they all got dressed again, Claire had to carry Matthew to his doorstep. He was babbling, making no sense, saying, *You make me crazy. I love you. I'm crazy. You make me crazy, Claire Danner.*

Claire had considered leaving Matthew draped across his front porch, but she was afraid he would choke on his vomit and die the way they were always warning you of in health class, so she tapped on the screen door, which brought Sweet Jane Westfield outside with her cigarette and her cup of tea. Claire thought Jane would be mad – they had stayed out all night, drinking – but Matthew had four older siblings, all out of the house by that time, and Sweet Jane was used to teenage shenanigans. She took Matthew inside and waved good-bye to Claire, and as Claire wandered down the Westfields' walk, she heard Matthew say to his mother, *That girl of mine makes me crazy.*

When Claire thought of Labor Day weekend, 1986, she thought, *That was when it started.* Matthew's alcoholism. But that might have been her feeling pointlessly responsible again. *No boundaries!* The truth was, in the years since they'd both left Wildwood, Matthew had known excesses Claire couldn't even imagine.

'Tell me about you,' Matthew said. 'Tell me why you're sad. Never in a million years did I expect to call and find you sad. I never think of you as being sad. Remember when you told me that once you were out of your parents' house, your life was going to be perfect?'

'Ha!' Claire said. She *had* told Matthew that. She had promised herself she would leave Wildwood Crest with a clean slate. And her life had been happy; it had been blessed. Until . . . when?

When had the trouble started? With Zack's birth – or before that? On the night of Daphne's accident? Where would Claire start if she wanted to explain about Lock? What would she say? *I love him the way I used to love you, with heedless abandon, with pure emotion in that aching, longing, dangerous way.*

'I went to a party last night,' she said. 'And I drank, and I had all this *stuff* on my mind. Then I had a fight with my best friend, Siobhan – it was her party – and the fight left me feeling horrible, and then I saw Jason coming down the stairs with this other friend of ours, this woman who is a complete knockout, and I accused him of sleeping with her and . . . God, it's a mess. I made a mess. Jason's not speaking to me and Siobhan's not speaking to me and our au pair probably isn't speaking to me, and I have one of my little girls upstairs vomiting and I just feel . . . bad about myself. And confused. I'm looking at my life and I'm saying, *What happened? What am I doing? How did I get here?* Do you ever feel that way?'

'All the time,' Matthew said. 'It's fair to say I feel that way all the time.'

'But you're a big star,' Claire said. 'Nobody gets mad at you.'

'Bess is mad. She's beyond mad. She's finished. My band is mad. Terry and Alfonso – they're disappointed and mad, and they have every right to be. I'm letting them down. I'm a big star, but guess what; I'm also a seriously flawed person. I can write songs and sing and play the guitar, but that doesn't mean I don't have weak spots and bad days like every other human being. We all fail, Claire.'

She was crying again. 'I miss you,' she said.

'I miss you, too,' he said.

'I have to hang up, but I'm going to see you, right? In August? You'll stay here with us?'

'Yes,' he said.

'You have to stop drinking,' she said. 'Just stop for one hour. Do you want me to call Bruce?'

'He knows all about it,' Matthew said. 'He's on his way over here as we speak.'

'You have to be sober for my concert, Matthew,' she said. 'For me, okay?'

'For you,' he said. 'Okay.'

'Okay,' Claire said. She hung up the phone and spent a moment enjoying the sun on her arms. She was feeling pain about the past twenty-four hours and pain from twenty years earlier. She was as confused now as she'd been then; the world and the people in it perplexed her. She perplexed herself.

'Mommy?'

She went inside.

The vacation could have gone either way. Lock and Daphne were alone for eight days and seven nights; things could have gotten better between them, or worse. They had taken two other vacations alone together since Daphne's accident, one to Kauai, one to London, and neither had done the trick, but there was always the lingering hope that this time would be different. This time the sunshine or the pool or the amenities of the world-class resort would inspire the change Lock had been waiting for. Daphne would snap (!) back into her old self; she would break out of the spell cast on her by her head injuries and wake up, like Snow White or Sleeping Beauty. *Where have I been all this time?*

In the end, the vacation didn't go one way or the other. Things between them remained the same. Which meant what? The two days at Andover were torture. Heather didn't want them there. She asked them to meet her off-campus, at a vegetarian restaurant in town. There were other students in the restaurant, some of whom waved to Heather and murmured her name, but Heather did not introduce Lock or Daphne to anyone. Lock couldn't say he blamed Heather, because Daphne, especially in front of people she had never met, was unpredictable. She began by harassing their waitress about her hair, which was knotted in dreadlocks.

224

'A nice white girl like you,' Daphne said, only seconds after ordering a leek and Gruyère tart, 'sabotaging your looks with that awful hair. You don't wash it, is that it? What do your parents say?'

The waitress chose to ignore Daphne; she flushed as she scribbled down Lock's and Heather's orders, and then she fled from the table while Daphne, inexplicably, clucked like a chicken. Heather glowered, mortified.

'Mom,' she said. 'Quit it.'

'Quit what?' Daphne said. 'I just wonder what her parents think.'

Lock tried to serve as a buffer between his wife and his daughter; he tried to shield Heather from Daphne's attacks, but Daphne landed a few jabs anyway. Heather's calves were too muscular, Daphne said. *You look like a boy. You should think about quitting hockey next year.*

'But Mom,' Heather said, 'hockey is why I'm here.'

'You don't want to turn into a lesbian, do you?' Daphne said. 'I don't want you to turn into a lesbian.'

'All right,' Lock said. 'That's enough.'

Heather seemed happier when it was just her and Lock alone, after Daphne went back to the inn to 'rest.' Heather took Lock onto campus, introduced him to her art history teacher, showed him her dorm room, where he visited with Heather's roommate Désirée, whose parents had kindly taken Heather to Turks and Caicos. Désirée's parents also had a house on Martha's Vineyard, and Heather mentioned spending the summer there, and Lock said, 'Yes, or you and Désirée could spend the summer on Nantucket. We have plenty of room.' But Heather scowled at this, and Lock knew he would never be taken up on his offer. His daughter, at the tender age of fifteen, was gone, and this made him feel unspeakably angry at Daphne. But Daphne's manner was beyond her. What had the doctors said? It was like someone else was inside Daphne, manning the controls. Some evil green alien, the wife-and-mother invader. Lock could not

225

blame Heather for wanting to spend the summer on the Vineyard; if given the chance, he might say yes to it himself.

Before Lock returned to the inn to shower and change – they were going to a restaurant thirty miles away, at Heather's suggestion – Heather said, 'You and Mom don't have to worry about me. I'm going to be fine.'

Lock looked at his daughter – her dark hair, her wide, pretty mouth, so much like Daphne's, her strong legs, her slender, feminine feet in espadrilles – and he nearly wept. He had expected to hear those words when she was ready to embark on her honeymoon, or when she was setting off for college, perhaps – but not now, at the age of fifteen. He thought he'd experienced and expelled all his sadness about losing his daughter's confidence and her company, but he was wrong. He felt it freshly now.

He was so consumed with keeping things between Heather and Daphne on an even keel – it was exhausting – that he didn't have a second to think about Claire. That changed once Lock and Daphne pulled away from Phillips Academy, once they were alone together, with what seemed like an endless stretch of alone-together time in front of them. Daphne stared out the window silently for a while, then started on a diatribe about Heather. Her legs were the legs of an eighteen-year-old boy, a cross-country runner, with those ropy muscles. If she stayed at that school, she would most certainly become a lesbian. They had to pull her out. She seemed so unhappy, anyway, didn't she? Positively morose. She hadn't smiled once the whole time they were there. And what to make of the vegetarianism? She had been raised on beef tenderloin! The school was to blame – so liberal, so forward-thinking, offering shameful alternatives to the way normal people lived. Had Lock happened to notice the hair on the girl who served them? Heather should move home. They could redecorate the basement, turn it into a hangout with an iPod station and the best speakers, a computer, a plasma TV, a refrigerator – full of hummus, if that was what she wanted!

Anything so she would come home! *She's so set on privacy and independence, we'll just promise her we'll never go down there.*

Lock was silent. The idea wasn't terrible. Lock wanted Heather home as much as Daphne did, but he knew it was never going to happen. In response to Lock's silence, Daphne started to cry, and Lock reached over for her hand, which she flung away in anger.

'We should have had more children,' she said. 'I can't believe I let you talk me out of it.'

It was pointless to remind her that after Heather was born, a cyst formed on one of Daphne's ovaries and she'd had both ovaries removed. Blame for the fact that Heather was an only child had, since the accident, fallen squarely onto Lock's shoulders.

At some point during the ride to the airport, Lock remembered Claire, although it would be inaccurate to say he'd forgotten her. Rather, he'd decided, out of fairness to Daphne and Heather, that he would do his best to contain his feelings for Claire. He would put them in a box – a small, gold treasure chest, as he envisioned it – and keep it closed and locked. However, as Daphne railed against him for first one offense, then another, Lock opened the box, just a crack – he pictured Claire driving to the grocery store, pulling a gather from her pot furnace, climbing into bed. In Lock's mind, she was alone, though in reality, he knew, this was never the case. More images flowed out of the box: He heard Claire's clogs on the stairs of the Elijah Baker House as he waited, two glasses of wine in hand, breath suspended, for her to pop her head around the corner. *Hey, you.* He thought about wiping away the tears that often appeared in the corners of her eyes after they made love. Claire cried for a variety of reasons: the sex was astonishing, the rush of emotion overwhelmed her, she hated to leave him, it hurt, physically, to rip herself away. And, too, there was guilt – about Jason, about Daphne, about the kids – and there was fear, fear of getting caught, fear of going to hell. Nearly every time they were together, they talked about stopping, about walking away in the name of a righteous life. But neither of them ever followed through.

It was cathartic to talk about but impossible to execute, leaving each other. They felt ecstatic, elated, anxious, guilt-ridden, despicable – but mostly, they felt alive. Each day was spring-loaded and tense with possibility – to see each other, to talk, to touch – and it was this emotion that was too intoxicating to give up.

The actual vacation, although parts of it were pleasant – the hot sun, the cool, clear blue water, the delicious food and drinks, the luxurious room, the attentive service – felt to Lock like a vacuum. It was an eight-day, seven-night tunnel of no Claire; it was something to be survived. He had promised Claire he would e-mail, and in fact, the resort had a business center he could have used at any time, but he felt that communicating with her – trying to put words to his emptiness and then subjecting himself to the added torture of awaiting a response – would be infinitely more painful than just putting his head down and enduring. He and Daphne spent long, silent hours by the pool, each of them reading, and while Daphne napped, Lock took walks on the beach, thinking not of Claire (always of Claire) but of what topics he could bring up at dinner that would not incite a verbal attack from Daphne. She did seem marginally better at the resort, though she found ways to insult the other guests (who were primarily British and therefore reserved and inclined to keep to themselves, especially when they heard Daphne lapse into her clucking). There were two evenings of intimacy and these were, perhaps, the most trying times for Lock. Sexually, Daphne was both aggressive and impossible to please. Lock, helped along by three rum punches, strove to remember Daphne as she used to be, before she took to assaulting his manhood at the same time that she was trying to excite him. It was during these intimate moments that Lock thought to himself, *I cannot stay married to this woman*. He would not be able to stand a lifetime of such sexual encounters, but he also knew he would never be able to cut Daphne loose, no matter how bad things got. There wasn't another man alive who would be willing to take Daphne on, and her parents had passed away, so what this

228

meant was that if Lock abandoned her, she would become Heather's lot, and Lock could not, would not, burden his daughter that way. He would stay with Daphne.

The best moments of the vacation were when Daphne would look up from her book, take a sip of her rum punch, and say, 'Thanks, babe' – this, the pet name that the two of them had used with each other, and with Heather, before the accident – 'for bringing me here. I'm having fun!'

The worst moment came at dinner on the final night. It was no surprise that Daphne had saved her poison spear for the final night; that was part of the torture: allowing Lock to believe that they'd made it – a whole week without overt hostility – and then sticking him in the final hour. Daphne was smarter, cleverer, and more cunning now than she had been before the accident.

Over a glass of very fine, pale, bubbling champagne, she said, 'I have a question for you.'

'Shoot.'

'Do you find Isabelle French attractive?'

Lock laughed, inadvertently spritzing some of his drink across the tablecloth. 'No,' he said.

'You're lying.'

'I am not lying.'

'Isabelle French is a beautiful woman. Anyone you asked would say so.'

'She's fine, nothing special. Other people may find her beautiful, but I don't particularly. I've known her a long time. Maybe I'm just used to how she looks. I don't notice it.'

'She's after you.'

'Don't be ridiculous, Daphne.'

'You heard what she did with Henry McGarvey at the Waldorf?'

'Of course.'

'If you touch her, I'll kill you.'

'I'm not going to touch her.'

'I mean it. I'll murder you in your sleep. Then I'll find a female judge who will let me off the hook.'

'Nothing is going on between me and Isabelle.'

'Really?' Daphne said. She tilted her head. Her eyes held a look of unusual clarity. 'Because I've noticed a change in you since you asked her to cochair the gala. You work late all the time now.'

'I've always worked late,' Lock said. 'It's the only time I get anything done. You know this. During the day, the phone rings off the hook.'

'Lock,' Daphne said. She leaned forward over her champagne flute. Another inch and she would topple it with her breasts. 'I am not a stupid woman.'

'No one thinks you are. Least of all, me.'

'And yet you're conducting an affair under my nose.'

Lock thought he might feel something at this declaration, but it fell into a pattern with Daphne's other rants: she started out with an 'innocent' question (did he find Isabelle French attractive?), then ramped up to a flat-out accusation. It was a little more troublesome in this instance because she happened to be partially correct. She sensed something.

'I am not having an affair with Isabelle French,' Lock said with conviction. 'And I do not like being accused of such on the last night of what has been a very pleasant vacation.'

Daphne looked amused. 'Tell me you love me.'

'I love you.'

'I've been thinking of hiring a private detective.'

'You have got to be kidding.'

She took a long sip of her drink – okay, now Lock's blood pressure was up a little bit – and then she said, 'Yes.'

He almost lashed out at her – she was infuriating, it was inconceivable that she was constantly unearthing new ways to rattle him. Would it never end? Would she ever level off? Would he ever truly be the fortress he thought he was, inured to her attacks? But she chuckled a little and turned her attention to the menu, and Lock let the stream of breath he had unconsciously been holding go, and thought, *Isabelle French. Jesus.*

When Lock arrived home from vacation, when he was finally, finally, *finally* back in the office, sorting through the neatly organized piles that Gavin had left on his desk, thoughts of Tortola and the hot sun and the cool water and the books he had read, and Daphne and her taunts of a private detective, all faded away. All Lock could think about was when he might see Claire.

How was your vacation? Gavin asked. Lock stared at him blankly, then said, *We had good weather.*

Lock called Claire's cell phone and said, quickly (even though he had prudently waited until Gavin left for the bank with a deposit), 'I'm back. Can you stop by later to pick up the . . . maybe seven o'clock?'

Daylight savings time had ended, though. Seven o'clock was too early – it was still light outside at seven. They had to stay in the office, hidden; they couldn't tool around in her car. Lock should push her back to eight, but he would never be able to wait that long.

So . . . Claire came at seven. Lock heard her running up the stairs, yes, running, and that echoed in his heart, his heart was running, God, only a few more seconds until . . .

He met her at the top of the stairs. He didn't even look at her, he didn't have to, he didn't care what she looked like, anyway – he just wanted her in his arms. He crushed her, and she was crying and he was struggling for air, overwhelmed as he was with love, relief, comfort, peace.

'That was too long,' he said. 'I'm sorry . . .'

'I nearly died without you,' she said. 'Everything went to pot . . .'

'I could barely breathe at times,' he said. 'I missed you so much.'

231

'Never go away again,' she said. 'Never leave me like that.'

'Okay,' he said. 'I won't.'

It was a rush, a torrent. The week following his return from Tortola he saw Claire four times. Four times! It was unprecedented, unsafe. But Lock told Daphne (truthfully), *You should see the work that stacked up on my desk while I was away.* And Jason had some kind of deadline at the end of the month and he was working even later than Claire stayed out. He was angry at her, anyway. They'd had an argument, and Jason was sleeping, alternately, in the guest room or on the sofa. Lock had heard about this, he'd heard about Edward and Siobhan (Siobhan wasn't speaking to Claire, either; they had not talked in almost seven days), and he'd heard about Zack's birthday and the encouraging news from the pediatrician. He and Claire had to catch up in bits and pieces because most of their time was spent holding each other, reassuring each other that they were really there. In a way it was the best week they'd ever had. Their emotions ran from rapture to delirium and back again; the despair of being apart was in their past. Guilt had been suspended, as had fear. Their first thoughts were not of being careful – twice, Lock had to keep Claire from embracing him in front of the twenty-paned window (the private detective, stupidly, haunted him). Their first thoughts were only of each other.

Gavin took advantage of the week Lock was away to steal, steal, steal, steal, steal. He skimmed off every check that came into the office, including a check for fifty thousand dollars from a prestigious women's shoe company in New York, which Isabelle French had enlisted to underwrite the gala. (He kept a thousand dollars for himself.) He had nearly ten thousand dollars in cash stowed away in the utensil drawer of his parents' kitchen. Gavin found taking money while Lock was gone almost too easy; he was able to cover his tracks, then double-check and triple-check that they were covered. It lacked the risk of skimming funds right under Lock's nose. It was almost more quickening to pilfer money from petty cash for his lunch (which he also did each day Lock was on vacation). Gavin was happy to see Lock return, not only because it put the fun back into his game, but because Gavin had missed his employer. Lock was a truly wonderful man – this had come into clearer focus after Lock had gone away. Gavin felt bad about deceiving him, but this guilt only added extra oomph to Gavin's treachery.

He fantasized all the time about getting caught. He had a favorite scenario in which he invited Lock and Daphne to his parents' house for dinner, and in an attempt to locate a serving fork or an extra dessert spoon, one of them opened the utensil drawer and discovered the money. And they said, *Where did you get all this money?*

Though they knew there could only be one place.

I am a thief. Gavin thought this all the time now. He had come around from considering it 'skimming.' Skimming was back when his cache was merely hundreds, but now that it was about to top five figures, it qualified as stealing. He was a thief. And clearly his mind had been ruined (as his mother had always feared) by movies and TV, because his self-image took on a more and more glamorous sheen. Instead of seeing himself as a rotten, dishonest brat who was freeloading off his parents and now taking important funds from little kids whose lives were infinitely more difficult than his had ever been, he put himself in a category with Brad Pitt in *Ocean's Eleven,* someone who disarmed elaborate security systems, cracked codes, slipped on velvet gloves.

There were fissures, however, cracks in his resolve, through which his panic escaped. He could not get caught! It wasn't that he had much to lose – the nitty, gritty facts were that if he got caught, he would have to move out of his parents' house, and he would lose his job and his three or four friends. But all of that was going into the rubbish bin, anyway. Once he had enough money (how much was enough? A hundred thousand? Could he actually take a hundred thousand and *not get caught?*), he was leaving. He was off to an island in Southeast Asia so remote it didn't even have a name (at least not one pronounceable to native speakers of English). It was important to Gavin, however, that he leave on his own terms – in glory, as it were. The people of Nantucket would learn he was a thief, but by then it would be too late. He would have vanished, never to be heard from again; he would have gotten away with it. It was imperative that Gavin get away with it – unlike the debacle at Kapp and Lehigh, where he'd had his hand slapped like a little boy, where his 'crime' had been categorized as naive and juvenile. It was important that he succeed in this one thing.

And, too, he was having fun. If he got caught, the fun would come to an abrupt halt.

One night, the week after Lock returned, Gavin experienced unprecedented panic. He was at dinner with Rosemary Pinkle, the recently widowed woman Gavin had befriended at the Episcopal church; they were both fans of the evensong service, and their friendship had grown to encompass monthly dinners out. These dinners sustained Gavin's altruistic side and reinforced his belief that he was not a complete loss in the human-kindness department. He listened to Rosemary's stories about her departed husband with careful attention; Rosemary and Clive Pinkle had traveled extensively and Rosemary's stories were fascinating. She did on occasion lapse into unexpected moments of melancholy – she shed tears, she broke down into sobs – at which point Gavin held her hand, hoping that should his father die first, there would be a young man in Chicago who would fill a similar role for his mother.

On the night in question, Rosemary was in high spirits. She was a gardener and heartened by the fine weather, and by the fact that the deer were staying away from her tulips. She and Gavin were eating at American Seasons, newly opened for the season, a further harbinger of summer. Just as Gavin was delving into his cream of sorrel soup, he was struck by a paralyzing thought. That afternoon at work, he had sent out a letter to the women's shoe company in New York, thanking them for their underwriting donation and confirming the 501 (c)(3) status of Nantucket's Children, making the donation tax-deductible. As Rosemary detailed to him how she had outsmarted the deer (she had sprinkled the mulch around the tulips with human hair, collected from a salon in town), Gavin questioned the amount he had typed in the letter. The check had been for $50,000; he had 'deposited' $50,000 and taken $1,000 as cash, making the net deposit $49,000. That number, $49,000, was the number that stuck in Gavin's mind – and he became more and more fearful as he pretended to eat his soup, and as he pretended to listen to Rosemary (the salon had been glad to get rid of the hair), that he had typed in $49,000 as the amount of the donation, instead of $50,000. The letter had been signed by Lock (who did not read it), stamped, and taken to the post office. However, if Gavin had indeed typed in $49,000 instead of $50,000, someone from the women's shoe company would call to inquire, and this would cause either Lock or Adams Fiske to look more closely into the matter.

Gavin tried, tried, *tried* to remember. He was hyperaware of every detail of his crime; he would have been paying attention when he wrote this letter, right? But that was the problem: he could not remember typing in the figure $50,000, and he did not remember double-checking it before he took it over to Lock's desk for a signature. Gavin did not remember typing $49,000, either, but this was the amount he subconsciously attached to the dona-tion. Gavin's heart was slamming in his chest. He was growing warm and he had to yank his tie free of his neck – it was strangling him – though of course he hated to do it, because there was noth-ing quite as distasteful as a man with a sloppy necktie. Gavin was positive now that if he had been working from his subconscious, if he wrote the letter on autopilot – which he must have, since he couldn't remember the most important detail of the letter – then he might have typed in $49,000 instead of $50,000. Lock did not read the letter because he never read the letters – they were all the same – and because Gavin had been looming over Lock's desk with barely concealed impatience. He wanted to get to the bank, he wanted a cigarette, and some of the letters Lock was signing had been waiting for twelve days. Lock had not noticed the amount. He was tired from his vacation, and if Gavin could put his two cents in, he seemed distracted, as if he had left his ability to focus back in Tortola. Plus, there was never a reason to check Gavin's work because Gavin never made mistakes. It was bound to happen sometime, though, and it had happened today. Gavin set his spoon on the plate resting under his soup bowl. He could not eat another bite.

Rosemary noticed this. In so many ways, she was like his mother – *Eat up, eat up!*

'Are you finished?' she said. 'Is it not good?'

'I don't feel well,' Gavin said. He could not get caught! Okay, say a representative from the women's shoe company *did* call. Chances were, Gavin would answer the phone. But what if the call came while Gavin was at lunch? What if the call came before Gavin got in in the morning or after he'd left in the evening? What if it came in while he was in the bathroom or on another call? Lock would answer! The sheer torture of waiting for that phone call would be enough to land Gavin in the funny farm.

The waitress came to clear his plate. Gavin said, 'It was very good. I just don't feel well.'

Rosemary leaned forward. She was attuned to people who didn't feel well. Her husband, Clive, had gone to bed early one night, complaining of heartburn, and had died in his sleep.

'Have some water,' she said.

The most crucial thing, the thing that was pressing with more and more urgency in his chest, and lower, in his bowels, was for him to go to the office and check the letter on his computer. Because what if he was mistaken? What if the amount *did* read $50,000? God, he would be so relieved! He would offer to pay for dinner, he would do more than offer: he would slip the waitress his credit card and ask her to run it without Rosemary's knowledge. Rosemary would be miffed (she always paid for dinner; in this, she was also like Gavin's mother), but she would be touched, too. He just had to excuse himself, dash to the office, check his computer, and race back. His heart sank; that would take too long. Rosemary would grow concerned, she would check on him in the bathroom or ask a male waiter to check on him, and he wouldn't be there – and how would he explain *that*? But staying here through his rack of lamb and then coffee and dessert was not an option.

He tugged at his tie some more, this time for effect. 'I hate to say this, but I think I have to go home.'

'Home?' Rosemary said.

'I think I'm going to be sick.'

'Oh, dear,' Rosemary said. 'You'd better go then, yes. Don't stay another second because of me . . .'

'I hate to walk out on you like this . . . ,' Gavin said.

'Go! I'll tell our waitress what's happened and settle the bill. Unless you want me to drive you home. Do you want me to drive you?'

'No!' Gavin said. He was hunched over, trying to convey the immediacy of his distress. 'I can drive. I'll just . . . I need to get home.'

'Go!' Rosemary said. 'I'll call in a little while, to check on you?'

He kissed her cheek. 'You're a doll. I'm so sorry to – '

'Go,' Rosemary said.

He humped through town, head down, pulling hasty, nervous drags off a cigarette, muttering to himself, praying this was all a mistake, a bad suspicion. Did all criminals suffer from such paranoia? They must! Forty-nine thousand dollars. Yes, the more he thought about it, the more certain he was that he'd blown it. But maybe not. God, he couldn't stand it. He hurried.

He fumbled with his keys at the door. His hands were shaking. He was not particularly quiet; it had not occurred to him that Lock would still be in the office – it was nearly eight o'clock – but when Gavin was halfway up the stairs, he heard voices. Lock was here. Shit! Gavin considered turning around and leaving, but no, he couldn't: he had to check that letter tonight! So what could he tell Lock he was doing? Getting a phone number, maybe, or an e-mail address. Would that be plausible? As Gavin rifled through possibilities in his mind, he became alerted to the fact that something unusual was afoot in the office. There was bumping and banging, heavy breathing, a woman's voice. Gavin stopped where he was on the stairs and flattened himself against the wall, the way he'd seen people do in the movies. Who was in the office? He and Lock were the only ones who had keys. Gavin cocked his head, straining to hear. The noises seemed to be coming from the conference room. A woman talking, or crying, or moaning. She was saying Lock's name. So Lock was here. A second later, Gavin heard Lock say, clear as a bell, 'Oh, Claire, Jesus!'

Okay, Gavin thought. Okay. He had walked in on something, a big-time something between Lock and Claire. Gavin felt like he was spinning. It just wasn't possible, was it? He had entertained the idea that Lock was hiding something – and an affair with Claire had crossed Gavin's mind, though he'd immediately dismissed it – but to have unearthed it now, like this, was hideous. He must leave. But Gavin was confused, both horrified and curious, like a rubbernecker at a traffic accident. He continued up the stairs, quietly, silently, velvet gloves, velvet slippers. He would peek, get visual confirmation, and then beat it.

He crept to the top of the stairs, at which point he heard, very distinctly, the sound of Claire crying. He peered around the corner into the conference room. There they were. What Gavin saw was Lock's back – he wore only his yellow dress shirt and a pair of boxers. His pants were in a pile a few feet away. He was standing at the conference table. Claire was sitting on the table with her bare legs wrapped around Lock's back and her head buried in his chest. She was crying; he was shushing her.

Okay, Gavin thought. Enough. Too much. He was leaving! He tiptoed like mad down the stairs; he could not wait to get outside. Carefully, he eased open the door (it was telling, he thought, that they had locked it behind them). They had a system, a ritual; this was a *thing* that Gavin had uncovered, a real thing! He might have felt excited by this – amused, smug, self-satisfied (he *knew* Lock was hiding something!). He might have felt relieved that he wasn't the only person he knew gone wayward; he might also have recognized the value of his new knowledge, its bargaining power. But first what Gavin felt was shock, followed quickly by sadness, disappointment, disillusionment. It was like learning there was no Superman, no such thing as a true hero. Lock and Claire. Gavin shook his head as he barreled through the dark night toward his car (his interest in the letter, like that, had been zapped).

He couldn't trust anyone anymore.

CHAPTER EIGHT

SHE TELLS HER

Claire tried to make amends. With Jason, this meant apologies on the hour – apologies in person, messages on his voice mail, a note stuck to the steering wheel of his truck. It meant placing herself in servitude. She cooked his favorite things: fried chicken, pasta with sausage and basil, his mother's corned beef, chocolate chip cookies. She folded his T-shirts, she had a beer cracked when he walked in the door, and she put the kids to bed herself every night so that he could watch TV. Still, Jason slept in the guest room or on the sofa; still he spoke to her in a furious, clipped tone, but by the following weekend, the debacle of the party had been absorbed into the sponge of their life together. There was too much going on to dwell on it. Jason returned to their bed, he reached for Claire as though nothing had happened, and afterward, as she lay awake, she was amazed at what a marriage was able to sustain.

It could sustain horrible fights; it could sustain her, desperately in love with someone else.

Claire's relationship with Siobhan was another story. Claire had not spoken to Siobhan in ten days. Ten days! It was long enough to make Claire think that perhaps Siobhan was gone for good. Claire had tried everything; she had even called Edward Melior about the catering bid.

Edward, who was always charming, was decidedly curt and businesslike on the phone. This might have been a reaction to Claire's strident tone (which she had promised herself she wouldn't take, but she had a hard time suppressing it).

'Edward? Claire Crispin. I heard you picked a caterer.'

'Yes . . .'

'I heard you picked À La Table.'

'Yes, we – '

'Unfortunately, Genevieve told Siobhan . . .'

'Yes, I know all about it.'

'It would have been a good idea to have called Siobhan right away, you know. So she didn't have to hear it on the street.'

'I did call. I left her a message on her office phone.'

'You did?'

'I did.'

'She doesn't check the office phone in the winter,' Claire said. 'You know that.'

'I don't know that. It was the number she put on the bid.'

'You could have tried to reach her at home.'

'I didn't feel comfortable doing that, Claire. For obvious reasons.'

'I'm the event cochair, Edward. You could have called *me* and told *me* about your decision. Then I could have called Siobhan and smoothed things over.' Claire paused. 'In fact, I have to say, I'm a little surprised that you didn't call me, you know, to check with me, before you handed Genevieve the golden apple.'

'It sounds suspiciously like you're pulling rank on me, Claire,' Edward said. 'Are you? Because I was under the impression that when you asked me to spearhead the catering, you meant that my committee and I were to meet, review the bids, and choose a caterer. It sounds as if what you actually meant was that I, as the head of the catering committee, should have acted more like a cardboard cutout while you, the cochair, picked the caterer that you wanted. And everyone knows you wanted Siobhan.'

'Of course I did, Edward.'

'Genevieve came in nearly forty-dollars-a-head under. Do you get it? We saved almost forty grand by going with À La Table.'

'I'm sure Siobhan would have come down in her price if we talked to her about it,' Claire said. 'The thing about using Island Fare is that you know you're getting a great product.'

'I don't like where this conversation is headed,' Edward said.

'Fine. It doesn't matter now, anyway. What's done is done. The real reason I'm calling is that I'd like you to call Siobhan and apologize.'

This was met with hearty laughter. 'For the record, Claire, I did contact you when the committee made a decision. I sent both you and Isabelle an e-mail. Isabelle got right back to me.'

'I'd really appreciate it if you – '

'Good-bye, Claire.'

There was no point in taking the problem to Lock or Adams, because Edward was right: he was put in charge of catering, it was his job to pick a caterer, he had a fiduciary responsibility to Nantucket's Children to take the best menu plan at the lowest price, and in this case, that bid was from À La Table. Claire could not argue with saving forty thousand dollars for what would be a similar catering experience. Edward had e-mailed both Claire and Isabelle when the committee made their decision; the fact that the e-mail came in during the ten-day period when Lock was gone and Claire had put a moratorium on checking her e-mail could not be held against Edward. Isabelle had gotten back to him within fifteen minutes. Claire had been copied on that e-mail as well. It said, simply: *Fine. Fully trust the committee's judgment.* Edward said he left Siobhan a message on her office phone, the phone number on the bid. This was reasonable. The fact that Siobhan had bumped into Genevieve at the farm market and Genevieve had chosen to gloat was just bad luck. That Claire had asked Edward to apologize to Siobhan was perhaps out of bounds, but Siobhan was her best friend and Claire desperately wanted to make things right. She had no boundaries.

Claire left messages on Siobhan and Carter's home phone, and she left messages on Siobhan's cell phone, both simple (*I'm sorry. Call me*) and more elaborate (there were two messages, left in tandem, that documented Claire's phone conversation with Edward). Siobhan did not answer; Siobhan did not return the calls. Claire finally stopped by Siobhan and Carter's house on Saturday morning, a week after the party. Liam answered the door and told Claire, with a straight face, that his mother was upstairs lying down. Claire considered sitting in her car across the street until Siobhan emerged, but that fell into the category of stalking, and knowing Siobhan, she'd call the police and get a restraining order.

The Irish were so damn stubborn! Siobhan was waiting for the one thing Claire was not willing to give her: a confession. *I am having an affair with Lockhart Dixon. The affair has been going on since September and I have been keeping it from you.* Claire saw Julie Jackson at pickup, and Julie gave her a weird (sympathetic? angry?) look. Claire smiled and waved as though everything were fine, but inwardly she groaned, praying that the substance of her and Jason's fight had not made its way around the party. How mortifying! They should put their house on the market now.

As Siobhan's silence entered its second week, Claire gave up. She even saw Siobhan's car outside the skating rink – Siobhan was watching Liam's or Aidan's hockey practice, so she was a sitting duck – but Claire didn't bother stopping. Claire had been ostracized on the playground as a child just like everybody else; she knew that she would not remain on the outs forever. She had lost her best friend, but so had Siobhan. Siobhan would come around eventually – this was what Jason said on the subject. He was barely speaking to Claire himself, but he had enough mercy to tell her this: if it went on much longer, he would call Carter and set up a family meeting, an airing of grievances. This sounded like something he'd learned from watching *The Sopranos,* but Claire appreciated his willingness to intervene if need be.

Claire consumed herself with Lock – four times in one week, five times in nine days. If he was the reason her life was going down the tubes, then she wanted, at least, to be with him. In the hot shop, she worked crazily on what she now thought of as the g.d. chandelier. She spent all day Monday and all day Tuesday trying to pull out a second arm, eight hours of work, 163 tries. She was rewarded with not one but two arms that made it into the annealer. Claire wasn't sure at first, but when she held them up to the sublime sphere of the body, she saw that they fell perfectly, better than perfectly; they dripped and twisted like the trajectory of a flower petal falling to the ground, like a happy or peaceful thought flowing from the mind to the page. Claire thought, *This g.d. chandelier is going to be the most gorgeous thing I've ever done.* Elsa, of Transom, had called again, asking for two dozen of the *Jungle Series* vases, and although the vases would have been easier, not to mention good money, Claire turned her down. *I don't have time right now.* Claire was cheating on Jason with Lock; she was cheating on her career with the chandelier; she was cheating on her *life* with the gala.

To: cdc@nantucket.net
From: isafrench@nyc.rr.com
Sent: April 29, 2008, 11:01 A.M.
Subject: Seating

Dear Claire,

Just to give you the heads up, I have called Lock and purchased a $25,000 table for the gala. I feel it's important that, as cochairs, we support the gala in the biggest way possible, and one way we can do that is by purchasing the most expensive tickets. I noticed, from looking at the list of tickets sold last year and the year before, that you and your husband bought $1,000 tickets and sat in the back. You will understand, no doubt, the importance of sitting up front this year – we can take tables side by side – in the $25,000 section. I just buy the table myself and invite people to sit with me. (It's expected, in turn, that they will make a large donation to the cause.) However, it is perfectly acceptable to ask the people sitting at your table to pay for their seats, which is what you may prefer to do. I have purchased my table now because summer is nearly upon us and the time has come to *start selling tickets* and it's always better/easier to do this when one has bought tickets oneself.

Thx!
Isabelle

Claire stared at the computer screen, dumbfounded.

That night, she had nothing to make for dinner, so she threw eggs into the skillet with chopped-up deli ham, shredded cheddar, half-and-half, chives, and halved cherry tomatoes, and she served this with buttered wheat toast. Jason regarded his plate with disbelief and said, 'What's this?'

She said, 'We didn't have anything else in the house and I didn't have time to go to the store.'

Jason said, 'Why didn't you call for pizza? I could have stopped on my way home and picked it up.'

At the mention of pizza, the kids started to clamor, even Zack, who didn't know what pizza was.

Claire stood up from the table and glared at Jason. 'Fine,' she said. 'Get pizza.'

*   *   *

That night, as Jason climbed into bed, he said, 'Do you want me to call Carter tomorrow so you can settle this thing with Siobhan?'

Claire reread the e-mail in the morning and found it just as egregious. She had cashed in a once-in-a-lifetime favor and gotten Max West to play for free, she had spent a month of Sundays in the hot shop, working on the g.d. chandelier – and now, *now,* Isabelle had basically set forth a mandate that Claire cough up *$25,000* for the concert. Claire got it: hard work and favors were one thing, but when it came down to it, one's contributions were measured in terms of cold, hard cash.

Twenty-five thousand dollars: it felt like a dare.

It was the first week of May, and every day had brought a cold, steely rain. This was comforting. Claire retreated to the hot shop and blew out a pair of vases; she was too aghast and distracted to work on the g.d. chandelier. The awful thing was, she could see Isabelle's point. Claire had agreed to be cochair, she had taken on that responsibility, and it would be naive of her not to understand that part of the responsibility was fiscal. But Claire could not swing it. Two tickets at $2,500 was $5,000; this would be an *extreme stretch* for them. (It would have been more palatable had Claire been producing income over the past four months with a paying commission, instead of slaving over the g.d. chandelier.) To take an entire table at $25,000 was out of the question, for a number of reasons. Let's say Claire paid for the table up front and then asked the people sitting with her to kick in for their tickets. She would (a) never have the guts to ask for the money and (b) never find anyone she was friends (or even acquaintances) with who would agree to pay that much, even if she were gutsy enough to ask. She was offended that Isabelle had checked on her past ticket purchases. Claire and Jason had not sat in the 'back' – they had sat in the middle, and last year they sat with Adams and Heidi Fiske. Adams Fiske, president of the board of directors, hadn't even bought a $2,500 ticket. He was back in $1,000-a-head land with all the other normal people.

246

Claire could not think of anyone she knew who would be willing to cough up $2,500 for their seat. Certainly not Carter and Siobhan (it was safe to say at this point that they wouldn't go at all), not Brent and Julie Jackson, not Tessa Kline, not Amie and Ted Trimble, not Delaney and Christo Kitt. Possibly Edward Melior – but Claire had just alienated him, so no. Possibly the clients of Jason's who owned the house in Wauwinet, but did Claire really want to sit – on one of the most important and glamorous nights of her life – with clients whom she barely knew? She did not. She wanted to be with her friends. So . . . she would not be taking a $25,000 table.

But to say so would be to say a bunch of other things as well. She would be saying that she didn't have the same means as Isabelle French, which would be a blow to her pride. But why? Claire had grown up in Wildwood Crest, New Jersey, where her family had been decidedly middle class, the middlest of middle class. In comparison, she and Jason lived the life of royalty – the house, their businesses, the opportunities for their four kids, the au pair. They had every material thing they needed and many they wanted, but they did not have $25,000 to spend on one evening out. No one Claire knew did – and that was perhaps the dicier issue: in not taking a $25,000 table, Claire felt she was cementing the differences between summer people and locals. Isabelle French and her compatriots from the city had more money than Claire and the wonderful people who shared her foxhole. They had a lot more money – why pretend it wasn't true? They were all donating to the cause – raising money for the hardworking families of Nantucket – just in varying degrees.

The more Claire thought about it, the more angry she became at Isabelle for even asking her to make such a colossal financial commitment. Claire became convinced that this was more of Isabelle's passive-aggressive behavior. Isabelle had asked Claire, knowing that Claire would either say she didn't have the money (which would underscore their class differences or, worse, make it seem as though Claire wasn't as gung-ho or dedicated to the cause as

247

Isabelle) or Claire would come up with the money and cut the legs out from under her family financially.

Horrible woman! Claire ranted.

She could not take this problem to Jason. He would see it only one way because he was a man, because he had no emotional attachments to money other than happiness (or relief) about what it could buy you. He would say, *If we had twenty-five thousand dollars to spend on a table up front at the gala, we would be buying a boat instead.*

So in the end, Claire called Lock. She was hesitant about doing so, because more and more lately, it felt like her problems were becoming ones that only Lock could solve. Or only Lock could understand. Or Claire had been brainwashed, somehow, because she believed in his authority (*There is no hell*), and hence he was the only person she wanted to take her problems to, despite her concern that he would soon see her as a person who constantly had problems that needed to be fixed. But this thing, Isabelle, the money, the gala: this fell squarely under his umbrella of expertise.

She called him at work. Gavin answered the phone, and his tone with her was different. Usually smug and impatient, he was now almost friendly. ('Claire! Hello!') He sounded like there was no one else he would rather have on the end of his telephone ('How *are* you?'); he treated Claire like a long-lost friend. *Lock stepped away from his desk, but let me find him. Hold on, here he is – Lock, it's Claire!* Weird.

'Hello?' Lock said. His voice was friendly but not intimate. Claire yearned for intimate, for a purr or a growl or a password or a nickname just for her – but this was impossible. Always, she got friendly, solicitous.

'I love you,' she said.

He chuckled. 'Glad to hear that,' he said.

'I just got an e-mail from Isabelle.'

'Uh-oh.'

'She bought a twenty-five-thousand-dollar table. She wants me to buy a twenty-five-thousand-dollar table. In the name of leading by example. As cochairs.'

'Right,' Lock said. He sounded uncomfortable.

'Do you see the impossible position that puts me in?'

'I do.'

'Do you?' It was only as Claire had him on the other end of the phone that she wondered if he *would* get it. Lock was masquerading as a normal year-round islander, but in fact he was a millionaire. He made a donation every year that was in the mid-six figures; he could buy ten $25,000 tables and not blink an eye. This thought (which was sort of novel, because she never gave any play time to Lock's net worth: she didn't care, she would take him prince or pauper) was followed by another series of thoughts . . . about what Lock planned to do in regard to *his* gala tickets. He could, she thought for one fleeting instant, buy a $25,000 table, and she and Jason could pay him for two seats (she had reconciled herself to the fact that $5,000 was the least she was getting off the hook for), and Lock could fill the rest of the table himself. This had the added bonus of putting Lock and Claire at the same table (and with little or no effort, side by side). They could put Jason next to Daphne and her beautiful tits, and everyone would be happy.

'I do . . . ,' he said.

And at the same time, she asked him, 'What are you planning on doing? Where do you sit, usually? You and Daphne?'

'Oh,' he said. Now he sounded really uncomfortable. 'Well, when Isabelle called – to get her table, that is – she asked Daphne and me to sit at her table. And I said okay.'

'You said okay?'

'I didn't see any reason not to. I got the sense that Isabelle is insecure, because of her divorce, you know. She didn't ask me to join her so much as implore me.'

'So you and Daphne will sit with Isabelle.'

'Yes.'

'Okay.' And because further words eluded her, she said, 'Thanks!' Her voice was cheerful and plastic. What she thought as she said it was, *Thx!* She hung up and stared at the phone, speechless.

A few seconds later, the phone rang. And Claire thought, *Lock, calling back.* He'd stepped out of the office with his cell phone and was hiding out in Coal Alley, where he could talk more freely. She almost didn't pick up – she was more stymied by Lock's news than by Isabelle's e-mail – but she lacked the willpower to resist him.

'Hello?' she said.

'Hi,' Siobhan said. 'It's me.'

The house he was renting in the hills was a mission-style bungalow with stained glass and real Stickley furniture, a framed sketch by Frank Lloyd Wright hanging in the powder room, and a gold nugget, allegedly mined in 1851, nestled in a shadow box in the study. Max loved the house. It belonged to a real California family; the husband owned a chain of Tex-Mex restaurants across the state, and the wife composed musical scores and jingles for TV commercials. There were five children, from teenager to toddler, but they – the family – were in Shanghai for a year. The house was cozy, a refuge, a nest, and despite the fact that neither the house nor anything in it belonged to Max, he felt comfortable in it, safe, and free to drink to his heart's content.

Bess had asked him for only one thing: that he use his influence to speed the divorce along. Dragging it out, prolonging it, insisting on mediation or court appearances, would only make things more painful for both of them, she said. She wanted out, now; she wanted a clean break. There was no need for negotiations; the only thing she wanted was the dogs.

'I'll give you three million dollars,' Max had said during their last phone conversation.

Bess was silent and Max took this to mean that she was stunned by his generosity. But then she tsk-tsked him – she did have something of the schoolmarm about her – and said, 'Oh, Max, I don't want your money.'

'Just take it,' Max said. 'It comes without strings. Three million.'

'I don't want it. Don't send it. If a check comes, I'll rip it up.'

Was she bluffing? How did she expect to live without money? Bob Jones was Accountant to the Stars, but his well wasn't bottomless like Max's. How would Bess afford the trappings of her virtuous lifestyle – the bushels of organic vegetables, the comfortable-but-not-inexpensive Donald Pliner shoes?

'Just take the money, Bess.'

'I don't want it,' Bess said. Her voice was very firm. Had any other divorce in the history of Hollywood proceeded like this – with one party offering a large sum of money, unbidden, and the other party turning it down?

'Is it not enough?' Max said. 'You want five million?' Silence. 'Ten million?' Max knew himself to be worth about sixty million dollars (and of course, Bob Jones knew this, too). 'Fifteen?'

'I don't want any money from you, Max. Just the papers. Please.'

Bess didn't want his money because she thought it was cursed. It wasn't good enough; it wasn't the kind of money that would bring her happiness. She was rejecting him, Max West, alcoholic, drug addict – and she was rejecting his money.

The divorce papers came in the mail; Max tossed his copies in the trash with the Pottery Barn catalog and the circular from Whole Foods. *Sayonara,* he said. *Adiós. Adieu. Arrivederci. Bayartai.* He could say good-bye in forty languages – that was something. Max made a pot of coffee and called Bruce. Bruce came over, and together they drank the pot of coffee on the deck, barely exchanging a word (Max loved and valued Bruce for this reason). Then Bruce left and Max pulled out the Tanqueray, but he didn't pour himself a drink. He felt okay without a drink, and how weird was that? He thought, *I should get divorced every day.*

When the box came from his mother, however, it was a different story. His mother, Sweet Jane, was moving out of her house in Wildwood Crest after fifty years; she was moving to a posh retirement community in Cape May. Max was paying for the move, and he was paying for the posh retirement community, but Max's three older sisters and his older brother had volunteered to go to Wildwood Crest to orchestrate the move. Max was expected to pay for everything but not do anything. His mother, with the help of one of his sisters – Dolores, probably – had gone through every closet and drawer in the house. Some stuff went to the dump; some stuff went into boxes. All of Matthew Westfield's stuff went into boxes because as soon as news got around that Jane Westfield was moving out, a clot of people began loitering across the street, waiting for the garbage. Who knew what Max West's high school report card might go for on eBay? The handwritten lyrics to 'Stormy Eyes' – scribbled on a McDonald's napkin – could be sold to the Smithsonian or the Hard Rock Cafe. So Sweet Jane and Dolores packed up every last scrap from Matthew's adolescence and mailed it to him.

He opened the box, and the box smelled like Claire. He went to the kitchen for the Tanqueray, a glass, and ice, and he walked out into the backyard and picked three of the best-looking limes off the tree. He made himself a very tall drink. The box smelled like Claire – or what he remembered as Claire's smell, but was probably some perfume that teenage girls used to wear in 1986 – because it was stuffed with notes from Claire, hundreds of notes, notes that had been handwritten (perfumed!), folded, and passed to him in the hallway, in class, at lunch, in the band room (where he hung out, plucking his guitar), or in the art room (where she hung out, sketching or firing pottery).

He unfolded one such note, carefully, because the paper was

252

twenty years old and as soft as fabric. It said: '*How can I tell you that I love you?*' The best song! *Everything Cat Stevens sings is so beautiful! You can sing like him – learn the song for me, please! I have a track meet against Avalon this* P.M. *but my dad is in A.C. tonight, so I'll be over late. Leave the door open!!! I love you xoxoxoxo*

Max took the whole drink in at once, not tasting anything except for the tang of fresh lime juice. Somewhere in the house was his . . . he stood up and meandered through the house, the first drink sharpening his need for the next one. Where was his guitar? He had, at last count, 122 guitars, but really only one, his Peal, mahogany and maple with abalone inlay. It had been his first guitar, acquired when he was fifteen from a rich summer woman who had bought it for her son, who didn't want it; she had sold it to Matthew for a hundred dollars. Max always used the Peal to play any new song he wrote; it was, in some ways, the only instrument he could truly hear. The guitar fit into his arms the way he imagined his own child would.

He poured himself another drink and tried the song. *How can I tell you that I love you?* He and Claire had been crazy for Cat Stevens; they bought every album and played them again and again, and Matthew figured out the chords and memorized the lyrics. Cat Stevens was outré by then; he had converted to Islam and disappeared from the public eye, but this didn't matter. Matthew and Claire had discovered him together, unearthed him, dusted him off; the songs were their currency, their gold, their treasure.

How can I tell you that I love you? Claire, in her track shorts, her long legs, milky white, with freckles behind her knees. He loved to watch her stretching those legs up and over the hurdles, with her arm out, perfectly timed. She sprinted, too. She was on a relay team, second leg; she took the baton, she handed it off. Claire's mother would attend the track meets but spend the whole time with her hands over her face: *I can't watch!* And Bud Danner never showed up at all. Matthew was her cheering section. He was her family.

Another drink. Their senior year, Claire would sneak out of her house in the middle of the night and run all the way over to East Aster and tiptoe brazenly past Sweet Jane's bedroom, right into Matthew's room. She would shed her clothes and climb into his bed – he could remember it as if it had happened the night before. He would wake up and find Claire, naked and warm, on top of him. They were seventeen. It was as sublime as love gets.

He read through nearly forty notes – it took him the whole bottle of Tanqueray. And there was other stuff to ogle, too: his diploma; programs from the holiday concert, the spring concert, their senior banquet, their prom; pay stubs from Captain Vern's, where he bused tables for two dollars an hour; tokens for skeet ball on the boardwalk; a cracked 45 of Billy Squier's 'My Kinda Lover'; an Algebra II quiz on which he'd scored an 84 (if he took the quiz again now, he'd get every question wrong). There were song lyrics, too – stupid, wrong lyrics, and lyrics he'd rethought, rewritten, and turned into Top 40 hits. At the bottom of the box, encased in a large wax-paper envelope, were a mess of snapshots, but he couldn't look at them. He'd had too much to drink, he was too sad, and the pictures were all of Claire.

They had talked recently and Max thought he'd heard a crack in her voice, a place where he might climb back into her life. Was he deranged? He didn't know. He hadn't seen Claire in years and years; she would be a different person now, the mother of four little kids. It was silly, but he thought of her kids as his kids, even though he had never set eyes on them. He was drunk, delusional, but what he was realizing was that Claire Danner lived in his heart and always had; she was a part of him. They were connected by their shared history, by having grown up together and given each other their first attempt at love. He wasn't New Agey like Bess, and he didn't even really believe in God, much to his mother's dismay, but he did believe in connections between people. He had written all those early songs for Claire. She was all he knew; she had been there at the beginning. His subsequent relationships had all failed. He let women down – his first wife, Stacey, his second wife, Bess, and Savannah in between.

Could he go back to Claire? Would she have him? Would there be anything left?

He strummed the Peal. The Peal, like Claire, was his true instrument, the original. He felt a song brewing inside him, gathering like a storm. An old song, a new song.

If her mother had said it once, she'd said it fifty thousand times: *Be careful what you wish for.*

As a child, Siobhan had wanted a horse. They did, after all, live on a farm, which her father had inherited, but it was a mediocre piece of land that could only sustain turnips and mean chickens. When Siobhan begged for a horse, her mother said, *Be careful what you wish for. If we get you a horse, you'll never have a moment's rest. You'll have to carry out feed and water, you'll have to groom the horse and deal with its droppings, you'll have to give it exercise, which means riding the horse, Siobhan. It will make you sore like you've never been in your young life. A horse will run your father and me to the poorhouse faster than we're going already, and your brothers and sisters will hate you from envy. Wish for a horse all you want, Siobhan, but the worst thing that could happen is for that wish to come true.*

Another gem from her dismal Irish upbringing! And yet here were her mother's words ringing true again. Siobhan had wanted to know what was going on between Claire and Lock Dixon – she had meant to find out! She had threatened and accused and withheld the sound of her voice from Claire's ear for two full weeks.

Now they were sitting on the cold sand of the south shore, two uneaten sandwiches between them. It was chilly on the beach, but Claire had been adamant about the place. The two of them alone, outside, surrounded by landscape that was bigger than they were.

There's something I have to tell you, Claire said.

And Siobhan thought, *Yes! Out with it!*

I'm having an affair with Lock Dixon. I'm in love with him.

The horse, her mother, the turnips and chickens, the envy of her brothers and sisters. Be careful what you wish for. Siobhan heard Claire's words and saw the expression on her face – one of naked pain, as though Siobhan were twisting her arm behind her back. Siobhan filled immediately with regret. And shock and horror. It was true, the unthinkable was true. The betrayal was real and complete. A commandment had been broken, and it lay shattered at their feet. It had been broken by the only person whose goodness Siobhan had wholly believed in. Siobhan didn't know if she was more disappointed in Claire for the transgression, or in herself for making Claire admit to it.

I'm having an affair with Lock Dixon. I'm in love with him.

In love with him?

Siobhan felt revulsion at the back of her throat, a gag reflex. She was going to be sick. This had been her hair-trigger reaction to every piece of bad news her whole life: vomiting. Gross and mortifying, but true. She had vomited outside the church at her mother's funeral, even though her mother had been dying for months; she had vomited in her apartment for two hours after she had broken her engagement to Edward Melior. Claire was in love with Lock Dixon, and Siobhan was going to vomit right there onto the cold sand. It was the body's most basic rejection. Her spirit screaming, *No!*

She coughed into her hand. Okay.

This was not a film with actors, it was not one of the afternoon soap operas – her sleeping with him sleeping with her. These were real people in real life; people hurting other people. Claire hurting, for starters, Jason. Poor Jason! Siobhan would honestly have bet her life savings that she would never have uttered those words in her mind, because Jason was *not* 'poor Jason.' He was too much of a callous son of a bitch, absolutely impossible, as macho and

Marlboro as the male species came, Jason was. He had let his guard down a little bit when the baby was born. Siobhan had seen him weepy and quivery-lipped, but what had he turned around and done then? He had blamed the whole thing on Claire. *She shouldn't have been in the hot shop. She knew better.* Jason was a Neanderthal. Carter was the refined brother; he did things like mince, julienne, and sauté; he had an artist's eye, a delicate touch. Jason had tormented Carter about the cooking for most of their adult lives – Carter was gay, cooking was for pussies. Real men did . . . what? Pounded nails into wood. Yes, Siobhan had had her trouble with Jason, they had exchanged words, and he did not appear anywhere on her list of favorite people. But he was family, and as with her brothers and sisters – some of whom she truly detested – she would take his side against someone who was not blood any day of the week.

Poor Jason.

Siobhan coughed again. The back of her throat tickled relentlessly; her stomach roiled. There would be no hope for the sandwich. Siobhan shivered and collected her jacket around her. The sky was leaden and very low. It was hard to believe it was almost summer.

'So?' Claire said. 'What do you think?'

What to say? The truth? *I'm bloody horrified. I'm trying not to get sick.* Be careful what you wish for. *The kids – what about your beautiful kids?*

Claire started to cry. 'You hate me. You think I'm awful.'

Siobhan loathed sitting in judgment like this. It didn't suit her. *She* was supposed to be the wicked one, the imp, the fiend.

'How long?' Siobhan said.

'Since the fall.'

Siobhan gasped but hoped it wasn't audible. That long. Since the beginning, practically. Well, Siobhan had suspected something at Christmas. Something – but not this. *I'm in love with him.* This was not Claire giggling over the phone about the cute guy slinging her bags of rubbish into the back of a truck. This was a real situation. Love. Love? Claire was easily swayed, easily influenced; she let people in too close too soon; she loved with abandon, unconditionally; she cared about people, worried about them, took on their shit. It was in her blood, some heinous legacy dumped on her by her parents. Was it any wonder that Lock Dixon, a man with what Siobhan could only assume was a miserable existence – the damaged, schizo wife – had taken advantage of this and invaded?

'Say something!' Claire pleaded.

Siobhan dug her toes into the cold, crumbly sand. 'I don't know what to say.'

'Say you understand.'

'I don't understand. Make me understand.'

'You think I'm betraying Jason and the kids. But haven't you ever been so in love that *nothing else mattered?*' Claire grabbed Siobhan's hands and squeezed them, but they were numb and bloodless, two dry sponges. 'Haven't you ever felt like your heart was upside down?'

Had she? She rummaged: Carter? Edward? Michael O'Keefe, with those blue eyes, the blue black hair, the tall leather boots? He rode horses. That was why young Siobhan had wanted a horse! She had been fatally in love with Michael O'Keefe. Was that what Claire was talking about? Probably, yes, but Siobhan had been how old then, eleven? They were grown women now; they knew better!

'Are you going to leave Jason?' Siobhan asked.

'No.'

'Okay,' Siobhan said. 'So if you have no plans to leave Jason, then how do you see this progressing? . . .'

'I have no idea.'

'You have to stop, Claire.'

'You sound like Father Dominic.'

'I'm sure I do.'

'I can't stop. I've tried.'

'You have?'

'I try every day.'

'So are you just going to keep . . .'

'I really don't know.'

'Because eventually, it's going to come to a point where . . . or something will happen that . . .'

'You are my dearest friend in all the world,' Claire said, 'and I trust you with my life. But you can't tell anyone. Not your sisters back in Ireland, not Julie, not Carter . . .'

'Jesus, Claire, of course not.' Siobhan said this automatically, without thinking of how this secret, this insidious worm, was going to gnaw away at her. Could she keep this a secret? Siobhan pushed her glasses up her nose. Her lenses were smudged with salty condensation.

'I can't believe I told you.' Claire was crying again. 'I feel like I just set free the last remaining smallpox virus. I feel like I just handed you the weapon you're going to murder me with.'

There was a way Siobhan was supposed to be acting; there were things she was supposed to be saying – comforting, reassuring things – that were eluding her. She had wanted the truth, the truth she now had. She had wanted the air clear; she had wanted Claire back. Be careful what you wish for.

Siobhan coughed into her hand. Her mother was everywhere with her maxims. The Irish had words for each blasted occasion, and the words were always right. Her mother's hand always landed on her back, rubbing away the world, no matter how bad things got. *This too shall pass away, Siobhan, my pet. This too shall pass.*

Siobhan looked at her friend. Absolution was beyond her, but was comfort?

'Everything is going to be okay,' she said.

'You think?' Claire said.

CHAPTER NINE

SHE BLOWS IT

Unlike coastal New Jersey, where Claire grew up, which had a mild spring, Nantucket went from slate gray skies and thirty-mile-an-hour winds to full-blown summer. The change of season was apparent all over the island; it was as though someone had raised the curtain and the show had begun. There were people everywhere; there was traffic; there were lines at the Stop & Shop and the post office; the sidewalks of Main Street were congested with people drinking coffee, buying wildflowers off the back of the farm truck, talking on cell phones, walking dogs, pushing strollers. The restaurants were opening one by one, and this year, Claire and Jason were invited to all of the splashy opening parties because Claire was cochair of the gala, because she was high-profile now, because her name had been linked to Max West's in the newspaper, because Lock had somehow added her name to each and every invitation list – who knew why?

It was becoming nearly impossible to see Lock. There were people occupying the houses next to and across the street from the Elijah Baker House, there were people visiting the Greater Light garden at all times of day and night, and the police had started trawling even the most remote beaches. The board members of Nantucket's Children were all in residence, and they popped in and out of the office at unexpected times. Once, when Lock and Claire were in the conference room having quiet, fervent sex, there had been an insistent knock on the door below. It caused them to jump and separate, to furiously pull on their clothes and button, zip, straighten. Lock tiptoed to the twenty-paned window, which was open (for ventilation purposes, it had to be, and because it was such a stubborn old dinosaur, it would remain open until October). Down on the sidewalk was Libby Jenkins, cochair from the previous year's gala, with her husband and another couple. Libby had consumed some wine, perhaps, and her voice was a touch slurred as she said, 'Damn, it's locked. The office is to die for, I'm telling you, all the original plasterwork from eighteen fifty . . .' Libby and her group drifted off down the street, but Claire was left spooked. She and Lock held each other, breathing heavily, until a safe amount of time had passed and Claire felt okay to whisper, 'Jesus.'

'I know.'

'This isn't a good idea, coming here.'

'The door is locked.'

'I know, but what if we forget one day?'

'Believe me, I won't forget.'

Claire knew this to be true. Lock checked and double-checked the lock, then checked it again.

'But Gavin has a key. And so does Adams.'

'Yeah, but . . . ,' Lock murmured.

'I feel like we're going to get caught,' Claire said.

'We won't get caught,' Lock said. 'Trust me.'

This sounded like one of his edicts that could not be argued with – *There is no hell* – but for some reason it did not sit right with Claire. It sounded false and presumptuous.

'Tell me,' Lock said. 'What choice do we have?'

Claire rested her head against his chest. 'I don't know,' she said. 'We could take a break.'

'Take a break?' he said. 'You mean not meet? Not see each other?'

'No,' she said. 'God, no.' When Claire was alone, doing yoga, doing the dishes, when she was in her hot shop, and she prayed for strength, this seemed like the answer. Take a break. Cool things off. But when she was with Lock, when he was there next to her, when she heard his pained voice say, *Not see each other?* – it was unthinkable. 'We just have to be careful. Really careful.'

'Assiduous,' Lock said. 'Steadfast in our commitment to keeping this a secret.'

Claire filled with fresh guilt. She had shared the secret with Siobhan, but she had not told Lock this. He would never in a million years understand why she had done it. He might, quite possibly, feel angry and betrayed enough to end things. And so it was official: Claire was lying to everyone. Siobhan now knew the truth, but since the day Claire had told her at the beach, the topic hadn't come up again. Siobhan never alluded to it, even when she and Claire were alone. It was as though Siobhan were the one with the hole in her head, and the information had fallen out and vanished. This was a relief to Claire, but puzzling, too. Why did Siobhan not want to talk it to death? Was she actually respecting Claire's private life, or did she find it too distasteful, disturbing, disgusting, disquieting, to discuss? And if they weren't planning on discussing it at all, ever, then why had Claire bothered to divulge the secret?

Everything in Claire's life was getting more complicated. She was so filled with conflicting emotions, she was amazed she was able to walk in a straight line.

'I should go,' Claire said. She hated these moments right before they separated, especially since every night lately had felt like it could be their last one together. She kissed Lock, desperately, then slipped down the stairs.

The worst thing about adultery was her growing envy and resentment of Lock's life at home with Daphne. As much as Claire tried to discount it, it did exist: Lock and Daphne had a child together whom they loved desperately, whose welfare they discussed, whom they were proud of and worried about. They had a home filled with art and antiques, and every acquisition had a story. They had the airline they liked to fly and their rental car company and their brands of shampoo and olive oil, the places they liked to get takeout, the TV show they watched on Sunday nights, the certain type of down pillow they slept on; they had their bathroom rituals, their sexual positions, their Internet provider, their friends from Seattle and Saint Louis, their photographs from trips to South Africa and Iceland, and a Red Sox game where Ramirez hit a home run and Lock caught the ball, and the night at the symphony when they heard Itzhak Perlman. They had a common vocabulary, years and years of shared experience, every night sleeping next to each other. Whereas Claire and Jason took the kids to Story Land on vacation, Lock and Daphne went to Tortola and stayed at a five-star resort, where the sand was like powdered sugar. It felt like Lock and Daphne's way of doing things was superior, if only because it was theirs. Claire wanted to have her own life with Lock. To have to live her life with Jason alongside the life that Lock was living with Daphne was excruciating. It was the worst thing.

Claire and Lock saw each other less frequently alone and more frequently with their spouses at various social functions. This was the problem. Claire hated seeing Lock and Daphne together – and it seemed that in early summer, Daphne was out with Lock every night instead of shut away at home, which was where she had always been in years past. Now she was at Lock's side, his wife; they were a couple, and Claire was confronted with their marriage again and again. She bristled when she saw Lock's arm around

Daphne's back, when he brought her a drink, when he reached out to straighten Daphne's necklace. Claire tried to concentrate on being with Jason, but Jason hated these social outings. She had to drag him, she had to set out his clothes so he would look presentable. He was like a sullen teenager, and his impatience was obvious: he spent most of his time sucking down beers at the raw bar, talking to the shucker, Mikey, whom he fished with, and checking his watch. How much longer until he could go home and watch TV?

At some point during each event, Claire and Lock would have to acknowledge each other, and this was painful and awkward: Lock and Daphne face-to-face with Claire and Jason.

'Claire,' Lock said, bending in to kiss her, then reaching across her to shake Jason's hand. 'Jason.'

'Hey, man,' Jason said.

'Claire,' Daphne said, smiling archly.

Claire licked her teeth. 'Daphne.' Air kiss. A glance to Daphne's chest – was she wearing something revealing? Daphne had no qualms about giving Claire the once-over, and then she would hurl veiled insults, one after another, like water balloons over the fence. *Look how much sun you've gotten – so many freckles! You always look so nice in that top. It's the same one you wore to Cinco, is it not? Did you tell me before that you bought it at Target? I never think to shop for my clothes there! God, this wine is atrocious. I can't believe you're drinking it! My palate is positively offended by it. And you're eating the cheese puffs – well, of course you can, you're so thin. I should follow you into the ladies' room to make sure you're not purging. We all wonder, you know.*

Claire would smile, laugh it off. What else could she do? Jason was mute at her side, barely paying attention, while Lock's eyes grew wider and sadder. He would take Daphne's arm and try to redirect her, lead her away, but that hurt, too, separating, seeking other conversations. Lock would later try to find Claire to apologize. *That's*

*just how she is. Believe me, I know – I have to live with her. I'm so
sorry. You look beautiful.*

Claire glared at Lock, wounded and livid.

'I love you,' he whispered in line at the bar.

She nodded, tight-lipped.

Little League ended, school let out, it stayed light until nine
o'clock at night, and it was impossible to get the kids into bed.
The days stretched out, impossibly long, and yet impossibly short.
With dropping off and picking up to and from camps, lessons,
trips to the beach, Claire had little time left to get into the hot
shop. The g.d. chandelier had only three arms; it was beautiful in
its incompletion, her best work without question, but that didn't
make it any less incomplete. No matter how sunny or filled with
possibility the early summer days made Claire feel, there was always a nugget of guilt and dread inside her, emitting radioactivity.
The g.d. chandelier. Must finish it!

She would get it done before July 10, she decided. July 10 was
the day the invitations to the gala were being mailed out. On the
evening of July 9, the gala committee would gather at Isabelle
French's house in Monomoy and they would stuff the invitations
into envelopes, stick on labels, and seal the envelopes up. Isabelle
herself was arriving on Nantucket on July 8 with the boxes of invitations in tow, so really, Claire's deadline for the g.d. chandelier was
July 8, because she couldn't live with the stress of having Isabelle
on the island and not being finished with the g.d. chandelier.

First, Claire looked at what she had: a glorious pink globe in the
center with three gracefully trailing arms. She needed five more
arms; then she needed to make the tiny bell-like cups to hold the
bulbs. Ted Trimble called each week to see if the chandelier was
ready to be wired.

Not yet, Claire said. *Soon.*

Claire went at the g.d. chandelier as if it was an exam she had
to take, or a paper she had to turn in. Being Catholic, she held the

belief that to create something truly great, truly holy, there must be sacrifice. And so for five days, she gave up all the things that she enjoyed. She gave up her evenings alone with Lock, she gave up a very fancy cocktail party at Libby Jenkins's house on Lincoln Circle, where she knew she would see Lock, she gave up three perfect, sunny afternoons at the beach, and she gave up the Fourth of July fireworks with her kids – Jason and Pan took them instead, with a gorgeous picnic that Claire had prepared but not eaten. In the days that she set aside to finish the g.d. chandelier, Claire ate pasty, tasteless foods – rice cakes, dry whole wheat toast, saltines with organic peanut butter, edamame, radishes – and something Pan made called Thai fire broth, which was insidiously spicy and which Claire drank only to stay awake.

With such sacrifice, with such a dedicated effort in the hot shop, Claire thought the remainder of the g.d. chandelier would come easily. She did very few things in her life with extreme self-confidence, but blowing glass was one of them. She could make glass do what she wanted; it was a gift. After so many years of blowing out globes for the *Bubbles* or making the glass do other wildly creative things for people like Jeremy Tate-Friedman of London and Mr. Fred Bulrush of San Francisco, Claire knew how the gather would behave. She had a clear idea of what she wanted the arms of the chandelier to look like: she had a sketch taped to the marvering table for reference. Her Catholic soul believed that since she had sacrificed sleep, yoga, sunshine, viognier, all food other than twigs and leaves, and the delighted cries of her children when the fireworks exploded overhead, she would be able to finish the chandelier. She would, through her own willpower, climb out of this hell.

But it was hard. She tried ninety-six times to get the fourth arm just right – and then she nearly dropped it, she was so weary. But it was fine, whole, undamaged. It went into the annealer and she was so tired she could have cried, but she made herself go back to the pot furnace for another gather.

266

Her arms ached, her sight blurred, she tried and tried again. Four more arms. They needed to fall and twist just so. She thought she knew the perfect angle, she could see it in her mind, but she could not make the hot glass take the angle; if it happened, it happened because of luck. But no, she couldn't think like that; she had to believe it was within her control. Time and time again, she tried; she was sweating, she was drinking gallons of water – gallons! – and yet she was always thirsty.

One afternoon, when Pan and the kids were at the beach, when she was roasting like a Thanksgiving turkey, she got the fifth arm – perfect, beautiful – into the annealer. Ten or eleven tries later, she got the sixth arm. Yes! Two arms in the space of an hour, and only two left to go . . . She could finish that very afternoon, the afternoon of July 6. She went back to the pot furnace for another gather and pictured herself driving out to the beach for a swim. She thought of the cool, cold water; then she thought of cool water trickling over the side of a stone fountain, a necklace of cool jade stones lying against her breastbone, a bowl of chilled cucumbers, music trilling out of a glass flute, a frosted glass of lemonade, chilled silver cups for mint juleps, ice swans, diamonds. A bead of sweat fell from the tip of Claire's nose, hit the steaming iron of her punty, and hissed, evaporated. She closed the door to the pot furnace, set her punty down, and staggered to the bench. She felt like she was going to vomit. She bent in half and retched onto the concrete floor. She pushed her goggles up onto her head, ripped off her gloves, and hobbled over to the water basin, where she dunked her hands and splashed her face. She fell back onto her butt.

Music from a glass flute. Who had asked for the glass flute? She couldn't remember, nor could she remember if she'd made it or not. It had to be possible. Lock loved the flute; she knew this because they listened to so much classical music on the Bose radio. She loved Lock; it was wrong, but it was true. How many weeks had she gone to confession, how many weeks had Father Dominic implored her to pray for the strength to stop, how many weeks had she said, *Yes, okay, I will,* but then found herself unable? She wondered how many other people she knew had a secret love. Anyone? Everyone? Not Siobhan. Siobhan thought Claire was a heathen. Claire's head ached; she had to lie down. She meant to ease her head back, but she misjudged the distance to the floor, and her head met the concrete with a cracking thud. Only two arms left.

Darkness. Heat. Hell.

She came to in the hospital, in an antiseptic white square box of a room, where she was lying, crookedly, on a blue vinyl table covered with paper. Jason was there, and a heavyset nurse Claire didn't recognize was holding a packet of cool blue gel to her forehead.

Jason said, 'Claire?'

'Hi?' she said.

'It happened again,' he said. His face was red and the skin around his eyes was puffy. She had seen him look this way before, but when? She couldn't remember.

'Two arms left,' she said. She didn't think Jason would know what she was talking about, but his face clenched in angry recognition.

'Would you excuse us?' he said to the nurse.

'A doctor will have to see her before she's discharged,' the nurse said. 'She has heatstroke. She's not free to go just because she's awake.'

'Fine,' Jason said.

The nurse slipped out. Claire looked at Jason. 'Heatstroke.'

'Again,' Jason said. 'You did it again.'

She waited a minute to see if he would go on or if it was her turn to speak. Everything was moving so slowly, it was practically going backward.

'You have to stop,' he said. 'The whole fucking thing. It's like a *cult* you've joined, the gala committee. It's like a planet you've

268

moved to. Planet Gala. It is taking over your life, and you have to stop.'

She meant to say, *Yes, okay, I will*, but instead she said, 'I can't.'

'You have to stop,' Jason said. 'I'd like to say you never should have started up again. Fine, I will say it: You never should have started up again. Because it's dangerous – you don't know when to stop, you push yourself until it just isn't safe. You should have learned your lesson the last time. You hurt yourself and we nearly lost Zack.'

Claire started to cry. There was a frozen slab of blue gel strapped to her forehead, she realized, making her head heavy and hard to move. Had Jason just said that? No, he had not said that. It was the heatstroke. It was her guilt.

She looked at Jason. His eyes seemed to be two different colors, but she couldn't remember which one was true. His eyes were blue, or green? Years ago, when she had made the nesting vases for the museum in Shelburne, she had created one that was the same color as Jason's eyes. But had it been blue, or green? Or both? 'I'm confused,' she admitted. 'I can't tell what's real and what's not real.'

'Because you have heatstroke!' he said. 'You were in the shop too long, it was fifteen hundred degrees, you were out of water, you pushed yourself too far, and you fell down again – again! – and you passed out, again. And you almost died. Again! You're like one of the kids, Claire. You do not listen!'

'I'm sorry,' she said. She remembered apologizing when it happened with Zack, on the operating table, as they took him by cesarean section. I'm sorry, I'm sorry, I'm sorry. *They don't know about the baby.* She had thought they were going to deliver him dead, but he had lived and he was fine. Kids developed at different paces, even siblings. Claire tried again to sit up.

'It's not like you even went back to work for a good reason!' Jason said.

'You mean a paying reason.'

'I mean a *good* reason! The gala! The auction item! Lock Dixon asked you! Who cares? It's not worth it. Let them get something else – a trip to Italy, a Hinckley picnic boat! It's not worth risking your life.'

'I'm not risking my life,' Claire said. But there they were, in the hospital.

'You've become like some *robot* that these people have *programmed*!'

'It's nearly over,' Claire said. She decided trying to sit up was pointless, so she lay back and closed her eyes. She was tired. 'In six weeks, it will be over. And I can't quit if Matthew is coming.'

'He doesn't care if you're in charge or someone else is.'

'The whole reason he agreed to do it is that it's *my* thing. So now he's coming, and if I quit, what does that say? That it wasn't important to me after all? That I don't care about it? I can't quit. I made a commitment and I intend to honor it.'

'Even if it costs you your marriage?' he said. 'Your kids?'

'Is it going to cost me you and the kids?' Claire said.

'I don't know,' Jason said. 'I just don't get it. You tell me you want to stay home with the kids, give the glass a rest for a while, you want to be a mom, spend time with Zack and all that – and then out of the blue, without even discussing it with me, you take on the gala, which is like a full-time job and then some. All those meetings – if they paid you by the hour, you'd be making a hundred grand. And on top of that, you're back in the hot shop, back at the glass, blowing out this piece that's going to be your magnum opus – great, whatever, I'm happy for you. Too bad you won't get paid a dime, but Lock Dixon asked you, and the committee, whoever the hell that is, expects it, and now you're on the hook.' He swallowed. 'They've stolen you from us, Claire. You're gone. Even when you're sitting at the dinner table, even when we're in bed and I'm on top of you, it feels like you're somewhere else.'

What could she say? He was right. She was amazed he'd noticed.

'I need you to stick with me for six more weeks,' she said. 'And then it will be done. Over.'

'You could have died, Claire,' he said. 'If Pan hadn't checked on you when she got home from the beach, I would be picking out your casket right now.'

'I'm sorry . . .'

'You're sorry? You were unconscious, Claire. Knocking yourself out, literally, over the goddamned chandelier.'

Two arms left, Claire thought involuntarily. Then she thought, *He's right. I've been brainwashed. I am not myself. How to return to myself? Quit? Leave Lock? Tell Isabelle to take her 'Petite Soirée' and go to hell?*

The door opened and the doctor swung in. 'Well,' he said, 'I hear you're lucky to be alive!'

They were at an impasse. Claire promised Jason she would stay out of the hot shop for one week, but doing so pushed her past her self-imposed deadline. And she only had two arms left – just two! She could do it, she knew she could; she had pulled two perfect arms in an hour and she had it down now, the formula, the rhythm. She said to Pan, 'I'm going to work for one hour. Will you check on me in an hour?'

Pan touched her front pocket, where she kept her cell phone. Claire knew this meant that Jason had told Pan to call him if Claire tried something like this.

'Never mind,' Claire said. 'I won't work.'

But of course she sneaked out only seconds after Pan pulled out of the driveway to take the kids to the beach. She found the door to the hot shop secured with a padlock.

She called Jason at work. 'You're a jerk, you know that?'

'You saw the lock?' he said.

She hung up. She nearly called Siobhan, but Siobhan would

take Jason's side – she had already taken Jason's side, saying, when she dropped off Tupperware containers of chicken salad and marinated cucumbers, *It's not worth what you're doing to yourself, Claire.*

So Claire called Lock, even though Lock was in the office and not free to talk. She told him what had happened – the chandelier, the heat, the sweat, the fall, the hospital, the fight, the padlock.

'He's a dictator,' she said of Jason. 'He thinks he's my father. He's not my father.'

'No,' Lock said. 'He's not.'

'Keeping me out of my own hot shop, keeping me away from my work, is wrong.'

'Wrong,' Lock said.

'What am I supposed to do?' Claire said.

'Leave.'

She looked out the window at her shackled hot shop. 'And go where?'

Lock was quiet.

Right, it was easy for him to take her side – anything to put him in opposition to Jason, anything to make Jason the bad guy and him the hero. Okay, now Claire was *defending* Jason. Jason wasn't letting her in the hot shop because he cared about her well-being. The chandelier *was* making her crazy. She *did* need a break. Leave? And do what? Fly to Ibiza? It was unfair for Lock to tell her to leave when he had no intention of leaving himself.

'Claire!' There was a voice in the hallway. Truly incredible: Jason was home, at two o'clock in the afternoon.

'I have to go,' Claire said, and she hung up.

She opened the bedroom door and found Jason standing there, his face a livid purple, his arm outstretched and trembling. In his palm was the key.

'Here you go,' he said. 'Take it.'

She took it. He turned on his heels and marched out.

She held the key until it started to sweat in her hand. This was what she wanted. Jason was trying to make her feel like it was wrong. It was wrong; all of it was wrong. She had been abducted. Where was the old Claire? Missing, dead, gone. She closed her eyes, and the thought that came to her was this: *Two arms left.* She filled a thermos with ice water and headed out back.

Forty-nine minutes and eighteen tries into it, she had her seventh arm. Into the annealer! One more arm! She was giddy with her impending triumph. Tomorrow was July 8 and Isabelle would arrive and Claire would be . . . done! The backbreaking work would be finished. Blowing the cups out would be as easy as blowing bubbles with the kids on the back porch.

Claire went back to the pot furnace and took another gather. The first key to success was getting the right amount of gather on the punty. This looked perfect. Claire took the gather to the marvering table and rolled it in the precious pink frit. The gather cooled against the table, so Claire went to the glory hole and reheated; then she took the gather to the bench and rolled it, grabbed her pliers and pulled and bent and twisted and rolled. She went back to the glory hole, got the piece good and hot again, tweaked it some more. She thought of the swoop she felt in her stomach when she saw Lock – that swoop was what she wanted to re-create with this glass. She thought the arm looked pretty good, pretty close . . . she heated it up, she tweaked it a little more, and feeling optimistic, she pierced the arm lengthwise with a long needle – this was delicate surgery, a procedure that had ruined dozens of good arms – so that there would be a thin tunnel through which to thread the wires. It was impossible to tell how good the arm was, however, until she held it up to the globe. Impossible that she would have pulled two perfect arms *in a row* – but yes! When the piece had cooled enough to pick up with tongs, Claire saw it was the missing piece of the puzzle. It fit – like Cinderella and the goddamned glass slipper. Impossible, but true!

Claire had hit a home run, she had pocketed the eight ball with two banks, she had won the pot with a royal flush, she had served an ace, she had skied a black-diamond run in knee-deep powder. Ringer! Hole in one! Touchdown! Goal!

Her self-righteous elation, however, was her worst enemy. She dropped the eighth and final arm on the way to the annealer – she was shaking with joy and nerves and, truth be told, thirst – and it shattered at her feet.

Later that night, as she lay in bed, all cried out, all done apologizing to her husband, and to God, and to herself, she recalled the myth of Sisyphus. It was his job to roll a boulder up a hill again and again and again; the task was never-ending. When Claire was a glassblowing apprentice, her mentor had told her that story. Satisfaction was not to be gained from finishing the task; satisfaction was to be gained from the process.

She feared that, like Sisyphus, she would never finish. The last arm of the g.d. chandelier was her boulder to push and push again. It was her punishment.

The caller ID said *Isabelle French,* and Siobhan couldn't help herself: she picked it up.

Then immediately regretted it.

Isabelle French wanted Siobhan to cater a party that very night – well, not a *party,* exactly, more like an evening at home. '*Une soirée intime,*' Isabelle said, and Siobhan thought it was a joke, her speaking French, because it was her last name. But no, Isabelle spoke in earnest: the *soirée intime* was the invitation stuffing for the summer gala.

'I'm thinking all-American picnic food,' Isabelle said to Siobhan. 'Fried chicken, deviled eggs. My grandmother's bread-and-butter pickles. If I give you the recipe, you'll make them?'

'Make them?' Siobhan repeated. She did not want to cater this

274

intimate evening at home. She wanted to turn down everything related to the summer gala. She did not want to make Isabelle's grandmother's bread-and-butter pickles.

'I know it's last minute,' Isabelle said. 'So I'll pay you for your time and effort. Say, three thousand dollars?'

Siobhan coughed. 'How many people?'

'I'm not sure exactly. Less than ten.'

Siobhan started scribbling down ingredients in her notebook. 'What time?'

'Seven.'

'I'll be there at six to set up,' Siobhan said.

She could be bought. Especially since Carter had lost six hundred dollars on Wednesday and four hundred on Sunday with the Red Sox. He had to stop gambling that fucking instant, she told him, or she was going to call a hotline. He promised he would, but that's how all addicts were, right? They promised until they were blue in the face, and carried on behind your back. Siobhan had opened a bank account that Carter knew nothing about, and all the checks from this summer were going right into it. He wouldn't be able to touch a penny.

Siobhan had catered at Isabelle's house before and had gotten all of her ogling out of the way the first time. The house was technically on the 'wrong side of the street' – not on the harbor, that is, but situated on a little hill overlooking the harbor. It wasn't a huge house, but it was spacious and airy and perfectly appointed. There was a koi pond in the front foyer, which would have shouted overstatement in anyone else's house, but in Isabelle's house it was a delightful surprise. She had a bright, well-equipped kitchen, which opened onto the enormous room she normally used for entertaining. The *soirée intime,* however, would take place out on the sunporch, where two gaming tables had been set up side by side and topped with smooth brown leather surfaces. Isabelle had ordered floral arrangements of purple and white irises, white gerbera

275

daisies, and fragrant Asiatic lilies that were as big as dinner plates. One wall of the sunporch was screened windows overlooking the water, and Siobhan was to set up the buffet along the back wall. She had made the fried chicken, as well as potato salad, marinated string beans, corn fritters, deviled eggs, and . . . the pickles. The pickles had been a snap, and they turned out perfectly (Siobhan was keeping the recipe to use again). She had also baked chocolate chip cookies and peach and blueberry hand pies. The all-American picnic had taken all day to prepare, but the first thing Isabelle did when Siobhan arrived was to hand her the check. Three thousand dollars.

'Thank you,' Siobhan said.

'Thank you!' Isabelle said. She leaned over and kissed Siobhan on the cheek, which took Siobhan by surprise. Isabelle was holding a rather full glass of wine, though she didn't seem drunk, just excited and nervous. Was the invitation stuffing a big deal? Siobhan had called Claire while she was filling the deviled eggs to give her the update. Claire was aghast to find that the invitation stuffing was being catered at all.

'She's calling it a *soirée intime,*' Siobhan said. 'An intimate evening chez French.'

'Oh, Jesus,' Claire said. 'Well, thank heavens I didn't offer to have it at my house. It would have been crying children and a bag of Fritos. And Jason kicking us out at nine o'clock so he could watch *Junkyard Wars.*' Siobhan had laughed at this; they had laughed together. Siobhan wanted to ask Claire if Lock would be attending the *soirée intime,* but she hadn't been able to mention Lock's name even once since the day Claire confessed they were having an affair.

Siobhan did not bring any help to Isabelle's house; Carter was doing a dinner party for forty people in Sconset – an event they now jokingly called 'La Grande Soirée' – and he'd taken Alec and two Dominican busboys-dishwashers with him. Isabelle gamely

276

pitched in, helping Siobhan carry dishes from the van to the buffet table on the sunporch.

When they were finished, Siobhan stopped to look at the invitations. They were set up on one of the gaming tables, a box of invitations, response cards, envelopes, a dish of water, a tiny sponge, and a roll of stamps at each place. Siobhan lifted one of the invitations carefully from the box; it was as heavy and creamy as a wedding invitation. Siobhan felt her ire rise up. The amount of money spent on these invitations (how many were there – two thousand?) was enough to pay for day care for one of 'Nantucket's Children' for a year.

'Lovely,' Siobhan said.

'Mmmmm,' Isabelle murmured. She sipped her wine, then picked up a sheet of vellum printed with names and waggled it in the air. 'These are the committee members,' she said. 'I notice your name is on here.'

'Is it?' Siobhan said. She checked the vellum – *Mrs. Carter Crispin* – and gave a little laugh. 'Well, I told Claire I'd help out, but I haven't done very much.'

'No,' Isabelle said. 'Half the people on the list are people I recruited, and most of them don't even speak to me. They won't help, won't lift a finger, they might not even *attend* – but because they agreed to serve on the committee, they will send a check. And they lend their name to our event. But they're ghosts.'

'Ghosts,' Siobhan said, eyeing the vellum.

'I know it drives Claire mad, having people on the committee who aren't willing to roll up their sleeves, but that's the way the game is played.'

There were footsteps – and a woman entered the sunporch, lugging a large instrument trapped in a black body bag.

'I'm playing in here?' the woman said to Isabelle.

'Dara! Hello! Yes, over there, in the corner, I think, don't you?' Isabelle turned to Siobhan. 'This is Siobhan, the caterer. Siobhan, this is Dara, the cellist.'

*   *   *

'A cellist!' Claire said. She had been inside for fifteen seconds, just enough time to take a glass of champagne from Siobhan's tray and catch strains of cello music floating in from the other room. 'She hired a *cellist?*'

'Flew her in from New York. She plays with the symphony.'

'No!' Claire said, but Siobhan didn't answer. It was her rule, strictly enforced, not to fraternize with guests of any event, and that included Claire.

'Let's go out after?' Siobhan whispered in an attempt to end the chitchat.

Claire said, 'I can't.'

Siobhan gave her a scowl, which Claire did not see, because at that moment Lock Dixon walked in. He smiled warmly at Siobhan.

'Hello, Siobhan.'

'Hello, Lock. Champagne?'

Claire was smiling, too, and drinking her champagne, and fidgeting with the straps of her sundress. Isabelle swooped in from God knows where.

'Lock!'

They kissed on the lips as Siobhan and Claire watched. There they were, Siobhan thought – the cook, the thief, his wife, her lover. Or something like that.

Lock said, 'Do I hear music?'

Isabelle said, 'Dara is here! I know how you love the cello!'

Claire turned to Siobhan. Siobhan looked into the koi pond, which babbled happily at their feet. Gavin Andrews walked in – stiff and smarmy as ever – followed by Edward Melior. Siobhan ground her molars together. Three thousand dollars was not enough compensation to deal with Edward. If she had thought for one instant that he would be here, she would never have taken the job. It seemed amazing to her that she had ever, *ever* kissed him, hugged him, rubbed his feet, chewed his ear, ruffled his hair,

278

slept with him, declared her love for him, agreed to marry him. She flashed back to the instant that she had flung his engagement ring at him, screaming, *It's over, Edward!* His face had screwed up in pain. That memory she found satisfying.

But because caterers were, among other things, actors, she smiled. 'Champagne? Gavin? Edward?'

Gavin took a glass with a sniff. Edward took a glass, then reached out, grabbed Siobhan's chin between his thumb and fore-finger, and kissed her flush on the mouth. Siobhan would have slapped him had she not strictly enforced the 'No hitting guests at any event' rule.

'Hello, beautiful,' Edward said.

She would have stabbed him in the gut with a serving fork. Re-grettably, the taste of him lingered on her lips – gin, he had been to a party before this – and she didn't have a hand free to wipe it away. Even worse, Siobhan felt a pulse between her legs. The kiss had aroused her. Impossible! She abhorred the man. Involuntarily, she thought of pressing him up against Isabelle's Sub-Zero refrig-erator. She thought about making him so hot that he begged for her. He had kissed her with authority, with ownership. How dare he! She hated his self-assurance. The tray of champagne wobbled in Siobhan's hands, and for a second she pictured it toppling into the koi pond. Damn Edward! She had not dropped or spilled any-thing in more than two years. Edward approached Isabelle and shook her hand. Siobhan stole a glance at him, at his shirt, neatly tailored across his shoulders, at the bulge of his wallet in the back pocket of his khakis.

They drank a lot. Only six people, and Siobhan could not keep the glasses full. And, too, she was busy making sure the food was per-fect. She warmed the fried chicken and softened the honey-pecan butter she had made to go on top of the chicken; she fried the corn fritters, last minute, on Isabelle's Viking range and brought them out piping hot. She offered the fritters to Edward first, and he popped one in his mouth and burned his tongue.

Siobhan clucked. 'Careful. They're hot.'

No question about her role: she was the hired help. This never bothered her; she had a strong work ethic and almost no pride of the deadly-sin variety. She liked to listen, to eavesdrop; she did it all the time on the job. Even when serving her best friend and her ex-fiancé, she was invisible, a fly on the wall. She, like Dara the cellist, was very pleasant background music.

First she watched Claire. Claire's cheeks were flushed; she drank quickly, she chinged her fork against her plate more than once, and she fussed with the napkin in her lap as if it was a bird she was trying to calm. She was sitting next to Lock. This was the first time Siobhan had seen them together, side by side, and it was revelatory. Siobhan knew the truth – she was the only one – but it was like looking at the optical illusion of the old lady and the young lady. At first your eyes saw only the old lady, but then, when someone pointed it out – aha! Yes! The beautiful young lady! How could I not have seen it earlier? It's so obvious! Lock and Claire were turned toward each other, they spoke addressing each other; under the table, Siobhan noticed from behind, their legs were touching, though just barely. It was happening under everyone's nose.

Siobhan was also acutely aware of Edward. He was drinking heavily, more gin, splash of tonic, a quarter lime – she knew how he liked it – and he was being funny and charming as always, but he was punctuating his stories with long, penetrating looks at Siobhan that seemed to rise and swell with the strains of the cello. Siobhan caught him looking once, and he did not look away. They were stuck there, hooked together. His look was saying . . . well, what else would it say? *I want you!* And Siobhan's look was, hopefully, both enticing and defiant. *You can't have me!*

Isabelle's voice sliced into Siobhan's thoughts. 'Claire, have you bought your table yet?'

280

There was a weighty pause. Isabelle asked the question loudly, at the exact time that Dara finished a movement, so that the room was suddenly silent and the question took on the import of an announcement or a challenge to be risen to.

Claire's answer was meek. 'Not yet.'

'But you will take a table, right? Twenty-five thousand dollars? That way you'll be up front, next to me. And Lock!'

Everyone looked uncomfortable except for Gavin, who merely looked interested. *Take a twenty-five-thousand-dollar table?* Siobhan thought. That was absurd. Well, not for Isabelle, and not for Lock – not for *Edward,* maybe – but for Claire, yes. Twenty-five thousand dollars was a new car. It was a year's worth of mortgage payments. It was not something Claire would – or could – toss away in one night. Isabelle, Siobhan decided, was an evil woman for asking Claire in front of everyone. Look at poor Claire – her cheeks were burning, and now the red splotches were popping out on her chest. Siobhan was in the process of offering the table more pickles. She had not dropped or spilled anything in more than two years, but what if the pickles were to end up in Isabelle's lap right now?

Adams Fiske said, 'Everybody donates what they're comfortable with. No one expects Claire to buy a twenty-five-thousand-dollar table.'

'Why not?' Isabelle said. 'She's chairing the event, as am I, and I'm taking a twenty-five-thousand-dollar table. It's expected that we lead by example.'

Lock took a breath as though he were about to speak, and Siobhan thought, *Yes, stick up for your girlfriend! Prove to me you love her!* But Edward, who honestly could not keep his wallet in his pants for one second, said, 'I'm in for a twenty-five-thousand-dollar table.'

Claire raised her face. She had been staring at the lonely deviled egg on her plate. 'Me, too,' she said.

'Claire?' Adams said.

Claire? Siobhan thought. *Are you out of your mind?*

'What?' Claire said. 'I am the cochair. Isabelle is right – it sets an example. And I've put money aside.'

She was lying; her gaze was fixed back on Mr. Egg. Siobhan whisked Claire's plate away and nudged her discreetly. Claire looked up. Siobhan shook her head. *You don't have to play these people's games.* It was like she was always telling Carter: Anteing up money you don't have doesn't make you ballsy. It makes you stupid.

Lock jiggled the ice in his glass and said, 'That's great, everybody. Thank you. It's great for the cause.'

They moved to the next table and got going on the invitations. It was dark now. Siobhan brought out dessert and coffee and cordials; Dara the cellist packed up and went out front to wait for her cab. Siobhan cleaned up in the kitchen. This was normally her favorite part of the evening – wrapping up leftovers for the boys, getting ready to go home. But tonight, right now, Siobhan was rattling around, distracted, upset. It was so many things: Claire, Lock, Edward, Carter and his gambling, Isabelle. Siobhan decided that from now on she was only going to take jobs from nice people, good people. She would not work for Isabelle French again.

There was a glass of champagne remaining on the silver tray, no longer chilled, but who cared? Siobhan drank it down. She felt better then – lighter, less serious. Claire's problems were not her problems. They were such good friends that it seemed this way sometimes – but no.

Siobhan felt hands on her waist and then a warm mouth on the back of her neck. She was well-trained in self-defense, and instinct nearly had her elbowing Edward in the sternum. She refrained, however, and managed just enough twitch to shrug him off.

'Go away, Edward.'

'You're beautiful, Siobhan. And you taste like a peach.'

The hot dishwater was fogging Siobhan's glasses, so that when she turned she couldn't really see him, but then her lenses cleared and he was on her, kissing her. Again she was aroused. Appalling! She had spent so long disdaining Edward and his annoying if tangential presence in her life that she had forgotten he was a skilled kisser. But she would never have spent four years of her life with someone who wasn't a skilled kisser or an extraordinary lover. Edward had been an extraordinary lover, very considerate, not as animalistic, maybe, as Carter, but attentive and confident – yes, she remembered this as he was kissing her. Then she pushed him away.

'Stop it, Edward.'

'I'm crazy about you. Look at me.'

She looked. She was very, very angry with him, but oddly her anger propelled her toward him rather than away from him. She wanted to punch him, to pound him. He had never been able to see her for who she really was – her own strong, clever, capable person – and she wanted him to see her now.

She led him into Isabelle's pantry, which was big enough for a king-size bed. God, what a hypocrite she was. So self-righteous with Claire, and now look at her . . .

The pantry was dim; it smelled very strongly of truffle salt, which was, coincidentally, one of Siobhan's favorite smells. Siobhan could hear the other guests chatting out on the sunporch; she should check on their drinks, light the citronella candles. She would, in a minute. Over Edward's shoulder, she spied tapioca, baking powder, baking soda, a jar of black peppercorns, a jar of pink peppercorns, a tin of Colman's dry mustard, and a small crystal jar of truffle salt, three ounces of the stuff, worth about forty dollars. Edward was looking at her expectantly. She liked this: she was driving the bus, she was in charge. She inhaled deeply, and Edward inhaled deeply also, as if they were playing a game of Simon says, but Edward either didn't notice the heady scent or he noticed it and didn't know what it was. The man understood nothing about food.

283

Was she going to kiss Edward again, here in Isabelle's pantry? She was not.

'Help me take some things out to the van,' Siobhan whispered.

He agreed happily. When he turned to leave the pantry, Siobhan popped the jar of truffle salt into the pocket of her chef's jacket. What was she doing? She felt like an incorrigible teenager, the kind who dyed her hair fuchsia, pierced her tongue, and hung around Piccadilly Circus. Thieving, from a client! She put the truffle salt back on the pantry shelf.

Edward was lingering by the kitchen sink. Siobhan pointed to covered dishes and platters drying upside down on dish towels, and Edward picked them up and followed her outside.

The night air surrounding Isabelle's house smelled like rugosa roses and honeysuckle, and the only sounds were the crickets. A car pulled up to the end of the driveway, and Edward and Siobhan both watched as Dara and the cab driver wrestled the cello into the back of the cab. Then the cab disappeared, and the lights that their movements had turned on turned off again, just like that. It was dark.

Siobhan set the platters safely in the back of the van, as did Edward. Then he grabbed her by the hips and they kissed, and his hands went right up inside Siobhan's chef's jacket. She was consumed, once again, with fury. Wasn't it just like Edward to assume that he could flip Siobhan like an egg, over easy? Wasn't it just in accordance with his view of the world to assume that she would feel the same way about him as he felt about her? She did not feel the same way! She was livid and she would tell him so. She had no intention of following Claire into the dark forest of adultery, despite the fact that Carter had been unfaithful (and untruthful) with and about the family's finances. Siobhan was going to make Edward see her and hear her – and then she would rip herself away.

But at that second, something happened. Edward stopped. He pulled back. He touched her face, ran his thumbs over her cheekbones, then over her lips. He pushed her glasses up, just as he used

284

to when they were dating. Siobhan had always loved this gesture. She had to admit that in all her life, no one had paid as close attention to her as Edward. She thought of the calla lilies he'd sent when Liam broke his arm. The bell had rung, and she opened the door, saw the delivery person with an armload of calla lilies, and knew they were from Edward.

'I still love you,' he said. 'I haven't stopped loving you for one second.'

'Oh,' Siobhan said. She knew this to be true, and yet the words caught her by surprise. Or else it was his tone of voice that caught her by surprise. It was very tender.

'You hurt me,' Edward said. 'When you left. When you turned right around and married Carter. My heart broke.'

Siobhan nodded. She was too stunned to speak.

'You didn't feel the way about me that I felt about you,' Edward said. 'You were right not to marry me in that case. But here it is, more than ten years later, and I'm still in love.'

Siobhan's anger shrank until it was like a pebble at her feet that she could kick away. She did not allow herself to revisit the demise of her relationship with Edward very often, mostly because she had behaved regrettably – throwing the ring in Edward's face and, six months later, marrying Carter in Ireland. She didn't like to see Edward because seeing him reminded her of the person she'd been then – a woman who would break an engagement and immediately take up with another man. Siobhan had not allowed Edward any closure; when he came to her house 'to talk,' Carter was there and Siobhan had asked Edward, curtly, to leave. Awful! She still had the ring – the beautiful and expensive symbol of Edward's love and commitment – in her jewelry box. The ring taunted her. She had not been able to get rid of it, to take it to a pawnshop or sell it on eBay, because . . . why? Because of something Siobhan herself did not understand. Because she had been waiting for something. She had been waiting, maybe, for tonight.

Siobhan pressed her head against Edward's chest. Edward was

a good man, a good person; he would be a wonderful father and an amazing provider. Siobhan had not loved him enough or in the right way, and there was no crime in that, but there was a crime in not behaving like a decent human being. Facing Edward all these years – even the blurred glimpse of him as they passed each other in their cars – had meant facing her worst failure.

She couldn't apologize, however. She didn't have the words at her disposal and she feared anything she said would sound lame or overwrought, not to mention ten years late. So she raised her face and she kissed him as softly as she possibly could, and the kiss stirred her, it excited her in a way she had forgotten she could be excited, and soon they were kissing crazily, they were two people in a movie, kissing and sucking and pawing each other. She was going to follow Claire into the dark forest! She was going to shag Edward. She would sin, but it would be ameliorated, in a way, by Siobhan's making things right with Edward. She would be giving him something he'd been waiting for for ten years.

Where? There, in the back of the van? The back of the van was cluttered with dishes. Her chef's jacket was now open, exposing her camisole underneath, and Edward's shirt was unbuttoned at the top. She could see he was ready to go, and she was certainly ready. Her mind flickered to Claire, Isabelle, Lock – all still inside, right? Blotting glue on the envelopes with the dainty sponges, peeling stamps, discussing the names of the people on the invitation list ('He's the one with the house on Shawkemo Road . . . whose wife died of . . . and then, the next summer, he married a twenty-five-year-old'). Was anyone looking for Edward or Siobhan? Most certainly not. Everyone inside was drunk, anyway.

'My car,' Edward said. 'The hood of my car.'

Siobhan thought he was kidding. It would be bad enough when she confessed to Father Dominic about the adultery, but imagine the look on Father's face when she told him it had happened on the hood of Edward's Jaguar! But Edward had a point: The hood of his car was tucked under the branches of a large tree. Even in

286

the dark, it was in shadows, and it was the car parked farthest from the house.

Yes! Hurry! They were sneaking now, tiptoeing over the crushed white shells of Isabelle's driveway. Siobhan felt lawless and heady. Was she really going to do this? It seemed so. Just the one time, and it was Edward, an old lover, not a new lover. Did that make it any less treacherous than what Claire was doing? Claire was in love; that was her justification. Siobhan was not in love with Edward; she had fallen out of love with Edward or had never been properly in love with him, she had lied to him about that or had misrepresented herself, the lie had broken his heart, and she felt guilty. And so now here she was, sinning in order to make things right. It made sense to Siobhan but it was also perfectly fucked up. Would she go to hell? Would she and Claire go together?

She smelled somebody's cigarette.

'Who's out there?' a voice shouted.

Edward whipped around. 'Hello?' he said. He held Siobhan with one hand, and the other hand flew to his shirt buttons. Siobhan clenched her chef's jacket together in front and peered around Edward.

Gavin Andrews came crunching around the corner. When he saw Edward and Siobhan, he shouted, 'Ahh!'

And Siobhan screamed, 'Ahh!'

Gavin put a hand to his heart. 'Jesus,' he said. 'You scared me! I thought there was a burglar out here!'

'A burglar?' Siobhan said, thinking automatically of the truffle salt. But she had put it back!

'No burglars,' Edward said. 'It's just us.'

'Yes,' Gavin said, taking a drag off his cigarette. 'I can see that.'

They stood for a moment in awkward silence. Okay, Siobhan thought. She was not going to shag Edward. Gavin Andrews, of all people, had arrived like a sign from God and put a stop to it. Now Siobhan had to worry about what this looked like. Did it look like she and Edward were about to shag on the hood of Edward's car? Oh, God, Siobhan hoped not. It was safe to bet that half the gossip on the island of Nantucket started with Gavin Andrews.

'I was helping Siobhan put dishes in her van,' Edward said. Somehow he had gotten his buttons done and his shirt straightened and he looked perfectly normal and presentable. But Siobhan looked like she had just fallen out of bed after a legendary ravishing. 'How's everything inside?'

'Oh,' Gavin said. He blew a stream of smoke through his nose. 'Fine.'

They had both had a lot to drink and it was very late, nearly midnight, but an opportunity like this didn't present itself often, so they took it. They drove to Altar Rock and looked at the moon. It had been nearly two weeks since they'd been alone together, and although they'd talked every day, they hadn't *really* talked, and so as Claire lay in Lock's arms, she told him all of the things that she'd been saving up for him – that she loved him, that she missed him, that her heart was lonely, starved, suffocating without him. She wasn't sure how much longer she could go on this way.

He kissed her neck. 'The Eiffel Tower,' he said. 'The post office.'

'I know,' she murmured. 'I know.' Play cards, eat Big Macs, go to the movies, do the things that other people did, do them together. She'd had a lot to drink, and it was affecting her. Here she was, in the middle of the night, in the most beautiful place in the world. Altar Rock, the highest point on the island, was not much more than a hill, but it looked out over the moors and ponds. This was her home, in the moonlight. She was only going to be alive once. Shouldn't she be happy?

She didn't know how much longer she could stay married to Jason and have Lock stay married to Daphne. She and Lock were in love, she, desperately and stupidly, blindly and completely. She was a slave, a goner. She would give up everything for him.

But was this true? Could she really imagine a future with Lock? What would that look like? Would she move out? (Inconceivable.) Would he move out? (More conceivable, but where would he go? He couldn't live with Claire *in Jason's house*.) Would they both move out and get a place together? Where would the kids go? With her, presumably. She could not imagine life without her kids, but neither could she imagine Lock living with her kids. She fantasized about a life with Lock, but she realized that this would have to take place in an alternate reality, one where they had no jobs, no responsibilities, no ex-spouses or children to care for, no friends, no connections. They would have to move to Ibiza, two displaced strangers, and start over. Claire felt like a marionette; Lock could swoop in and clip all the strings that were tying her to her current life, but then she would collapse, lifeless. She would be a person without form. The worst thing about adultery was that it made you see your life for what it was: something that was nearly impossible to escape. Claire cried a little at this, and Lock squeezed her and whispered, 'Hey, it's okay. I'm here. I love you.'

'I know,' she said. They saw each other so infrequently now that when they did have time together, it became weighted and tangled with emotion. This was Claire's fault. She had worries to soothe and problems to fix. She was becoming tiresome, even to herself.

'I should go,' she said.

He released her. She wanted him to say, *Not yet,* or *So soon?* But he simply agreed. 'Yes,' he said. 'It's late.'

Claire's head was buzzing from the alcohol. Claire checked on each one of her kids, all of them sleeping, even Zack in his crib. Jason was snoring softly in their bed. He had taken the kids for pizza and ice cream and to the playground at Children's Beach. *Mom has another meeting!* He seemed resigned to life without her; he was making the most of it, enjoying it, even – and Claire had

289

a somber vision of Jason packing the kids up and whisking them away. Leaving her alone. God, she deserved it. She lay awake fretting about this (where would they go? Yellowstone? Bar Harbor? They would go someplace Jason could fish), and then she worried about other things: Lock, the chandelier, money.

She had made a promise she couldn't keep. She had agreed to take a $25,000 table. Part of her had known all along that she would do this, that she would never be able to eat crow and say, *Sorry, I can't afford it.* It was a matter of pride – in front of Isabelle, in front of Lock. She had lied and told everyone at the table (as well as Siobhan, who was floating around the table) that she had set money aside. This had sounded feasible. But it was not remotely feasible – Claire had gone over their finances again and again. She and Jason had sizable IRAs, which could not be touched, and they had $42,000 in savings. There was no way Claire could demolish more than half of their savings on the gala. She had told herself that after the gala she would make an effort with her business and solicit a new commission from Mr. Fred Bulrush or Jeremy Tate-Friedman. But now Claire couldn't even pay the electric bills for the shop, much less get ahead to the tune of $25,000. She had considered going to the bank and taking out a loan and paying it off over the next calendar year. That seemed like the most responsible course of action . . . until she thought of Matthew.

Matthew had millions and millions of dollars. Now that Bess was out of the picture, there was nobody and nothing for him to spend it on. It couldn't hurt to ask. She vacillated between this train of thought and the fear that indeed it *could* hurt to ask: Matthew could flip out, call her a vulture. She hadn't spoken to him in twelve years, she had called him out of the blue and asked him to play a free concert, and he had said yes. Wasn't he doing her enough of a favor? She would pay him back, with interest, but to this he might respond that he wasn't a bank, and he wasn't a loan shark. He had, once upon a time, been her friend, but he didn't appreciate being preyed upon now.

In this vein, she had talked herself out of calling several times.

But now it was dark, it was quiet, she had had some drinks, and she had enunciated a promise that could not be denied. She dialed Matthew's number.

'¿Hola?'

'Matthew? It's Claire. Claire Danner.'

'Buenas noches, chica. I knew it was you because you're the only person who still calls me Matthew. Other than my mother.'

'Am I?'

'You are. How are you? It must be the middle of the night there.'

'It is,' Claire said. He sounded sober. This was a good thing. Sober at nine thirty at night. Home, and not out at the clubs, drinking, or carousing with seventeen-year-olds to take his mind off Bess. 'I didn't wake you, did I?'

'No, no,' he said. 'I was just lying on the sofa with my Berlitz.'

'Which language?'

'Spanish. You can never know enough Spanish. And Portuguese. You may think the two languages sound alike, but they are in fact quite different.'

'You got a D in Spanish,' Claire said. 'What's the deal?'

'Gives me something to do. Keeps me out of trouble. I'm shooting air baskets, grabbing at straws. I don't know what I'm doing. Well, I'm coming to see you. Six weeks!'

'I can't wait. I miss you.'

'I miss you, too.'

Claire swallowed. 'Listen, I called because I have the world's biggest favor to ask you.'

'The answer is yes, whatever it is.'

'I need to borrow twenty-five thousand dollars.'

Silence.

Oh, God! Claire thought.

'I got myself into a real mess with this gala. I'm the cochair and my other cochair is a very wealthy woman named Isabelle

French. And she has managed to bully me into taking a twenty-five-thousand-dollar table for the gala. And I don't have twenty-five thousand dollars, and I can't even broach the possibility with my husband or he will kill me. So I ran through all these other options, and the one that seemed the least painful was to borrow the money from you. But I'll pay you back. I swear.'

Silence.

Oh, God! Claire thought. Had he hung up? What if he didn't play the gala at all now? The possibility had not occurred to her until this very second.

'Matthew?'

'I'm looking for my checkbook.'

'You are? You mean you'll lend it to me?'

'Well, we can call it a loan, but to paraphrase my favorite ex-wife, if you send me a check, I'll rip it up.'

'But Matthew . . .'

'Claire, relax. It's just money.'

'Right, but it's a lot of money.'

'Do you remember when we were kids,' he said, 'and your grandmother sent you a hundred bucks for your birthday?'

Claire racked her brain. A check from her grandmother? Sixteenth birthday? Was that what he was talking about?

'Yes.'

'What did you do with it?'

'I . . . we . . . got our ears pierced.'

'Right. You paid for me to get my ear pierced, and you paid extra for a diamond stud. You told me I would never be a proper rock star unless I had a diamond stud. And you bought yourself fourteen-karat studs, which were cheaper.'

'Yes,' Claire said. She actually did remember this: driving to the mall in Rio Grande and sitting in a chair at the Piercing Pagoda. They convalesced in Sweet Jane's kitchen, both of them holding ice cubes to their earlobes, trying not to cry.

'How many times did you give me five bucks so I could put gas in the Volkswagen?'

'Yeah, but that was only five bucks.'

'How many times did you pay for Kettle Korn or Slushees? How many times did you pay for beer?'

'You had a job. You paid sometimes, too.'

'You paid for dinner before the prom.'

'My father gave me the money.'

'But what I'm saying is, when I didn't have it, you paid for me, no questions asked. You gave me everything you had. There was no line drawn between what was yours and what was mine.' He paused. 'I'd like it if things could still be that way. So I'm going to write this check, and I don't want to hear about you paying me back.'

'Oh,' she said. 'Jesus.' She thought she might cry, but she was too relieved to cry. 'Thank you.'

'Does this twenty-five-thousand-dollar table mean you'll be sitting up front?'

'Front and center.'

'Good,' Matthew said. 'Then it's worth it.'

When she hung up, it was one in the morning, but Claire felt like it was full daylight, bright and sunny. Her chest cavity, she realized, had been filled with concrete, but now the heaviness was gone and she could breathe. Matthew would send the check in the morning, and Claire would have her $25,000 table. Problem solved.

Should she press her luck? Something was telling her yes. She wasn't at all tired, and the effects of the alcohol were fading. She pulled a Coke out of the fridge, exchanged her sandals for her clogs, and left the house, quietly, for the hot shop.

She spent a long time looking at the chandelier. Maybe that was the difference. She turned it in her hands, scrutinizing, meditating. Other times when she came into the hot shop, she was in a hurry, stressed, worried: Would she finish today? How long would it take? How many tries? Her forearms were in a constant state of fatigue and ache; the muscles were becoming ropy. But now Claire studied the chandelier, she pictured the arc and dip and twist of the final arm, and she saw how the piece would look, completed.

She pulled it on the first try, as she knew she would. She rolled the gather in the frit, and as she pulled and twisted, the final arm came into being. She pierced it with a steady hand. She held it up – yes, no question about it – then gently set the arm in the annealer. Tomorrow, she would blow out the cups. Piece of cake.

She went back into the house. Quarter to two. Suddenly she was very sleepy. She shed her clothes, washed her face, brushed her teeth, did her ritualized rinsing of the sink basin and wiping of the granite vanity top. Then she fell into bed, feeling light, clean, and empty, as though she didn't have a care in the world.

Once the invitations had been mailed, response cards arrived every day, some bearing credit card numbers, some bearing checks. Gavin kept the checks in a neat pile on his desk, and when he got a stack of ten, he went to the bank to deposit – and skim. Claire dropped off a check for $25,000. Gavin could not help mentioning this to Lock.

'Claire took a twenty-five-thousand-dollar table.'

'She did?'

'Yes.'

Lock rose from his desk and came over to look at the check, as Gavin knew he would.

'Well, she said she was going to.'

'And she did,' Gavin said.

The influx of money from the gala tickets made Gavin giddy. His stockpile was getting bigger and bigger. He had moved it out of the utensil drawer (in anticipation of his parents' arrival on August 1) and stuffed it in a green L.L. Bean duffel bag under his bed. It was so much money, he was afraid to count it. And yet he was no longer afraid of getting caught. The letter to the women's shoe company, as it turned out, had been perfectly fine. (He marveled that he had ever feared otherwise.) His affairs were in order; his trail was covered. Meanwhile, the people all around him were committing indiscretions – first Lock and Claire, and then, the other night, Siobhan Crispin and Edward Melior. He should get out of theft, he thought, and into blackmail.

Isabelle called, now, every day – to see who had responded, who had merely sent donations, who had requested seating with whom.

'Did the Jaspers respond?'

'They did not.'

'What about Cavanaugh?'

'Sent a donation.'

'How much?'

'A thousand dollars.'

'That's it?'

'That's it.'

Isabelle sighed. 'They have more money than Beckham. They could have sent ten times that much. But they didn't – because of me.'

Gavin did not know how to respond. He felt he was growing closer to Isabelle. He felt that perhaps she was calling so often because she wanted to talk to him.

'Did Kimberly Posen respond?'

'Not coming. Sent a donation.'

'Not coming?'

'No,' Gavin said. 'But she sent twenty-five hundred.'

This was met with silence. 'She used to be my best friend,' Isabelle said. 'I'm her daughter's godmother.'

'Oh.'

'You're sure she's not coming?'

'I'll check again,' he said.

Gavin wanted to make Isabelle happy; he wanted to give her good news. When she next called, he said, 'Your friend Dara Kavinsky is a yes and so is Aster Wyatt.'

'Dara is the cellist,' Isabelle said. 'And Aster did the invitations. He's my graphic designer. Why is it the only people who are coming are the people on my payroll?'

As the days passed, Gavin found himself thinking more and more about Isabelle French. She was sexy, he decided, alluring, classy . . . and disillusioned. He was perhaps the only person in the office who realized that everyone Isabelle had personally invited to the gala had said no and sent a donation. *It's because of my divorce,* Isabelle said. *It's like a disease: people are afraid they'll catch it. I hate being single.* Was this a clue for Gavin to ask her out? She had been so nice to him at the invitation stuffing. She had seated him next to her, she had touched the back of his hand in a way that sent a shiver up his arm – and at one point she had nudged him with her foot under the table. Gavin had ended up being the last to leave. There was a full moon, and Isabelle invited him to walk outside to see her moon garden. She had a circular plot planted with night-blooming white flowers – evening primrose, she said, and four-o'clocks – which were waxy and luminous in the moonlight. And she had a 'moon fountain' – a sphere made of honey onyx, a little bigger than a bowling ball, that glowed from within as water trickled over it and made it spin. The moon garden was the kind of magical place that Gavin was hoping to discover in his travels. He was in awe; to his embarrassment, he'd teared up. Isabelle was holding his arm – she was wearing heels in the grass and they'd both had a lot to drink – and he wondered if he should kiss her. But in the end he'd been too intimidated. A woman with enough aesthetic imagination (and money) to create a moon garden (she'd designed the fountain herself, she said) was beyond him.

Now, of course, he regretted his cowardly decision, and he wondered if he would ever summon the balls to ask Isabelle out. He entertained a fantasy where he bedded Isabelle French. (At her house, because he could never in a million years take Isabelle to his parents' house. Or maybe he could – before the first of August – and pretend it was his. Would she buy this?) He and Isabelle could become lovers; he would not need the duffel bag full of money because she would support him. But here his enthusiasm waned. Despite his lack of ambition, he did not want to be a kept man. And so he returned to the notion of grabbing a fistful of cash out of the duffel bag and taking Isabelle for a romantic dinner at the Chanticleer, then seducing her. Cut.

The escalating flirtation with Isabelle made the incessant ringing of the phone more palatable. But the calls were mostly from teenagers, asking how to get Max West tickets. In the beginning, Gavin took great pleasure in saying, 'This isn't Madison Square Garden, you know. It's a charity benefit. The tickets are a thousand dollars apiece.'

Gasp. 'A thousand dollars?'

'Yes,' Gavin said. 'Would you like to buy a pair?'

Click.

Now, however, he had tired of that song and dance; it made him feel like Scrooge or the Grinch, announcing such an outlandish price, quashing hopes. Then there were calls from the tent people, the tables-and-chairs people, the underwriters (how much signage, where, for how long?), the production people (lights, speakers, ferry reservations, would the crew house have a grill?), and the caterer, Genevieve, whose purpose in calling, it seemed, was merely to double-triple-check that she still had the job. (Perhaps the rumors of Siobhan and Edward's being together had made it farther afield.) Gavin was single-handedly piecing together the gala. He secured ferry reservations for the enormous truck that was bringing over the tent; he confirmed that there would be housing, meals – and a grill! – for the production crew; he got the alcohol permit from the town. He tried to talk Isabelle off the ledge.

'The van Dykes are a yes,' Gavin said. 'Do you know them?'

'No,' Isabelle said. 'They must be friends of Claire's.'

Gavin, pointedly, did not keep any notes. With each phone call, he became more and more indispensable. Claire was effusive. *God, thank you, Gavin, what would we do without you? You deserve a raise! In September, when this is over, I'm going to bring it up at a board meeting. I'm going to tell them what an enormous help you've been. I could not do all this myself – I simply do not have the time.*

Daphne called. Since discovering Lock and Claire in the office, back in April, Gavin had done his best to keep his conversations with Daphne short and to the point. *Oh, hi, Daphne, would you like to speak to Lock? He just stepped out. I'll tell him you called!* Gavin could not gossip with the woman while keeping a huge secret from her himself. He had limits. He even, at times, experienced guilt. Daphne had no idea about her husband's infidelity, or rather, she had every idea but she had identified the wrong target. Was it cruel keeping the news of Lock and Claire from her, or was it kind? Gavin chose kind. He was old enough now, mature enough, sophisticated enough, to realize that really, what you didn't know – what you might never know – couldn't hurt you.

This day, Daphne did not want to talk to Lock. She was adamant about that from the beginning.

I'm calling to talk to you, Gavin. I want to tell you something.

Surprisingly, the 'something' she had to tell him was not about a third party – not about the postmaster dating a twenty-year-old Bulgarian house cleaner, not about Jeanette Hix's being addicted to diet pills, which gave her insomnia, which led her to prowl the Cumberland Farms at four in the morning and shoplift a ninety-nine-cent bag of caramel Bugles.

Instead, Daphne said, *Lock tells me you're doing a fantastic job. You, my friend, are a wizard. I hope you're planning a nice, long vacation after this is over, someplace exotic. You deserve it, darling. I'm proud of you.*

Well, thank you, Daphne, Gavin said. He hung up the phone, impressed. A conversation with Daphne, and not one sideways reference, not one barbed word. Only sincere praise, or a passing along of praise, because she wanted him to know. He was proud of himself.

One night, when Gavin was getting ready to leave at five o'clock (heading home, where he would sit on his parents' deck looking at the ocean, drinking wine, smoking, listening to Mozart, reading his Lonely Planet guide to Southeast Asia . . . Vietnam was sounding better and better), Lock stopped him.

'Gavin?'

Gavin stopped by the door. Lock's tone of voice was ominous. Was this it, then? Gavin wasn't prepared! Think! Whip out the weapon. He had the knife sharpened in his mind; all he had to do was wield it!

Gavin smiled expectantly, his mind a whirlwind. What was it he had planned to say? *Before you contact the authorities, let me say one thing: I know about you and Claire. I came into the office one night in April. I saw you two . . . together.*

Lock was slow to speak. He looked pained. God, this was torture! Gavin stood there, caught in the force field of the insidious thing he had done – stealing from the very cause he was working so hard to promote! – and he was overcome with remorse and nearly unbearable disgrace. Lock was going to put a name to his acts – theft, robbery, embezzlement. This acknowledgment alone would kill Gavin. Committing the crime was one thing, but having it exposed was quite another. Had he learned nothing from taking advantage of Diana Prell in the broom closet, or from the debacle at Kapp and Lehigh? Gavin experienced what could only be described as a pure, unadulterated shame. He was, as they said in certain Asian cultures, *losing face.* Gavin understood this turn of phrase now. Even as he stood, waiting for Lock to lower the hatchet, his face was stiff and burning. He could not look Lock in the eye, so he gazed beyond Lock, out the twenty-paned window into the late summer afternoon.

Lock rose and approached him. Instinctively, Gavin backed up, but he was not fast enough to get away. Lock caught him, clapped him on the shoulder.

'I know things haven't been easy around here,' Lock said.

Gavin's eyebrows shot up. He thought of Rosemary Pinkle and how disappointed she would be. She was such a nice woman and she believed in Gavin. Tomorrow he was supposed to join her for drinks in her garden with a niece she wanted him to meet.

'With the gala, I mean. All the phone calls. Isabelle pushing you one way, Claire pulling you the other.'

Gavin nodded, uncomprehending. His parents were due in next week. They would not appreciate arriving to scandal. Gavin wasn't quite sure what they thought of him – he had never been quite sure – but he knew it wasn't terribly good. He hadn't measured up, somehow.

'And I just want to say thank you. You're doing a great job.' Lock squeezed Gavin's shoulder in emphasis, so firmly that it hurt.

'I am?' Gavin said reflexively. He breathed out his fear.

'I'm so grateful. If this gala comes off in the legendary way I think it will, it's in no small part because of your hard work.'

'Oh,' Gavin said.

'But you're not off the hook yet,' Lock said.

'No?' Gavin said.

'The worst is probably still to come.'

'You think?' Gavin said.

'Yes,' Lock said.

CHAPTER TEN

HE BLOWS IT

There was only one time previously in his life that had been as frenetic and difficult as this summer. He had been in the process of buying a company, one bigger than his own; he had someone else handling the financing so that he could focus on the negotiations, which were primarily with an older gentleman named Gus MacEvoy, who owned the other, bigger company, and who was reluctant to sell. Most of Lock's dealings were classic M&A stuff, pages right out of his business school textbook, but that didn't make it any less stressful or consuming. And to make matters more complicated, Daphne was at home with Heather, who was eighteen months old and driving Daphne crazy. Daphne had undergone surgery to remove her ovaries a few months before, and she was still in pain and was suffering from a hormonal imbalance. When Lock got home (with all that was going on in the office, this was sometimes not until eight or nine at night), Daphne

301

was alternately whimpering, fuming, or despondent. Her life, she said, was tedious beyond belief. It was *Sesame Street* and peeka-boo and endless putterings up and down the street while Heather picked a dandelion, or put a pebble in her mouth, or ran ahead, stumbled, and cried. Heather threw her food instead of eating it. Heather spilled things, she broke things, she ripped pages out of Daphne's magazines, she fussed unless Daphne read *The Runaway Bunny* three hundred consecutive times. She had to be held. She screamed in protest every time she had her diaper changed. Daphne took her to the playground, and one of the other mothers made a sideways comment because Daphne was reading the *New Yorker* while Heather was playing in the sandbox.

I was not cut out to be a mother, Daphne said. *I want to put her up for adoption.*

Lock had laughed. He thought Daphne was kidding. *We're not going to do that,* he said.

Well, you don't get a vote, Daphne said. BECAUSE YOU'RE NEVER HOME!

Those days had been hard, but they'd survived. Lock bought the company with Gus MacEvoy's blessing; Heather grew quickly into a charming little girl – for a while there, her mother's best friend.

And, Lock told himself, he would survive this summer. The gala would make them enough money to fund all of their programs and initiatives and start an endowment, and he and Claire would be able to get back on track.

Right now, however, the relationship was floundering. Claire blamed him, and to avoid further arguing, he accepted the blame. He apologized; there was little he could do.

What had happened was this: He and Daphne had been eating dinner on their deck. It was hot, so they'd ordered sushi, washing it down with silver gin fizzes. This sounded pleasant in the telling, but Daphne was growing more belligerent and demeaning with each sip of her drink, talking about this person and that person, wondering aloud about the sexual preferences of these near strangers, and then, ultimately, wondering about Lock's sexual practices with Isabelle French. Rather than engage Daphne in that fight once again, Lock stood up to clear the dishes. And there, ascending the stairs from the front door, was his daughter, Heather. Lock nearly dropped the plates. She had come home.

The Vineyard, Heather said, was crowded and noisy, there was traffic, there wasn't anything for teenagers to do, and Désirée's parents never wanted to drive them anywhere because of the traffic, so they sat in the house, bored, and they bickered. Désirée said, *If you hate it here so much, why don't you just go home?* So . . . here she was.

Lock hugged her. 'You can always come home, sweetie. Your rooms are all ready for you. God, am I glad to see you!' Daphne was still on the deck, possibly carrying on her invective with herself. Lock didn't want her to see Heather yet; he didn't want her to ruin it. Heather might leave as suddenly as she'd come. As it was, she would be here for more than four weeks. It was a gift he'd never expected.

It did not sit well with Claire. She was, naturally, happy for Lock, happy that Lock was happy. But Heather's presence put a limit on when they could see each other. Now, after work, Lock went right home. He and Heather drove to the beach and they swam. Lock was teaching Heather to surf-cast; she caught a bluefish on the second night. Heather had to train for field hockey, which would begin as soon as she went back to school, so she rose early and went running, but Lock didn't like to think of her out on the dirt roads around their house alone – the roads where Daphne had had her accident. So Lock began getting up early and going with her; he needed to lose weight, anyway. He couldn't meet Claire late at night when he had to get up at six in the morning to go running. He couldn't meet Claire because he and Heather were surf casting or he and Heather were renting *Night at the Museum* or he was taking Heather to the Pearl for dinner. Or Heather was at the movies with her friends and from there was going to the Juice Bar for ice cream and from there was going to hang out on the strip. When the hanging out was over (eleven o'clock, her curfew), Lock had to pick her up.

'That's perfect,' Claire said. 'You can stay with me until eleven. Tell Daphne we're working on the seating chart.'

'Right,' said Lock. 'But Heather might need me before eleven. If she wants to go home early.'

'You're kidding me, right?' Claire said.

He had expected her to be more understanding. She had four children; she was a slave to their schedules as much as he was to Heather's.

'I have to be available for her,' Lock said. He was terrified that Heather would get bored and take off, that she would find fault with him or with Daphne and leave. Claire's kids were younger; they were not at the point yet where they could use their own wings. *But just wait until they do,* Lock said. *It will throw you for a loop. You will understand, then, where I'm coming from.*

Claire said, 'I feel like I've been replaced.'

'I feel funny doing this when Heather's on the island,' he said. 'She's always been away – at school, or on the Vineyard. Now that she's here, I feel worse about it somehow, like I'm betraying her.'

Claire narrowed her eyes. 'How dare you say that.'

'What?'

'I have children, too. I have four sweet, adorable children at home, but I don't throw them down in your path to make you feel guilty, do I? I leave the kids out of it. Heather isn't any different because she's yours; she's not better or more special than my children.'

'I wasn't saying she was.'

'You were so. You said you felt like you were betraying her. All of the kids are getting betrayed, Lock – I've had to live with it since last fall.'

He kissed her head. 'You're right. I'm sorry.'

She pulled away. 'You are so hurtful. You are so arrogant. God, it infuriates me.'

He was tempted to let her go. Even a few weeks ago, this would have been unthinkable. He needed Claire; his happiness depended on her. But Heather was his daughter, his only child. Did he have to keep explaining it?

'I'm afraid she's going to leave,' he said. 'I have to do everything humanly possible to keep her here.'

Claire pinched the bridge of her nose. 'I'm going,' she said.

Lock checked his watch. 'Okay,' he said. Claire flew down the stairs. 'I love you,' he called out. She slammed the door.

He saw her again a few days later, and he apologized. They were both under a lot of stress, he said. Once the gala was over, things would get back to normal.

'What exactly *is* normal?' Claire said.

He laughed, but she did not find it funny. He changed the subject. 'I saw you bought your table for the concert.'

'Matthew paid for it.'

'Matthew?'

'Max West. He sent me a check.'

'You're kidding me.'

'I didn't have the money. Not even close.'

'You said you had money set aside.'

'I lied.'

'Jesus, Claire, if you needed money, you could have asked me.'

'What?'

'You could have asked me. I would have happily bought your table.'

'And what exactly would you have told Daphne?'

'She wouldn't have noticed.'

'She wouldn't have noticed?'

'It all goes through our accountant,' Lock said. 'I wish you had asked me. Instead of hitting up your old rock-star boyfriend.'

'Did you actually just utter that sentence?' Claire said.

'What?' Lock said. 'I would have liked to come to your rescue. I wish you'd asked me instead of Max.'

'You're picking a fight with me.'

'I'm confused. Why did you feel you had to lie to Isabelle?'

'Isn't it obvious?'

'No, it isn't. There was no pressure for you to take a twenty-five-thousand-dollar table.'

'Yes, there was.'

'You imagined there was.'

'Don't be an ass, Lock. There was pressure. "We have to lead by example, I am leading by example, we have to sit up front together . . . " '

She was doing a fair imitation of Isabelle's voice, and Lock smiled.

'Don't laugh. It's not funny. I was bullied into it.'

'Well, you didn't end up paying. You should be happy.'

'Happy?' she said. She was angry now. Her lips were pale and bloodless and her cheeks were blazing. He needed to let this subject go. Was he affronted that she hadn't asked him for the money? Yes, he was, a little bit.

He grabbed her. 'I want to be the person who fixes your problems. I want you to turn to me.'

'But I can't,' Claire said. 'I love you madly and badly, but I can't depend on you for anything because *you're not mine*. And you'll never *be* mine, will you?'

That was the question. The affair had seemed so right when it started; it had been the answer to his prayers. But with each passing day it got more complicated. He felt himself sinking and he wanted to sink, he wanted to become utterly consumed with Claire – but he couldn't take the final step and leave Daphne. He was certainly not willing to do it with Heather at home.

306

'I'm giving you everything I have,' he said.

'You're giving me everything you have,' Claire said. 'But it's not enough.'

'It's not?' he said.

The next day, Benjamin Franklin, treasurer of the Nantucket's Children board of directors, walked into the office and asked Lock to see the financial records since the audit. Lock glanced at Gavin's desk. Gavin was out for the afternoon: his parents were arriving on the island that evening, and Gavin needed time to spruce the house up, get his father's Cherokee serviced, buy flowers and wine for his mother, et cetera, et cetera. Gavin would know where the financials were; he would be able to explain it all to Ben Franklin. Wouldn't you just know that Ben Franklin would come while Gavin was out? Frustrating!

'Why do you want to see them, Ben?' Lock asked. This was, after all, an unusual request. Ben Franklin was reluctant at best about being treasurer, lazy at worst; he liked Gavin to do all the work for him. And Ben wasn't the sharpest knife in the drawer anymore. Lock studied him. Did he even know what he was asking?

Ben chuckled. 'My granddaughter Eliza works at the bank as a summer teller.'

'And?'

'And I'd like to look the books over. To see what it is you're trying to hide.'

'Hide?' Lock said. 'Gavin keeps the most impeccable books you've ever seen.' He stood up, and Ben trailed him to Gavin's desk. Lock opened the filing cabinet. *Financials 2007–8:* a manila folder with the bank statements. He pulled it and handed it to Ben.

'And I need the donor log,' Ben said. 'And a copy of the most recent budget.'

'Yep, yep, yep,' Lock said, trying not to sound impatient. One of Ben's twenty million grandchildren worked at the bank as a summer teller, and for this reason Ben wanted to see the financials? It was a complete nonsequitur. Lock logged on to Gavin's computer, pulled up the files, and printed them out. Ben Franklin and Lock were silent as the pages printed; Lock was preoccupied with thinking who on the current board might replace Ben as treasurer. It was a thankless job; nobody wanted to do it. Lock handed the sheets to Ben. 'There you go, sir. I'm sure you'll find them all in order.'

Ben tipped an imaginary hat. 'I'm sure I will.'

They made a pact: no more fighting. Things had become tense between them.

I feel like you're squeezing me in, Claire said.

It's felt that way to me since we started, Lock said. *I always have to accommodate your schedule. And you're a frightfully busy woman. Now I'm busier because of Heather. I squeeze you in, you squeeze me in. We squeeze each other in. Nothing in this relationship is as one-sided as you think it is, Claire.*

No? she said. She was dying to challenge him. Just seeing his name on the display of her cell phone made her feel combative. It wasn't right.

So they'd called a truce. They shook hands. Just get through the next three weeks, past the gala, get Heather back to Andover, the kids back in school. Start over. Agreed? Agreed.

The work for the gala was almost done. It was time to enjoy it, Lock said. After all, it was a party.

A party! Yes, he was right. The g.d. chandelier was completed. Ted Trimble had it now and he was – very carefully – wiring it. Claire had eight spaces at her table to fill. Since Matthew had paid for the table, Claire was able to give seats away. She invited Siobhan and Carter first and – surprise! – Siobhan was thrilled. Claire invited Adams and Heidi Fiske and Christo and Delaney

Kitt. She invited Ted and Amie Trimble as a thank-you for wiring the chandelier. Already, Claire was feeling better. She was feeling excited. She would be up front, surrounded by her dearest friends. This was *her* event. Max West would play, and Pietro da Silva would auction off the first piece she had created in nearly two years. She was the cochair. This was *her* party, thrown in a tent as big as an airplane hangar. Whoo-hoo!

She needed a dress. She took a full morning off with Siobhan, and together the two of them hit the town. It was impossible to buy certain things on Nantucket – a set of plain blue cotton sheets, for example, or gym socks, children's underwear, a plastic colander, a softball, anything in bulk. But if you were looking for a party dress, Nantucket was utopia. Claire and Siobhan shopped at Hepburn, Vis-à-vis, David Chase, Eye of the Needle, Erica Wilson. So many sensational dresses! Siobhan wanted something black, something dramatic, something that would stand in contrast to her chef's jacket. She found a knockout dress at Erica Wilson, a halter dress with a fitted skirt and beading. Absolutely gorgeous. But everything looked good on Siobhan; she had healthy coloring and a tiny little body. Claire was harder to outfit. She tried on everything: some things looked truly hideous, clashing with her red hair, making her look like a cadaver. She found a few things she liked, nothing she loved.

They ate lunch on the patio at the Rope Walk – lobster rolls, fried clams. Claire felt like a tourist, which was nice, if odd. They were drinking wine to boot – Claire a glass of viognier (she ordered it automatically now) and Siobhan a fat glass of chardonnay.

Siobhan raised her glass. 'This is fun,' she said. 'This is what I miss.'

'Me, too,' Claire said.

'No,' Siobhan said. 'I mean it.' She covered Claire's hand with her own, smaller hand. Claire knew Siobhan's hand intimately – its elfin size, the nails bitten to the quick, the simple wedding band in white gold. 'When all this is over, do I get you back?'

'Don't be silly,' Claire said. 'You have me now.'

Siobhan pushed her darling square prescription sunglasses up her nose. 'Do I get you back, Claire?'

Claire sipped her wine. Her stomach squelched at the smell of fried food in the air. Here, on their carefree day of shopping, Siobhan was asking for something. She wanted Claire back with Jason, ensconced in the Crispin clan, fitted snugly in her place. *Do I get you back?* Meaning: No more Lock.

Their onion rings arrived at that second, and then a woman from the next table asked if Siobhan would take a picture of her and her family. Claire leaned back in her wrought iron chair and looked out at the brilliant blue harbor, the circling seagulls, the white snap of sails, the wispy clouds. The day sparkled. *This is fun. This is what I miss. Do I get you back, Claire? Do I get you back?*

Claire sipped her viognier and enjoyed the sun on her face, despite the inevitability of freckles. The family said, in chorus, 'Cheese!' The question floated away, without an answer.

Eleven days to go. Claire woke up suspicious. Something wasn't right. She rolled over. Jason was gone. He was at the Downyflake; through a fog of sleep, she'd heard him get up, dress, leave. Out in the kitchen, she found her cell phone and called him. It was considered a major foul to interrupt Jason at breakfast, but she had a persistent, nagging worry that something was amiss.

She pictured him in a crowded airport, fed up, leaving. Had he left?

'Hey,' Jason said. He sounded uninspired, impatient – but this she expected. He was marking off the days on the family calendar until the gala. This past Sunday, reclining in his chair at the beach, he'd muttered under his breath (when Claire thought he was asleep), *In two weeks the goddamned thing will be over.*

'Is . . . everything okay?'

'Everything's fine.'

310

'You're at the Downyflake?'

'Of course,' he said. 'Where else would I be?'

Claire made the kids breakfast. She was preoccupied, but she could do it in her sleep. Should she call Siobhan and check on her? No, she was losing her mind. She was looking for something to go wrong.

J.D. said, 'Mom!'

Claire looked up, alarmed. 'What?'

'I want to go to Nobadeer. Pan keeps taking us to Eel Point, and it's a *baby* beach.'

'Think of Shea,' Claire said. 'And Zackie.'

'I want waves,' J.D. said. 'I haven't used my boogie board once all summer.'

'Well, I'm sorry,' Claire said.

'You don't care about me.'

'That's not true.'

'You only care about Zack.'

'J.D., you know that is not true. It hurts me when you say that.'

'It hurts me that I can't go to Nobadeer.'

'I can't let Pan take you there. Zack would drown in ten seconds. And even worse is your sister – she'll be out in those waves, trying to keep up with you, and – ' Claire shuddered. 'I can't even stand to think about it.'

'You take me, then.'

'I'm sorry?'

'Why can't you take me?'

The obvious answer was that she was busy. She had been doing another set of vases for Transom – for income, to appease Jason – and out of the blue, Mr. Fred Bulrush of San Francisco had called. *I heard you were back at it.* How had he heard? Claire had no idea – she had yet to call him back – but it would be nice to get a commission and see some real money. Claire was supposed

311

to meet Isabelle at noon to go over the seating chart, though really this was fruitless: Isabelle would seat people where she wanted, no matter what Claire said. So why *not* spend the afternoon at Nobadeer with J.D.? She loved spending time with the kids one-on-one, though she rarely got the chance. Why not take advantage today? Get sandwiches and sodas at Henry's and take her oldest son to the waves? She could read the new Margaret Atwood novel while J.D. rode his boogie board.

'Okay,' she said. 'I'll take you.'

'I want to go,' Ottilie said.

'Me, too,' said Shea.

'No,' Claire said. 'This is just an outing for J.D. You two are going with Pan. I'll pack extra Oreos.'

Ottilie scowled; Shea was appeased by the cookies. Claire's phone rang. It was Lock – calling at five minutes to eight? Fear gripped Claire's knees. Here it was: the bad news.

'Hello?' Claire said.

'I have bad news,' Lock said.

Claire killed the burner under the bacon. 'What is it?'

'Genevieve can't do it.'

'Can't do what?'

'The gala.'

'She can't *cater* the gala? Ten days and counting, and she can't – '

'That's right. Something about her mother in Arizona – she's sick, terminal, I guess. Genevieve has to get there now, today, she doesn't know when she'll be back, she can't prep an event for a thousand people, and she has no second, no one to take over. We have to find someone else.'

'Like who?'

'Well, I thought you might call Siobhan.'

'Siobhan,' Claire said.

'Yes. That's the obvious answer, right?'

'Right,' Claire said. But was it? The catering question had been painful from the beginning – it had caused a rift in Claire and Siobhan's unriftable friendship – and only now had things settled. Only now did Siobhan seem comfortable with the outcome. To reopen discussions of Siobhan and Carter's catering was unfair. But if Genevieve couldn't do it, someone had to step in, and if Claire overlooked Siobhan as that person – if Siobhan wasn't asked first – there would be a fresh hell to face.

'Okay,' Claire said. 'I'll call.' She hung up the phone and looked at J.D. 'Get your suit on.'

J.D. breathed a sigh of relief. 'Thank God,' he said. 'I thought you were going to bag on me.'

'Bag on *you?*' she said. 'Never.'

She picked up Zack, washed the syrup off his face and hands, and carried him into her bedroom, where she dialed Siobhan.

'Hey,' Siobhan said.

'Hey,' Claire said. 'You know, I woke up with a funny feeling that something awful was going to happen, and it has.'

'Are the kids okay?' Siobhan said.

'Everyone's fine. It's a different kind of awful.'

'Tell me.'

'Genevieve flaked.'

'Huh?'

'She canceled. Her mother is sick in Arizona. She has to go. She bagged the gala.'

Silence. Then laughter. Siobhan was chuckling musically. There were two ways in which this was not funny: it was not funny that Genevieve's mother was dying (Claire had lost her mother to cancer, and so had Siobhan), and it was not funny that the gala had no caterer.

'I hate to ask you this, but – '

'Oh, no!' Siobhan said. 'No way!'

'You won't do it?'

'Are you kidding me?' Siobhan said. 'I have seats right up front and a kick-ass dress. Why the hell would I trade that in so

313

I can spend the next ten days slaving and sweating and swearing? Bad enough I have the Pops to do on Saturday. I have no desire to turn around on Sunday and start prepping for another monster job.'

'It's a lot of money, though, Siobhan.'

'I am happy to say, I don't care.'

'So you won't do it?'

'Don't sound so shocked.'

'I'm not shocked. But I thought you wanted this job.'

'No,' Siobhan said. 'After all the crap I've been through . . . I mean, I realize I'm "on the committee" and that means I should be there in the final hour to bail you guys out, but Edward had a chance to hire me, and he passed. He chose Genevieve. The fact that Genevieve flaked is utterly predictable. I find it gratifying that she flaked because that means I was *not* bad-mouthing her back in April but rather speaking the truth about her. She's unprofessional and she should never have been given the job. When someone comes forty-dollars-a-head under, there's a reason.'

'Okay, well, if you're not going to do it, who else should I call? I have to get someone today.' Claire's phone beeped. The display said, *Isabelle French*. 'Oh, shit, Isabelle's on the other line. I'll call her back. Who else should I ask?'

'To feed a thousand people in ten days?' Siobhan said. 'Nobody I know. It's August, Claire. People are booked and overbooked. If someone is free, there's a reason, and you shouldn't hire them.'

'Great,' Claire said. 'So you're telling me the only people I want are people who aren't available?'

'Pretty much.'

Isabelle's number beeped in again. Claire should switch over, but she wasn't ready for that brand of hysteria.

'Okay,' Claire said. She knew she should be panicked. They had no caterer for the gala – no food, no drink. But Claire felt calm. She had woken up with a bad feeling, and here it was, realized. J.D. walked into the bedroom in his bathing suit with a towel around his neck. Should she bag on him and instead spend all day in the office with Isabelle, dialing every caterer in the phone book? Was this the right thing to do? The right choice was usually the more difficult one. Who had told her that? Father Dominic? Her mother? But putting the gala before her family and disappointing her son could not be the right choice here. So in this rare case, the right choice was the less difficult one. 'Listen, I'm taking J.D. to Nobadeer, just the two of us. Want to meet me there with the boys?'

'I am up to my tits in Pops,' Siobhan said. 'But what the hell, I'll come for an hour.'

The hours Claire spent at the beach were like hours spent dreaming. The sun was hot, the water refreshing, and J.D. was happy and exhilarated by the waves and by his cousins. Siobhan came for an hour and brought Claire half a chicken salad sandwich, a cup of gazpacho, and a bottle of fancy Italian lemonade. Claire's phone rang off the hook – Isabelle, Lock, Edward, Genevieve – but Claire didn't take a single call. She would deal with the catering problem later, and quite possibly, by the time she gave it her full attention, it would be solved. It was liberating to let it go; it was fortifying to spend four hours being herself – a woman who loved the beach, the mother of a ten-year-old boy. She even tried to boogie-board a few times – it was too hot to stay out of the water. She rode the waves to shore, enjoying the swell and the rush, enjoying even the sand in her suit and the salt stinging her eyes.

They left the beach at quarter to five, in time to get home and relieve Pan. Claire was so relaxed that she let J.D. sit in the front seat next to her. His dark blond hair was damp, his bare torso suntanned and rippling with emerging muscles. He, like Jason, would be handsome and strong. J.D. switched the radio station fifteen times – ah, to finally be in control of the music! – and he polished off his Coke, then casually hung his elbow out the open window.

As they turned the corner onto their street, J.D. said, 'Mom, that was awesome. You rock.'

Claire grinned. Her face was tight and warm from the sun. Ten, she decided, was the perfect age for a boy. J.D. did not need the constant caretaking that the other kids needed, but his heart and mind were still those of a child.

'You were great company,' she said.

There was an unfamiliar car in their driveway. As Claire pulled in, her good mood evaporated. It was not an unfamiliar car at all; it was a green Jaguar convertible, the car Lock drove in the summertime. Lock was not a man who got excited about cars. As the director of Nantucket's Children, he always said, he should be driving a twelve-year-old minivan. But this car he loved. The XKR was sleek, curvy, and fast, in a prestigious racing green. He would not park it on the street; it spent all summer in the yacht club parking lot. Now here it was in Claire's driveway. Lock sat in one of the Adirondack chairs next to Claire's mudroom door. He was wearing a khaki suit, a pink seersucker shirt, a darker pink tie, and loafers without socks. A hanging geranium twirled above his head; a few pink petals had dropped onto the creamy shoulders of his jacket. How long had he been sitting there? He was pitched forward, his forearms on his knees, staring expectantly out at Claire's cul-de-sac. Willing her to appear? Well, yes, obviously. Claire had never known Lock to idly wait anywhere, for anything. The man was a model of efficiency, always on the phone, or reviewing paperwork, or drafting letters, or reading relevant articles in philanthropic magazines or the *Economist* or *Barron's*. It was almost like this wasn't really him.

'Who's that guy?' J.D. asked.

Claire was frozen. She could barely twist her wrist to remove the key from the ignition. She was stunned by Lock's presence. He had stopped by unannounced only one other time, and that was back in January, when he had entered her hot shop while she was working. Back then, she had been surprised, yes, certainly, but back then a part of her had been expecting him. Back then, he was always on her mind; thoughts of him followed her everywhere, so the fact that he had appeared out of the blue seemed right. That day had marked the first time Lock had told her he loved her. It had been magic, his appearing to declare that; it had been supernatural. But now, today, Claire was tense, on guard; she was a little repulsed. Part of this was because she looked awful. As she got out of the car, this came into clearer focus: the fronts of her legs were sunburned, she was wearing a damp cotton beach cover-up that had at one time been white but was now the color of old chewing gum, and her hair was like a clump of seaweed, tangled and salty. Her feet were sandy and she could feel freckles popping out all over her face. She did not want Lock to see her this way, looking like something that had washed up on the beach. Nor did she want to see Lock in all his seasonal pink, sockless, his thinning hair windblown from a ride in his convertible. She had done a thorough job of blocking him out of her mind and had success-fully forgotten all about the catering nonsense.

But now she would have to deal with it.

This wasn't what petrified Claire, however. What petrified Claire was the notion that Lock had not come on official gala fix-the-catering nonsense but had come, finally, to whisk Claire away. The Jaguar was the white horse. Lock had been watching for her so eagerly, and stood so suddenly when she emerged from the car, that Claire thought, *Oh, God, he's going to do it – ask me to run away with him.* He wanted her to climb into the Jag and drive off with a wave, leaving J.D. baffled on the porch.

Claire opened the back of the Pilot, pulled out the sandy towels, and took her time shaking them. She slid out the boogie boards, handed them to J.D., and said, 'Would you rinse these, please, sweetheart?'

J.D. was looking at Lock; Lock was looking at Claire.

J.D. took the boogie boards to the hose on the side of the house.

317

Claire trudged up the porch stairs in her dime-store flip-flops. He would never ask her to go with him, she realized. And suddenly that was all she wanted. For him to ask, for him to beg.

'Hi,' she said.

'Hi,' he said.

She wondered about her other children and Pan. They weren't home yet; the inside of the house was too quiet. Claire busied herself with folding the damp towels.

'You've taken me by surprise,' she said, moving to the mudroom door.

'I was on my way home from work,' Lock said. He smiled tightly. 'I've been trying to reach you all day. We have to talk.'

She turned to him. She couldn't breathe. Really, if he asked her, if he meant it, if he promised her all the right things, if he'd thought it through very carefully and still made it romantic and spontaneous, the chance of a lifetime, the chance for happiness with a man who understood her better, differently, would she go with him? No, never. But she might.

'About the catering,' he said.

As they entered the house, Claire wondered: Was it a mess? In her mind the house was always a mess, with the flotsam of their lives littering every surface – bills, mail, magazines, the girls' ponytail holders, Zack's pacifiers and bottles with half an inch of sour milk left, sunglasses, keys, the nails and screws and spare change that Jason emptied from his pockets each evening. Yes, it was all there, the family's life exposed: someone's used Band-Aid was on the counter, and Claire swept it into the trash. Claire had never been to Lock's house, but she gathered it was one of those homes where everything was tucked away so that the place was left with as much personality as a hotel room.

Claire's answering machine was blinking. Eight messages.

Claire opened the fridge. 'Would you like some cold grapes?'

'You don't have to entertain me,' Lock said.

Claire pulled out the colander of grapes anyway and set it on the bar. 'How about a beer?'

Lock shrugged. 'After the day I had? Sure.'

Okay, so he was going to talk about his day, one hell of a day he had, while Claire was at the beach, boogie-boarding and drinking sparkling Italian lemonade. J.D. marched in, and Claire said, 'Outdoor shower, please.'

'I'm going.'

Lock offered his hand. 'Hey, you must be J.D. I'm Lock Dixon.'

J.D. shook his hand, looked him in the eye, smiled. 'Nice to meet you, Mr. Dixon.'

'I'm a friend of your mother's.'

'We work together,' Claire said. 'We're working on the gala together. Mr. Dixon runs Nantucket's Children.'

'Okay,' J.D. said. He disappeared out the back door.

'He has nice manners,' Lock said.

Claire pulled one of Jason's beers out of the fridge and flipped off the top. 'Glass?'

'No thanks.'

He was here in the house, he had met and approved of the oldest child, he was drinking Jason's beer, and Claire was supremely uncomfortable with all of it.

'Give me the lowdown,' she said.

He removed his jacket and hung it on the back of the barstool. He rolled up the sleeves of his seersucker shirt neatly. Here was Lock Dixon relaxing with a beer after work. Claire watched him. He was her lover, but he was a complete stranger.

Claire heard stampeding feet in the mudroom. The rest of the gang traipsed in, Zack crying, Pan looking beat up and weary. The girls, like J.D., stopped what they were doing (bickering), dropped their sodden towels on the floor, and stared at Lock.

'Who's that?' Shea demanded.

'This is Mr. Dixon,' Claire said. 'Mommy's helper on the gala.'

Lock waved at Pan. 'Nice to see you again.'

Pan smiled and handed Zack off to Claire. He was hot and unhappy and his diaper was leaking and full of sand.

Claire wasn't sure what to do. This wasn't exactly how she wanted Lock to see her life.

'Is that your car?' Ottilie asked.

'It is,' Lock said.

'I like it!' she said.

'I have to talk to your mom right now,' Lock said. 'But next time I come, I'll give you a ride.'

'Can I ride, too?' Shea asked.

There was a knock at the door. The front door, which meant UPS or a neighbor's child selling raffle tickets.

'Okay,' Claire said to the kids. 'To the shower, please.' She was using her Julie Andrews voice. *They're only young once! Must enjoy them!* She wanted Lock to see that she was a good mother, the best mother, despite her obvious shortcoming. 'Excuse me one second,' she said, and she went to the door.

There was another knock before Claire could reach the door – crisp, insistent. Claire peeked out the window – another car in the driveway, a cherry red Land Rover with roo bars. So not the Girl Scouts. The first thing Claire saw when she opened the door was the hair, long and lustrous.

'Isabelle!' Claire said. Now she was officially aghast. Zack's diaper was so heavy it was falling off. Claire could hear the girls pounding on the door of the outdoor shower to get J.D. out.

'Hello,' Isabelle said, with a mixture of surprise and distaste, as though it were Claire who had ambushed her at home and not the other way around. She stepped inside. 'Is Lock here?'

'Yes,' Claire said. She looked down at her cover-up, her legs, her feet. Isabelle was looking very tan and lithe in a white eyelet sundress, and Claire was wearing a trash bag with four hot, sandy, hungry children running around like wild Indians. When she had woken up this morning and felt like something bad was going to happen, she could never have predicted that it would be something this specifically *bad*. But as Isabelle walked past her into the great room without so much as a word of apology, or, for that matter, greeting, Claire got ahold of herself. Lock and Isabelle had shown up without warning and had plopped themselves down in her home. She would not allow herself to feel self-conscious about how she looked or about the fact that there was no babbling koi pond at the entryway or that she didn't have a pitcher of gin and tonics and hors d'oeuvres ready. She would deal with these people graciously, then send them off.

First, however, she had to deal with the Indians.

'I have to change a diaper,' she said. 'Lock, will you pour a glass of wine for Isabelle, please? There's a bottle of cold viognier in the fridge.' This was, incredibly, true, and Claire was secretly thrilled. She took Zack upstairs, rinsed him off in the sink, changed his diaper, and dressed him in an adorable blue terry cloth playsuit. When she came back down, Lock and Isabelle were seated at the bar with their drinks, popping cold grapes, while the three kids stood, wrapped in towels, dripping onto the floor and looking like refugee boat people.

'Go get dressed,' Claire said, 'and I'll let you watch a little TV before dinner.'

'What's for – '

'Steaks,' Claire said. 'And corn.'

The children slinked off, casting furtive looks at the strangers in the kitchen. As soon as the kids were gone, Isabelle got down to business.

'We have a serious problem,' she said.

Out the mudroom window, Claire saw Jason's truck pull into the driveway. She felt a wash of relief.

'We'll find another caterer,' Claire said.

'I've called everyone on Nantucket. I spent all day on the

321

phone and so did Gavin and so did Lock. No one is available. I called all the restaurants; I even called the head of the high school cafeteria.'

'I find that hard to believe,' Claire said.

'Someone said the woman did private catering on the side. I called fourteen places on the Cape, all the way down to Wareham, and nobody can do it. The party is too big, they don't have the staff, it's too expensive to get here, we don't have a prep kitchen . . .'

'It's not looking good,' Lock said. 'To bring someone in from New York, which is what we may have to do, will be prohibitively expensive. And again, the problem of the prep kitchen.' He took a swill of beer. Claire needed a drink herself, but Lock had not poured her one. Claire pointedly poured herself a glass of wine. She looked at Lock and Isabelle, sitting side by side in their perfect summer clothes like two people who had escaped from a Renoir painting. They were a natural pair. Claire could see this suddenly, clearly, without feeling one way or the other about it. They should be together. Isabelle was unmarried, or nearly so; the two of them were much better suited for each other than Claire and Lock. She wasn't able to follow this train of thought, however, because at that moment, Lock dropped the bomb.

'We need you to try one more time with Siobhan.'

The 'we' bugged her royally. 'We,' meaning Lock and Isabelle, meaning the people who had slaved over the problem while Claire was at the beach, meaning Nantucket's Children – it didn't matter.

'I did,' Claire said. 'She said no.'

'We need you to try *again* again. We need you to beg. No food, no drink. Or food and drink that is so expensive, we don't make one red cent on this gig, after all the work we've done. You get it? We're up against the wall. Desperate.'

'Desperate,' Claire repeated. She looked at Isabelle, who had her head bowed in folded hands, in a posture of prayer. It fell to Claire and Claire alone – again! Would it never end?

The mudroom door slammed. Jason stepped into the kitchen. He looked at Isabelle, then Lock, then Isabelle again. Claire felt a sting of jealousy, but how could Jason keep from staring at Isabelle when she had all that beautiful long hair and the even tan and the thin gold bracelet at her wrist and the perfectly shaped nails polished to look like glass? She was the most put-together woman who had ever graced their house.

'That Jaguar yours?' Jason said.

'The Rover is mine,' she said.

'Jason, this is Isabelle French, my cochair for the gala. Isabelle, my husband, Jason Crispin.'

'Pleasure,' she said, and they clasped hands.

'Jason,' Lock said, standing. Jason and Lock shook hands.

'The Jag is yours?' Jason said.

'It is.'

'Sweet.' Jason eyed their drinks. 'Can I get you another? Lock, another beer? Isabelle, more wine?' Jason was suddenly the consummate host.

Claire said, 'We're having a meeting. The caterer for the gala, Genevieve, can't do it. Her mother is very sick. We have no caterer.'

'You should ask my brother,' Jason said to Lock. 'And Siobhan. They'll do it.'

'I did ask them,' Claire said. 'They said no.'

'Ask again,' Jason said, popping a beer. 'Or I'll ask.'

'That would be great,' Isabelle said. 'It would honestly be so great if you would ask again. We're up against the wall.'

'No problem.' Jason clapped Lock on the shoulder. 'Are you two staying for dinner? Claire, what's for dinner?'

Was this really happening? Claire couldn't be sure. Maybe she was still asleep in her chair on the beach.

'Steaks,' she said. 'And corn.' She raised her eyebrows at Lock. If she wasn't careful, she was going to say something grossly inappropriate. 'You're welcome to stay if you'd like.'

'No, thanks,' Lock said. 'I have a dinner at the yacht club.'

'Oh, funny,' Isabelle said. 'So do I.'

Funny? When Claire smiled, her teeth were cold. Her face was stiff from the sun and the salt. She wanted Lock and Isabelle out of her house. They could go on to the yacht club for dinner; that was fine. Claire wanted to sit with her kids on the back deck and shuck the corn, and while the corn was boiling and the steak grilling, she wanted to take a long, hot outdoor shower. Jason could call Carter and Siobhan and ask about the catering yet again at Isabelle's behest, but they would say no and Claire would be able to end her day with a fat, satisfying *I told you so.* Claire smiled at Isabelle and Lock a little more broadly. They weren't finished with their drinks, but she didn't care.

'I'll walk you out,' Claire said.

Isabelle downed her wine in one gulp. 'Everything is going to work out,' she said. 'I can feel it.' She slid off her stool, and at the door she linked her arm through Lock's. Lock glanced at Claire. Claire could not look at him.

'I'm sorry we just barged in on you,' Lock said. 'I tried calling.'

'I know,' Claire said. 'I was avoiding my calls.'

'We're in a legitimate bind,' he said.

'I realize that,' Claire said.

'We both found your little disappearing act today discouraging and immature,' Isabelle said. 'You were at the beach! You should have been helping us. You are the cochair.'

She couldn't wait for them to leave. *Get in the car,* she thought. *Please! Leave!*

'Did you?' she said. 'Well, I'm sorry.'

'You don't sound sorry.'

'I took my son to the beach. I had a nice day.'

Lock cleared his throat. He looked like he wanted to shrug Isabelle's arm off, but he was too polite.

'The gala is in – '

'I'm well aware of when the gala is, Lock.'

He sighed and searched her face for . . . what? Love? Tenderness? A sign that she was contrite for not sitting on the phone all day, dialing caterers? At that second, she thought, *Run away with Isabelle, since she's so devoted to the cause!* Lock and Isabelle found her immature and discouraging. What was discouraging was that they had dumped the catering disaster in her lap, and now she would have to own it.

They made their way down the porch steps, Isabelle's arm wrapped through Lock's like a snake. Isabelle trailed Lock to his car, and after he got in, she stood at the driver's side, talking to him sotto voce. Talking to him about Claire.

Jason was in the kitchen. 'Claire!' he said.

Claire wanted Jason next to her at the front door. He was the other half of her united front: the happy Crispins.

'Claire!' he called.

'What?' she said. If he wanted dinner, he could start by lighting the grill.

'Look at this.'

She turned to see Jason crouching down, holding Zack by both hands. But then he let go, and Zack took one, two, three, four, five steps, bumped into the cabinet that held the pots and pans, and fell onto his butt.

Claire shrieked, 'He walked!'

Zack grinned at his parents, then started crying.

'He walked!' she said.

'He walked,' Jason said. 'He's a walker.' He grabbed Claire's hand and pulled her in tight, kissed her throat. She hugged him – and suddenly she was so, so happy, happier than she'd been in a long time.

'He's a walker,' she said. And she hoped that this was all she would remember about today.

* * *

The morning after Claire had offered Siobhan the gala catering job and Siobhan turned it down – once and for all, she hoped that was clear – Siobhan was awakened by a voice in her walk-in closet. She looked at the clock: ten past six. Fucking absurd. Siobhan climbed out of bed, naked as a jaybird, and stood in front of the closet door to make sure.

Yes, Carter was in there. On the phone. He had something to hide. Growing up, Siobhan and her siblings had pulled blankets over their heads, spoken in pig Latin, stretched the cord of the phone all the way to the stairs of the root cellar, then slammed the door for privacy. Gossiping about Michael O'Keefe at first, and then, in later years, about where they hid the beer. They didn't do it to save their father's ears.

Siobhan did not knock – though with the boys always under-foot, knocking before entering a room was law – because the closet was not a proper room. Siobhan flung open the door, and there was Carter, naked as the day he was born, sitting his hairy ass on her velvet footstool, the newspaper in his lap. On the phone with Tomas, his bookie in Las Vegas (where it was three in the morning!), betting on the bloody Red Sox. What Siobhan heard Carter say was, *Put down five thousand even. Schilling is pitching.*

How to describe the scene that ensued? It was cinematic. It was Shakespearean. Siobhan snatched the phone from Carter's hand and ran like a jackrabbit into the master bath. She eyed the oval pool of the toilet, and her gag reflex kicked in. She was going to be sick. She heard Carter coming. There wasn't time! She flushed the phone down the toilet.

What the hell? Carter said.

Siobhan canceled their credit card. *Stolen*, she said. When she hung up, Carter was staring her down. Five thousand dollars! She fired Carter right there and then – fired Carter from the business that they owned together, the business in which he was the head chef. Siobhan had no idea if she had the legal right to do this, but she could not have been more fucking emphatic: *You are no longer part of Island Fare. Do not prep any more jobs. Do not set foot in the kitchen. You are throwing every red cent we have earned into some stinking Vegas cesspool.*

Carter tried several tacks. He apologized with the desperate mien of a druggie begging his dealer for one last score. He cried. *Please, baby, please, one more game. It's a sure thing, I promise. Schilling is pitching, baby!* Siobhan was so livid, she could not speak. She stormed into the kitchen for coffee, and Carter followed, crying, both of them naked. She poured coffee, but she missed her cup; it spilled all over the counter and dripped onto the floor and this sent Siobhan over the edge. In the most venomous whisper she could summon, she said, *You're trying to ruin us!*

No, baby, I'm not . . .

Have you no shame? she asked. Because, really, they had a mortgage and, besides that, two little boys upstairs who would, unlike Siobhan or Carter, go to college someday. Carter was confused by the question. Shame? Siobhan said, *Look at you. Pathetic.*

At this, he became belligerent – *You can't tell me what to do! You can't fire me from my own business!* – and stormed out, though not before stopping in the garage to collect his surfboard.

Siobhan called Claire. If this had happened last August, Siobhan would have regaled her with all the gory details, right down to her visceral disgust at finding Carter resting his unmentionables on the velvet footstool she had inherited from her grandmother. But now, of course, things had changed; she and Claire were operating on a need-to-know basis, and all Claire needed to know was that yes, Island Fare would cater the gala. They were eager to do it.

Claire yipped and made some other yee-ha cowboy noises. *Yesterday was so bad,* Claire said. *But then Zack walked, he took his first steps, and now you're going to cater the gala, just like the two of us planned in the beginning! It feels so right, it's all coming full circle! Hooray!* Claire was eager, then, to get off the phone; she

327

couldn't wait to call Isabelle and Lock and *tell them the happy news!*

Claire did not think – would never, under current circumstances, have thought – to ask, *Why the sudden change of heart? Why, when Siobhan had been so adamant the evening before, was she so eager now? Had something happened?* Claire didn't ask, and really, it was just as well. Siobhan didn't need a lot of caretaking. She was a hardscrabble girl, tough as a turnip, mean as an underfed chicken; she was a survivor. She would make this work all alone; she would be better off without the liars and the cheaters and the gamblers to bring her down. She would be just fine.

CHAPTER ELEVEN

SHE HIDES IT AWAY

The days leading up to the gala were a blur, and Claire couldn't remember which things happened in which order – and in fact, many things happened simultaneously – but each and every detail of these days was charged and important.

On Monday they filled the last table of ten. They had one thousand guests. Gavin answered the phone and took the credit card for the final table, and it was he who led the celebration – high-fiving Lock and hugging and kissing Isabelle, Claire, and Siobhan, all of whom were in the office, ironing out the catering details.

Also on Monday, the late summer issue of *NanMag* was released, featuring the article about Nantucket's Children and the summer gala. The text of the article was long, and preachy about the cause in some places, but no worries – few people would actually read it. What mattered were the photographs! There was a shot of Lock standing in front of the Elijah Baker House, surrounded by half a dozen children; there was a shot of the chandelier (unwired), taken in Claire's hot shop; there was an old snapshot that Claire had dug up of herself and Matthew in high school – they were in the sand dunes on Wildwood Beach, Matthew holding his guitar, Claire staring moodily at the ocean; there was a photograph of Claire and Lock sitting side by side (though not touching) on the edge of Lock's desk.

They were in the office when they looked at the article – Isabelle was actually the one who got ahold of the copy of *NanMag,* hot off the press – and all of them skimmed through it together, Lock holding the magazine while Gavin, Isabelle, Claire, and Siobhan read over his shoulder. Lock read certain lines aloud. ('The summer population may believe their beautiful island is immune to the tough realities that face other communities – substandard housing, latchkey kids, petty crime by teenagers, gangs, drug use – but they are wrong. For example, in the winter months, Nantucket has the highest incidence of heroin use per capita in the commonwealth – and too often, it's the island's children who pay the price.') Claire studied the picture of her and Lock. It was, as far as she knew, the only picture of them ever taken. Did they look like a couple? They did not, she decided. They were completely mismatched, a French film dubbed in Italian, a giraffe with tiger stripes. Claire was still stinging from the way the catering situation had fallen out; Isabelle's words 'discouraging and immature' replayed in her mind.

Claire didn't have the heart to be tart or snotty with Isabelle, however, because Isabelle was morose enough as it was. Not one of the people she had personally invited to the gala had deigned to come. She was candid about this, more candid than Claire might have been in the same situation. *They sent checks,* she said, *but they won't come.* Claire thought for a minute or two that Isabelle was going to blame the declines on Max West, but it became clear from her near-teary demeanor that she took it personally. They

330

weren't coming because of her, because of whatever had transpired last fall, at the Waldorf.

Thankfully, Isabelle was distracted by the magazine article.

Siobhan said to Claire, 'Your hair looks good.' These were the only nice words Siobhan had uttered since coming up to the office. She was exhausted from doing the Pops, which had ended very late on Saturday night and took all day Sunday to clean up, and Carter had been no help. He was sick, Siobhan said. Siobhan had agreed to cater the gala, but she did not seem happy about it. She let everyone in the office know that she was not happy, and everyone in the office, including Claire, cowered and deferred to her because she represented their one and only hope.

'Thank you,' Claire said sweetly, though she disagreed: she thought her hair – which she had tried hard to straighten – made her look like Alfred E. Neuman.

'Your hair looks good, too,' Gavin said to Lock. And everyone laughed. Except Isabelle.

It took Claire a few minutes to notice, but Isabelle was silently seething. Finally she let an audible hiss leak – and she stepped away from the group.

'Nice article,' she said flatly. 'It really showcases all the work you've done on the event, Claire.'

The room fell silent. Claire reeled with surprise – not that Isabelle was offended that she hadn't been photographed or mentioned as cochair, but that neither she nor Lock (nor Gavin, who had proofread the article weeks ago) had *noticed* that Isabelle had not been photographed or mentioned as cochair. What Claire thought was, *Ohhhhhhh, shit*. What Claire said was, 'We all know how much work you've put into this, Isabelle. I can't believe there's not more in this article about *you* . . .'

'There's *nothing* in the article about me!' Isabelle spat.

Claire scanned the article. 'Surely your name is listed as – '

'It's not!' Isabelle said. 'I've been completely overlooked.'

'It's a faux pas on *NanMag*'s part,' Gavin said. 'We should call them right now and complain. Maybe they'll print a correction in the next issue.'

'A correction?' Isabelle said. 'What good will that do?' She snatched up her Peter Beaton bag and stormed out.

Lock closed the magazine. Gavin, Siobhan, and Claire went to collect their things, but nobody said a word. What to say? Isabelle was right. She – the woman who had hired a cellist from the New York Symphony to play at the invitation stuffing, the woman who had wooed Manolo Blahnik into underwriting the event to the tune of fifty thousand dollars, the woman who had painstakingly made a hundred phone calls on the day of the catering crisis – had been overlooked.

Would she quit? Claire wondered. Now, in the final hour? Would she not show?

Lock said, 'Let's give her time to cool down. I'll call her later.'

Lock was on the phone with Isabelle – in the middle of a long, teary (on Isabelle's part) conversation – when Ben Franklin walked into the office. It was nearly six; Gavin had gone home. Ben stood in front of Lock's desk with the financials clenched in his hands for several minutes as Lock attempted to placate Isabelle. ('No one is selling you short. Everyone on the committee understands how hard you've worked, how much of yourself you've poured into this event . . .')

Lock put his hands over the receiver. 'I can't help you now, Ben. I'm trying to talk someone off the ledge here.'

Ben's face was stoic. This lack of emotion, and the way he was holding forth the financials, made him seem like nothing so much as a butler.

'It's important,' he croaked. 'Eliza was right.'

'I'll call you in the morning,' Lock said. 'First thing.'

Ben nodded and, turning on his heels, left the office.

$$* \quad * \quad *$$

On Tuesday, at the office, the phone wouldn't stop ringing. Everyone wanted gala tickets!

'We're sold out,' Gavin said. 'I'm sorry. I'll have to put your name on the waiting list.'

By noon, the waiting list was forty-six people long. What *was* this? Had everyone read the article in *NanMag*? Or were people just such procrastinators that they didn't think about Saturday's plans until the Tuesday before? Either way, they were out of luck. Gavin thought this rather smugly. Despite the fact that it wasn't at all his type of music, he was attending the gala as Isabelle's guest. He had called her on Monday afternoon to see if she was okay, and she had asked him.

Will you be my date for the gala? Isabelle had said.

At first he thought she was kidding. He had laughed.

She said, *No, I'm serious.*

Are you sure there isn't someone else who –

No! Isabelle said. *Absolutely not! I'd like to go with you.*

Isabelle French – the beautiful, wealthy cochair of the event – would be attending with Gavin Andrews, handsome (Best Looking, 1991, Evanston Day) and single office assistant. He was on fire! He wished to God that he had known this was going to happen. If he had known, he would never have . . .

Lock came back from lunch at one o'clock and said, 'Damn! I forgot to call Ben Franklin!'

Gavin coughed. His throat was . . . blocked. Ben Franklin?

'Ben Franklin?' he said.

'Yeah,' Lock said. 'He took a look at the financials. Nice that he takes an interest *now,* for the first time ever, when I am insanely busy with other things.'

Insanely busy with other things. Yes: Gavin had been so busy answering the phone and taking care of other gala business and thinking of sex with Isabelle French that he hadn't even noticed the financial records were missing. Gavin's breathing was shallow; he needed the bathroom. Jesus, he had to get out of here before he was arrested. Go home, get the duffel bag with the money, and leave. Get to Hyannis, at least, then decide where to go. He should have had a better plan! But he had expected to go undetected for a lot longer than this. Ben Franklin took the financials? Unthinkable. Ben Franklin was completely clueless. Even if he looked at the financials, would he know what was going on? Would he see the cash taken from every deposit? Would he be able to figure it out?

Gavin had to leave. The less fanfare attending his departure, the better. He should just say he was going to Even Keel for an iced coffee and never return.

But the fact of the matter was . . . Gavin didn't *want* to leave. He didn't want to leave this office, which had kept him busy and engaged – and had, for the past few weeks, anyway, felt like the center of the universe. The work he was doing fulfilled him; he went home happy. To leave the office now, with the best, most exciting moments to come, with the concert, which Gavin was attending with Isabelle French, on the horizon, would be horrible. To leave Nantucket forever would be even worse. And his parents! Just last night the three of them had had dinner together at the Pearl, and both his parents had remarked on how well he seemed to be doing. Gavin had finally received some much-sought-after approval. Furthermore, it struck Gavin for the first time that his parents were older people – his father now had a hearing aid – and there was no one in the world to care for them but him.

What have I done? Gavin thought. Stupid, idiotic, moronic, immature, insecure, dishonest, small-minded, shortsighted, and pathetic: that only began to describe the little game he'd been playing since last October. What was money? Money was nothing. What Gavin wanted was esteem, and just as he was starting to get it legitimately, his crimes were catching up with him.

How to undo? he wondered. There must be a way.

'I'm going to call Ben right now,' Lock said. 'Hold my other calls.'

Gavin nodded briskly. He had no time to undo. He had to get out of there. But then he heard footsteps on the stairs, and Heather slunk in around the corner, the picture of teenage discontent.

'Dad,' she said.

Lock, who was dialing, hung up the phone. 'Jesus, I forgot!' He jumped up. 'Those are what you call whites?'

Heather shrugged. She was wearing a pink Lacoste shirt, a pair of almost-faded-to-white denim shorts, and a green grosgrain-ribbon belt. And Tretorns that had been laced up backward so that they tied by her toes.

'We have a father–daughter tennis match,' Lock said to Gavin. 'Couldn't have come at a worse time, but we have to play, don't we?'

'You say so,' Heather said.

'We have to! Greta and Dennis Peale? We'll kill them!' He turned to Gavin. 'Are you okay to hold down the fort?'

'Okay,' Gavin said.

Claire was on her way to the rec fields to 'supervise' the construction of the tent. Claire would not be consulted about a single decision, but the gentleman at the town parks and rec department, which owned the fields, wanted a representative from Nantucket's Children 'on hand' in case there were any questions. Claire had called Isabelle to see if she wanted to do this or to help Claire do this, but Isabelle did not answer her phone. She was still pissed about the magazine article. So Claire decided she would go and sit alone in the baking sun while the crew from Tennessee assembled the four-thousand-square-foot tent.

She sat at a picnic table, drinking diet iced tea, playing solitaire. She tried to make the cards say something: Stay with Lock, or leave him? Continue to pray for strength, or just exhibit it, reclaim her life, work on her marriage? She loved Lock and she hated him. The worst things about adultery, it seemed, were countless.

At noon, when the crew broke for lunch, she left.

On the way home, she stopped by Siobhan's commercial kitchen to see if she could help somehow. She couldn't construct a tent, but with direction she could whip up a batch of curried mango chutney.

Claire walked into the kitchen without knocking. Why would she knock? She expected a kitchen full of people – Siobhan, Carter, Alec, Floyd, Raimundo, Vaclav. It was, after all, the middle of August, and Island Fare had a herculean task ahead of them. By not knocking, however, Claire interrupted something. She blew into the kitchen – which had all of the fans running, possibly masking the noise of her entrance – and caught Siobhan and Edward by surprise. Edward Melior? It just wasn't possible. But yes – he and Siobhan were at the long stainless steel counter, standing very close to each other. Siobhan saw Claire first and jumped and pushed Edward away, or so it seemed, and Edward whipped around and saw Claire – and whereas his face registered guilt, it also registered relief. Claire was not Carter.

'Hi,' Claire said brightly and casually, as though there were nothing about finding Edward Melior in Siobhan's prep kitchen that shocked her. On the counter were the makings for the crispy pork wontons. Claire pointed to the stack of wonton wrappers and said, 'Yum, my favorite.'

Siobhan said, 'What are you doing here?'

And Edward said, 'Hey, Claire. How's it going with the tent?'

Claire plucked a water chestnut out of a five-pound can and ate it. 'Tent's going up!' she said. What was going on here, exactly? Siobhan could not abide having Edward's name mentioned in conversation – and yet here they were, alone together. Claire had wondered if something had happened between the two of

336

them at the invitation stuffing at Isabelle's house – they had both stepped away from the table for a long time. But when Claire had asked, *How was it with Edward the other night?* Siobhan had shrugged and said, *Laborious. As usual.* Claire was bowled over by Edward's presence here. And where was Carter? Was she *missing* something?

'What are you doing here, Edward?' she asked.

'Oh,' Edward said. He smiled; he had a smile for every occasion, and this one was his 'pretending to be innocent' smile. 'I was just helping Siobhan fill the wontons.'

'Really?' Claire said. This was the Edward who would eat peanut butter on a roof shingle and who couldn't tell white Burgundy from lighter fluid?

'She's in the weeds,' Edward said. 'And who wouldn't be? She is saving our asses, taking the gala on at the last minute.'

'Indeed she is,' Claire said. She glanced at Siobhan to see how she liked being talked about in the third person. Siobhan's mouth was a tight little pucker, and her freckled nose twitched like a rabbit's. 'I came for that very same reason. To see if I could help. Can I help?'

'I'm fine,' Siobhan said. 'I think I'll just finish up here myself.'

'Yes,' Edward said. 'I have a showing at one, anyway.'

'Are you sure you don't want any help?' Claire said.

'I'm sure.'

Edward jingled change in his pocket. 'I may just stay and help Siobhan finish this.'

'I thought you had a showing at one,' Claire said.

'I do.'

'You should go,' Siobhan said.

'Don't you want me to stay?' Edward asked.

There was an uncomfortable pause.

'Go!' Siobhan said. 'Both of you!'

On Wednesday, Gavin went to work, against his better judgment. It was a gamble, one that was almost as quickening as the act of stealing the money in the first place. Had Lock spoken to Ben Franklin? Would the office be stormed by federal agents? Would Gavin be led away in handcuffs? These were real possibilities, he knew, but Gavin's gut instinct was that he would be safe for at least one more day, and he hoped this was all he would need to figure things out. He had been up all night thinking it through, and he had arrived at a shocking conclusion: He didn't want to leave Nantucket. He didn't want to flee to Southeast Asia or anywhere else. And so he had to figure out a way to put the money back. To unsteal it. This was harder than it might seem. He had pilfered the money over the course of a hundred transactions. He couldn't just deposit the lump sum now. The duffel bag, which contained $52,000, was in the backseat of his Mini Cooper, which was parked, locked up tight, on Union Street. What Gavin needed was for Ben Franklin to back off. Once the gala was behind them and all the summer people went home, Gavin would find a way to quietly square the books. But he couldn't do it now, with everyone breathing down his neck.

Lock strolled in at five minutes to nine. He looked at Gavin and grinned. 'We won at tennis,' he said.

And Gavin, who had decided in the wee hours that the most important thing was not to call any attention to his plight, threw this resolution out the window immediately. 'Did you ever catch up with Ben Franklin?' he asked.

'No,' Lock said. 'To be honest with you, I don't have time to deal with him right now.'

'I hear you,' Gavin said. 'He's not quite right upstairs anymore, anyway. You know that, don't you?'

'I do know it,' Lock said. 'I'll advise Adams to find a new treasurer in the fall. But nobody will want to do it.'

'Nobody,' Gavin echoed. The phone rang.

'Time to get to work,' Lock said.

On Wednesday, Ted Trimble called to say that the chandelier was wired.

'Do you want to come get it?' he asked Claire.

'Yes,' she said.

From the car, Claire called Lock at the office. Things had been stilted and businesslike between them since the catering fiasco, but if anyone should go with her to get the chandelier, it was Lock. And so she asked: Would he go with her to Ted Trimble's shop and pick up the chandelier? Would he help her deliver it to the rec fields? (They would store it in the concession stand, normally used for Little League games, because it could be locked.)

If I move it myself, Claire said, *I'll break it. I'm so nervous about Saturday, I'm shaking.*

You have no reason to be nervous, Lock said.

And yes, he said. He would come help her.

Ted Trimble's shop was unoccupied when Claire pulled in. A note on the door read: *Claire, it's upstairs!* Claire walked up the hot stairs into a cavernous room filled with light fixtures and wires and extension cords and bulbs and stove burners and sections of slant-fin radiator. There were two desks in the center of the room, back-to-back: one for Ted's secretary, Bridget, and one for his wife, Amie, who did the bookkeeping – but neither Bridget nor Amie was around. The fans were running and the radio was on; it was murderously hot. Claire hadn't had time to get lunch, and the climb up the stairs made her dizzy.

She heard Lock call up from the bottom of the stairs. 'Hello?'

'I'm up here,' she said. She did not see the chandelier. She

339

heard Lock reach the top of the stairs, and she said, 'I can't find it.'

'It's right here,' he said.

She turned as he lifted the chandelier from a white box. Lock held the chandelier from the top, where Ted had affixed a silver chain; at the end of the chain was an inverted sterling silver bowl that held the wires. The chandelier dangled from Lock's hands; it twirled, even in the still heat of the room.

'God,' Claire said.

'It's gorgeous,' Lock said. He traced the arc of one of the chandelier's arms with his finger. 'It is absolutely gorgeous.'

Claire knew what the chandelier looked like; she had its shape and form memorized. She had spent more time with this piece than with any other piece in her career. And yet when Lock held it, when she gazed at it from afar, it was like seeing it for the first time. That deep, luscious pink, those twisting, draping arms – it was glorious. It was graceful; it was, as far as glass went, a work of genius.

Claire felt her eyes burning with tears. She was thinking of all the hours that had gone into the creation of that goddamned chandelier – the effort, the energy, the hours that she could have spent, *should have spent,* doing other things: tending to her children, her marriage, her life. The chandelier was the opposite of where she had failed; it was where she had succeeded. And in two days, she would sell it to the highest bidder.

'I don't know if I can let it go,' she said. 'I don't know if I can part with it.'

'It will be in safe hands,' Lock said softly. 'It will be in my hands. I will pay whatever I have to in order to get it.'

This sounded like one of the nicest things anyone had ever said to Claire; the words were meant to comfort and to compliment. Claire thought back to the first auction meeting, when Lock began his campaign to get her back to work. It had been an idea then – and now it was a resplendent reality, dangling from Lock's hands.

Just as their attraction to each other that first night had been a tiny seedling of thought, of curiosity. And now what was it? It was as complicated and as fragile as the chandelier.

What was left unspoken, of course, was that the chandelier would hang in the house that Lock shared with Daphne; it would grace the meals they ate together. It would never hang in the house that Lock owned with Claire. Lock would never own a house with Claire; they would never be together. This, suddenly, was as obvious and oppressive as the heat in the room. Even though Lock would most likely buy the chandelier, Claire would never see it again.

'I have to get out of here,' she said. 'This heat is making me dizzy.'

'Right,' Lock said. 'I'll help you get this to the rec fields.'

They tucked the chandelier back into the box and padded it with Bubble Wrap. They closed the box and sealed it with electrical tape. It was safe. Lock carried it down the stairs with Claire following behind on unsteady feet. Lock set the box in the back of Claire's Honda Pilot.

Claire said, 'Would you drive?'

'Sure.' He took her car keys, got behind the wheel of her car, adjusted the seat. They were alone in her car on legitimate gala business; every other time they had been alone in her car, it had been illegitimate business, the business of their love affair, and this thought made it too awkward to speak, even though Claire had things she wanted to tell Lock: about Isabelle's adamant silence, about her own anger over what had happened with the catering. Claire couldn't speak, but she wanted him to speak. She had fallen in love with him – the silver belt buckle and the bald spot and his deep reservoir of kindness and generosity and the new idea of herself that he had given her. The viognier, the Bose radio, the gardens at Greater Light, kissing him on the chilly cement steps – she had felt like a teenager again, like a person, a woman desirable to him and to herself. It was not tawdry or careless. It was real. She

341

wanted a life where she could reach out and straighten his tie, where they could share a sandwich, where they could stand in line together at the post office, his chin resting on her head. The worst thing about adultery – their kind, anyway – was that that life was never going to happen, and it was so, so sad.

She stared at him. His cheek, his ear, the creases at the corners of his eyes – she knew every inch of him intimately. But he said nothing. Nothing!

The silence was oppressive. If Claire opened her mouth, she knew what would come out. *This is pointless. We have no future. We'll never be together, not properly. Continuing is emotional suicide. What are we doing? How can it possibly be worth it?*

We have to stop.

We should never have started.

Lock pulled into the parking lot of the rec fields. The tent was up now, a white elephant, a spaceship.

Lock cleared his throat. 'It was nice to see you.'

At eight thirty the next morning, there was no sign of Pan, and Claire, because she was busy cleaning up breakfast and deciding how to attack the problem of Isabelle – should *she* apologize for the *NanMag* article even though she didn't write it? – let the kids run around outside in their pajamas. Claire knocked, tentatively, on Pan's door. This was highly unusual. Claire couldn't remember another time when Pan had been even five minutes late; it simply never happened.

There was a groan from inside, which Claire took as a cue to open the door. Pan lay in bed with her hair in her face. The room was stuffy; Pan never opened her windows because she found even summer nights too cold.

'Are you okay?' Claire said. In her mind, she launched automatically into a Hail Mary. Not two days before the gala, not today, when Claire had a list a mile long; not tomorrow, when Matthew was coming; and certainly not Saturday, when Claire would be unavailable from start to finish.

Pan groaned. Claire approached the bed. There was a half-eaten bowl of rice on the dresser.

'Pan, are you sick?'

Pan pushed her hair out of her face. 'I feel hot,' she said.

Claire gasped. Pan was covered with red spots.

On the way home from the doctor, with Pan leaning limply against the car door – Tylenol, the doctor had said, baths with baking soda, bed rest – Claire called Isabelle at home. No one answered, so Claire left a message on the machine.

'Hey, Isabelle, it's Claire. Listen, will you call me when you get this message, please? It seems odd I haven't heard from you this week, and I just want to make sure we're all set with the event.' Pause. Mention the elephant in the room? 'I know you were upset about the magazine article, and honestly, no one was more shocked that you weren't mentioned than I was. It's awful. An egregious oversight. I'll say something to Tessa. Okay, call me, please.'

Claire hung up, then dialed Isabelle's cell phone.

Again, no answer. Again, Claire left a message.

'Hey, Isabelle, it's Claire.' She paused, thinking: *I find your behavior discouraging and immature.* 'Call me when you get a chance!'

On Thursday, when Lock walked into the office, he stopped first at Gavin's desk. Slowly, Gavin raised his eyes from his work.

Lock said, 'Is it true that you're going to the gala with Isabelle?'

'Yes.'

'Daphne told me that, but I didn't quite believe it. Isabelle invited you?'

'I didn't invite myself.'

'Of course not. Well, good, I'm glad you're going with Isabelle. You've worked hard, and you deserve it.'

'I'm sure it seems odd to you . . .'

'Not odd at all,' Lock said. 'Have you decided what you're wearing on Saturday?'

Gavin said, 'Navy blazer, white shirt, madras pants, loafers.'

'Tie?' Lock said.

'No,' Gavin said. 'But you should wear one, as the director.'

Lock nodded and moved on to his desk. Gavin let his breath go. The most crucial thing, he'd decided last night, was to get the money out of his car and into the bank, into the Nantucket's Children operating fund. If it was in the fund, no one could accuse him of stealing it. But Gavin couldn't just show up with $52,000 to deposit, could he?

Claire had said she would come at two o'clock to help, but she didn't show up until four, at which point Siobhan was at the end of her rope.

Claire said, 'Sorry I'm so late. You're not going to *believe* what happened!'

Did the woman think she was the only person with problems? Did she think she was the only person who was insanely busy? One thing was for certain: since she'd decided to cochair the gala, Claire had cornered the market on drama. Siobhan said nothing, and Claire stood there expectantly, waiting for Siobhan to bite. Siobhan would not bite! Siobhan was tired of the way things worked in this friendship, with Claire's problems constantly taking top billing. She would not ask! She was in the middle of poaching six hundred lobsters, a hot and thankless fucking job: you had to rip the claws off the poor buggers before you dropped them in, otherwise the whole mess tasted like rubber bands.

Siobhan would make Claire rip the claws off. Just thinking this made Siobhan smile, which Claire took as her cue to proceed.

'Isabelle isn't speaking to me because of that stupid article in *NanMag*.'

Siobhan didn't know how angry at Claire she really was until she decided, in that split second, to take Isabelle French's side. 'Well, she wasn't mentioned at all. Not once.'

'I know,' Claire said. 'But that's not my fault. How can she blame me?'

Siobhan didn't answer. She held up a lobster; there was a tub of them, crawling all over one another, on the floor. They were really quite unappetizing-looking creatures.

'Here,' she said. 'Rip the claws off, remove the rubber bands, throw it into the pot.'

Claire made a face. 'I can't do that.'

'You came to help,' Siobhan said. 'This is what I need done.'

'What about making the gazpacho?'

'I finished that an hour ago,' Siobhan said. 'If you'd been here at two like you said – '

'I know,' Claire said. 'Sorry. But guess what, on top of every-thing else?' She paused. Waiting for what? A drum roll? 'Pan has the chicken pox!'

Siobhan laughed, though this, she realized, was cruel and may have been crossing the line. 'The chicken pox?'

'She's very sick,' Claire said. 'And contagious to boot, though my kids all had the vaccine. But she can't work. What am I going to do about a sitter?'

'Who's watching them now?'

'Jason. He should be at work, but he agreed to help. What am I going to do about the gala, though? Nightmare.'

Nightmare? She wanted nightmare? Siobhan could redefine nightmare: Carter had spent three days surfing and skulking around the house like a derelict, doing little more than drink-ing beer and eating the junk Siobhan bought for the children –

Go-Gurts, barbecue-flavored Fritos, Slushee pops. Then she caught him on a suspicious phone call on their land line. He'd claimed it was Jason, but the call log showed a number with an unfamiliar area code, and that did it, the camel was on its knees: Siobhan threw him out. She loved repeating the phrase *threw him out,* though in reality what she had said was, *Please make yourself scarce, Carter Crispin. Go away, take a trip, leave the island for a few days, get out of my hair until this gala mess is behind me. Then we can start over, I can focus, we can talk, and we will work this out and find you some much-needed help. Okay?*

And Carter had said, *Okay.*

Siobhan gave him three hundred dollars from her secret till. On the one hand, she couldn't believe he hadn't offered to stay and help her with the gala. How in God's name would she pull it off alone? But on the other hand, she was glad he was respecting her. She had fired him, she was the boss. He would do exactly as she said.

He packed a small bag. Siobhan watched him, both defiant and sad. She loved the man, yes, she did, but he was little more than rocks in her pocket right now.

Where will you go? she asked him.

He shrugged. And did not meet her eye. *Probably the city.*

New York City, she thought at the time. It was only after he was gone that she understood he'd meant Atlantic City.

With Carter gone, Siobhan had been forced to leave the boys at home alone. They were nine and seven and would be able to survive for weeks as long as they had potato chips, a working bathroom, and the TV remote. However, Siobhan felt guilty, guilty, guilty. It was a beautiful summer day and her two healthy sons were sitting in their darkened bedroom, eating tooth-rotting, heart-stopping junk and turning their brains to mush on reruns of *The Suite Life of Zack and Cody.* She might have brought them with her to the kitchen, but in her past attempts to get them to help, to foster an appreciation of her work and perhaps spark an interest in learning to cook themselves, they had complained incessantly, eaten her *mise en place,* and played obnoxious practical jokes like making tea sandwiches out of their boogers. Siobhan could not jeopardize this job by bringing Liam and Aidan to the kitchen, and yet since she left them, she had done nothing but worry – that they might choke on a pretzel rod, or electrocute themselves, or engage in a fight that left them both bleeding, that they might notice the beautiful day and venture out to the beach on their bicycles, which would lead either to their drowning in the ocean or to their getting hit by a car in the road. It was not safe to leave a seven- and a nine-year-old alone, but Siobhan did not have a live-in au pair, with chicken pox or otherwise. She was her own au pair. She was, for the next few days, a single parent, as well as the sole owner and operator of this catering business, which was attempting to pull off a seated dinner for a thousand people. Six hundred lobsters to poach – was she insane? Genevieve at À La Table would have bought the lobster meat frozen (to buy it fresh was prohibitively expensive). However, frozen lobster meat was watery and bland, and despite her diminished circumstances, Siobhan wouldn't compromise.

Claire ripped the arms off the lobster with no small amount of gusto. 'You know, this is cathartic. I need to let off a little aggression.' She ripped the arms off another.

Twelve months ago, Claire would never have been able to rip the arms off a living creature, and now here she was – enjoying it! What did *that* say? Siobhan shook her head.

'I was pretty shocked to find Edward here the other day,' Claire said. 'Is there something going on between you two that I should know about?'

'Something going on?' Siobhan said.

'Yeah. Are you two . . . friends again?'

Siobhan reached into the boiling cauldron with her twelve-inch tongs, pulled out the steaming scarlet lobsters, and dropped them into a sink full of water to cool. She would literally be here all night shelling them, and that thought alone was enough to make her cry.

She turned on Claire with all the fire she could muster. 'I'm not like you.'

'What is that supposed to mean?'

'I am not a cheat like you. I am not a Madame Bovary in love with someone else!'

'I only asked if you were friends!' Claire said. 'I didn't say anything about – '

'You insinuated.'

'I did not! I just thought it was strange. You have to admit, it *was* strange, you and Edward here alone . . .'

'Adultery is a sin, Claire. It's evil. You want to know what I think? There it is. You are committing an evil sin. Against Jason and against your children and against yourself. You are betraying yourself. You are a good person, a person who remembers the mailman's birthday, a person who picks other people's rubbish up off the beach. But now you're a different person. Look at you – dismembering the crustaceans!'

'You asked me to! You said this was what you needed done . . .'

'It's like all of a sudden you don't care about your soul,' Siobhan said.

'My soul?'

'You're going to tell me you love Lock Dixon. You're going to tell me Jason is emotionally unavailable and that the most intimate moments you have are when he reads to you from *Penthouse Forum*. It doesn't matter. You took a vow, my darling, to love him. *Forsaking all others!* Remember that? I was standing there! You're breaking that vow every time you kiss Lock, every time you call him.' Siobhan was on a roll; she was pulling lobsters and dumping them as she spoke, and the steam was heating her up. The truth was bubbling out of her. Claire had lost her moral compass, or it

348

was going haywire. 'Either you stop this thing with Lock, or I'm telling Jason.'

Claire stared at her. 'What?'

'I'm serious. End it. Or I'll end it for you.'

'I can't believe you're saying this.'

'I mean it. I will tell Jason everything I know. I'll tell everybody.'

'You wouldn't do that.'

'I would so. Because I love you, Claire. And I can see how this is changing you and making you crazy and weak. It's ruining you. You have to put a stop to it.'

Claire stared, shaking her head. Siobhan stared back for a defiant moment. She had not planned to lay down an ultimatum, but now that it was out, it felt right. Siobhan had had her chance to sleep with Edward, but she hadn't gone through with it, and she was glad. Her soul was clean – or sort of. There had been the kissing and the groping at Isabelle's house, and then when Siobhan had agreed to take on the catering of the gala, Edward had called to thank her. He had called in his official capacity as head of the catering committee, but they had ended up talking for nearly an hour, and Siobhan told him about Carter's gambling. Edward made Siobhan promise that she would call him if she needed help, and Siobhan said, *Any time you want to swing by the prep kitchen, I'll be there working by myself.* He had come the very next day. He had held her hand and touched her cheek, and they had kissed again, once, softly, and it might have gone further had Claire not come barging in. Siobhan had, in fact, called Edward that very morning on her way to the kitchen to tell him about Carter's exodus to A.C., and about leaving Liam and Aidan alone, and Edward had offered to cancel all of his appointments in order to take the kids out to Great Point in his Jeep. Siobhan had turned him down – the kids didn't know Edward, and news of any outing they took with Edward would make its way straight back to Carter. But it had felt good to have him offer. It was comforting

349

to know that Edward would do anything for her – anything – because he loved her so. Siobhan was such a bloody hypocrite – but God, who wasn't? She was acting in bad faith with Edward, using him as a stanchion when her own husband was failing. She didn't love Edward, and implying that she might was disingenuous and would stop right now, this second. She would sell the engagement ring and give all the money – every penny – to charity. She was going to walk the path of virtue! And by way of her moral policing, she would make Claire walk it, too.

Someday, Claire would thank her.

Besides, the ultimatum had been issued. She couldn't back out of it now. Anyone with children would know that.

Lock was nearly ready to leave for the day when Ben Franklin walked into the office. It was six thirty and the light through the twenty-paned window was slanted and golden, which meant that summer was ending. Summer ending, already? Well, yes, the summer gala was always the last thing on the social calendar, and the charity benefited from the sense of nostalgia people felt when their departure from the island was imminent. Heather would return to Andover on Monday: Lock couldn't stand to think about it. Because of the chaos surrounding the next few days, he and Daphne were taking Heather out to dinner to the Galley tonight. Their reservation was in an hour. Lock was not exactly happy to see Ben Franklin walk through the door, but he had been meaning to connect with the man all week and, for various reasons, had missed him.

'Hello, Ben, hello!' Lock said, standing up. 'Good thing you caught me. I was just on my way out the door.' He reached across his desk for Ben's hand, but Ben's arms were loaded down with the financials. 'Can I help you with those?' Lock said.

Ben dropped them unceremoniously on Lock's desk. 'There's money missing,' he said. 'A lot of money.'

The house was clean. So the objective, on Friday, was to keep it that way.

'We have a visitor coming,' Claire told the kids.

'A rock star,' Jason said.

The day had the feeling of a holiday. Jason was staying home from work. He had been a real trouper since Pan got sick, but his good, accommodating mood seemed to be tied to the fact that the day of the gala was almost upon them and hence almost past them. He was still x-ing out the squares on the calendar with his heavy-lined black Sharpie. *Three days until I get my wife back! Two days!*

Once again, Claire had been awake all night. Siobhan was breaking every best-friend rule in the book. She was going to blow the whistle on Claire; she was personally determined to save Claire's soul. This was so ludicrous that at first Claire hadn't known whether to believe her – but yes, she had to believe her. *I'm doing this for your own good.* Claire had to admit, her relationship with Lock wasn't strong right now. They were too consumed with the gala, and Lock was busy courting his daughter; they had not connected, they had not been intimate. But could she leave him? Could she go back to the person she had been before all this – Claire Danner Crispin, mother of four, local artisan, generally good and moral person? Could she go back to Jason and Siobhan, snap herself back into her rightful place? What would her life be like without Lock? She couldn't imagine anymore. The conclusion that Claire had come to while she was lying in bed was that she would tell Siobhan she had ended the affair, and then continue it secretly. She would be back to lying to everyone.

Claire had thought the day before the gala would be busy, but she was wrong. Everything had been taken care of: the tent was up, the production team was hanging lights, setting up the audio, prepping the stage. The contract musicians were flying in that afternoon; Edward had an associate picking them up and delivering them to their hotel. Gavin had organized the table numbers, the seating chart, the who-went-where. The chandelier was safe and sound in the concession stand. Tomorrow it would be unpacked and put on display.

Claire had called Bruce Mandalay one final time to make sure Matthew was on his way.

'His flight leaves in an hour,' Bruce said. 'He'll be there at seven o'clock, your time. You just have to make sure you get all of the alcohol out of your house.'

'Yes,' Claire said. 'Absolutely.'

'He went out to the bars for the first time in months the night before last. He found himself a fight and spent the night in jail. It hit the tabloids today.'

'Oh no!' Claire said.

'He needs to get out of town,' Bruce said. 'Nantucket will be good for him.'

Claire took the beer and half a bottle of viognier out of the fridge. She took the beer out of the fridge in the garage. She took the vodka out of the freezer. She took the gin, Mount Gay, Patron, Cuervo, vermouth, amaretto, and Grand Marnier out of the liquor cabinet, leaving only club soda, tonic, lime juice, and a sticky jar of maraschino cherries. She put all the alcohol in the supersecret storage place where they hid the kids' Christmas presents, and she locked the door.

Matthew would be there in a matter of hours.

Claire called the office. It was the day before the gala – surely there were things to do?

'Everything is under control,' Gavin said.

'Have you heard from Isabelle?' Claire said. 'I left a message with her Tuesday, and again yesterday, and I sent an e-mail, but I haven't heard back. I'm afraid she won't come to the gala.'

'She's coming to the gala,' Gavin said.

He sounded pretty confident about that, and Claire relaxed a little.

'So there's nothing for me to do?' she said.

'Nothing,' he said.

Jason was taking the kids to the beach.

'Sure you don't want to come?' Jason said.

'No,' Claire said. 'I'd better stay here and wait.'

Wait for what? Matthew wasn't due in until seven that evening. Claire wiped down the countertops yet again. The house was clean, the guest room as immaculate and comfortable as the Four Seasons. Claire had stocked her kitchen with chocolate milk and Nilla wafers, and the freezer was full of cherry Italian ice. Claire checked on Pan. Her fever was down to 100.7 and her spots were starting to itch, a good sign. She was sitting up in bed, reading *Harry Potter.* Claire brought her a fresh glass of ice water and a mug of Thai fire broth.

'I'm sorry I can't work,' Pan said.

'Don't be sorry. We'll figure something out.'

Claire left the room. She had calls out to four different baby-sitters, and she was now waiting to hear back. She would figure something out! Earlier in the week, Claire had bumped into Libby Jenkins, one of the gala cochairs from last year, in town. Libby had asked, 'How're you doing?'

And Claire had said, 'Great. We're right on track.'

Libby had said, 'Don't worry. It's still early. Everything tends to fall apart at the last minute.' She laughed.

Claire had laughed along, thinking, *Clearly the woman has no interest in bolstering my self-confidence.*

As it was, things were held together with string and chewing gum. Matthew was coming off a bad drinking binge, the au pair had the chicken pox, Isabelle wasn't speaking to her, and Claire was being blackmailed by her best friend. In typical fashion, Claire had succumbed to Siobhan; rather than fight her, she had caved in. Rather than say, *No, I will not let you blackmail me,* she had said, *Yes, I will let you blackmail me. I will end things with Lock.*

Just let me get through the weekend, Claire said.

Okay, Siobhan agreed. They had parted amicably. They had kissed good-bye.

No doubt the place where Claire could be most helpful today was in the catering kitchen, helping Siobhan. But Claire did not want to work under Siobhan's judgmental eye. Claire would be chopping cilantro, and Siobhan would be thinking, *Sinner! Cheater! Lying Madame Bovary! Aren't you worried about your soul?*

Claire checked her e-mail: nothing. Isabelle had not turned up. Claire checked her outfit. She had finally found the perfect dress at Gypsy. It was a Colette Dinnigan of green and gold lace. It was formfitting but flirty and feminine – silky, lacy, sexy. Claire checked her high heels, and the jewelry she planned to wear. She confirmed her hair appointment at the salon. In the morning, forty women were gathering to decorate – tablecloths, flower arrangements, candles, tasteful and discreet balloons. Lock would make a speech, then give a short PowerPoint presentation. Adams would do the thank-yous. Pietro da Silva would auction the chandelier. Matthew would perform.

Claire sunk into the sofa. There was nothing to do but wait. Wait for things to go wrong.

He had played for Queen Elizabeth, Princess Diana, Nelson Mandela, Jacques Chirac, Julia Roberts, Robert De Niro, Jack Nicholson, the sultan of Brunei, the Dalai Lama; he had played Bill

Clinton's second inauguration and Super Bowl XXVIII; he had played at both the Oscars and the Grammys. He had played Shea, Fenway, Madison Square Garden, Minute Maid Park, the L.A. Forum, Soldier Field, the Meadowlands. He had sung with Buffett, Tom Petty, Dylan, Clapton, Ray Charles, Jerry Lee Lewis, Harry Connick Jr., Harry Belafonte, and the Boss; he had recorded sound tracks for sixteen major motion pictures, two HBO series, and five commercials, including ones for Coca-Cola and RadioShack. And Max West, aka Matthew Westfield, thought he had never been so nervous as when he arrived on Nantucket to see Claire Danner again.

Well, maybe once: On the dark school bus, in December 1986, the bus that was taking the chorus from the elderly folks' home in Cape May back to their high school in Wildwood. Matthew and Claire were juniors; they had been best friends since they were twelve. He had slept next to her, platonically, in bed; he had seen her pee, he had seen her puke beer out her nose. She had broken up with Timmy Carlsbad, and he had listened to her cry for three weeks. He had broken up with Yvonne Simpson, and Claire had fallen down the stairs on her way to get the phone at two in the morning when he called to tell her. On that night on the school bus, Matthew was feeling good. He had performed three numbers with the barbershop quartet, and the old people's eyes had lit up. They had smiled; they had clapped and called out, *Bravo! Encore!* It was his first taste of being a star, and he was high from it. He thought, *I never want this feeling to end.* He had brought those people – whose lives were nearing their dismal end – happiness, just by singing. So let's say it was all timing: Claire laid her head on his shoulder, put her hand on his leg, and said, 'You were great. I'm proud of you.'

He had immediately gotten an erection, which was, at sixteen, not an uncommon thing. He had in fact masturbated while thinking of Claire more than once, though he never would have admitted it to her or anyone else. She was his closest friend, close enough to be his sister. He shouldn't feel this way about her, but he did. His dick was a shaft of glowing steel; her head on his shoulder and her hand on his leg were bright, burning spots, his heartbeat was an amplified bass line. Surely she could feel it? Should he kiss her? He wanted to kiss her. But either she would become angry, which he didn't want, or she would laugh, which he couldn't bear. He sat through one, two, three agonizing moments. Was he brave enough? He was sixteen, but he had the wisdom, somehow, to know that another moment like this wasn't likely to come along anytime soon: the dark bus, him a star.

He lifted her head. He kissed her – it remained the singular kiss of his life.

Romantic nonsense? This was the question Matthew had asked himself over and over again since October, when he had learned he would be seeing Claire again. Was it all just romantic nonsense, a fixation from his youth? Would she even be recognizable to him as the same person when he saw her? Would she still have any of the qualities that he treasured and had kept in his heart all these years? Had she aged? Had she changed? This was the kind of nervousness he supposed people felt when they attended high school reunions – which he never did, for obvious reasons.

Jesus, the anticipation was killing him!

His pervasive thought, of course, was that he needed a drink – and he did keep alcohol on the plane for emergencies such as this one. But he had had it all removed specifically for this flight because he knew himself. He knew he would want a drink, but he didn't want to have been drinking when he saw Claire. He had nearly derailed two days earlier. He had gone out with Archie Cole, the drummer from Sugar Shack, who was so young and clueless he didn't realize Max was an alcoholic. They got completely hammered on gin and tequila, and Archie picked a fight with a complete bozo at one of the clubs, and Max, in an attempt to help Archie out, got socked in the eye and ended up in the slammer. It was typical idiot stuff; he had to stop!

356

The plane landed, but they were delayed on the runway.

Matthew whipped out his cell phone and sent her a text message. *Just landed. I'm nervous.*

A second later, his phone beeped. The message from Claire said, *Don't be nervous. I'm here alone.*

There was a special part of the airport for private planes. Matthew sat, searching out the window, fidgeting. *Let me off!* Where was she? She was there somewhere.

Finally they opened the hatch and let the stairs down, and the pilot said, 'Welcome to Nantucket Island.' And Terry and Alfonso, who had been asleep, woke up and descended before him. Sometimes when Max West's plane landed, the press or a private citizen got wind of it, and there was a crowd of fans, waiting, screaming, and waving signs, and it never failed to make Matthew feel like one of the Beatles. But this time, tonight, when he descended, there was only one person waiting. She had gotten security clearance, because she was standing there at the bottom of the stairs, alone as promised. Matthew looked at her, and his mind went blank. She smiled at him – grinned, really, like a seventeen-year-old girl – and wrung her hands.

What did he think? He couldn't think. He was gazing upon something beautiful that he had lost, but that now, amazingly, was found. Claire. She was herself, the red hair, the thin white wrists, the green eyes. She reached out for him, and he hugged her and his eyes filled with tears. They did not speak. He lifted her up off the ground. She was as light as a feather. It was miraculous, as miraculous as if she'd been dead all these years but had somehow been brought back to life. His Claire.

In the car, she talked and he gawked. He sat in the front seat of her SUV, which smelled like rug shampoo. Terry and Alfonso were in the back; Alfonso was smoking, finally, gratefully, after Claire had assured him it was okay, and he was careful to blow the smoke

357

out the window. Matthew held Claire's hand – he couldn't help himself, because his primary emotion was fear that she would vanish. He had last seen her, Jesus, twelve years earlier, at a concert at Boston Garden. She had come backstage with Jason, who was, at that time, her fiancé. Matthew had been married to Stacey then, though he was drinking heavily and their marriage was on the rocks. Stacey had been jealous of Claire, and their meeting backstage was chaotic and awkward. Matthew had been drunk or high; he had paid too much attention to Jason – trying to impress or intimidate him – and not enough attention to Claire, though Stacey accused him otherwise. Then Claire disappeared into the crowd, and Matthew was too high to feel the loss of her. He felt it months later, his first time at Hazelden.

He would not lose her again! She was whole and perfect, an artifact unearthed. She did not know it as she chimed along about the gala, but he had no intention of letting her go.

She dropped Terry and Alfonso off at their hotel, and then they were alone. She thanked him, yet again, for coming to play, and he said, 'I would do anything for you, Claire Danner, and you know it.'

At a stop sign, she reached across the car and touched his face. 'What happened here?'

He had a dark purple crescent beneath his eye, and some yellowing on his swollen upper cheek, where he'd taken that punch.

'I was out of line,' he said. 'Got what I deserved.'

'You were drinking?' Claire asked.

'Drinking and stupid,' Matthew said. What he needed was someone to keep him on the straight and narrow. Someone like Claire! 'It won't happen while I'm here. I promise.'

'Okay,' she said.

They pulled into her driveway. The house was large and lovely, lit from within. He had pictured Claire in just such a house, happy and bright. She deserved it.

'Here already?' he said. He should have asked her to drive

around some, show him the island, even though it was nearly dark. He didn't want to go inside and face the husband and the kids. He wanted Claire to himself.

'Here already,' she said.

Max West was a rock star, but since Bess and the dogs had left, he had gotten used to being alone. Claire lived in a house full of people: her husband, a slew of kids. So many people!

'Matthew, this is Jason,' Claire said. 'You remember my husband, Jason Crispin?'

Matthew did not remember Jason. He could not have picked Jason out of a crowd of two – they had met so long ago, and Max had been wasted, and nothing about Jason was remarkable. He was a big guy – well, bigger than Matthew – and rock solid with muscles, he was tan, he had blond hair, and there was a day's growth on his face. He was a handsome enough guy, Matthew supposed, but was he special enough for Claire? Max didn't think so. Could Max take him in a fight? That remained to be seen.

'Hey, man, how're you doing?' Jason said. He had an aggressive handshake and that eager glint in his eye that everyone got when they met *Max West*. 'Good to see you again. I am a *huge* fan!'

Matthew smiled. So underwhelming. Not special enough for Claire, not even close. The most interesting thing about Jason was that he was drinking something from a blue plastic stadium cup. Was it beer? And if it was, would Underwhelming Jason offer Matthew one? Because being in Claire's actual house and meeting her actual family was making him anxious, and when he got anxious, he got thirsty. He needed a drink.

Underwhelming Jason noticed Matthew's gaze. He tipped his cup and said, 'Iced tea. Can I get you one?'

Iced tea? Matthew nearly groaned. Bruce had called.

'No, thanks, man,' Matthew said. 'I'm all set.'

Meanwhile, Claire had the children lined up like Russian dolls, ready to meet him, and she was running through the names. Jaden,

Odyssey . . . or did she say Honesty? He missed the third one's name completely but caught that the baby's name was Zack. The kids were beautiful, gorgeous, with their golden red hair, their summer tans, their gap-toothed smiles. These were his kids.

'It's nice to meet you!' Matthew said to his kids. 'I brought presents!' He unzipped his duffel and pulled out the black Louis Vuitton shopping bag that his assistant, Ashland, had handed him on the tarmac at LAX. He'd sent her, at the last minute, to Rodeo Drive to get the kids gifts. *They're little kids,* he'd said. *Or maybe some of them are grown. Two boys, two girls. Get a range.*

The kids ravaged the packages as if it was Christmas morning. He, Matthew, was Santa Claus. Claire and Jason looked on politely. Claire said, 'You didn't have to bring them anything, Matthew. They have everything under the sun.'

'But we don't have one of these!' the oldest boy – what was his name? – shouted. He held up a silver Colibri lighter.

'What is that?' Claire said. 'Let me look at it.' She flipped it open. Flame. 'It's a lighter.'

Matthew filled with dread. There was a typical rock-star move: buy a ten-year-old boy a hundred-dollar Italian lighter so he can take up smoking weed in the basement with style.

'Mom, give it back!' the kid said. 'I want it!'

'You're going to burn the house down,' Claire said. She was laughing, sort of. It was strained. Matthew could not look at Jason. The worst thing was that now Matthew would have to fire Ashland. A lighter? What had she been thinking?

'What else is there?' Matthew asked nervously. A bong? A handgun?

There were two Louis Vuitton silk scarves for the girls, as well as some Chanel eye shadow in the blue palette. Claire looked like she was going to pop a vein. She would never run off with him now. In the box for the baby, Zack, was a remote control Ferrari Testarossa. That was a hit with everyone except the baby. Jason, especially, seemed enthralled. Max exhaled, relaxed a little bit. Okay, Ashland could keep her job.

'Can I get you something to drink?' Claire said. 'We have iced tea, water, milk, chocolate milk, juice – OJ, pomegranate, and apple-cranberry – or I could make coffee. Espresso, cappuccino, regular, decaf . . . ?'

Matthew was dying to ask for a beer. Just one cold beer – the situation was unusually stressful, so he deserved one beer. He wouldn't get drunk. He was a gin man; beer, for him, was like juice. But he couldn't bring himself to ask; Claire would be disappointed in him, and she would know how weak he really was, unable to last ten minutes without a drink. He opted for coffee, and Claire made a pot.

The evening wore on. Matthew wanted to be with Claire, and Claire alone – it was Claire, after all, that he'd come to see – but Claire's house was a circus, it was the boardwalk on an August night, it was an obstacle course. Matthew was introduced to the nanny, a Thai girl named Pan, who had the chicken pox. She stood across the room bowing to him, and he thought of Ace in Bangkok. (In the end, he had given her five thousand dollars to help her pay for college.)

'Sawadee kop!' Matthew said. He could say hello in forty languages. Did Claire know this? Pan giggled and ducked back into her room. Matthew would much rather have talked to Pan, but Underwhelming Jason was right there at his side, dogging him.

'That's right, man, you toured in Asia. What was that *like,* man?'

What was it like? Matthew could talk about this all day. He had played for people with totally different belief systems – Buddhists, Muslims, Hindus – but Underwhelming Jason, like every other American man, wanted to talk about the girls, the perks, the money. Matthew needed a drink. He needed some quiet time, alone, with Claire. He found it hard to believe that mankind had created the iPod, a ten-ounce slab of plastic that could play twenty thousand songs, but had been unable to invent a way to travel back in time twenty years, to the happiest days of your life, and allow you to stay there. *Claire!*

She fussed over him – put out a bowl of Nilla wafers, his favorite, and brought him a bag of frozen peas for his eye. It grew later, and finally she excused herself to put the kids to bed.

'It's so good to see you,' she said before she went upstairs. 'I'm really glad you're here.'

'But you're coming back downstairs, right?' he said. Desire had thickened his voice. He sounded, to his own ears, like he was tipping his hand.

Jason grew silent and looked at Claire.

'Yes,' Claire said. 'I'll be back down to say good night.'

He was nuts, he thought, believing that he might have some time alone with Claire when her husband was in the house. It would be smarter to wait until the morning, when Underwhelming Jason went to work. However, much to Matthew's delight, Jason retired first (he was an early riser, he said, by way of apologizing, it seemed). Matthew shook Jason's hand, giddy to see him go. The feeling of being in a time warp intensified. How many late nights had Matthew and Claire sat up watching a movie, waiting for Sweet Jane to go to bed so they could fool around?

Left alone to his own devices, Matthew hunted through the fridge for a beer. Nothing. There was a bar in the living room, a beautiful built-in bar with rows of sparkling glasses, but the cabinets were empty of everything but mixers and garnishes. Claire had done her homework. It was an act of love, he knew, a demonstration that she cared about his well-being, but it was maddening. He wouldn't survive another minute without a drink, so he sneaked quickly to the fridge in the garage. Empty!

He returned to the living room, defeated, and shaking from too much caffeine. The Thai au pair appeared in her nightgown. He noticed her necklace – a tiny silver bell – and he reached out to touch it. 'That's pretty,' he said.

'Thank you,' she said. She was covered with plump red spots. 'I get you anything?'

I need a drink! he thought. He could enlist the au pair to help him! But Claire would know, she would find out, and she would be so disappointed, or maybe, like Bess, she operated on zero tolerance and she would ask him to leave.

'I'm all set,' he said. 'Thanks!'

Pan bowed, and Matthew repaired to the back deck. The tender, bruised skin around his eye throbbed with pain. He was a rock star, and the world was his oyster. He could have anything he wanted. But could he have Claire? He was as spoiled as a child – Bess had said this time and again. He was used to instant gratification. The best things in life, she'd said, are the things you have to wait for.

Well, he had waited twenty years for Claire. He could wait ten more minutes, couldn't he? Was she feeling the same way he was? Would she leave with him? He wanted to know, now!

Tomorrow, he thought, he would have a drink.

He was *here,* in her *house*. She still had a hard time believing it. The Second Coming of Matthew.

He was waiting for her on the back deck, his elbows resting behind him on the railing, his legs angled forward. He was in jeans and bare feet, watching for her.

She grinned. He was here! It was him!

'God,' he said. 'You are still so beautiful.'

That voice. It had always been his voice more than his looks that had captivated her.

He put an arm around her and she leaned into him. It was

363

friendly and comfortable; they were sliding back into their old identities, their teenage selves.

'It is *so* great to see you.'

'I know,' she said. 'Honestly? It's like we were never apart.'

He gave her a squeeze. They didn't say anything else for a while, though there were things she might have asked him, things she wanted to know – about Bess, about his drinking problem, about his famous affair with Savannah Bright – but it was better, somehow, to pretend for a minute that none of that had ever happened. She wanted to forget Lock and Jason and the kids inside and just try to locate her old self. She wanted to be that girl on the boardwalk, in the dunes eating lobster, jumping into the passenger side of the yellow Bug. She wanted to rest in Matthew's arms and pretend, for five minutes.

He smelled the same. Was that possible? He had, as a teenager, smelled like whatever brand of discount laundry detergent Sweet Jane favored, and secondhand smoke from his older sisters' cigarettes. And that was how he still smelled. She looked up at his face, a face she had most frequently seen, in the past twelve years, on the screen of VH1. He started humming in her ear, and then the humming turned into singing. He was very softly singing 'Stormy Eyes' in her ear. A private concert for Claire. He had written the song for her the week before they parted ways. 'Stormy Eyes' became his first hit.

He held her face. She was crying now – of course she was crying. He couldn't sing that song to her and not expect her to cry. And then he kissed her. He kissed her slowly, carefully, and she thought of Matthew on the dark bus, a sudden, surprise superstar. 'Sweet Rosie O'Grady.' Matthew, with his guitar slung across his back; Matthew the night they played strip poker and he got so, so jealous. *That girl of mine makes me crazy.* Matthew standing beside the examining table: Claire was pregnant, she knew it, Matthew was going to have to sell the Peal, and she was going straight to hell. *Anemia!* Matthew onstage at the Pony, Claire standing behind him, banging the tambourine against her hip like Tracy Partridge – he was already gone from her, she could see it, even before Bruce introduced himself, before they drove to New York in Bruce's Pinto and Bruce bought Claire a cheeseburger and Coke at a turnpike rest stop. She could have held on tighter, she knew that, but she let him go, and look what happened. He became a star. And as a star, he'd come back to her. Here he was.

Could all these thoughts be contained in a single kiss? It seemed impossible, but yes.

He pulled away. 'I love you, Claire. I want you to come with me when I leave.'

She was confused. 'And do what?' she said.

'Live with me. Marry me.'

'Matthew?' she said. The idea struck her as funny, and then it struck her as sad. He was so lost. And she was lost, too, more lost than he knew.

'Will you?' he said.

'Oh,' she said. Oh, oh, *oh!* Dear, darling grace of God. He was asking her for real. He meant it. 'I wish I could. Believe me when I say, a part of me wishes I could.'

'Your kids can come with us. We'll get a tutor – lots of people do it on the road. It will be good for them to see other countries, to learn other languages, experience other cultures.'

'Matthew,' she said, 'I have a life here.'

'You'll have a life with me. Please? I need you.'

'You need someone, but that someone isn't me.'

'It is you. You're telling me you don't feel it?'

She felt something. What was it? Vestiges of old heartache, intense nostalgia, delight at seeing him, at touching him, at hearing him tell her she was still beautiful. A part of her wanted to run away with him; a part of her wanted to escape the turmoil she'd created, just leave, run off, go on tour, take the kids or leave them behind, get out of there. She had a lot of feelings, but she did not mistake any of them for love.

365

She kissed him on the tip of his nose. He still had the scar – measles, age seven. She hadn't seen him in forever, but she knew him so well; she knew what was best for him. He had not wanted to go to California to record the album; he didn't want to leave her. She said, *If you don't go now, you'll miss your big chance!* They fought about it; she insisted. *You have to go!* He couldn't figure out why she was pushing him away. Things should have been the other way around: he should be wanting to go, she should be begging him to stay. Things were backward. He went, he wrote 'Stormy Eyes,' he became a rock icon.

He may have forgotten all this. She would remind him in the morning. She laid her head against his chest. In there, his heart was rattling.

'Everything is going to be okay,' she said. Someone had told her this recently, but who was it?

Matthew relaxed. He may have believed her.

CHAPTER TWELVE

SHE KNOCKS IT DOWN

She woke up with a burst of adrenaline, as if someone next to her had rung the bell. This was it. Post time!

Jason had gone to the Downyflake; he would have breakfast, check on things at the work site, and be back by ten so that Claire could head to the tent to decorate. He'd left a note on the counter: *Look outside.*

She looked: there was a crowd of people on the cul-de-sac in front of their house. What were they doing there?

'Autographs,' a voice said behind her. Claire turned. Matthew peered over her shoulder out the window. 'They're here for me.'

'They are?' Claire said. 'Really?' This she had not predicted – that people would know Matthew was staying here, that they would come here, camp out with their cell phones and their iPods, hoping to see him, touch him, talk to him.

'Really,' Matthew said.

'It happens everywhere you go?'

'Everywhere.'

'Your eye looks better.'

'Does it?'

'No,' she said. He smiled, but she knew he was hurting. The problem, she decided, was that they had never had proper closure. Their relationship was a campfire that had smoldered for years; it had not been doused. Matthew was lonely without Bess, he was a hostage to his alcohol addiction, and he was grabbing for Claire because she was stable. Or so he believed. But they couldn't go back to Wildwood Crest in 1987, no matter how much either of them wanted to.

'What would you like for breakfast?'

'A Bloody Mary.'

'Matthew.'

'I'm kidding.'

'You promised me you'd be sober for tonight.'

'I'm kidding!'

Claire grabbed his arm. Upstairs, she heard Zack crying. 'I would make you miserable.'

'I don't believe that,' he said.

She touched his cheek, carefully, below his black eye.

'I love you, Claire,' he said.

And she said, 'I know.'

She was a get-it-done machine. She had yet to nail down a babysitter, but as she was flipping a tower of pancakes for Matthew and the kids, it dawned on her. She stepped outside. The gawkers were gathered on the cul-de-sac like a Greek chorus. Claire approached three teenage girls and asked if any of them could babysit that night. All three had planned to crash the gala to hear Max West sing, but one – the oldest, most together-looking one, Hannah, her name was – agreed to babysit if she could get her picture taken with Max West.

'Done,' Claire said. 'We'll need you at five.'

She was the Energizer Bunny. She was stage manager, den mother, multitasking superwoman. She tied five hundred silver balloons to the backs of chairs, she centered flower arrangements and smoothed tablecloths, she reviewed the timetable with Gavin, she inspected the greenroom – no alcohol in there, right? Right. She folded programs, she called Jason twelve times – Shea had a birthday party from one to three, the present was wrapped, he just had to drop her off and pick her up, and Zack could sleep in the car. J.D. was going to the Fiskes' house; Ottilie was not allowed to wear the eye shadow Matthew had brought, no matter how convincingly she made her case. No TV for the kids today, and no cigarettes for Jason.

'I'm going to need you to be charming tonight. Talk to people, make conversation, even though you hate it, okay, Jase?'

'Okay, boss,' he said.

Claire avoided the prep kitchen. Siobhan would put her to work, and although she didn't have time to punch out five hundred rounds of brioche with a biscuit cutter, she would be too cowardly to turn Siobhan down.

Claire did not see Lock, nor did she see Isabelle.

When she drove back to the house to pick up Matthew, she found him commingling with the gawkers on the cul-de-sac. Had any of them given him alcohol or weed? She was suspicious, but she didn't have time to investigate.

'We have to go!' she said.

In the car, Matthew said, 'Are you breathing?'

Claire said, 'If we don't haul ass, we're going to be late.'

He said, 'I don't think I've ever seen you like this.'

They picked up Terry and Alfonso and drove back to the tent for the sound check. This time, Claire did look for Lock and she did look for Isabelle – no luck – and she felt a flash of self-righteous indignation. Where were they? Why weren't they helping – the executive director and the event cochair? Claire checked the greenroom again while Matthew was onstage. *No alcohol in here, right? Right.* Claire went to her hair appointment. She had her head tipped back in the sink and hot water rushing over her scalp when the stylist said, 'You seem kind of tense.'

Right, Claire thought. Could she even begin to explain? Today was the day, tonight the night; it was the culmination of a year's work. So much had happened, so much had changed. She had changed. She had spent hundreds of hours and thousands of dollars (thousands of hours and tens of thousands of dollars). She had experienced all of the stress and heartache promised to her at the beginning, and then some. And in eight hours, it would be over. Claire would be in bed. The thought should have been the source of enormous joy and relief, but instead, Claire felt depressed. All that anticipation and buildup and preparation, and like everything else, it would end. They would be left with . . . what? A pile of money. Hope and happiness for kids who needed it. That was the whole point.

Gavin arrived at Isabelle's house at five o'clock. They had time for one drink, and then they had to go: Gavin had myriad responsibilities at the tent. The gala would not come off properly without him there, directing. He should skip the drink and proceed posthaste to the tent, but Isabelle had been adamant – *Come at five, we'll have time for one drink* – and Gavin found her impossible to deny.

She was sitting on the bench by the koi pond in the foyer when he arrived. He didn't have to knock; the front door was wide open and she was waiting for him, dressed in a stunning red valentine of a gown, with her hair like a waterfall over her shoulders. She raised her face when he walked in, and he could tell she'd been crying.

'Are you okay?' he said.

She all but collapsed in his arms. Hopes for a light, breezy – and quick – drink went down the drain.

'I just got off the phone with my ex-husband,' she said.

He didn't have time for this. He had to get to the tent; there were fifty volunteers currently donning black T-shirts and eating a staff meal of hot dogs and macaroni salad, donated by the Stop & Shop, waiting for him to give them their orders. Gavin knew nothing about the business of ex-husbands, or of emotional intimacy in general. Call him self-absorbed – that was probably true – but no one else's problems had ever captured his full attention. But in this case, his reticence was founded. He had to get to the tent! Run the gala! Isabelle was the cochair; she should know this.

'Is everything okay?' he said.

'He called ostensibly to wish me good luck tonight,' she said. 'But every time we talk, we get sucked down into the same old emotional quagmire.'

Gavin was holding her tentatively. She was warm in his arms, and she smelled like powdered sugar.

'I made such a fool of myself last fall,' she said. 'There was another man. I was in love with him; he said he was in love with me. In fact, he said he was in love with me first, and that was why I fell in love with him. But he was a compulsive liar. He couldn't leave his wife, never had any intention of doing so, despite frequent promises to the contrary, and then he claimed that he was staying with her for financial reasons, that he loved me but he couldn't let her put him through the wringer. And he had kids, a retarded daughter in a home, and two boys at Collegiate. He didn't want to lose them . . .' She stopped. 'Can I get you a drink?'

'Uh,' Gavin said, 'sure.' He took a deep breath. The koi pond made bubbly noises at his feet, and he watched the fish darting through the water. It might have been better if he'd been born a fish. The world of human beings, of relating to them in a meaningful way, bewildered him. (Lock and Claire, Edward and Siobhan, the guys who'd led him astray at Kapp and Lehigh, poor Diana

371

Prell in the broom closet, even his own parents – he had never understood them.) He didn't know how firmly or gently to hold Isabelle. She had thrust herself upon him, but he'd been holding her now for a few minutes. Should he let her go or pull her closer? 'But we should probably leave soon.'

She raised her face to him. 'Would you kiss me?'

It was official: he was flustered. How many times had he chastised himself for not kissing Isabelle on the night of the invitation stuffing, when they were alone, standing close together under the intoxicating spell of the moon garden? That had been a painful moment of cowardice on his part, a missed opportunity. But this was different. The sunlight was intense, and Gavin's every muscle and tendon was alert with the pressing need to *get going!* He was always on time (his father's fault: *To be early is to be on time, to be on time is to be late, to be late is to be forgotten*). There was no time for kissing, and yet Isabelle was poised – eyes fluttering closed, face raised, lips parted ever so slightly. Gavin was a man; he did not need to be asked twice. He kissed her. The kiss was soft and sweet; she was a cookie, a confection. He had in the past been too aggressive with women, but that was perhaps because other women had not been as delicious as Isabelle.

She smiled at him. 'Thank you,' she said. She laid her head against his chest. He touched the shining curtain of her hair. 'I'm looking forward to tonight.'

'Yes,' he said. 'Me, too.'

Gavin was the man in charge. He had the clipboard with one thousand names and one hundred table numbers. He had the timetable. He had the notes for Lock's remarks and Adams's remarks. He had organized the volunteers. He was the point person for the production staff, for Siobhan and her crew, and for Max West in the greenroom.

'If you have a question,' Lock heard a woman wearing a black volunteer T-shirt say, 'ask that cute guy in the madras pants.'

Lock had a question. He had a series of questions. There was, according to Ben Franklin, more than fifty thousand dollars missing from their bank account. Fifty thousand dollars! Lock had spent the whole day poring over the financials – while Gavin was at the tent, organizing – just in case Ben Franklin was truly losing it. But no: Lock saw the cash skimmed from every deposit, and it made him sick. Not only would Gavin be fired (and possibly arrested), but Lock might lose his job as well, for not paying attention. Or he might be implicated in the whole scheme. It was unthinkable, that Lock's name would be dragged through the mud for this.

Lock was the first person to get a drink at the bar. He ordered glasses of white wine for himself and Daphne, and a Coke with a cherry for Heather, but the whole time he kept his eye trained on Gavin, who was clearly in his element with his clipboard and his earpiece. Basking in his own self-importance. How could Lock feel anything but grossly betrayed? Betrayed one minute and hypocritical the next. Lock was hiding his own cache of sins – and it was for this reason alone that Lock had decided to wait until after the gala to confront Gavin. He would do it quickly and kindly – not only to minimize negative press toward Nantucket's Children, but also for Gavin's sake.

Lock drank his first glass of wine quickly. Across the green expanse of field, he saw Claire. She was stunning. Damn it! The sight of her pained him. The dress she wore was light green and gold, and it draped around her body in such a way that Lock could easily picture her nude underneath the lacy material. Her legs looked amazing because of her high heels, and she negotiated with the heels gracefully, even in the grass. Her hair had been straightened and smoothed, and it fell around her face in beautiful lines. She was luminous, a movie star. Everyone was looking at her; everyone wanted to talk to her. Lock felt a surge of jealousy – she was his!

Lock got another drink. He had to be careful; he didn't want to have too much before he gave his remarks, thanked everyone for coming, and started the PowerPoint presentation. But his mind was careening one way and then another; it was a sled without a rider, whoosh, down the mountain, down a double fault line – Gavin, Claire, Daphne, Heather. Around him, the cocktail hour was in full swing. Everyone was chatting and laughing. He had to get out there and shine – that was his job. He wanted, first, to find Daphne and Heather. Daphne needed monitoring, and Lock didn't want to squander a single second with Heather: she was leaving for school in two days. But there were people to talk to. They appeared, one after another, popping up in his path, hands to shake, connections to establish or reinforce. He wanted to keep his eye on Claire. And Gavin.

He oozed schmooze, but his mind was a runaway. He spied Isabelle French looking lovely in a red dress. Isabelle was another wild card; she had been so upset, so offended by the slight in the magazine. She had told Lock that she would see the gala through to the end, but then she was resigning from the board. Withdrawing her financial support. It would be another stain on Lock's record.

Lock saw Daphne and Heather talking to one of their neighbors. Daphne held her wineglass aloft for Lock to see. He repaired to the bar to get her another drink. Daphne! Claire! Isabelle! Gavin!

Gavin!

When Lock approached the bar, Gavin was standing there alone. He was slouching against the bar in an uncharacteristically casual way, as though he were playing a part in a western. When he saw Lock, he grinned. 'This is great,' he said. 'All these people. It's amazing.'

Lock had overestimated his own kindness. He could not stand to listen to Gavin utter one word about how exciting the gala was when the man had single-handedly robbed the cause of more than fifty thousand dollars. As Lock looked at Gavin now, the pieces of the puzzle fell into place – Gavin's skittishness around the office, his sense of proprietorship over the finances, his anxiety about getting to the bank at lunchtime, and the way that, when he returned from the bank, he looked like the cat that had eaten the canary. Lock had actually wondered if Gavin had a crush on one of the tellers at the bank, so obvious was the change in his demeanor, from businesslike to slaphappy. It had been Ben's granddaughter Eliza who had called Gavin into question in the first place. She took special notice of the Nantucket's Children transactions because her grandfather was on the board of directors. Why did Gavin walk with so much cash? Thousands of dollars, she told Ben.

Doesn't seem right, she said.

And Ben said, *No, my dear, it doesn't.*

Lock had promised himself he would wait until Monday to discuss the financials with Gavin, but because of his anger and the wine and the zooming trajectory of his thoughts, he found he could not wait. It was just the two of them, alone, at the bar; no one else was around. What were the chances? It was a sign.

'I have to talk to you about something,' Lock said.

The smile fell off Gavin's face like a man jumping off a building. 'I have the money in a duffel bag,' he said. 'In my car. I want to give it back.'

Lock stared. He was not prepared for the admission nor for the offer of restitution. He had the money in his *car?* He wanted to give it *back?*

'It's not going to be that easy,' Lock said.

Gavin cleared his throat. 'I know about you and Claire,' he said.

Now Lock was the one to lose his composure, or almost. But at that moment the bartender slid Lock's drinks across the counter, and Lock was able to divert his attention long enough to accept the drinks and pitch a couple of bucks into the tip bowl. Know about Claire? No! How? Lock's eyes sought out Heather. Jesus.

'I don't know what you're referring to,' Lock said.

Gavin sighed. 'I came into the office one night when you were there with her. I saw everything, heard everything . . .'

Saw everything, *heard* everything? Lock's sensibilities were offended. One night when he and Claire were making love, Gavin had been present, watching?

'Okay,' Lock said with preternatural calm. He had made a tactical error; he should have waited, as he'd planned.

'I will tell Daphne,' Gavin said. 'I will tell Heather. I will tell Jason Crispin. I will tell Isabelle. I will send the ugly truth through this tent, and by the time dinner is served, everyone will know.'

'You would do that?' Lock said. 'Of course you would. You've been stealing from the cause for *months,* so it's no surprise that you would blackmail me to keep yourself from getting in trouble.'

'I want to give the money back,' Gavin said. 'It was a mistake.'

A mistake? Lock checked his surroundings to see if anyone was listening. Was the bartender listening? Lock had to seal this up, somehow; he couldn't handle it now.

'Let's talk about it on Monday,' Lock said. 'You and me, in confidence. You'll come in at seven?'

Gavin nodded once, briskly. Was he appeased? Would he keep his mouth shut? Did he trust Lock to save him? Why would he? It was safe to say that trust between them, now, was out of the question. What linked them was fear.

Gavin took his glass of wine and his clipboard and disappeared into the crowd. *A mistake?* When you committed a crime or broke a commandment – either a religious commandment or one of your own making – and you did so willingly, with both eyes open, was it fair to call it a mistake?

Maybe it was.

Never again! Never again! Never again! Siobhan was shouting in her mind, but whispering under her breath. She would never again cater two titanic events back-to-back, she would never cater again without Carter, she would never cater again, period! She would sell the business and go back to making sandwiches and scooping ice cream at the pharmacy on Main Street. She would marry Edward Melior and live a life of leisure; she would go to lunch instead of making lunch and serving lunch. Because this was hell. The tent she was working in was hot and airless. She had been up all night for three nights running, prepping the dinner, and because she didn't have enough staff, and because her husband was a compulsive gambler, she had ignored the passed hors d'oeuvres. She had five hundred pieces of three different things, which was, put mildly, not enough.

Claire poked her head into the catering tent. Siobhan noted, unhappily, that Claire looked fantastic. She was freaking Heidi Klum in that sensational dress, and she had finally found a stylist who knew what to do with her hair – but Claire strolling in all cool and beautiful infuriated Siobhan. To make matters worse, Claire was wearing the strand of pearls that their father-in-law, Malcolm, had given her when she gave birth to J.D., the first child to carry on the Crispin name. She was flaunting her own good fortune by wearing those pearls; she was announcing herself as the 'have' to her sister-in-law, the 'have-not.' Siobhan felt like Cinderella. The little adulteress was out sipping viognier while Siobhan slaved inside a plastic bag.

Claire said, 'There aren't enough hors d'oeuvres, Siobhan. People are complaining and they're getting very drunk. They've decimated the cheese table and the raw bar. The only things left are some lemon wedges and rinds of Brie. You have to send out more food, pronto.'

Pronto? Siobhan wanted to slap her.

'I don't have anything ready,' Siobhan said. 'Let them get drunk.'

'What?' Claire said. She looked around the tent. Siobhan's staff was furiously plating dinner. 'Where is Carter?'

Finally she had noticed that Siobhan was doing this *all alone!*

'If I had to guess, I would say Harrah's in Atlantic City.'

'What?' Claire said.

'I kicked him out. It's a long story that I do not have time to explain,' Siobhan said. 'Do you have anything else to say, or are you only here to ride my ass?'

'Siobhan – '

'Nice pearls!' Siobhan spat.

Claire got the key to the concession stand from the security guard. It was time to bring out the chandelier.

'I'd be careful carrying it in those shoes,' the security guard said.

'Point taken,' Claire said. She should have had someone help her, but she couldn't find Lock or Jason. Claire scanned the crowd. She saw Jason standing at one of the tall cocktail tables, talking to Daphne Dixon. Daphne looked gorgeous in a coral halter dress that put her 'beautiful tits' on display. Claire sighed. The sight of Jason and Daphne together unsettled her, but there was no time to pry them away from each other. And where was Lock? Okay, forget it: Claire would get the chandelier herself. There was a table outside the entrance of the tent where the chandelier was to sit and garner everyone's admiration on the way into dinner.

Claire made her way across the field, her heels catching in the grass every now and again. There hadn't been rain, thank God, but a field was still a field. Flats would have been a better call, but the dress called for heels. She would pay for her vanity tomorrow when her feet ached.

A couple stood outside the locked concession stand, deep in

conversation. Claire did not look at them closely – she had no desire to interrupt – but then the woman made a noise and Claire did look over. It was Isabelle and . . . Gavin.

'Isabelle!' Claire called out in spite of herself. 'God, I tried to reach you all week!'

Isabelle sniffed and adjusted the straps of her dress. Her dress was beautiful and simple, a red sheath with satin piping. 'Hello, Claire,' she said.

Claire looked between Isabelle and Gavin. 'I don't mean to interrupt,' she said. 'I just came to get the chandelier.'

'Oh, right,' Isabelle said.

'Is everything okay?'

Claire wondered if Isabelle was crying because of the article in *NanMag*. Was it that big of a deal? Or maybe she was upset that none of her friends had come to the event. Maybe she was crying over her bad divorce. Whatever it was, she had chosen a curious person to comfort her. Gavin. It gave Claire pause.

'I'm sorry,' Claire said. 'I really didn't mean to interrupt. Just ignore me.'

Claire unlocked the concession stand. Behind her, the party raged. Despite the fact that there were no hors d'oeuvres to speak of, the gala was going smoothly. She had not had the nerve to pop into the greenroom to check on Matthew; if she found him drinking, she would unhinge. It was better not to know. Besides, if she popped in to see him and they got into a difficult conversation, he might start drinking. She would stay away and hope for the best.

The concession stand had no lights, so Claire had to grope through the gathering dark for the chandelier. When she found the box, she became aware of Isabelle and Gavin loitering by the open door.

'I've got it,' Claire said. 'I'll unwrap it at the table.'

She hesitated before the doorway, indicating that they should make room, which they did, and Claire stepped through. Should she say anything else to Isabelle? Isabelle, even in the worst of times, had been upbeat and indomitable. She handwrote notes on hundreds of invitations, despite her shame; she got on the phone and interrogated caterers, including the head of the high school cafeteria. Claire should congratulate her, thank her – try one last time to connect with her. Tomorrow, Isabelle French would be out of her life forever.

But Claire stopped herself. Isabelle most certainly did not want to be comforted by Claire. For all Claire knew, she could be the reason Isabelle was crying.

Claire had the chandelier, and right now she needed to concentrate on delivering it safely to the tent. All the way across the field in these heels? Claire proceeded slowly, carefully; the box was heavy.

She set the chandelier down on the designated table and unpacked it, using scissors to free it from its cocoon of protective Bubble Wrap. A card beside the chandelier read, *Pulled-taffy chandelier in fuchsia. Artist: Claire Danner Crispin. Starting bid: $25,000.* People standing around the table oohed and aahed when the chandelier was finally revealed. Claire tried not to smile, but even sitting on the table, the chandelier was magnificent! She had worked so, so hard.

'It's my first piece in nearly two years,' she said to no one in particular. At that moment, she wished fervently that Lock would win it. She had made it for him.

She touched the perfect arc of the first arm (four and a half hours, sixty tries).

'Good-bye,' she whispered. 'Good-bye.'

He'd had three six-packs since arriving for the sound check, so eighteen beers, but it was nothing to worry about. Terry and Alfonso weren't happy with him, he could tell, but they weren't going to blow the whistle on him, either. It was just beer. They were relieved he hadn't pulled the Tanqueray out.

He could have whatever he wanted. There was a nineteen-year-old Nepali kid named G-Man in the greenroom whose job it was to fetch Max and the band whatever their hearts desired. What Matthew desired was beer, and beer he got, Heineken after Heineken, in cold green bottles. *Namaste!*

He popped open another beer. Number nineteen. The worst thing about drinking beer was that he constantly had to urinate. On his last trip to the PortaJohn, he had felt light-headed. Whether this was because of the beer or because of his deep melancholy at leaving the next day, he had no idea. He wanted to leave with Claire, but he had not been able, yet, to persuade her. He entertained fantasies of just staying on Nantucket, of living with Claire and Jason and their kids, like some kind of eccentric uncle. The fact of the matter was, he needed a family; he should have started one of his own, but his lifestyle hadn't cooperated. Too many drugs, too many late nights, too little chance for routine and consistency.

Matthew sneaked peeks out of the tent, across the field. Claire was in his crosshairs. He tried to appreciate the other women, but his eyes always landed on Claire. That green dress. It was impossible to believe that Claire was even prettier at thirty-seven than she had been at seventeen, but yes, it was true. She had grown into herself. She had so much confidence now, such a way about her, a kindness mixed with competence. She floated, lit from within.

At that second, Matthew saw Claire talking to a balding man in a pink tie. Claire tucked herself under his ear and whispered something. He, in turn, touched the small of her back, as though he was used to touching her. It was the head honcho of the charity. The guy had come into the greenroom and introduced himself a few minutes ago, but Matthew couldn't remember the man's name. Dock? Dick? The man had not seemed particularly starstruck to meet *Max West,* as so many people were, but he had been grateful and businesslike. Now, Matthew saw this Dick guy and Claire were on intimate terms. God, the way he'd touched her just now, his hand on the small of her back, practically cupping her ass, made Matthew burn with jealousy. He couldn't trust himself, especially not when he'd been drinking. Was this Dick person the reason Claire had turned him down?

Matthew called G-Man over. 'Would you get me a Tanqueray, splash of tonic, with a very fresh lime?' he asked. 'Please?'

It was going too fast! Already it was time to sit for dinner. Everybody was starving. The cocktail hour – always legendary – had been a bit lean in the food department.

Claire took a deep breath and looked around the tent. This was *it!* The gala! The tent was lit by white Christmas lights and candles; the tables were decorated with crisp white linens, crystal goblets, and simple arrangements of pink tea roses in silver bowls. The tent shimmied with the sound of people talking and laughing. This was a beautiful party. Adams opened a bottle of champagne and poured some for Claire and then kissed her cheek and said, 'You did a great job.'

'It wasn't only me,' Claire said. She peered at the next table. Lock was sitting between Heather and Isabelle. Daphne was on the other side of Heather, and Gavin – who Claire now understood was Isabelle's date! – was sitting on the other side of Isabelle. Dara, the cellist, was at the table with a date, and Aster Wyatt, the graphic designer, was there with his boyfriend. None of Isabelle's other friends had shown up. Isabelle looked positively morose. Claire raised her champagne flute in Isabelle's direction. *We did it!* she mouthed. Isabelle looked away.

Claire's heart faltered. She took a feeble sip, then set her glass down. Tomorrow, she reminded herself, it wouldn't matter what Isabelle thought.

Everything tends to go wrong at the last minute. They were past the point where everything could go wrong, weren't they? But Claire worried about dinner. Siobhan had not managed to get hors d'oeuvres out; even Genevieve and her troop of sixteen-year-olds could have done better. When the waiter set down Claire's plate, however, her mind was put at ease: the food was beautiful. The beef tenderloin was rosy, the lobster salad creamy, the wild rice studded with dried cherries and golden raisins, like jewels. Claire checked around her: service seemed even. Claire believed she could hear a collective sigh of relief, and then expressions of excitement and joy. Dinner!

As dinner was being cleared, Lock stood up from his place. Claire's stomach clenched; she wasn't ready for this. Lock took a microphone from one of the production guys and said, in a booming voice that quieted everyone, 'Good evening!'

Applause. People were feeling good now; they had been warmed by the cocktail hour, and they'd eaten. The evening was about to take off like a rocket ship.

'I'm Lockhart Dixon, executive director of Nantucket's Children, and I would like to *thank you* for coming to our summer gala!'

More applause.

'Nantucket's Children was founded in 1992, when it came to the attention of our late founder, Margaret Kincaid, that the face of Nantucket was changing. There were children of working islanders whose basic needs were not being met. The island needed affordable housing options, better after-school programs, day care . . .'

Lock went on; Claire knew the spiel. She looked around at the attractive, wealthy people surrounding her. Did *they* get it? Nantucket's Children was about kids whose parents worked as hard as they could to make a life here. Nantucket's economy depended on this workforce; the island had a responsibility to care for these children. Lock finished his speech and raised his hands, and the lights in the tent dimmed. The video started on a screen that dropped down over the stage: kids of all shapes, sizes, and colors playing ball, studying, riding bikes, walking in groups on the beach. The sound track played 'Lean on Me,' and Claire misted up. A picture of J.D. flashed on the screen, showing him sitting with a special-needs preschool student, a book open between them. The Read to Me program, funded by Nantucket's Children. Claire felt conflicted: to cochair this gala had been so hard, so draining, and it had led her to such a complicated place. She looked at the kids' faces on the screen. The point of the gala was to raise money; money would make a difference. She had taken the job as cochair because she wanted to help, because she wanted to return some goodwill to the universe. But it had back-fired. Or had it?

Claire's nerves attacked her thighs, her knees. She knew what was coming. She looked over at Isabelle's table and was alarmed to see Isabelle stand up, push her chair in, and stroll to the back of the tent. Where was she going? Didn't she know the thank-yous were next on the program? Gavin stood and followed Isabelle out.

Adams ambled up onto the stage and took the microphone from Lock. Claire turned around, searching in vain for Isabelle. She was gone. Claire tried to signal to Adams, but he was off and running on his president-of-the-board speech. He thanked Gavin – polite applause, though now Gavin was missing, too – and then he thanked Lock, and Lock returned to the stage to take a bow. Claire looked at Daphne – she was, as ever, scowling – and then Daphne stood up and walked out. The applause was deafening, or so it seemed to Claire. She was gripped with fear. Here was the moment she had been waiting for, or one of the moments, and she was dreading it. *No!* she thought. Her face blossomed into two red posies. *Calm down.* She had done harder things than this. She had kept her cool while they performed an emergency C-section and pulled Zack out: Living? Dead? Healthy? Impaired? She had been introduced during the unveiling of *Bubbles III* at the Whitney Museum; she had been photographed by the *New York Times*. She had banged the tambourine against her hip in front of a packed house at the Stone Pony. She must have had chutzpah then. Well, if she'd had it, she'd lost it. She worked alone in the hot shop, she raised her family; she was not the kind of person who could accept a bouquet of flowers in front of an intimidating crowd like this. Her heels would snap, she would fall, there would be a stain on her dress in an embarrassing place, there would be something stuck in her teeth. She checked again for Isabelle – gone. In the bathroom. And Daphne, gone. And Matthew, too, would miss her shining moment. Was it even worth having a shining moment if the right people weren't there to watch?

Isabelle!

'It is now my distinct pleasure,' Adams said, 'to introduce the two women who made this evening possible. These women have been working for nearly a year – they have raised money, called in favors, turned over their lives in service to Nantucket's Children and the summer gala. Please put your hands together for our gala cochairs. Ladies and gentlemen, Claire Danner Crispin and Isabelle French!'

Later, Claire would say she'd heard the crash. The sound was trapped in her subconscious. The sound of glass breaking. And so even as Claire walked up onstage to accept an armload of lilies and delphiniums (prom queen, Academy Award, Miss America), her spirit was in a free fall. About to land with a sickening thud.

The plan for the auction was as follows: Pietro da Silva would walk in from the back of the tent, holding the chandelier aloft. And for additional drama, Ted Trimble had rigged a battery pack so that the chandelier would be illuminated. Pietro da Silva was a professional auctioneer; he moonlighted for every charity on the island, and he liked to make things interesting. Strolling through a darkened tent with the precious chandelier aglow had been his idea. Auction as theater. Why not? The price would go up.

Claire was in a state of heightened agitation. The flowers of the bouquet brushed against her face. She was aware that Isabelle had *not* come up onstage with her; Claire had posed for the photographers of both island newspapers with Adams alone. Did the audience find it strange that Isabelle was missing? Claire wasn't sure, nor was she quite sure what was wrong inside her heart, but something was definitely wrong. Onstage, with the lights in her eyes, she tried to locate Jason. Where was Jason? She thought of Jason as she had first known him, his young face glowing warm and orange from the bonfire up at Great Point; he had brought a cooler of cherrystone clams, and he shucked them there on the beach and fed them to Claire, each one a tiny, sweet, perfect present. That Jason was gone, and in his place she now had . . . what? The man who had grabbed her hand when Zack took his first steps, who kissed her throat, the man who had returned to sleep beside her, even though she had strayed so far away from herself. Jason! Where was her husband? She felt that something awful had happened. One of their children had burned to cinders in the hot shop! Where was Jason? His spot at their table was empty. Shea was throwing up in bed, all alone; Ottilie had been stolen from the house by a stranger who had been stalking her for months. In the back of the tent, all the way in the back, Claire saw Siobhan, her face as pale and pinched as a pie crust, genuflecting in her white chef's jacket. Someone was dead.

When Claire stepped off the stage, Lock was waiting for her with a stricken face. *Everything tends to go wrong at the last minute.* Here it was, the last minute.

'The chandelier fell,' Lock said. 'It broke.'

It fell, Claire thought. *It broke.*

'Broke?' she said.

'Smashed,' Lock said.

Not possible, Claire thought. The security guard had been hired specifically to make sure that nothing happened to it.

The crowd quieted as Lock led Claire out of the tent by the arm. They did not know what had happened, but they sensed tragedy.

Adams spoke into the microphone with rousing enthusiasm. 'Enjoy your dessert! Max West will begin his concert in a matter of minutes!'

It was not a tragedy: the chandelier, after all, was only a thing. And yet when Claire saw it, lying lopsided in the grass – broken, smashed, ruined – she cried out, and then she just plain cried, blubbered, sobbed. She turned to Lock and said, 'Where is Jason?'

Hands came around her. 'I'm right here, baby. God, I am so sorry.'

Claire collapsed into him. She was crying so hard that Jason couldn't understand what she was saying. She had to concentrate on taking a breath, repeating herself.

'I want you to call the babysitter. Ask her. Are the kids okay?'

'I'm sure they're fine.'

'Call her!' There was something terribly wrong; Claire felt it. The lighter! J.D. had set the house on fire with the goddamned lighter. He had been flicking it on and off under his covers. Claire should have taken the evil thing with her when she left the house. The covers of his bed caught fire, and the rest of his room. The rest of the upstairs, where the children were sleeping. They would die of smoke inhalation. Hannah, the babysitter, had decided to crash the concert after all. She had left the children alone, and now they were dead.

Jason called. Claire was limp against him, shivering. Everyone gathered in a loose circle: Lock, Adams, Ted and Amie Trimble, Brent and Julie Jackson. Not Siobhan, though Claire had seen her a few moments earlier. Not Isabelle. Not Gavin. Not Daphne.

Jason hung up his phone. 'The kids are fine,' he said. 'They're all asleep.'

387

'Even Zack?'

'Even Zack.'

'And Hannah's there? You talked to Hannah?'

'Hannah's there, Pan's there. The kids are safe.'

Okay. She was allowed, now, to let go – her anger, her rage, her disappointment, her heartbreak. The house was not on fire; her children were safe in bed. The chandelier was only a *thing,* an inanimate object, a *thing,* Claire! She chastised herself for her hot fountain of tears, but they were not to be stopped. Hundreds of hours of work, all that stress and strain, a trip to the hospital – she'd nearly *died* because of that goddamned chandelier! She'd returned to the hot shop only to create it, it was a labor of love, the best kind of charity, and now it was gone. She turned on the gathered crowd in fury.

'How did it happen?' she demanded. 'Who knocked it over? It didn't just fall over all by itself! And where is the security guard? He was supposed to be *watching* it!'

No one answered. Isabelle, Claire thought. She left the tent, and then, seconds later, the chandelier fell. She had been so disillusioned with Claire from the beginning . . .

'Where is Isabelle?' Claire asked.

'She's back in the tent,' Adams said. 'Eating dessert.'

'I can't find Gavin,' Lock said. 'I thought he was having a cigarette, but I've looked everywhere. He's vanished.'

Vanished? Claire thought. Gavin wasn't her favorite person, but there was no reason for him to break her chandelier. Topple it and run, like some kid who had put a baseball through a window.

'Someone probably knocked it over by accident,' Jason said.

By accident? Claire thought. By what, carelessly swinging a purse? It would have to have been a pretty big purse. By carrying a tray loaded down with dessert samplers? Siobhan had been in the back of the tent, crossing herself: *In the name of the Father, and the Son, and the Holy Spirit. Do you not care about your soul, Claire?* Claire had seen her – but now where was she? Where

388

was she now, when Claire needed her? Siobhan was angry; Claire knew it. She was resentful. She had not wanted to cater the gala. She had wanted to be eating and drinking and wearing her sexy black dress, not waiting on everyone hand and foot, like a servant. She had sat in judgment on Claire; she had quite possibly decided on her own to make Claire hang.

'I can't believe nobody saw what happened,' Claire said. 'Where was the security guard?'

'There were crashers,' Adams said. 'A bunch of girls trying to get in without tickets. He was dealing with them.'

Claire strode up to the bar and cornered the bartender. Hunter, his name was. He had worked for Carter and Siobhan for years. 'Did you see who did it?' Claire asked him. 'You must have seen something.'

He held up his palms. 'My back was turned,' he said. 'I saw nothing.'

There were only a few people who had seen what happened, and one of them was Max West, who had been standing outside the door of the greenroom, drinking a cold, stinging Tanqueray and tonic. Max had had his eyes glued on the opening of the big tent; he was trying to hear what was being said inside.

The blue Solo cup was filled to the top with forbidden gin. Everything, for Max, was swaying and shimmering. He had finally arrived at that place he liked to visit when he was drinking, that place where he wasn't sure what was real and what wasn't, that place where the world and the people and events and circumstances in it seemed to have been created for his bemusement. Constantly, while drunk, he tilted his head in wonder.

He had seen the chandelier fall, had seen who knocked it over, but he was afraid to open his mouth, to blow the whistle, because it just as easily could have been his fault. He had been lurching after only a few steps; he, too, was capable of causing a catastrophic accident. The chandelier fell, it smashed in the grass, although the word 'smash' indicated sound, and all Matthew heard was a muted crunch. Matthew looked at the chandelier in the grass. Should he pick it up? He thought, *I have to stop drinking.*

Back in the greenroom, he threw back two shots of espresso and tried to get Bruce on the phone. Bruce was at the gym in Burbank, on the treadmill; he was hesitant to get off. (He had to lose twenty pounds, his doctor said, or he was going to have a heart attack.)

'Is this an emergency, Max?' Bruce said.

Matthew said, 'Yes.'

Matthew tried to explain it as concisely as he could: The auction item, a chandelier that Claire had *made,* had broken, and the charity would need something to auction in its place. What can we give?

'It has to be something really good,' Matthew said. 'They expected this chandelier to go for, like, fifty grand.'

'Fifty thousand dollars?' Bruce said. 'Jesus, Max! Haven't you done enough for this woman? You're playing a free concert. And you bought her table, right, for twenty-five grand? That's enough, Max. That's plenty. Why do you feel you have to give her anything else?'

'I don't have to,' Matthew said. 'I want to.' How to explain it? He would do anything for Claire. He was on a mission here! 'What can we give them?'

Bruce sighed. 'How about two tickets to your London concert on Christmas Eve with two backstage passes?'

'That's a start. But it has to be bigger than that. Think big, Bruce!'

'How about we add first-class airfare, seven nights in a suite at the Connaught, and Christmas Eve dinner at Gordon Ramsay's place with you, Elton John, and Paul McCartney?'

'I'm having Christmas Eve dinner with Elton John and Paul McCartney?'

'You are.'

'Genius,' Matthew said. 'Thank you, Bruce. That should do it.'

Gavin hurried down the grassy strip on the edge of Old South Road with only the tip of his cigarette for illumination. He was running, but because he was pitifully out of shape, he would lose his breath, hack out a cough, and be forced to stop and walk. He had called the airline from his cell phone and booked himself, under an assumed name, on the last flight off the island.

He was leaving Nantucket. He had dumped all the money – minus five hundred dollars to get him wherever he was going – into the backseat of Ben Franklin's Lincoln Continental. He told himself it wasn't stealing, since he had given the money back – it was just some awful game he'd had fun with for a while. It killed him to leave Isabelle, but she deserved better than him; she deserved someone powerful and clever, not some two-bit criminal. Leaving now, he was doing Isabelle a favor. And Lock and Claire, too. He could ruin their lives, rip apart both their families – but what would that accomplish? Nothing but heartbreak.

He sneaked out while Isabelle was in the bathroom. He stood on the far side of the parking lot for a few minutes; he couldn't tear himself away until he learned what would happen to the auction. What happened was this: Pietro da Silva and Max West got up onstage and offered the most outrageous auction package the island had ever seen – concert tickets, backstage passes, airfare, hotel, Christmas Eve dinner with Max, Sir Elton John, and Sir Paul McCartney, or, as Max West self-deprecatingly joked, 'two knights and a knave.' It went for a hundred thousand dollars, and Max West offered it again for another hundred thousand. Two hundred thousand dollars! Gavin found his heart soaring. So much money for the charity! So much more than they'd expected! It was weird, the elation that Gavin experienced at the gala's success. It was backward. He ran.

He was almost to the turnoff for the airport when the lights came up behind him. He threw down his cigarette, squashed it in the grass, then felt ashamed of himself for littering. The lights were not the lights he'd been fearing. Or were they? He debated between turning around to check and simply bolting. How much speed did he have left? Enough to make it to the airport? The airport wouldn't be safe now, anyway. He would have to hide, but where?

The lights were spinning and flashing. Yes, definitely police lights, but possibly not for him. He turned. A cruiser pulled up right alongside him. There were two cops in the front seat and an old man in the back. Ben Franklin.

'Gavin Andrews?' the driver said.

It was over, then. Gavin sunk his hands deep into the pockets of his madras pants and looked back toward the tent. He was half a mile away, but he could still hear the strains of Max West's singing. The tune, whatever it was, was catchy.

'Put your hands where we can see them!' the second police officer barked.

Gavin raised his hands over his head, the way he'd seen it done in the movies. Everyone Gavin knew was committing crimes large and small, engaging in scandals, acts of corruption, delinquency, and plain old bad faith – but he was the one who had gotten caught.

It figured.

He had never sounded better. Although Claire was shrouded with sadness and rage, she could still tell how good he sounded. Matthew – Max West – was putting on a terrific show; he was playing all his hits, and the guests were all dancing and singing along at the top of their lungs. Claire was dancing with Jason, Ted and Amie Trimble, and Adams and Heidi Fiske. They were surrounding her in a circle, buffering her, as though she were the one who might break.

The chandelier was gone. Every time Claire thought this, it sickened her. It was Hemingway's novel, left on a train. It was Degas's ballerinas, gone up in smoke. The worst thought was that other people might not view her loss that way; they might see it as nothing more than broken glass, easily swept up, easily replaced by concert tickets and dinner with celebrities, which had in fact brought in four times as much money as the chandelier might have. Max West, everyone said, had swung in on a vine. He had saved the day. But that didn't begin to mend the gash in Claire's spirit. She had dedicated the better part of a year to the chandelier, it was the finest work she'd ever done, and it would fall into oblivion. There was no consolation for that.

She felt a tap on her shoulder: Lock. Everyone was dancing, but Lock was just standing there, staring at her with an expression that threatened to give it all away.

'I need to talk to you,' he said.

'Now?'

'Yes,' he said.

She didn't want to miss even one second of the concert, but then Max segued into a cover of 'Dancing Queen,' and since it wasn't actually his song, Claire felt okay stepping out.

As they strolled through the tent, Lock tried to take her hand. Claire glared at him.

'What are you doing?' she said. 'Are you drunk? Where's your wife? Your daughter?'

'Daphne left because she thought I was paying too much attention to Isabelle,' he said. 'And Heather went downtown to meet her friends.'

'Where are we going?'

'I want to show you something,' he said. 'In the concession stand.'

'I don't think that's a good idea,' Claire said.

'Please? Five minutes.'

She followed him across the shadowy field to the dark concession stand. He pointed to the box. 'I packed it up for you,' he said. 'The remains. What was left.'

'This is what you wanted to show me?'

'I knew it would be important to you,' he said. 'Important that it not get thrown away.'

She peered into the box. It was too dark to see clearly, but she could make out the lopsided form of the broken chandelier and a pile of shards. The box was a casket now.

'You didn't have to keep the shards,' she said. 'They're dangerous.'

'I didn't have the heart to throw them away.'

This was a gesture on his part, an effort he'd made to say he understood her loss, but he didn't.

He put his arms around her. 'I love you, Claire. All this year, what we've been through – it was for that reason. I love you.'

She rested her hands on his jacket lapels. She thought back over the past year – the times she met him secretly, the moments right before they parted when she was sure she would die from longing, the confusing time she spent with Father Dominic, asking herself, over and over again, *How can a good person do something so bad?* She would have liked to believe that what she was acting on now was the strength she'd prayed for. But the truth was, her feelings for Lock were weakened and confused. She thought about the afternoon he came to the house to talk about the catering; he had been so foreign to her on that day, so distinct from the man she loved, the man she wanted to climb the Eiffel Tower with, reincarnate Frank Sinatra for, even stand next to in line at the post office. On that pleasant, sunny afternoon, Claire couldn't wait for Lock to leave. She thought about the morning when Lock helped her transport the chandelier. They had sat side by side in the car – Lock driving, Claire riding – as they might have if they were a real couple, but those minutes had been silent and awkward because what was meaningful between them was lost, at least to Claire. And then, last night, when Matthew made his plea – *I want you to come with me. Marry me* – Claire had thought, *I could never leave Jason. I could never leave the kids.* But Lock she could leave with ease. It was Lock she had wanted to run away from.

'We are so lucky that the only thing that broke was the chandelier,' she said. She raised her head and looked at him. For much of the past year, he had seemed wonderful and mysterious; he had seemed all-knowing, a repository of wisdom and right answers and sound judgment. He had served as her savior. She had been needy in ways she didn't even know about, and he had filled her up. But he was wrong about there being no hell; there was a hell, and they had narrowly avoided it. 'We could have ruined our lives. My marriage could have broken up, or yours could have. Our kids, your job, our friends, our lives – they all could have ended up in the trash.' Claire thought of herself living with Lock in a rental house with Claire's children in strange rooms, displaced and resentful. After six months, Lock would be going to work at night to escape *her;* she, in turn, would be making secret phone calls to Jason. Claire shook the image from her head and filled up with an emotion that was as thick as syrup, an emotion she could only describe as bittersweet. God, she had loved Lock Dixon so completely, with such bright intensity that it had blinded her. But now, finally, it had burned itself out.

'Claire . . .'

She smoothed his tie. The worst thing about adultery, in the end, was that it had shaken her belief in the things she had always held sacred – love, marriage, friendship. 'I need something from you,' she said.

'Yes, of course,' Lock said. 'God, anything.'

He was earnest, supplicant, hurting. He had been hurting since she'd met him; he was the injured bird on the side of the road, the one no one would stop to save but her. He was the tar in her hair, on her hands, weighing one side of her head down, impossible to get out. He was the one person she had been unable to say no to. Until now.

'I need you to let me go.'

Lock nodded. He was stunned, maybe, or maybe in his infinite wisdom he was saying, *Yes, you're right. Go now, while you can.* Claire didn't ask. She hurried back toward the bright tent, toward the music.

Siobhan knew what her childhood priest, Father Kennedy, would say: They were all, every last one of them, sinners. That included Carter, her gambling husband, and Claire, her adulterous best friend. That included Siobhan herself.

The whole thing had happened so fast, the way it had when Liam broke his arm: one second he was handling the puck, and the next second he was up against the boards, then down on the ice, his arm dangling off him.

Siobhan had been setting out dessert samplers and listening to Lock Dixon up onstage, giving his sappy 'save the children' speech. To Siobhan, the whole idea that this evening, with its cocktails and canapés and women in their summer diamonds, had anything to do with the actual children and working families of Nantucket was fucking nonsense. This evening was about the guests celebrating their own wealth and good fortune; it was about seeing a famous rock star up close. It wasn't about doing the right thing so much as being *seen* doing the right thing. Some people under the tent probably had no idea which charity their money was even benefiting! The whole world of charity benefits, Siobhan decided, was shallow and obnoxious. But perhaps that was *too* cynical: Siobhan was just tired, bone-weary, and suffering from a foul, foul mood caused by visions of Carter at the roulette wheel.

She had just stepped out of the tent when the security guard – a doughy guy from the UK – rushed past her. There were people, crashers, Max West fanatics, trying to jump the fence. For most of the evening, there had been people lingering outside the tent, getting fresh drinks, sneaking a cigarette, going to the bathroom. But now, everyone was packed inside, listening to the speeches, waiting for Max West to hit the stage. The only people behind the tent were her bartender, Hunter, and, at the bar, Mr. Ben Franklin, who appeared to be talking to himself. Siobhan felt a stab of empathy; she had been talking to herself all night long, and nothing she'd said had been very nice.

Siobhan looked to her right and saw Isabelle French pick up Claire's chandelier. It was dangling from Isabelle's left hand. Isabelle was saying something to Gavin that Siobhan couldn't hear. Siobhan thought back to the night of the *soirée intime* and how awful Isabelle had been, harassing Claire about taking a $25,000 table. It had been no better than sorority hazing.

Siobhan did not like the sight of Isabelle holding Claire's chandelier so carelessly. Siobhan did not think before she spoke. She barked at Isabelle in the meanest shanty Irish voice she could muster.

'Put that *down!*'

Her voice was too loud and too sudden; it was a gunshot in the dark. It caused Ben Franklin to spill his drink all over the bar. And Isabelle – naturally skittish, drunk, holding carelessly on to the cord – swung around, and the chandelier swung with her.

Siobhan cried out. Gavin cried out. The chandelier narrowly missed hitting the edge of the table.

Isabelle turned on Siobhan accusingly. 'What?'

'Put it down,' Siobhan said.

Gavin took the chandelier from Isabelle and set it safely back on the table.

Isabelle looked like she was about to burst into tears. 'I'm going to the bathroom.'

Gavin said, 'I'll wait for you right here.' Siobhan glared at him, thinking of his coming out to spy on her and Edward that night. He was creepy. He would not look at Siobhan now, would not offer an apologetic word on behalf of his 'date.' In so many ways, the two of them deserved each other. Gavin lit up a cigarette, flipped open his cell phone, and disappeared into the shadows.

Siobhan touched the chandelier gingerly; it was as delicate as spun sugar. To think that Isabelle had nearly cracked it. Inside the tent, the slide show was playing. Adams would be next with the thank-yous, and Claire would be last, the biggie. Siobhan knew she should not begrudge Claire her moment of recognition, but begrudge it she did. It wasn't fair that Claire got everything. She was the artist, she was the gala cochair; she was the nice to Siobhan's naughty. She had received the first-child pearls from their father-in-law, Malcolm; every time Claire wore them, like tonight, it was a slap in the face to Siobhan. Siobhan loved Claire better than any other woman in the world, but along with that love came resentment. You want naughty? Siobhan indulged in a mean little fantasy where she trashed the chandelier. She had not dropped or spilled anything in more than two years, since the full sherry glasses went over in Martin Scorsese's lap during the film festival. Siobhan was due for an unfortunate accident.

Siobhan pictured herself the villainess in this story, then shivered. Awful. She was so absorbed in the thoughts of a horrible sinner that she did not notice Daphne Dixon coming out of the tent until Daphne was practically on top of her. What she saw only registered in the corner of her eye as a flare, a flame-colored blur. And that was what Siobhan meant by 'fast' – one minute Siobhan was standing alone by the chandelier, contemplating the injustices of her life, and the next minute there was Daphne, drunk, stumbling out of the tent, headed for Siobhan. She looked like she wanted to tell Siobhan something – oh, dear Lord, what was she going to say? – or maybe she just needed someone to hold her up. Daphne was a lot bigger than Siobhan, and she had a frightening amount of momentum. She knocked into Siobhan, Siobhan knocked into the table, the table tilted, the chandelier slid to the ground. Crash, in the grass, and then whipped by its own chain.

Oh no, broken. So broken. Siobhan untangled herself from Daphne. Daphne got to her feet unsteadily; she took her shoes off – were her shoes the problem? – and staggered away.

'Daphne! Daphne, come back here!'

Daphne did not turn around, though she stumbled again. She was very drunk. Siobhan's first thought was that she could not let Daphne get into a car. Siobhan chased Daphne out to the parking lot. She caught up to her and grabbed her arm.

'You're not driving,' Siobhan said.

'It was an accident,' Daphne said. 'Accident, accident, accident. Don't worry. It wasn't your fault.'

Siobhan tightened her grip on Daphne's arm and flagged the security guard, who was threading his way through the parking lot. Should she tell him about the chandelier, smashed to bits in the grass? Who had knocked it over? *Don't worry. It wasn't your fault.* Damn right it wasn't! But Siobhan had been standing in the wrong place; she should have been in the airless catering tent, doing dishes. Siobhan had the sick feeling it *was* her fault. Siobhan had knocked it over, right? She wasn't sure; it had happened so fast. *Accident, accident, accident.* Yes, it was an accident. Claire and Siobhan should have absolutely insisted that Daphne get into a cab so many years ago. Claire had always felt guilty about that, but Siobhan hadn't, though now Siobhan could see that Claire was right. *Don't worry. It wasn't your fault.* But it was their fault. Their inaction had been negligent, criminal. They had let Daphne drive home, despite the fact that she was wearing the lampshade. They might as well have handed her a loaded gun. If they had only stopped Daphne, every-thing now would be different.

Or would it?

'This woman needs a cab,' Siobhan said to the security guard. 'She shouldn't be driving.'

'I'm fine,' Daphne spat.

'Please put her in a cab,' Siobhan said. 'She's been drinking.'

The security guard wheeled Daphne toward the exit. 'Will do. Ma'am, where do you live?'

Siobhan headed back to the tent, gravel crunching under her kitchen clogs. They were, all of them, sinners.

When Siobhan returned, the tent was rumbling with applause. She approached Hunter, at the bar, who was mopping up Ben Franklin's drink.

'If anyone asks,' Siobhan said to Hunter, 'tell them your back was turned.'

Hunter nodded.

Siobhan entered the back of the tent as Claire rose to accept her flowers. Siobhan would tell her what had happened later, privately. After all the hours Claire had devoted to the chandelier, it had taken only ten seconds to destroy. Less: five seconds, three seconds. How would Claire forgive her? (She would, Siobhan knew, because she was Claire.) Siobhan thought of the blue velvet bag in the secret compartment of her jewelry box, empty now. She had sold the ring for seventy-five hundred dollars – and donated it, anonymously, to Nantucket's Children, even though she very much needed the money. *Carter!* What was Carter doing, right this second? Was he thinking of her, sensing her angst and torment – or was he stoned from throwing the dice? She had to get him help. But where? From whom? She would have to suck up the little pride she had left and ask Lock Dixon; he would have the answer. Forgiveness.

Siobhan closed her eyes and crossed herself: *In the name of the Father, and the Son, and the Holy Spirit.* It was all she could think of to do.

It was five minutes to ten and he was growing hoarse. That, really, was the worst effect of drinking before a show: he didn't forget words or lose the melody, but his voice deteriorated. He still had two songs to sing.

He nuzzled the microphone. 'This last song is for my . . . friend, Claire Danner.' The word 'friend' was lame and insufficient, but he couldn't very well tell a thousand of Claire's friends and peers that he had fallen back in love with her. Still, he added, 'When I wrote this song twenty years ago, I wrote it for her.' He looked down into the audience. Claire's eyes were glassy. She blinked; tears fell. Matthew strummed the first chord, and the band eased into 'Stormy Eyes.'

He wanted her to come up onstage; he wanted her to sing the last verse with him. Nobody realized this, but Claire could sing. High school chorus, soprano section. He tried to wave her up; she shook her head. She was dancing with Underwhelming Jason. Dick wasn't around. Matthew felt hopeful.

At the end of 'Stormy Eyes,' the concert was officially over. The lights went out. The crowd screamed. They wanted more. Matthew smiled. At a thousand dollars a ticket, he had expected a different crowd – more genteel, more reserved – but this group rivaled sixty thousand New Yorkers at Shea Stadium in the noise department.

'All right!' Matthew said into the microphone. He had an encore, one final song, and he had given it a lot of thought. He had, in fact, arranged for this song even before he arrived on the island. He had called each of the contract musicians himself – one second tenor, one baritone, one bass – and made sure they all knew barbershop.

Nobody would understand but her, and that was okay because she was the only one who mattered. He waited until the crowd grew quiet, absolutely silent, and then he hit the first, perfect note.

Sweet Rosie O'Grady, my dear little Rose.

It was how he'd gotten her before. It was all he had left.

And yes, she was smiling ear to ear, and yes, tears were streaming down her face, and yes, it was as though they were the only two people in the place – Matthew Westfield and Claire Danner, high school sweethearts from Wildwood Crest, New Jersey.

But as the quartet closed in on the end of the song, as their four voices blended with a beauty and a poignancy that Matthew himself could scarcely believe – *and Rosie O'Grady loves me!* – Claire looked him right in the eye and shook her head.

No, she said. *I can't.*

Matthew clipped the note. The lights went out. The audience keened. He was intensely jealous then, as jealous as he'd ever been, not of Underwhelming Jason and not of Dick, but of having a life that you couldn't, or didn't want to, leave behind.

No, he thought. *You shouldn't.*

It was time for him to go.

Claire woke up to Jason kissing the back of her neck.

'What time is it?' she said.

'Six.'

'Too early.' She closed her eyes.

He let her sleep until nine, an unbelievable luxury. When she came out into the kitchen, the kids had all been fed and the breakfast dishes were washed. Pan was sitting on the sofa, reading to Zack. She was still spotted, but she felt better. Jason was standing at the counter, making sandwiches. Claire watched him in amazement: he lined up the bread and slathered one with mayo (Ottilie), one with mustard (J.D.) and one with mustard and butter (Shea). When he saw Claire, he stopped what he was doing and poured her a cup of coffee.

Claire kissed him and said, 'Thank you for letting me sleep.'

'Picnic for the beach today,' he said.

'Okay,' Claire said. 'Where's Matthew?'

'He left.'

'He *left?*'

'His plane took off at seven. For Spain. I drove him to the airport.'

'He told me his flight was at ten,' Claire said. 'He didn't even say good-bye.'

Jason cleared his throat and started laying down slices of ham. 'He told me to tell you he loves you, but that he understands.'

Claire nodded.

Jason closed the sandwiches, then sliced them with the big knife. 'You pulled off a great event, despite everything. You should be proud of yourself, Claire.'

Claire took her coffee out to the back deck, stood at the railing, and looked out over the golf course. It was a glorious day.

Her head should have hurt, but it didn't. Her heart should have hurt, but it didn't, either. The chandelier was broken. On the way home from the gala, Claire had asked Jason to stop by the grocery store. Claire was about to toss the box into the Dumpster, but she found she couldn't part with it so unceremoniously. The chandelier, broken or whole, represented a year of her life; and weren't there things about the past year that had been valuable? Wasn't there anything she could salvage? She could, she decided, salvage the chandelier. She thought of Mr. Fred Bulrush in San Francisco, for whom she had made the pulled-taffy candlesticks. She would repair the chandelier, and he would buy it. If it was lopsided, if it had hairline cracks, if it had dings and scars, if it contained a story of love and betrayal and ecstasy and regret, so much the better. *It's like all of a sudden you don't care about your soul. Stand in line together at the post office. You must pray for strength. We need someone who can give it a dedicated effort. There's been an accident. O my God, I am heartily sorry for having offended you, and I detest all my sins. They don't know about the baby. I've been watching for you for . . . oh, about five days. Live with me. Marry me. When all this is over, do I get you back? He's a walker! Ladies and gentlemen, Claire Danner Crispin! . . .*

It would mark her triumphant return.

ACKNOWLEDGMENTS

Virginia Woolf said it best: For a woman to write, she must have 500 pounds sterling and a room of her own. In other words, the time and the space.

For the time, I must first thank my au pair, Suphawan 'Za' Intafa. Za can most accurately be described as an angel sent straight from heaven. There would be no book (indeed, no life) without Za. I'd also like to thank my mother, Sally Hilderbrand, who showed up in a time of 'revising crisis' to bail me out. And while I'm at it, I'd also like to thank my grandmother Ruth Huling, who bailed my mother out over thirty years ago. I promise to follow their wonderful, selfless example and be there for my daughter, Shelby, when the time comes.

For the space, I'd like to thank Anne and Whitney Gifford for the keys to Barnabas. Barnabas was both an inspiration and a lifesaver. Thanks also to Jerry and Ann Longerot for their 'cabin' on Lake Michigan in my final, desperate days of need.

Thank you to Mark Yelle, of Nantucket Catering Company (the man my children simply call 'the Chef'), for explaining the ins and outs of the catering business. I borrowed all of Siobhan's fabulousness from Eithne Yelle, though I will say, Siobhan is fictional(!).

I have the pleasure of sitting on three nonprofit boards on

Nantucket – the Nantucket Boys & Girls Club, the Nantucket Preservation Trust, and the Friends of the Nantucket Public Schools. I have chaired events and chaired events, and I am happy to say those experiences have been enriching from start to finish. My appreciation goes out to Irene McMenamin Shabel and Mary Dougherty of Philadelphia, for sharing their wealth of information about philanthropy in the big city. The Arthur Ashe Youth Tennis and Education foundation doesn't know how lucky it is!

In New York, thank you to my incomparable agents and muses, Michael Carlisle and David Forrer of Inkwell Management. They take incredibly good care of me. At Little, Brown, thank you to my editor, Reagan Arthur, for her insight, intelligence, and patience – and thank you also to Oliver Haslegrave, Michael Pietsch, and David Young. Across the pond, thank you to Ursula McKenzie and most especially Jo Dickinson, who made this a better book all the way around.

Finally, at home, I'd like to thank the people in my foxhole. First of all, my soul mate, my darling, my defender, my reality check, and my partner in crime, Amanda Congdon. And all the other people who, daily, lend me their friendship, laughter, and support: Elizabeth Almodobar, Margie Marino, Sally Bates Hall, Wendy Rouillard, Wendy Hudson, Rebecca Bartlett, Debbie Bennett, Leslie Bresette, Betty Dupont, Rence Gamberoni, Evelyn MacEachern, Holly McGowan, Nancy Pittman, the aforementioned Anne Gifford and Eithne Yelle, my absolutely beloved Manda Riggs – and, in many cases, their significant others, especially my pal Richard Congdon, who basically provided the soundtrack for a year of weekends.

As ever, thank you to Heather Osteen Thorpe for the first, crucial read, and for checking in with me nearly every day.

As for my husband, Chip Cunningham, and our three children, Max, Dawson, and Shelby – what can I say? I'm yours once again.